WHAT IF?

#3

SURINAM TURTLE PRESS

1. The Master of Mysteries — Gelett Burgess
2. The White Cat — Gelett Burgess
3. Two Oclock Courage — Gelett Burgess
4. Ladies in Boxes — Gelett Burgess
5. Find the Woman — Gelett Burgess
6. The Picaroons — Gelett Burgess & Will Irwin
7. The Heart Line — Gelett Burgess
8. The Triune Man — Richard A. Lupoff
9. The Time Armada — Fox Holden
10. A Shot Rang Out — Jon Breen
11. The Smiling Corpse — Philip Wylie
12. Sacred Locomotive Flies — Richard A. Lupoff
13. Welsh Rarebit Tales — Harle Cummins
14. Sideslip — White & Van Arnam
15. Blondy's Boy Friend — Philip Wylie
16. The Technique of Mystery — Carolyn Wells
17. Marblehead — Richard A. Lupoff
18. Deep Space — Richard A. Lupoff
19. Lady Mechante — Gelett Burgess
20. Away From The Here and Now — Harris
21. Tracer of Lost Persons — Robert Chambers
22. Hairbreadth Escapes of Major Mendax — F. Blake Crofton
23. The Book of Time — H.G Wells and Richard A. Lupoff
24. The Case of the Little Green Men — Mack Reynolds
25. Star Griffin — Michael Kurland
26. J. Poindexter, Colored — Irvin S. Cobb
27. Pair o' Jacks — Jack Woodford
28. Evangelical Cockroach — Jack Woodford
29. Money Brawl — Jack Woodford and H. Bedford-Jones
30. The Basil Wells Omnibus — Basil Wells
31. The Disentanglers — Andrew Lang
32. Tarnished Bomb — Malcolm Jameson
33. Satans of Saturn — Otis Adelbert Kline
34. A Gellett Burgess Sampler — Alfred Jan
35. John Carstairs, Space Detective — Frank Belknap Long
36. The Illustrious Corpse — Tiffany Thayer
37. Astonishing! Astounding! — Malcolm Jameson
38. The Town from Planet Five — Richard Wilson
39. Win, Place and Die! — Milton K. Ozaki
40. Dead Men's Money — J.S. Fletcher
41. Prince Pax — Charles Sylvester Viereck
42. Tree of Life, Book of Death — Grania Davis
43. Bogart '48 — John Stanley and Kenn Davis
44. The Case in the Clinic — E.C.R. Lorac
45. The Time Column — Malcolm Jameson
46. What If? #3 — Richard A. Lupoff

WHAT IF?

#3

Stories That Didn't Win a Hugo,

But Should Have

Compiled and Edited by

Richard A. Lupoff

Surinam Turtle Press

RAMBLE HOUSE

2013

ISBN 13: 978-1-60543-729-3

Edited by: Richard A. Lupoff and Fender Tucker

Cover Art by Gavin L. O'Keefe

Surinam Turtle Press #46

WHAT IF? #3

CONTENTS

A Note on Publishing History

What If: Stories that Should have Won the Hugo was conceived in the 1970s. The idea was not to second-guess the members of the science fiction community who voted for the awards, nor to suggest that they had selected unworthy recipients. It was simply to suggest that year after year there were multiple worthy nominees in each category. Many fine works were unavoidably passed over, and these anthologies would offer a degree of recognition (and monetary compensation) to their inevitably disappointed authors.

In fact, two anthologists had hit on the same idea at virtually the same moment. I was one; the other was my friend, George R.R. Martin. When our almost identical proposals were compared, it was discovered that I had initiated the project a split second before George, and he graciously withdrew from the field.

The first volume of *What If: Stories that Should have Won the Hugo* was published in 1980, and included one story from each year, 1952 to 1958. The critical response was enthusiastic. The second volume, with stories from 1959 through 1965, was published in 1981. Critical response was again enthusiastic.

My contract at the time called for four volumes in the series. When I delivered the manuscript for the third volume of *What If: Stories that Should have Won the Hugo,* covering the years 1966 to 1973, my own editor at Pocket Books, David Hartwell, was so enthusiastic that he asked me to extend the series to an eventual fifth volume.

Months passed, during which I selected stories for the fourth volume and secured publication rights from their authors.

Then came one of the more bizarre days in my career. I received two letters. One came from the publicity department at Pocket Books. An advance copy of Volume 3 in the form of a set of galley proofs had been sent to the influential *Pub-*

lishers Weekly. Pocket Books had received a copy of *PW's* review. The reviewer has praise for the entire series to date, and adjudged the third volume as surpassing even its admirable predecessors.

The second letter was a personal one from David Hartwell. He informed me that sales had been disappointing. As he put it, he could sell more copies of a competent but unexceptional first novel by a previously unknown author than a collection of short stories by as prominent a figure as Theodore Sturgeon. Consequently, my contract was being cancelled and the series was being discontinued.

By now the third volume was literally "in press." Cover proofs had been printed. No matter. *What If: Stories that Should have Won the Hugo* was no more.

Well, in this business there's no point in sulking. I turned to other projects. Thirty years passed. Thanks to the exigencies of fate, my files for *What If: Stories that Should have Won the Hugo* were lost. And then—lo! and behold—an internet book dealer offered a set of those three-decades-old galley proofs for sale. His price was only slightly exorbitant. There was a certain irony in my having to buy those proofs—apparently the only surviving copy of my anthology—from this dealer. But so it was, and so *What If: Stories that Should have Won the Hugo, Volume 3,* is published at last.

In fact, stories had already been selected and rights purchased for *What If: Stories that Should have Won the Hugo, Volume 4,* but barring the recovery of those long lost files, it seems unlikely that the phantom fourth volume of the series will be resurrected.

Unlikely? Yes.

But impossible?

Come on now—you've got to be kidding!

Richard A. Lupoff
2013

Shining Examples

AN INTRODUCTION BY RICHARD A. LUPOFF

THE YEAR 1964 represented the end of an era for science fiction; 1965, the opening of another. A specific event signaled the change, but this event merely capsulized a larger evolutionary development that had been taking place over the preceding dozen years.

The event was the founding of an organization called Science Fiction Writers of America (SFWA). The purpose of SFWA was the improvement of the lot of science fiction writers, chiefly in their relationships with publishers. It was to be accomplished primarily through the exchange of information among writers. The idea of making the organization a strong one, capable of carrying out collective action in the fashion of a guild or even a labor union, was considered at the time, as it has been periodically ever since, but it was rejected then and has been at every later reconsideration. There *have* been a few attempts at collective action—a sporadic and rather ineffective boycott of a notoriously crooked magazine publisher, a collective move against a paperback house widely known for its unreliable practices in the area of reporting sales and paying royalties, a loud and piercing wail against another publisher when that publisher revised its contract so as to make its authors into indentured servants for life.

In the royalties case, the publishing house was purchased by a larger and more reliable outfit and the new owners reached an amicable agreement with SFWA. In the case of the obnoxious contract, the document was withdrawn and a less noisome (although still far from ideal) form was substituted.

In the case of the magazine publisher, agreements were repeatedly reached and repeatedly breached, with the publisher seeming to rely on the notion that he presented too small and too shifty a target to be hit. Apparently he was right.

Almost as an afterthought the founders of SFWA decided to institute an annual literary award. The award was named the Nebula. A physical trophy was designed by Judith Ann Lawrence, a graphic artist whose husband was the science fiction writer James Blish. Lawrence's design, from an idea proposed by author Lloyd Biggle, called for a lucite cube containing a glittering representation of a spiral nebula, as well as a geological sample. There were four literary Nebulas: for short story, novelette, novella and novel.

While SFWA was the first *successful* writers' association in the field, it was by no means the first attempted. As early as 1952 there had been an organization called Science Fantasy Writers of America, patterned on the Mystery Writers of America and similar organizations in other fields. This first SFWA had failed, but in the early 1960s two attempts were made to start such an organization.

Operating from Los Angeles, A.E. van Vogt attempted to start a group known as the Science Fiction Writers Protective Association. Simultaneously an East Coast group, with its roots divided between New York City and the little town of Milford, Pennsylvania, was working toward a similar goal.

The East Coast group, with a lineage dating to the original New York Futurian Society of 1938, included Damon Knight, James Blish, Judith Merril, Virginia Kidd and others associated with the annual Milford Science Fiction Writers Conferences.

The Milford group managed to get their organization rolling first. Rather than risk a destructive rivalry, van Vogt graciously cancelled his plans and urged his group's prospective members to join SFWA instead. Thus SFWA came into being. Damon Knight was its first president and has remained a leading member ever since.

If you've read the first volumes of *What If: Stories that Should have Won the Hugo,* you will have noticed that the fans who give out Hugos have been maddeningly inconstant in their designation of categories. There were years in which a single fiction award was given, in which none were given, in which two were given and in which three were given.

In the first year in which Nebulas were presented—awards given in the year 1966 but for works published in 1965—the only Hugos for fiction were in the novel and short-story lengths. Just one year later the fans had recognized the intermediate or novelette length, and a year after that they had added the novella category and brought their structure into alignment with that of the Nebulas. There was some backsliding a few years later, but order was restored. Since 1973 (awards for 1972), the Hugos and Nebulas have recognized the same four lengths, borrowed, incidentally, from the awards given by the Mystery Writers of America.

With two award series marching in precise lockstep, you may reasonably ask if the Nebula doesn't make the Hugo superfluous (or vice versa). That's a good question, and I'll get to it in a little while. Skim until you come to my answer if you're impatient.

But if you're willing to stick with me while I talk about a few other things, I'll appreciate it a lot.

I said a few paragraphs ago that the founding of SFWA and the establishment of the Nebula awards marked a longer-term evolutionary process in the development of science fiction. What was the nature of that process?

The founding of the Hugo awards in 1953 had coincided with the final crest in the publication of pulp magazines. In the course of a single year the number of science fiction pulps fell from an all-time high of over forty to fewer than ten. With minor revivals and minor slumps alternating since then, the figure has remained under ten.

The pulp era is one fondly remembered by older science fiction hands as a time of innocence and unbridled (if often primitive) energy. In magazines with names like *Planet Stories, Out of this World Adventures, Science Wonder Quarterly* and *Marvel Tales,* authors like "Doc" Smith, Jack Williamson, Edmond "World Wrecker" Hamilton and Leigh Brackett spun their wondrous webs. These were the days of grand space opera, astonishing adventures and mind-dazzling concepts. They were often short on subtlety and polish, but who cared?

Well, the entire so-called Serious Literary Establishment cared. This Establishment—comprising critics, editors, librarians and literature teachers at every level from primary school to university—took a collective look at the pulp magazines with their lurid titles and their garish covers, perhaps took a quick peep at a crude story or two, and decided that this science fiction stuff was subliterate trash.

School kids were told that science fiction was *not* suitable matter for book reports. In some institutions pulp magazines were forbidden material, and anyone caught with a copy of *Super Science Novels* was lucky to get off with a mere reprimand and the seizure and destruction of the wicked publication.

I am not exaggerating. It happened to me. More than once. The school administration may have held more power, but *I* had more endurance. I kept reading science fiction. The school I attended no longer exists, and I'm still here, still reading science fiction and frequently writing it myself. And I did have the satisfaction, before my old school closed its doors forever, of returning for a visit and being welcomed as a Distinguished Alumnus upon the occasion of the publication of my first science fiction novel!

The death of the pulps was brought about by certain financial convulsions within the publishing industry; these had nothing to do with science fiction as a literary form (the death of the pulps extended to all categories including mysteries, westerns and love stories). The science fiction readers *were* still there. The science fiction *writers* were still there. All that was needed was a medium to bring them together.

That medium was an obvious one: the book, primarily the paperback but also the hardbound volume. Two publishers very heavily committed to science fiction were already on the scene. These were Ace Books, owned by veteran pulp publisher Aaron A. Wyn and edited by Donald Wollheim; and Ballantine Books, masterminded by the husband-wife team of Ian and Betty Ballantine.

Ace Books specialized in mass-appeal, pulp-type adventure books. Ballantine pushed ahead with more literary science fiction. In later years both publishers broadened their lines to include both types of fiction and were joined by virtually every other publisher in the field of popular fiction.

In the field of hardcover publishing, the heyday of the fan-owned presses was also approaching its end. Gnome Press, Shasta Press, Fantasy Press and Fantasy Publishing Company, Incorporated, faced increasing competition from general commercial publishers: Doubleday, Harper & Row, St. Martin's Press, Scribner's.

Science fiction rapidly emerged from the shadow of its pulp-magazine background. As if the famous dictum that form follows function had been reversed so that function followed form, Literary Establishmentarians started taking science fiction seriously.

The fiction hadn't changed.

There remained the customary mix of a few splendid works, a great many fair-to-good and a few execrable botches. A statistician would look at this and say, sure, that's just the normal distribution curve. A science fiction fan would say, sure, that's just Sturgeon's Law: Ninety percent of everything is crud.

That's the way things were in the pulpiest days of the 1930s and '40s; that's the way in the "book era" of science fiction, that was inaugurated in 1953.

But critics, professors and librarians didn't see it that way! To them, pulp magazine equaled subliterate trash. A *prima facie* case. No need to even examine the prose.

But *books . . .*

Well, books weren't *necessarily* good literature, but they at least *might* be worthwhile. One might reasonably risk a look inside the covers of even a gaudy Ace Double Novel. A Richard Powers-covered Ballantine Book looked better. And, of course, anything bound in boards, with the logotype of a Simon & Schuster or a G. P. Putnam's Sons on the spine, was on the face of it respectable.

And once librarians, professors and critics stopped dismissing science fiction out of hand and actually started reading it before they made their judgments, they discovered—well, not "Doc" Smith or Ed Earl Repp. It was too late for them, and even the sophisticated critics didn't have the subtle perception to recognize a primitive genius, which Smith, at least, surely was.

But they *did* discover some of the more modern writers.

Christopher Isherwood discovered Ray Bradbury as the result of reading a Doubleday edition (hardcover) of *The Martian Chronicles.* This we know because Bradbury himself tells the story of his meeting Isherwood in a chance encounter and handing him the very copy.

And they discovered Arthur C. Clarke and Kurt Vonnegut (although some Lit'ry Establishmentarians lacked—and still lack—the elementary wit to perceive that Vonnegut writes science fiction), and in later years they recognized Frank Herbert and Ursula Le Guin. And—please God!—they will one day discover the genius of Avram Davidson's short stories and Philip K. Dick's novels.

One no longer needed to hide the latest *Startling Stories* inside a copy of *Time* magazine to avoid curious stares on the Lexington Avenue IRT. One no longer had to tear the brass-brassiered space maidens from the cover of *Planet Stories* for fear of being misunderstood by one's parents.

It was possible not merely to read Pohl and Kornbluth's *The Space Merchants* without suffering acute embarrassment, but also to actually check the thing out of a library and turn in a book report on it!

Respectability was ours.

All of this, as I have suggested, was not an instantaneous event by any means, but a gradual development taking place over a number of years.

Well, here we were. 1965. A new series of annual literary awards. Others had come and gone, some before the Hugo had been instituted, and of these only the old International Fantasy Award had achieved any real acceptance. But the IFA had begun to fade once the Hugo was established, had ceased to exist after 1955 and disappeared for a second and final time after a brief revival in 1957. The Jules Verne Prize had come and gone three separate times and had never really caught on. The Spectrum Awards had struggled briefly and disappeared with hardly a trace. What chance had the Nebulas?

A very good chance, it turned out, and for a very good reason. The Hugos were successful where the International Fantasy Awards, Jules Verne Prize and Spectrum Awards had failed because the Hugos had a sizable and reasonably objective constituency: the membership of the World Science Fiction Conventions held each year.

The Nebula also had a sizable constituency, and a prestigious one: the membership of the Science Fiction Writers of America.[1] From the beginning, most eligible writers saw fit to join SFWA, and within a few years the membership of the organization reached a level close to five hundred, where it has remained ever since. An examination of any year's SFWA membership directory will show almost all of the "star" names in the field and almost all of the solid, journeyman professionals. There are also a certain number of "who's-that?" names as well—beginners, occasional writers, minor talents. But out of those "who's-that?" writers will doubtlessly emerge most of tomorrow's headliners.

---

[1] There has been a good deal of confusion over the years, growing from the word "America" in the title Science Fiction Writers of America. It doesn't mean that writers of non-US nationality are excluded. It refers to science fiction writers whose works have been *published* in America. The writers themselves can be of any nationality. The official explanation of this policy is that SFWA tries to look out for the best interests of its members, and that whatever clout the organization possesses applies to American publishers. There's really not much that SFWA can do if a member's story is pirated by a Lower Slobbovian publisher.

Even so, there has been agitation within SFWA to de-jingoize the title by changing it to "Science Fiction Writers' Association." I personally favor the move, but I'm just one member out of five hundred and so far our side has not prevailed.

Almost at once, the Nebula was accepted is a significant award. It was presented, from the outset, at an annual dinner meeting of SFWA, held alternately in New York and California, the two areas where the greatest number of SFWA members reside. Almost at once, publishers recognized its value and began plastering "Nebula Award Winner," sometimes even "Nebula Award Nominee," on the covers of recognized works. The same prestige has also been attached to Hugo winning and nominated works but to no other award series so far.

As I have mentioned, the Nebula categories were pegged to the standards already established by the Mystery Writers of America for their annual awards. After several years of vacillation, the science fiction fans brought their Hugo awards into alignment as well, so that the structure of novel/novella/novelette/short story has been accepted for nearly a decade.

There has, unfortunately, continued to be a certain amount of confusion over the old problem of what constitutes a year. SFWA presents its awards in the spring of each year, dating them for the year of publication. Thus, the first set of Nebulas, presented in the spring of 1966 for works published in 1965, were called 1965 Nebula awards. The equivalent Hugos, presented at the World Science Fiction Convention over Labor Day weekend of 1966, were called 1966 Hugos—but were given for works published in 1965.

As in other volumes of *What If: Stories that Should have Won the Hugo,* I will simply shove such problems aside and pay attention to actual date of publication of any story.

This third volume of *What If: Stories that Should have Won the Hugo* covers a period of eight years, from 1966 to 1973. An intriguing question is: To what extent have Hugo and Nebula award winners overlapped?

If the winners had been substantially identical, it would seem that one series or the other would be superfluous. And with the Nebulas awarded three to four months before the Hugos, one might have expected the latter to fall by the wayside. If the winners had been almost completely different, one might ponder a long while over the meaning of that phenomenon.

There seems little doubt that writers apply somewhat different standards in making their choices than do the fans. The constituencies of the two series overlap substantially. Most members of SFWA are present or former fans and members of the World Science Fiction Conventions. But convention membership in recent years has run to the order of five thousand, while SFWA's membership is slightly under five hundred, or almost exactly ten percent that of the conventions. Is the SFWA membership a statistically valid microcosm of convention membership? If so, the award winners should be essentially identical.

In fact, this has not been the case. A shining example is provided by Thomas M. Disch. In a survey of past science fiction awards. Professor Harlan McGhan noted that Disch had been nominated for Nebula awards on seven occasions between 1965 and 1980. In the same period, Disch was nominated for the Hugo only once, and that was not until 1978.

Median's conclusion: Disch is a "writer's writer."

My inference: McGhan is probably correct. The Hugo electorate tends to be younger than the Nebula electorate and more concerned with blazing action or ingenuity of scientific speculation. The Nebula voters, being writers themselves, are more concerned with such writerly matters as ingenuity and impact of dramatic structure, subtlety and depth of characterization, and sophistication of style and narrative technique.

That theory may be a pack of hooey, but it's mine.

It is also interesting to note that Disch, despite his many nominations, has yet actually to win either a Nebula or a Hugo.

Let's take a look at the performance of the Hugo and Nebula electorates in the years 1965-1973. (We'll use these years because they represent the period from the inception of the Nebula through the entire period covered in this volume of *What If?*)

In this period of nine years, with four literary awards in each series, there should be thirty-six possible matches. In fact, the statistics aren't quite that straightforward. There were a number of occasions upon which "no award" was the result of the voting, or upon which a tie was reported. Furthermore, while the four Nebula categories were present from the start, the fans remained skittish for a while, and the Hugo categories kept appearing and disappearing, combining and then separating again.

In fact, there were only thirty-one instances in these nine years when a Hugo and a Nebula award were given in parallel. Of these thirty-one. there were twelve matches and nineteen disagreements—a rate of agreement just under thirty-nine percent! In specific years, the results have ranged from complete or near complete agreement to complete or near-complete disagreement.

In later years, the rate of agreement between Nebulas and Hugos would rise somewhat. But there is still a good deal of difference between the two lists of winners. The Nebula has decidedly not rendered the Hugo superfluous. Nor has the Hugo rendered the Nebula redundant. Each has its place.

1966

DANIEL KEYES'S "Flowers for Algernon" appeared in *F&SF* in April, 1959, and won the Hugo for short fiction the following year. It was a popular award, but its sequel was even more remarkable. Keyes expanded the story into a novel, which was published by Harcourt in 1966, and it won both the Hugo and Nebula for best novel of the year. Dramatized as *Charly,* the story went on to even more success. Keyes remains to this day an author known for that single work, although his association with science fiction has been a long one, dating back to a stint as editor of *Marvel Science Stories* in 1951 and including contributions to *Other Worlds, Galaxy, If* and other magazines over the years.

For the Nebula, *Flowers for Algernon* was tied with *Babel-17* by Samuel R. Delany,

The third finalist in Nebula balloting was *The Moon is a Harsh Mistress* by Robert A. Heinlein, and here a further complication arose. The Heinlein novel had been serialized in *If,* the installments divided between 1965 and 1966. In which year should the novel have been eligible for awards? SFWA sidestepped the question by ignoring the serial and declaring the first book edition (Putnam) eligible for the Nebula. *That* was clearly dated 1966. But the book lost anyway!

The fans decided that most of the magazine version of the Heinlein had appeared in 1966 (or at least bore 1966 indicia) and declared *that* version "official." And *The Moon is a Harsh Mistress* won the Hugo. All of which may prove something, but it is rather difficult to tell just what.

There were any number of noteworthy novels published in 1966. Aside from works by Heinlein, Keyes and Delany, we read *Make Room! Make Room!* by Harry Harrison, a chilling early population-and-pollution novel and probably Harrison's finest effort. Ballantine brought out *World of Ptavvs,* the first novel by the immensely popular Larry Niven. The prolific Jack Vance had several novels. Berkley brought out *Night of Light* by Philip José Farmer.

And Farrar Strauss published *The Crystal World* by J.G. Ballard, a novel of shimmering beauty and haunting strangeness. Ballard was the *ne plus ultra* of the *New Worlds* experimental "new wave" school, and *The Crystal World* may well have been his ultimate achievement. He had, of course, written many short stories and several novels before *The Crystal World,* and has continued to this day to produce occasionally striking pieces of prose.

The Crystal World was a magnificent achievement. Yet. it failed to make the final Nebula ballot, or the Hugo ballot at all. Was it too much a novel of technique? Too demanding, too uncompromising? Did it lack dynamic characterization? Whatever the reason, it failed. In the intermediate lengths, the Nebulas were won by Jack Vance for "The Last Castle" from *Galaxy* and "Call Him Lord" by Gordon Dickson from *Analog.* The Nebula for short story was won by Richard McKenna for "The Secret Place," and thereon hang not one but several tales. First of all, McKenna had died in 1964. "The Secret Place" was a posthumously published work, and as far as I know it was the first such work ever to win a Nebula or Hugo.

Second, McKenna had had an odd attitude toward science fiction. A retired navy man, he had decided to become an author, attended college, and then tried his hand at science fiction. In a posthumously published essay, McKenna informed us that his choice of science fiction had been based not on love for the form but on the fact that its literary standards were rather low and its "crackability" for a new writer consequently high. Once he'd learned what he could from science fiction McKenna was quite willing to abandon the form in favor of "real" fiction.

Well, he accomplished exactly what he set out to accomplish, leaving as his *magnum opus* the much-acclaimed novel

The Sand Pebbles. But in the meantime he had produced a number of good science fiction works. He wrote at least one real classic, "Casey Agonistes," but although it is usually published as science fiction or fantasy, this story in my opinion is realistic fiction masquerading as science fiction. All right: that is as it is.

Thirdly, "The Secret Place" made its first appearance in Damon Knight's anthology *Orbit 1.* The *Orbit* series was the second continuing series of original anthologies in the science fiction field, following Frederik Pohl's *Star Science Fiction.* Time and again stories from *Orbit* dominated Nebula award ceremonies, and it came to be charged—sometimes jocularly, sometimes with more than a touch of serious rancor—that a little in-crowd centering on the town of Milford, Pennsylvania was running SFWA and the Nebulas to suit its own purposes. There was, in fact, something to the charge. A medium-sized colony of science fiction authors and editors had settled in Milford, some of them maintaining full-time residence there, others commuting in and out from New York City, The Milford group included Damon Knight (founder and first president of SFWA), Kate Wilhelm, Virginia Kidd, James Blish, Judith Ann Lawrence and Judith Merril.

Knight had also founded the Milford Science Fiction Writers Conference. This summer literary workshop was attended by a variety of major and not-so-major writers including the already-noted Milford residents plus Avram Davidson, Samuel R. Delany, Terry Carr, Carol Carr, Frederik Pohl (who attended once and swore off for life), Kurt Vonnegut (who celebrated the experience in his tales of Kilgore Trout), Harlan Ellison and Richard McKenna.

Without claiming that any casual relationship obtained, one can observe that, repeatedly, Milford Conference-generated stories would appear in *Orbit* and then go on to win Nebula awards, with Damon Knight hovering ever in the background as founder-host of the Milford Conference, founder-president of SFWA and editor of *Orbit.*

The whole thing did smack of cronyism to say the least,

and Knight may appear a Machiavellian figure. I do not accuse him. I'm only saying that it looked awkward.

In their Hugo awards for the fiction of 1966, the fans affirmed SFWA's choice of "The Last Castle" by Vance. The fans gave only one intermediate-length award, so they called "The Last Castle" a novelette, while SFWA had called it a novella. The fans did *not* agree with the writers in their choice of short-story winner, awarding the Hugo to Larry Niven for "Neutron Star" rather than to McKenna for "The Secret Place."

But I think they both erred egregiously in overlooking "Light of Other Days" by Bob Shaw, a story which had appeared in *Analog.*

Although not a member of the *New Worlds/* "new wave" circle, Shaw in certain ways does resemble Barrington Bayley. Both are writers of many years' standing; both are British; both have produced any number of good-to-excellent works; and yet both have failed, for some hard-to-identify reason, to gain the full degree of recognition and acceptance that they truly deserve.

Shaw made his first sale in 1954, when he was barely twenty years of age, and has continued for over twenty-five years to turn out short stories and novels. The astonishing thing about "Light of Other Days," to me, is its *shortness.* I remembered it, from 1966, as being a very substantial story. When I reread it in making my selections for *What If: Stories that Should have Won the Hugo,* I was again impressed by the amount of narrative information and emotional impact it contains.

But when I "measured" the story—that is, worked out its length in number-of-words preliminary to calculating the check I would send the author—I was astonished at how few words the story contains. How could Shaw get his act going, do so very much and do it so very well, and then finish so fast?

In a market where stories are usually purchased on the basis of so-many-cents-per-word, the author's vested interest lies in making his stories *longer* rather than shorter. Which may account for a certain excessive verbiage one detects in all too many works. But for an amazing economy and an overwhelming impact, one could do no better than study "Light of Other Days."

Light of Other Days

BOB SHAW

LEAVING THE VILLAGE behind, we followed the heady sweeps of the road up into a land of slow glass.

I had never seen one of the farms before and at first found them slightly eerie—an effect heightened by imagination and circumstance. The car's turbine was pulling smoothly and quietly in the damp air so that we seemed to be carried over the convolutions of the road in a kind of supernatural silence. On our right the mountain sifted down into an incredibly perfect valley of timeless pine, and everywhere stood the great frames of slow glass, drinking light. An occasional flash of afternoon sunlight on their wind bracing created an illusion of movement, but in fact the frames were deserted. The rows of windows had been standing on the hillside for years, staring into the valley, and men only cleaned them in the middle of the night when their human presence would not matter to the thirsty glass. They were fascinating, but Selina and I didn't mention the windows. I think we hated each other so much we both were reluctant to sully anything new by drawing it into the nexus of our emotions. The holiday, I had begun to realize, was a stupid idea in the first place. I had thought it would cure everything, but, of course, it didn't stop Selina being pregnant and, worse still, it didn't even stop her being angry about being pregnant.

Rationalizing our dismay over her condition, we had circulated the usual statements to the effect that we would have *liked* having children—but later on, at the proper time, Selina's pregnancy had cost us her well-paid job and with it the new house we had been negotiating for and which was far beyond the reach of my income from poetry. But the real source of our annoyance was that we were face to face with the realization that people who say they want children later always mean they want children never. Our nerves were thrumming with the knowledge that we, who had thought ourselves so unique, had fallen into the same biological trap as every mindless rutting creature which ever existed.

The road took us along the southern slopes of Ben Cruachan until we began to catch glimpses of the gray Atlantic far ahead. I had just cut our speed to absorb the view better when I noticed the sign spiked to a gatepost. It said: "SLOW GLASS—Quality High, Prices Low—J.R. Hagan." On an impulse I stopped the car on the verge, wincing slightly as tough grasses whipped noisily at the bodywork.

"Why have we stopped?" Selina's neat, smoke-silver head turned in surprise.

"Look at that sign. Let's go up and see what there is. The stuff might be reasonably priced out here."

Selina's voice was pitched high with scorn as she refused, but I was too taken with my idea to listen. I had an illogical conviction that doing something extravagant and crazy would set us right again.

"Come on," I said, "the exercise might do us some good. We've been driving too long anyway."

She shrugged in a way that hurt me and got out of the car. We walked up a path made of irregular, packed clay steps nosed with short lengths of sapling. The path curved through trees which clothed the edge of the hill and at its end we found a low farmhouse. Beyond the little stone building tall frames of slow glass gazed out towards the voice-stilling sight of Cruachan's ponderous descent towards the waters of Loch Linnhe. Most of the panes were perfectly transparent but a few were dark, like panels of polished ebony.

As we approached the house through a neat cobbled yard a tall middle-aged man in ash-colored tweeds arose and waved to us. He had been sitting on the low rubble wall which bounded the yard, smoking a pipe and staring towards the house. At the front window of the cottage a young woman in a tangerine dress stood with a small boy in her arms, but she turned disinterestedly and moved out of sight as we drew near.

"Mr. Hagan?" I guessed.

"Correct. Come to see some glass, have you? Well, you've come to the right place." Hagan spoke crisply, with traces of the pure highland which sounds so much like Irish to the unaccustomed ear. He had one of those calmly dismayed faces one finds on elderly roadmenders and philosophers.

"Yes," I said. "We're on holiday. We saw your sign."

Selina, who usually has a natural fluency with strangers, said nothing. She was looking towards the now empty window with what I thought was a slightly puzzled expression.

"Up from London, are you? Well, as I said, you've come to the right place—and at the right time, too. My wife and I don't see many people this early in the season."

I laughed. "Does that mean we might be able to buy a little glass without mortgaging our home?"

"Look at that now," Hagan said, smiling helplessly. "I've thrown away any advantage I might have had in the transaction. Rose, that's my wife, says I never learn. Still, let's sit down and talk it over." He pointed at the rubble wall then glanced doubtfully at Selina's immaculate blue skirt. "Wait till I fetch a rug from the house." Hagan limped quickly into the cottage, closing the door behind him.

"Perhaps it wasn't such a marvelous idea to come up here," I whispered to Selina, "but you might at least be pleasant to the man. I think I can smell a bargain."

"Some hope," she said with deliberate coarseness. "Surely even you must have noticed that ancient dress his wife is wearing? He won't give much away to strangers."

"Was that his wife?"

"Of course that was his wife."

"Well, well," I said, surprised. "Anyway, try to be civil with him. I don't want to be embarrassed."

Selina snorted, but she smiled whitely when Hagan reappeared and I relaxed a little. Strange how a man can love a woman and yet at the same time pray for her to fall under a train.

Hagan spread a tartan blanket on the wall and we sat down, feeling slightly self-conscious at having been translated from our city-oriented lives into a rural tableau. On the distant slate of the Loch, beyond the watchful frames of slow glass, a slow-moving steamer drew a white line towards the south. The boisterous mountain air seemed almost to invade our lungs, giving us more oxygen than we required.

"Some of the glass farmers around here," Hagan began, "give strangers, such as yourselves, a sales talk about how beautiful the autumn is in this part of Argyll. Or it might be the spring, or the winter. I don't do that—any fool knows that a place which doesn't look right in summer never looks right. What do you say?" I nodded compliantly. "I want you just to take a good look out towards Mull, Mr. . . ."

"Garland."

". . . Garland. That's what you're buying if you buy my glass, and it never looks better than it does at this minute. The glass is in perfect phase, none of it is less than ten years thick—and a four-foot window will cost you two hundred pounds."

"Two hundred!" Selina was shocked. "That's as much as they charge at the Scenedow shop in Bond Street."

Hagan smiled patiently, then looked closely at me to see if I knew enough about slow glass to appreciate what he had been saying. His price had been much higher than I had hoped—but *ten years thick!* The cheap glass one found in places like the Vistaplex and Pane-o-rama stores usually consisted of a quarter of an inch of ordinary glass faced with a veneer of slow glass perhaps only ten or twelve months thick.

"You don't understand, darling," I said, already determined to buy. "This glass will last ten years and it's in phase."

"Doesn't that only mean it keeps time?"

Hagan smiled at her again, realizing he had no further necessity to bother with me. "Only, you say! Pardon me, Mrs. Garland, but you don't seem to appreciate the miracle, the

genuine honest-to-goodness miracle, of engineering preci-
sion needed to produce a piece of glass in phase. When I say
the glass is ten years thick it means it takes light ten years to
pass through it. In effect, each one of those panes is ten light-
years thick—more than twice the distance to the nearest
star—so a variation in actual thickness of only a millionth of
an inch would . . ."

He stopped talking for a moment and sat quietly looking
towards the house. I turned my head from the view of the
Loch and saw the young woman standing at the window
again. Hagan's eyes were filled with a kind of greedy reverence which made me feel uncomfortable and at the same
time convinced me Selina had been wrong. In my experience
husbands never looked at wives that way, at least, not at their
own.

The girl remained in view for a few seconds, dress glowing warmly, then moved back into the room. Suddenly I received a distinct, though inexplicable, impression she was
blind. My feeling was that Selina and I were perhaps blun-
dering through an emotional interplay as violent as our own.
"I'm sorry," Hagan continued, "I thought Rose was going to
call me for something. Now, where was I, Mrs. Garland?
Ten light-years compressed into a quarter of an inch
means . . ."

I ceased to listen, partly because I was already sold, partly
because I had heard the story of slow glass many times before and had never yet understood the principles involved.
An acquaintance with scientific training had once tried to be
helpful by telling me to visualize a pane of slow glass as a
hologram which did not need coherent light from a laser for
the reconstitution of its visual information, and in which
every photon of ordinary light passed through a spiral tunnel
coiled outside the radius of capture of each atom in the glass.
This gem of, to me, incomprehensibility not only told me
nothing, it convinced me once again that a mind as nontech-
nical as mine should concern itself less with causes than effects.

The most important effect, in the eyes of the average indi-

vidual, was that light took a long time to pass through a sheet
of slow glass. A new piece was always jet black because
nothing had yet come through, but one could stand the glass
beside, say, a woodland lake until the scene emerged, perhaps a year later. If the glass was then removed and installed
in a dismal city flat, the flat would—for that year—appear to
overlook the woodland lake. During the year it wouldn't be
merely a very realistic but still picture—the water would rip-
ple in sunlight, silent animals would come to drink, birds
would cross the sky, night would follow day, season would
follow season. Until one day, a year later, the beauty held in
the subatomic pipelines would be exhausted and the familiar
gray cityscape would reappear. Apart from its stupendous
novelty value, the commercial success of slow glass was
founded on the fact that having a scenedow was the exact
emotional equivalent of owning land. The meanest cave
dweller could look out on misty parks—and who was to say
they weren't his? A man who really owns tailored gardens
and estates doesn't spend his time proving his ownership by
crawling on his ground, feeling, smelling, tasting it. All he
receives from the land are light patterns, and with scenedows
those patterns could be taken into coal mines, submarines,
prison cells.

On several occasions I have tried to write short pieces
about the enchanted crystal but, to me, the theme is so inef-
fably poetic as to be, paradoxically, beyond the reach of poetry—mine at any rate. Besides, the best songs and verse had
already been written, with prescient inspiration, by men who
had died long before slow glass was discovered. I had no
hope of equaling, for example, Moore with his:

Oft in the stilly night,
Ere slumber's chain has bound me,
Fond Memory brings the light,
Of other days around me . . .

It took only a few years for slow glass to develop from a
scientific curiosity to a sizable industry. And much to the

astonishment of we poets—those of us who remain convinced that beauty lives though lilies die—the trappings of
that industry were no different from those of any other.
There were good scenedows which cost a lot of money, and
there were inferior scenedows which cost rather less. The
thickness, measured in years, was an important factor in the
cost but there was also the question of *actual* thickness, or
phase.

Even with the most sophisticated engineering techniques
available thickness control was something of a hit-and-miss
affair. A coarse discrepancy could mean that a pane intended
to be five years thick might be five and a half, so that light
which entered in summer emerged in winter; a fine discrepancy could mean that noon sunshine emerged at midnight.
These incompatibilities had their peculiar charm—many
night workers, for example, liked having their own private
time zones—but, in general, it cost more to buy scenedows
which kept closely in step with real time.

Selina still looked unconvinced when Hagan had finished
speaking. She shook her head almost imperceptibly and I
knew he had been using the wrong approach. Quite suddenly
the pewter helmet of her hair was disturbed by a cool gust of
wind, and huge clean tumbling drops of rain began to spang
round us from an almost cloudless sky.

"I'll give you a check now," I said abruptly, and saw
Selina's green eyes triangulate angrily on my face. "You can
arrange delivery?"

"Aye, delivery's no problem," Hagan said, getting to his
feet. "But wouldn't you rather take the glass with you?"

"Well, yes—if you don't mind." I was shamed by his
readiness to trust my scrip.

"I'll unclip a pane for you. Wait here. It won't take long
to slip it into a carrying frame." Hagan limped down the
slope towards the seriate windows, through some of which
the view towards Linnhe was sunny, while others were
cloudy and a few pure black.

Selina drew the collar of her blouse closed at her throat.
"The least he could have done was invite us inside. There

can't be so many fools passing through that he can afford to neglect them."

I tried to ignore the insult and concentrated on writing the check. One of the outsize drops broke across my knuckles, splattering the pink paper.

"All right," I said, "let's move in under the eaves till he gets back." You worm, I thought as I felt the whole thing go completely wrong. I just had to be a fool to marry you. A prize fool, a fool's fool—and now that you've trapped part of me inside you I'll never ever, never ever, *never ever* get away.

Feeling my stomach clench itself painfully, I ran behind Selina to the side of the cottage. Beyond the window the neat living room, with its coal fire, was empty but the child's toys were scattered on the floor. Alphabet blocks and a wheelbarrow the exact color of freshly pared carrots. As I stared in, the boy came running from the other room and began kicking the blocks. He didn't notice me. A few moments later the young woman entered the room and lifted him, laughing easily and whole-heartedly as she swung the boy under her arm. She came to the window as she had done earlier. I smiled self-consciously, but neither she nor the child responded.

My forehead prickled icily. *Could they both be blind?* I sidled away.

Selina gave a little scream and I spun towards her. "The rug!" she said. "It's getting soaked." She ran across the yard in the rain, snatched the reddish square from the dappling wall and ran back, towards the cottage door. Something heaved convulsively in my subconscious.

"Selina," I shouted. "Don't open it!" But I was too late. She had pushed open the latched wooden door and was standing, hand over mouth, looking into the cottage. I moved close to her and took the rug from her unresisting fingers.

As I was closing the door I let my eyes traverse the cottage's interior. The neat living room in which I had just seen the woman and child was, in reality, a sickening clutter of shabby furniture, old newspapers, cast-off clothing and smeared dishes. It was damp, stinking and utterly deserted.

The only object I recognized from my view through the window was the little wheelbarrow, paintless and broken.

I latched the door firmly and ordered myself to forget what I had seen. Some men who live alone are good housekeepers; others just don't know how.

Selina's face was white. "I don't understand. I don't understand it."

"Slow glass works both ways," I said gently. "Light passes out of a house, as well as in."

"You mean . . . ?"

"I don't know. It isn't our business. Now steady up— Hagan's coming back with our glass." The churning in my stomach was beginning to subside.

Hagan came into the yard carrying an oblong, plastic-covered frame. I held the check out to him, but he was staring at Selina's face. He seemed to know immediately that our uncomprehending fingers had rummaged through his soul. Selina avoided his gaze. She was old and ill-looking and her eyes stared determinedly towards the nearing horizon.

"I'll take the rug from you, Mr. Garland." Hagan finally said. "You shouldn't have troubled yourself over it."

"No trouble. Here's the check."

"Thank you." He was still looking at Selina with a strange kind of supplication. "It's been a pleasure to do business with you."

"The pleasure was mine," I said with equal, senseless formality. I picked up the heavy frame and guided Selina towards the path which led to the road. Just as we reached the head of the now slippery steps Hagan spoke again.

"Mr. Garland!"

I turned unwillingly.

"It wasn't my fault," he said steadily. "A hit-and-run driver got them both, down on the Oban road six years ago. My boy was only seven when it happened. I'm entitled to keep something."

I nodded wordlessly and moved down the path, holding

my wife close to me, treasuring the feel of her arms locked around me. At the bend I looked back through the rain and saw Hagan sitting with squared shoulders on the wall where we had first seen him.

He was looking at the house, but I was unable to tell if there was anyone at the window.

1967

THE THIRD SET of double awards, those for the year 1967, represented a continuing de-emphasis on the traditional science fiction magazines as sources of winners. However, neither the fans nor the writers strayed very far from home. There were no trophies presented to baffled authors or editors summoned away from Grove Press or *The Atlantic Monthly.* The authors and editors honored were all members of the main-line, traditional science fiction community, regardless of their roles as identifiable rebels and iconoclasts within that community.

The winning novels, for instance, were both by newer, more experimental writers. The Hugo winner was Roger Zelazny's *Lord of Light:* the Nebula winner, Samuel R. Delany's *The Einstein Intersection.* Zelazny's book was published by Doubleday and Delany's, by Ace, both with one benefit of prior magazine publication. Both were of somewhat experimental, "lit'ry" natures; both reflected the growing change of consciousness that was taking place at the time. The Zelazny book was steeped in Asian religious tradition; Delany's was a surrealistic and self-conscious manipulation of reality and form.

It's interesting to note that even the unsuccessful nominees shared in this turning away from traditional science fiction themes and attitudes. Difficult and even painful novels by Robert Silverberg and Piers Anthony made both ballots, while in the Hugo voting, at least, there was a longshot bid by Chester Anderson's *The Butterfly Kid,* one of the first and best of the psychedelic novels.

The balloting in the shorter lengths was even more remarkable. The appearance of Damon Knight's *Orbit 1* in 1966, and the winning of a Nebula by Richard McKenna's

"The Secret Place," had established the original anthology as a potential source of award-winning fiction. The following year Doubleday published *Dangerous Visions,* a large anthology of original fiction edited by Harlan Ellison. From this single volume, four stories made the final Nebula ballot and five appeared on the final Hugo ballot. Two Nebula awards were won by stories from *Dangerous Visions,* as were two Hugo awards, while Ellison himself won a Hugo for a short story that had appeared in *If* magazine.

It was a dazzling performance, subject only to the smallest of doubts in view of Ellison's immense political talents, which have been demonstrated repeatedly since 1967 (and had been demonstrated well before that year). Please note that I am in no way suggesting dishonest dealings. Rather, there is the suggestion of a situation comparable to the whole unfortunate Knight-Milford-*Orbit*-Nebula matter. With Harlan Ellison, we observe a man so persuasive, so media-wise, on occasion so charismatic, that one wonders if votes are not cast "because it's Harlan's story" or "because it was in Harlan's book."

At any rate, those winners, starting this time with the short story, were Ellison's own "I have No Mouth and I Must Scream," from *If* (the Hugo winner), and Delany's "Aye, and Gomorrah" from *Dangerous Visions* (the Nebula winner).

Fritz Leiber won both Hugo and Nebula awards for his novelette "Gonna Roll the Bones," a thoroughly popular decision despite such other strong entries as Ellison's "Pretty Maggie Moneyeyes" and Philip K. Dick's unforgettable "Faith of Our Fathers."

The novella category was thoroughly complicated. In Hugo balloting there was another of those uncomfortable dead heats, between Philip José Farmer's "Riders of the Purple Wage" (from *Dangerous Visions)* and Anne McCaffrey's "Weyr Search" (from *Analog)*. And in the Nebula balloting for novella, the winner was "Behold the Man," by Michael Moorcock.

"Behold the Man" was a major achievement, both in its original form and in its later expansion to novel-length. The controversy was not literary but legalistic, for the story first appeared in *New Worlds* magazine in England in 1966. In the United States, Donald Wollheim and Terry Carr were co-editing an annual *reprint* anthology of best stories of the year, and they selected "Behold the Man" for their 1967 edition.

It was this second appearance of the story as a reprint in an anthology with wide circulation in the US that brought first the Nebula nomination and then the award itself to "Behold the Man."

There was a good deal of grumbling, but the award stuck, and no one has attempted to make a retroactive revision to it.

Meanwhile, one of the truly outstanding stories of the year got overlooked. This was "The Star-Pit" by Samuel R. Delany. It appeared in *Worlds of Tomorrow,* one of the minor magazines of the era (actually a spinoff of *Galaxy),* and made the Hugo ballot, but it was completely passed over by the Nebula voters.

Like much of Delany's work, "The Star-Pit" is a complex and difficult story with multiple levels of meaning and numerous ambiguities. I find myself still somewhat puzzled by it, still seeing its meaning differently on each reading after more than a dozen years. I believe that this a reflection of the story's excellence.

The Star-Pit

SAMUEL R. DELANY

I

TWO GLASS PANES with dirt in between and little tunnels from cell to cell: when I was a kid I had an ant-colony.

But once some of our four-to-six-year-olds built an ecologarium with six-foot plastic panels and grooved aluminium bars to hold the corners and the top down. They put it out on the sand.

There was a mud puddle against one wall so you could see what was going on under water. Sometimes segment worms crawling through the reddish earth hit the side so their tunnels were visible for a few inches. In hot weather the inside of the plastic got coated with mist and droplets. The small round leaves on the litmus vines changed from blue to pink, blue to pink as clouds coursed the sky and the pH of the photosensitive soil shifted slightly.

The kids would run out before dawn and belly down naked in the cool sand with their chins on the backs of their hands and stare in the half-dark till the red mill wheel of Sigma lifted over the bloody sea. The sand was maroon then, and the flowers of the crystal plants looked like rubies in the dim light of the giant sun. Up the beach the jungle would begin to whisper while somewhere an ani-wort would start warbling. The kids would giggle and poke each other and crowd closer.

Then Sigma-prime, the second member of the binary, would flare like thermite on the water, and crimson clouds would bleach from coral, through peach, to foam-white. The kids, half on top of each other, lay now like a pile of copper ingots with sun streaks in their hair—even on little Antoni, my oldest, whose hair was black and curly like bubbling oil (like his mother's); the down on the small of his two-year-old back was a white haze across the copper if you looked that close to see.

More children came to squat and lean on their knees, or kneel with their noses an inch from the walls, to watch, like young magicians, as things were born, grew, matured, and other things were born. Enchanted at their own construction, they stared at the miracles in their live museum. A small, red seed lay camouflaged in the silt by the lake/puddle. One evening as white Sigma-prime left the sky violet, it broke open into a brown larva as long and of the same color as the first joint of Antoni's thumb. It flipped and swirled in the mud a couple of days, then crawled to the first branch of the nearest crystal plant to hang exhausted, head down from the tip. The brown flesh hardened, thickened, grew black, shiny. Then one morning the children saw the onyx chrysalis crack, and by second dawn there was an emerald-eyed flying lizard buzzing at the plastic panels.

"Oh, look, da!" they called to me. "It's trying to get out!"

The speed-hazed creature butted at the corner for a few days, then settled at last to crawling around the broad leaves of the miniature shade palms.

When the season grew cool and there was the annual debate over whether the kids should put tunics on—they never stayed in them more than twenty minutes anyway— the jewels of the crystal plant misted, their facets coarsened, and they fell like gravel.

There were little four-cupped sloths,, too, big as a six-year-old's fist. Most of the time they pressed their velvety bodies against the walls and stared longingly across the sand with their retractable eye-clusters. Then two of them swelled for about three weeks. We thought at first it was some bloating infection. But one evening there were a couple of litters of white, velvet balls half hidden by the low leaves of the shade palms. The parents were occupied now and didn't pine to get out.

There was a rock half in and half out of the puddle, I remember, covered with what I'd always called mustard-moss when I saw it in the wild. Once it put out a brush of white hairs. And one afternoon the children ran to collect all the adults they could drag over. "Look, oh da, da, ma, look!" The hairs had detached themselves and were walking around the water's edge, turning end over end along the soft soil,

I had to leave for work in a few minutes and haul some spare drive parts out to Tau Ceti. But when I got back five days later, the hairs had taken root, thickened, and were already putting out the small round leaves of litmus vines. Among the new shoots, lying on her back, claws curled over her wrinkled belly, eyes cataracted like the foggy jewels of the crystal plant—she'd dropped her wings like cellophane days ago—was the flying lizard. Her pearl throat still pulsed, but as I watched, it stopped. Before she died, however, she had managed to deposit, nearly camouflaged in the silt by the puddle, a scattering of red seeds.

I remember getting home from another job where I'd been doing the maintenance on the shuttle-boats for a crew putting up a ring station to circle a planet that was itself circling Aldebaran, I was gone a long time on that one. When I left the landing complex and wandered out toward the tall weeds at the edge of the beach, I still didn't see anybody.

Which was just as well because the night before I'd put on a real winner with the crew to celebrate the completion of the station. That morning I'd taken a couple more drinks at the landing bar to undo last night's damage. Never works.

The swish of frond on frond was like clashed rasps. The sun on the sand reached out two fingers of pure glare and tried to gouge my eyes. I was glad the home compound was deserted because the kids would have asked questions I didn't want to answer; the adults wouldn't say anything, which was harder to answer than questions,

Then, down by the ecologarium, a child screeched. And screeched again. Then Antoni came hurtling toward me, half running, half on all fours, and flung himself on my leg, "Oh, da! Da! Why, oh why, da?"

I'd kicked my boots off and shrugged my shirt back at the compound porch, but I still had my overalls on. Antoni had two fists full of my pants leg and wouldn't let go, "Hey, kid-boy, what's the matter?"

When I finally got him on my shoulder he butted Iris blubber wet face against my collarbone, "Oh, da! Da! It's crazy, it's all craaaa-zy!" His voice rose to lose itself in sobs.

"What's crazy, kid-boy? Tell da."

Antoni held my ear and cried while I walked down to the plastic enclosure.

They'd put a small door in one wall with a two-number combination lock that was suppose to keep this sort of thing from happening. I guess Antoni learned the combination from watching the older kids, or maybe he just figured it out.

One of the young sloths had climbed out and wandered across the sand about three feet.

"See, da! It crazy, it bit me. Bit me, da!" Sobs became sniffles as he showed me a puffy, bluish place on his wrist centered on which was a tiny crescent of pin-pricks. Then he pointed jerkily to the creature.

It was shivering, and bloody froth spluttered from its lip flaps. All the while it was digging futilely at the sand with its clumsy cups, eyes refracted. Now it fell over, kicked, tried to right itself, breath going like a flutter valve. "It can't take the heat," I explained, reaching down to pick it up.

It snapped at me, and I jerked back. "Sun stroke, kid-boy. Yeah, it is crazy."

Suddenly it opened its mouth wide, let out all its air, and didn't take in any more. "It's all right now," I said.

Two more of the baby sloths were at the door, front cups over the sill, staring with bright, black eyes. I pushed them back with a piece of sea shell and closed the door. Antoni kept looking at the white fur ball on the sand. "Not crazy now?"

"It's dead," I told him.

"Dead because it went outside, da?"

I nodded.

"And crazy?" He made a fist and ground something already soft and wet around his upper lip.

I decided to change the subject, which was already too close to something I didn't like to think about. "Who's been taking care of you, anyway?" I asked. "You're a mess, kid-boy. Let's go and fix up that arm. They shouldn't leave a fellow your age all by himself." We started back to the compound. Those bites infect easily, and this one was swelling.

"Why it go crazy? Why it die when it go outside, da?"

"Can't take the light," I said as we reached the jungle. "They're animals that live in shadow most of the time. The plastic cuts out the ultraviolet rays, just like the leaves that shade them when they run loose in the jungle. Sigma-prime's high on ultraviolet. That's why you're so good looking, kid-boy. I think your ma told me their nervous systems are on the surface, all that fuzz. Under the ultraviolet, the enzymes break down so quickly that—does this mean anything to you at all?"

"Uh-uh." Antoni shook his head. Then he came out with, "Wouldn't it be nice, da—" he admired his bite while we walked, "—if some of them could go outside, just a few?"

That stopped me. There were sunspots on his blue black hair. Fronds reflected faint green on his brown cheek. He was grinning, little, and wonderful. Something that had been anger in me a lot of times momentarily melted to raging tenderness, whirling about him like the dust in the light striking down at my shoulders, raging to protect my son. "I don't know about that, kid-boy."

"Why not?"

"It might be pretty bad for the ones who had to stay-inside." I told him. "I mean after a while."

"Why?"

I started walking again. "Come on, let's fix your arm and get you cleaned up."

I washed the wet stuff off his face, and scraped the dry stuff from beneath it which had been there at least two days. Then I got some antibiotic into him.

"You smell funny, da."

"Never mind how I smell. Let's go outside again." I put down a cup of black coffee too fast, and it and my hangover had a fight in my stomach. I tried to ignore it and do a little looking around. But I still couldn't find anybody. That got me mad. I mean he's independent, sure: he's mine. But he's still only two.

II

Back on the beach we buried the dead sloth in the sand, then I pointed out the new, glittering stalks of the tiny crystal plants. At the bottom of the pond, in the jellied mass of ani-wort eggs you could see the tadpole forms quivering already. An orange-fringed shelf fungus had sprouted nearly eight inches since it had been just a few black spores on a pile of dead leaves a few weeks back.

"Grow up," Antoni chirped with nose and fists against the plastic. "Everything grow up, and up."

"That's right."

He grinned at me. "I grow!"

"You grow?" Then he shook his head, twice: once to say no, and the second time because he got a kick from shaking his hair around—there was a lot of it. "You don't grow. You don't get any bigger. Why don't you grow?"

"I do too," I said indignantly. "Just very slowly."

Antoni turned around, leaned on the plastic and moved one toe at a time in the sand—I can't do that—watching me.

"You have to grow all the time," I said. "Not necessarily get bigger. But inside your head you have to grow, kid-boy. For us human-type people that's what's important. And that kind of growing never stops. At least it shouldn't. You can grow, kid-boy, or you can die. That's the choice you've got, and it goes on all your life."

He looked back over his shoulder. "Grow up, all the time, even if they can't get out."

"Yeah," I said. And was uncomfortable all over again. I started pulling off my overalls for something to do. "Even—"

The zipper got stuck. "God *damn* it!—if you can't get out," *Rnrnrnmrnrn*—it came loose again.

The rest got back that evening. They'd been on a group trip around the foot of the mountain. I did a little shouting to make sure my point got across about leaving Antoni alone. Didn't do much good. You know how family arguments go:

He didn't want to come. We weren't going to force—

So what. He's got to learn to do things he doesn't want—

Like some other people I could mention!

Now look—

It's a healthy group. Don't you want him to grow up health—

I'll be happy if he just grows up period. No food, no medical—

But the server was chock full of food. He knows how to use it.

Look, when I got home the kid's arm was swollen all the way up to his elbow!

And so on and so forth, with Antoni sitting in the middle, looking confused. When he got confused enough, he ended it all by announcing matter-of-factly, "Da smell funny when he came home."

Every one got quiet. Then someone said, "Oh, Vyme, you didn't come home that way again! I mean, in front of the children."

I said a couple of things I was sorry for later and stalked off down the beach on a four-mile hike.

Times I got home from work? The ecologarium? I guess I'm just leading up to this one.

The particular job had taken me a hectic week to get. It was putting back together a battleship that was gutted somewhere off Aurigae. Only when I got there, I found I'd been already laid off. That particular war was over—they're real quick now. So I scraped and lied and browned my way into a repair gang that was servicing a traveling replacement station, generally had to humiliate myself to get the job because every other drive mechanic from the battleship fiasco was after it too. Then I got canned the first day because I came to work smelling funny. It took me another week to hitch a ride back to Sigma. Didn't even have enough to pay passage, but I made a deal with the pilot I'd do half the driving for him.

We were an hour out, and I was at the controls when something I'd never heard of happening, happened. We came *this* close to ramming another ship. Consider how much empty space there is; the chances are infinitesimal. And on top of that every ship should be broadcasting an identification beam at all times.

But this big, bulbous keeler-intergalactic slid by so close I could *see* her through the front viewport. Our inertia system went nuts. We jerked around in the stasis whirl from the keeler. I slammed on the video-intercom and shouted, "You great big stupid . . . *stupid* . . ." so mad and scared I couldn't say anything else.

The golden piloting the ship stared at me from the viewscreen with mildly surprised annoyance. I remember his face was just slightly more negroid than mine.

Our little Serpentina couldn't hurt him. But had we been even a hundred meters closer we might have ionized. The other pilot came bellowing from behind the sleeper curtain and started cursing me out.

"Damn it," I shouted, "it was one of those . . ." and lost all the profanity I know to my rage, ". . . golden . . ."

"This far into galactic center? Come off it. They should be hanging out around the star-pit!"

"It was a keeler drive," I insisted. "It came right in front of us." I stopped because the control slick was shaking in my hand. You know the Serpentina colophon? They have it in the corner of the view screen and raised in plastic on the head of the control knobs on the ship. Well, it got pressed into the ham of my thumb so you could make it out for an hour, I was squeezing that control rod that tight.

When he set me down, I went straight to the bar to cool off. And got in a fight. When I reached the beach I was broke, I had a bloody nose, I was sick, and furious.

It was just after first sunset, and the kids were squealing

around the ecologarium. Then one little girl I didn't even recognize ran up to me and jerked my arm. "Da, oh, da! Come look! The ani-worts are just about to—"

I pushed her, and she sat down, surprised, on the sand.

I just wanted to get to the water and splash something cold on my face, because every minute or so it would start to burn.

Another bunch of kids grabbed me, shouting, "Da, da, the ani-worts, da!" and tried to pull me over.

First I took two steps with them. Then I just swung my arms out. I didn't make a sound. But I put my head down and barreled against the plastic wall. Kids screamed. Aluminium snapped, the plastic cracked and went down. My boots were still on, and I kicked and kicked at red earth and sand. Shade palms went down and the leaves tore under my feet. I remember the stems of the crystal plants broken like glass rods beneath a piece of plastic. A swarm of lizards buzzed up around my head. Some of the red was Sigma, some was what burned behind my face.

I remember I was still shaking and watching water run out of the broken lake over the sand, then soak in so that the wet tongue of sand expanded a little, raised just a trifle around the edge. Then I looked up to see the kids coming back down the beach, crying, shouting, afraid and clustered around Antoni's ma. She walked steadily toward me—steady because she was a woman and they were children. But I saw the same fear in her face. Antoni was on her shoulder. Other grownups were coming behind her.

Antoni's ma was a biologist, and I think she had suggested the ecologarium to the kids in the first place. When she looked up from the ruin I'd made, I knew I'd broken something of hers too.

An odd expression got caught in the features of her—I remember it oh so beautiful—face, with compassion alongside the anger, contempt alongside the fear. "Oh, for pity's sake, Vyme," she cried, not loudly at all. "Won't you ever grow up?"

I opened my mouth, but everything I wanted to say was

too big and stayed wedged in my throat.

"Grow up?" Antoni repeated and reached for a lizard that buzzed his head. "Everything stop growing up, now." He looked down again at the wreck I'd made. "All broken. Everything get out."

"He didn't mean to break it," she said to the others for me, then knifed the gratitude I felt toward her with a look. "We'll put it back together."

She put Antoni on the sand and picked up one of the walls.

After they got started, they let me help. A lot of the plants were broken. And only the ani-worts who'd completed metamorphosis could be saved. The flying lizards were too curious to get far away, so we—they netted them and got them back inside. I guess I didn't help that much. And I wouldn't say I was sorry.

They got just about everything back except the sloths. We couldn't find them at all, no matter how long we searched.

The sun was down so they should have been all right. They can't negotiate the sand with any speed so couldn't have reached the jungle. But there were no tracks, no nothing. We even dug in the sand to see if they'd buried themselves. Never did find them, though. It wasn't till more than a dozen years later I discovered where they went.

For the present I accepted Antoni's mildly adequate, "They just must of got out again."

Not too long after that I left the procreation group. Went off to work one day, didn't come back. But like I said to Antoni, you either grow or die. I didn't die.

Once I considered returning. But there was another war, and suddenly there wasn't anything to return to. Some of the group got out alive, Antoni and his ma didn't. I mean there wasn't even any water left on the planet.

When I finally came to the Star-pit, myself, I hadn't had a drink in years. But working there out on the galaxy's edge did something to me—something to the part that grows I'd once talked about on the beach with Antoni.

If it did it to me, it's not surprising it did it to Ratlit and the rest.

(And I remember a black-eyed creature pressed against the plastic wall, staring across impassable sands.)

Perhaps it was knowing this was as far as you could go.

Perhaps it was the golden.

III

Golden? I hadn't even joined the group yet when I first heard the word. I was sixteen and a sophomore at Luna Vocational. I was born in a city called New York on a planet called Earth. Luna is its one satellite. You've heard of the system, I'm sure; that's where we all came from. A few other things about it are well known. Unless you're an anthropologist, though, I doubt you've ever been there. It's way the hell off the main trading routes and pretty primitive. I was a drive-mechanics major, on scholarship, living in and studying hard. All morning in Practical Theory (a ridiculous name for a ridiculous class, I thought then) we'd spent putting together a model keeler intergalactic drive. Throughout those dozens of helical inserts and supernertia organus sensitives, I had been silently cursing my teacher, thinking, about like everyone else in the class, "So what if they can fly this jalopy from one galaxy to another. Nobody will ever be able to ride in them. Not with the Physic and Physiologic shells hanging around this cluster of the Universe."

Back in the dormitory I was lying on my bed, scraping graphite lubricant from my nails with the end of my slide rule and half reading at a folded-back copy of *The Young Mechanic* when I saw the article and the pictures.

Through some freakish accident two people had been discovered who didn't crack up at twenty thousand light-years off the galactic rim, who didn't die at twenty-five thousand.

They were both psychological freaks with some incredible hormone imbalance in their systems. One was a little oriental girl; the other was an older man, blond and big boned, from a cold planet circling Cygnus-beta: golden. They looked sullen as hell, both of them.

Then there were more articles, more pictures, in the economic journals, the sociology student-letters, the legal bulletins, as various fields began acknowledging the impact that the golden and the sudden birth of intergalactic trade were having on them. The head of some commission summed it up with the statement: "Though interstellar travel has been with us for three centuries, intergalactic trade has been an impossibility, not because of mechanical limitations, but rather because of barriers that till now we have not even been able to define. Some psychic shock causes insanity in any human—or for that matter, any intelligent species or perceptual machine or computer—that goes more than twenty thousand light-years from the galactic rim; the complete physiological death, as well as recording breakdown in computers that might replace human crews. Complex explanations have been offered, none completely satisfactory, but the base of the problem seems to be this: as the nature of space and time are relative to the concentration of matter in a given area of the continuum, the nature of reality itself operates by the same, or similar laws. The averaged mass of all the stars in our galaxy controls the 'reality' of our microsector of the universe. But as a ship leaves the galactic rim, 'reality' breaks down and causes insanity and eventual death for any crew, even though certain mechanical laws—though not all—appear to remain, for reasons we don't understand, relatively constant. Save for a few barbaric experiments done with psychedelics at the dawn of spatial travel, we have not even developed a vocabulary that can deal with 'reality' apart from its measurable, physical expression. Yet, just when we had to face the black limit of intergalactic space, bright resources glittered within. Some few of us whose sense of reality has been shattered by infantile, childhood, or prenatal trauma, whose physiological and psychological orientation makes life in our interstellar society painful or impossible—not all, but a few of these golden . . ." at which point there was static, or the gentleman coughed, ". . . can make the crossing and return." The name golden, *sans* noun, stuck. *A few* was the understatement of the millennium. Slightly less than one human being in thirty-four thousand is a golden. A couple of people had pictures of emptying all mental institutions by just shaking them out over the galactic rim. Didn't work like that. The particular psychosis and endocrine setup was remarkably specialized. Still, back then there was excitement, wonder, anticipation, hope, admiration in the word; admiration for the ones who could get out.

"Golden?" Ratlit said when I asked him. He was working as a grease monkey out here in the Star-pit over at Poloscki's. "Born with the word. Grew up with it. Weren't no first time for me. Though I remember when I was about six, right after the last of my parents had been killed, and I was hiding out with a bunch of other lice in a broke-open packing crate in an abandoned freight yard near the ruins of Helios on Creton VII—that's where I was born, I think. Most of the city had been starved out by then, but somebody was getting food to us. There was this old crook-back character who was hiding too. He used to sit on the top of the packing crate and bang his heels on the aluminum slats and tell us stories about the stars. Had a couple of rags held with twists of wire for clothes, missing two fingers off one hand; he kept plucking the loose skin under his chin with those grimy talons. And he talked about them. So I asked, 'Golden what, sir?' He leaned forward so that his face was like a mahogany bruise on the evening, and croaked, 'They've been *out,* I tell you, seen more than ever you or I. Human and inhuman, kid-boy, mothered by women and fathered by men, still they live by their own laws and walk their own ways!' " Ratlit and I were sitting under a street lamp with our feet over the Edge where the fence had broken. His hair was like breathing flame in the wind, his single earring glittered. Star-flecked infinity dropped away below our boot soles, and the wind created by the stasis field that held our atmosphere down—we call it the 'world-wind' out here because it's never cold and never hot and like nothing on any world—whipped his black shirt back from his bony chest as we gazed on galactic night between our knees. "I guess that was back during the second Kyber war," he concluded,

"Kyber war?" I asked. "Which one was that?"

He shrugged. "I just know it was fought over possession of couple of tons of di-allium, that's the polarized element the golden brought back from Lupe-galaxy. They used y-adna ships to fight it—that's why it was such a bad war. I mean worse than usual."

"Y-adna? That's a drive I don't know anything about."

"Some golden saw the plans for them in a civilization in Magellanic-9,"

"Oh," I said. "And what was Kyber?"

"It was a weapon, a sort of fungus the golden brought back from some overrun planet on the rim of Andromeda. It's deadly. Only they were too stupid to bring back the anti-toxin."

"That's golden for you."

"Yeah. You ever notice about golden, Vyme? I mean just the word, I found out all about it from my publisher, once. It's semantically unsettling."

"Really?" I said. "So are they. Unsettling I mean." I'd just finished a rough, rough day installing a rebuilt keeler in a quantum transport hull that just wasn't big enough. The golden having the job done stood over my shoulder the whole time, and every hour he'd come out with the sort of added instruction that would make the next sixty-one min-utes miserable. But I did it. The golden paid me in cash and without a word climbed into the lift, and two minutes later, while I was still washing the grease off, the damn five-hundred-ton hulk began to whistle for take-off. Sandy, a young fellow who'd come looking for a temporary me-chanic's job three months back, but hadn't given me cause to fire him yet, barely had time to pull the big waldoes out of the way and go scooting into the shock chamber when the three hundred meter doofus tore loose from the grapplers. And Sandy, who, like a lot of these youngsters drifting around from job to job, is usually sort of quiet and vague, got loud and specific. ". . . two thousand pounds of non-shockproof equipment out there . . . ruin it all if he could . . .

I'm not expendable, I don't care what a . . . these golden out here . . ." while the ship hove off where only the golden go. I just flipped on the "not-open" sign, left the rest of the grease where it was, left the hangar and hunted up Ratlit.

So there we were, under that street lamp, silting on the Edge, in the world-wind.

"Golden," Ratlit said under the roar. "It would be much easier to take if it were grammatically connected to something: golden ones, golden people. Or even one gold, two golden."

"Male golden, female goldine?" I suggested.

"Something like that. It's not an adjective, it's not a noun. My publisher told me that for a while it was written with a dash after it that stood for whatever it might modify."

I remember the dash. It was an uneasy joke, a fill-in for that cough. Golden *what?* People had already started to feel uncomfortable. Then it went past joking and back to just "golden."

"You illiterates always want to mess up the language," Ratlit chided. "Just think about that, Vyme. Just golden, one, two, or three of them."

"That's something to think about, kid-boy," I said.

Ratlit had been six during the Kyber war. Square that and add it once again for my age now. Ratlit's? Double six and add one. I like kids, and they like me. But that may be because my childhood left me a lot younger at forty-two than I should be. Ratlit's had left him a lot older than any thirteen-year-old has a right to be.

"No golden took part in the war," Ratlit said.

"They never do." I watched his thin fingers get all tangled together.

After two divorces, my mother ran off with a salesman and left me and four siblings with an alcoholic aunt for a year. Yeah, they still have divorces, monogamous marriages and stuff like that where I was born. Like I say, it's pretty primitive. I left home at fifteen, made it through vocational school on my own, and learned enough about what makes things fly to end up—after that disastrous marriage I told you about earlier—with my own repair hangar on the Star-pit.

Compared with Ratlit I had a stable childhood.

That's right, he lost the last parent he remembered when he was six. At seven he was convicted of his first felony after escaping from Cretan VII. But part of his treatment at hospital *cum* reform school *cum* prison was to have the details lifted from his memory. "Did something to my head back there. That's why I never could learn to read, I think." For the next couple of years he ran away from one foster group after the other. When he was eleven, some guy took him home from Play Planet where he'd been existing under the boardwalk on discarded hot dogs, soublakia, and phelafel. "Fat, smoked perfumed cigarettes; name was Vivian?" Turned out to be the publisher. Ratlit stayed for three months during which time he dictated a novel to Vivian. "Protecting my honor," Ratlit explained, "I had to do *something* to keep him busy."

The book sold a few hundred thousand copies as a precocious curiosity among many. But Ratlit had split. The next years he was involved as a shill in some illegality I never understood. He didn't either. "But I bet I made a million, Vyme! I earned at least a million." It's possible. At thirteen he still couldn't read or write, but his travels had gained him fair fluency in three languages. A couple of weeks ago he'd wandered off a stellar tramp, dirty and broke, here at the Star-pit. And I'd gotten him a job as grease monkey over at Poloscki's.

He leaned his elbows on his knees, his chin in his hands. "Vyme, it's a shame,"

"What's a shame, kid-boy?"

"To be washed up at my age. A has-been! To have to grapple with the fact that this—" he spat at a star—"is it,"

He was talking about golden again.

"You still have a chance." I shrugged. "Most of the time it doesn't come out till puberty."

He cocked his head up at me. "I've been pubescent since I was nine, buster."

"*Excuse* me."

"I feel cramped in, Vyme. There's all that night out there to grow up in, to explore."

"There was a time," I mused, "when the whole species was confined to the surface, give or take a few feet up or down, of a single planet. You've got a whole galaxy to run around in. You've seen a lot of it, yeah. But not all."

"But there are billions of galaxies out there. I want to see them. In all the stars around here there hasn't been one life form discovered that's based on anything but silicon or carbon. I overheard two golden in a bar once, talking: there's something in some galaxy out there that's as big as a star, neither alive nor dead, and sings. I want to hear it, Vyme!"

"Ratlit, you can't fight reality."

"Oh, go to sleep, grandpa!" He closed his eyes and bent his head back until the cords of his neck quivered. "What is it that makes a golden? A combination of physiological and psychological . . . what?"

"It's primarily some sort of hormonal imbalance as well as an environmentally conditioned thalamic/personality response."

"Yeah. Yeah." His head came down. "And that X-chromosome heredity nonsense they just connected up with it a few years back. But all I know is *they* can take the stasis shift from galaxy to galaxy, where you and I, Vyme, if we get more than twenty thousand light-years off the rim, we're dead."

"Insane at twenty thousand," I corrected. "Dead at twenty-five."

"Same difference." He opened his eyes. They were large, green and mostly pupil. "You know I stole a golden belt? Rolled it off a staggering slob about a week ago who came out of a bar and collapsed on the corner. I went across the Pit to Calle-J where nobody knows me and wore it around for a few hours, just to see if I felt different."

"You did?" Ratlit had lengths of gut that astounded me about once a day.

"I didn't. But people walking around me did. Wearing that two-inch band of yellow metal around my waist, nobody in the worlds could tell I wasn't a golden, just walking by on the street, without talking to me a while, or making hormone tests. And wearing that belt, I learned just how much I hated golden. Because I could suddenly see, in almost everybody who came by, how much they hated me while I had that metal belt on. I threw it over the Edge." Suddenly he grinned. "But maybe I'll steal another one,"

"You really hate them, Ratlit?"

He narrowed his eyes at me and looked superior.

"Sure, I talk about them," I told him. "Sometimes they're a pain to work for. But it's not their fault we can't take the reality shift."

"I'm just a child," he said evenly, "incapable of such fine reasoning. *I* hate them." He looked back at the night. "How can you stand to be trapped by anything, Vyme?"

IV

Three memories crowded into my head when he said that.

First: I was standing at the railing of the East River—runs past this New York I was telling you about—at midnight, looking at the illuminated dragon of the Manhattan Bridge that spanned the water, then at the industrial fires flickering in bright, smoky Brooklyn, and then at the template of mercury street lamps behind me bleaching out the playground and most of Houston Street; then, at the reflections in the water, here like crinkled foil, there like glistening rubber; at last, looked up at the midnight sky itself. It wasn't black but dead pink, without a star. This glittering world made the sky a roof that pressed down on me so I almost screamed . . . That time the next night I was twenty-seven light-years away from Sol on my first star-run.

The second, I was visiting my mother after my first few years out. I was looking in the closet for something when this contraption of plastic straps and buckles fell on my head. "What's this, ma?" And she smiled with a look of idiot nostalgia and crooned, "Why that's your little harness, Vymey. Your first father and I would take you on picnics up at Bear

Mountain and put you in that and tie you to a tree with about ten feet of cord so you wouldn't get lost." I didn't hear the rest because of the horror that suddenly flooded me, thinking of myself tied up in that thing. Okay, I was twenty and had just joined that beautiful procreation-group a year back on Sigma and was the proud father of three and expecting two more. The hundred and sixty-three of us had the whole beach and nine miles of jungle and half a mountain to ourselves; maybe I was seeing Antoni caught up in that thing, trying to catch a bird or a beetle or a wave—with only ten feet of cord. I hadn't worn clothes for anything but work in a twelvemonth, and I was chomping to get away from that incredible place I had grown up in called an apartment and back to wives, husbands, kids and civilization. Anyway, it was pretty terrible.

The third was after I had left the proke-group—fled them. I suppose, guilty and embarrassed over something I couldn't name, still having nightmares once a month that woke me screaming about what was going to happen to the kids, even though I knew one point of group marriage was to prevent the loss of one, two, or three parents being traumatic—still wondering if I wasn't making the same mistakes my parents made, hoping my brood wouldn't turn out like me, or worse like the kids you sometimes read about in the paper (like Ratlit, though I hadn't met him yet), horribly suspicious that no matter how different I tried to be from my sires, it was just the same thing all over again . . . Anyway, I was on the ship bringing me to the Star-pit for the first time. I'd gotten talking to a golden who, as golden go, was a pretty regular gal. We'd been discussing inter- and intragalactic drives. She was impressed I knew so much. I was impressed that she could use them and know so little. She was digging in a very girl-way the six-foot-four, two-hundred-and-ten-pound drive mechanic with mildly grimy fingernails that was me. I was digging in a very boy-way the slim, amber-eyed young lady who had seen it *all*. From the view deck we watched the immense artificial disk of the Star-pit approach, when she turned to me and said, in a voice that didn't sound cruel at

all, "This is as far as you go, isn't it?" And I was frightened
all over again, because I knew that on about nine different
levels she was right.

Ratlit said, "I know what you're thinking." A couple of times
when he'd felt like being quiet and I'd felt like talking I may
have told him more than I should. "Well, cube that for me,
dad. That's how trapped I feel!"

I laughed, and Ratlit looked very young again.

"Come on," I said. "Let's take a walk."

"Yeah." He stood. The wind tore at our hair like fingers.
"I want to go see Alegra."

"I'll walk you as far as Calle-G," I told him. "Then I'm
going to go to bed."

"I wonder what Alegra thinks about this business? I always find Alegra a very good person to talk to," he said
sagely. "Not to put you down, but her experiences are a little
more up to date than yours. You have to admit she has a
modern point of view. Plus the fact that she's older." Older
than Ratlit, anyway. She was fifteen.

"I don't think being 'trapped' ever really bothers her that
way." I said. "Which may be a place to take a lesson from."

By Ratlit's standards Alegra had a few things over me. In
my youth kids took to dope in their teens, twenties. Alegra
was born with a three-hundred-milligram-a-day habit on a
bizarre narcotic that combined the psychedelic qualities of
the most powerful hallucinogens with the addictiveness of
the strongest depressants. I can sympathize. Alegra's mother
was addicted, and the tolerance was passed with the blood
plasma through the placental wall. Ordinarily a couple of
complete transfusions at birth would have gotten the new-
born child straight. But Alegra was also a highly projective
telepath. She projected the horrors of birth, the glories of her
infantile hallucinated world on befuddled doctors; she was
given her drug. Without too much difficulty she managed to
be given her drug every day since.

Once I asked Alegra when she'd first heard of golden, and
she came back with this horror story. A lot were coming

back from Tiber-44 cluster with psychic shock—the mental condition of golden is pretty delicate, and sometimes very minor conflicts nearly ruin them. Anyway, the government that was sponsoring the importation of micro-micro surgical equipment from some tiny planet in that galaxy, to protect its interests, hired Alegra, age eight, as a psychiatric therapist. "I'd concretize their fantasies and make them work 'em through. In just a couple of hours I'd have 'em back to their old, mean, stupid selves again. Some of them were pretty nice when they came to me." But there was a lot of work for her; projective telepaths are rare. So they started withholding her drug to force her to work harder, then rewarding her with increased dosage. "Up till then," she told me, "I might have kicked it. But when I came away, they had me on double what I used to take. They pushed me past the point where withdrawal would be fatal. But I *could* have kicked it, up till then, Vyme." That's right. Age eight.

Oh yeah. The drug was imported by golden from Cancer-9, and most of it goes through the Star-pit. Alegra came here because illegal imports are easier to come by, and you can get it for just about nothing—if you want it. Golden don't use it.

The wind lessened as Ratlit and I started back. Ratlit began to whistle. In Calle-K the first night lamp had broken so that the level street was like a tunnel of black.

"Ratlit?" I asked. "Where do you think you'll be, oh, in say five years?"

"Quiet," he said. "I'm trying to get to the end of the street without bumping into the walls, tripping on something, or some other catastrophe. If we get through the next five minutes all right, I'll worry about the next five years." He began whistling again.

"Trip, bump the walls?"

"I'm listening for echoes." Again he commenced the little jets of music.

I put my hands in my overall pouch and went on quietly while Ratlit did the bat bit. Then there was a catastrophe. Though I didn't realize it at the time.

Into the circle of light from the remaining lamp at the other
end of the street walked a golden.

His hands went up to his face, and he was laughing. The
sound skittered in the street. His belt was low on his belly the
way the really down and broke g . . .

Ratlit would say that was ungrammatical, though. And I
just thought of a better way to describe him; the resemblance
struck me immediately. He looked like Sandy, my mechanic,
who is short, twenty-four years old, muscled like an ape, and
wears his worn-out work clothes even when he's off duty. "I
just want this job for a while, boss. I'm not staying out here
at the Star-pit. As soon as I shave up a little, I'm gonna make
it back in toward galactic center. It's funny out here, like
dead." He gazes up through the opening in the hangar roof
where there are no clouds and no stars either. "Yeah. I'm just
gonna be here for a little while."

"Fine with me, kid-boy."

That was three months back, like I say. He's still with me.
He works hard too, which puts him a cut above a lot of characters out here. There's something about Sandy . . . On the
other hand Sandy's face is also hacked up with acne. His hair
is always snap short over his wide head, but in these aspects,
the golden was exactly Sandy's opposite, come to think of it.
There was still something about him . . . The golden staggered, went down on his knees still laughing, then collapsed.
By the time we reached him, he was silent. With the toe of
his boot Ratlit nudged the hand from the belt buckle.

It flopped, palm up, on the pavement. The little fingernail
was three quarters of an inch long, the way a lot of the
golden wear it. (Like his face, the tips of Sandy's fingers are
all masticated wrecks. Still, something . . .)

"Now isn't that something." Ratlit shook his head. "What
do you want to do with him, Vyme?"

"Nothing," I said, "Let him sleep it off."

"Leave him so somebody can come along and steal his
belt?" Ratlit grinned. "I'm not that nasty."

"Weren't you just telling me how much you hated

golden?"

"I'd be nasty to whoever stole the belt and wore it. Nobody but a golden should be hated that much."

"Ratlit, let's go."

But he had already kneeled down and was shaking his shoulder. "Let's get him to Alegra's and find out what's the matter with him."

"He's just drunk."

"Nope," Ratlit said. " 'Cause he don't smell funny."

"Look. Get back." I hoisted the golden up and laid him across my neck, fireman's carry. "Start moving." I told Ratlit. "I think you're crazy."

Ratlit grinned. "Thanks. Maybe he'll be grateful and lay some lepta on me for taking him in off the street."

"You don't know golden," I said. "But if he does, split it with me."

"Sure."

Two blocks later we reached Alegra's place. The golden was light, so I didn't have much trouble. Halfway up the tilting stairs Teehalt said, "She's in a good mood."

"I guess she is." The weight across my shoulders was becoming pleasant.

I can't describe Alegra's place. I can describe a lot of places like it; and I can describe it before she moved in because I knew a derelict named Drunk-roach who slept on that floor before she did. You know what never-wear plastic look like when they wear out? What non-rust metals look like when they rust through? It was a shabby crack-walled cubicle with dirt in the corners and scars on the window pane when Drunk-roach had his pile of blankets in the corner. But since the hallucinating, projective telepath took it over, who knows what it had become.

Ratlit opened the door on an explosion of classical beauty. "Come in," she sang, accompanied by symphonic arrangement scored on twenty-four staves, with full chorus. "What's that you're carrying, Vyme? Oh, it's a golden!" And before me dizzying tides of yellow swirled and melted. "Put him down, put him down quick and let's see what's wrong!"

Hundreds of eyes, spotlights, glittering lenses; I lowered him to the mattress in the corner. "Ohhh . . ." breathed Alegra.

And the golden lay on orange silk pillows in a teak barge drawn by swans, accompanied by flutes and drums.

"Where did you find him?" she hissed, circling against the ivory moon on her broom. We watched the glowing barge, hundreds of feet below, sliding down the silvered waters between the crags.

"We just picked him up off the street," Ratlit said. "Vyme thought he was drunk. But he don't smell."

"Was he laughing?" Alegra asked. Laughter rolled and broke open on the rocks.

"Yeah," Ratlit said. "Just before he collapsed."

"Then he must be from the Undok expedition that just got back." Mosquitoes darted at us through the wet fronds. The insects reeled among the leaves, upsetting the droplets that fell like glass as, barely visible beyond the palms, the barge drifted on the bright, sweltering river.

"That's right," I said, backpaddling frantically to avoid a hippopotamus that threatened to upset my kayak. "I'd forgotten they'd just come in."

"Okay," Ratlit said, his breath clouding in front of his lips. "I'm out of it. Let me in. Where did they come back from?" The snow hissed beneath the runners, as we looked after the barge, nearly at the white horizon.

"Undok, of course," Alegra said. The barking grew fainter. "Where did you think?"

White eclipsed to black, and the barge was a spot gleaming in the distance of galactic night, flown on by laboring comets.

"Undok is the furthest galaxy reached yet," I told Teehalt. "They just got back last week."

"Sick," Alegra added.

I dug my fingers against my abdomen, trying physically to grab the pain.

"They all came back sick—"

Fever heated blood-bubbles in my eyes, and I slipped to the ground, my mouth wide, my tongue like paper on my lips . . .

Ratlit coughed. "All *right,* Alegra. Cut it out! You don't have to be so dramatic!"

"Oh, I'm dreadfully sorry, Ratty, Vyme." Coolth, water. Nausea swept away as solicitous nurses hastily put the pieces back together until everything was beautiful, or so austerely horrible it could be appreciated as beauty. "Anyway," she went on, "they came back with some sort of disease they picked up out there. Apparently it's not contagious, but they're stuck with it for the rest of their lives. Every few days they suddenly have a blackout. It's preceded by a fit of hysterics. It's just one of those stupid things they can't do anything about yet. It doesn't hurt their being golden."

Ratlit began to laugh. Suddenly he asked, "How long are they passed out for?"

"Only a few hours," Alegra said. "It must be terribly annoying." And I began to feel mildly itchy in all sorts of unscratchable places, my shoulder blades, somewhere down my ear, the roof of my mouth. Have you ever tried to scratch the roof of your mouth?

"Well," Ratlit said, "let's sit down and wait it out."

"We can talk," Alegra said, patly. "That way it won't seem like such a long . . ." and hundreds of years later she finished ". . . time."

"Good," Ratlit said. "I wanted to talk to you. That's why I came up here in the first place."

"Oh. fine!" Alegra said. "I love to talk. I want to talk about love. Loving someone" (an incredible yearning twisted my stomach, rose to block my throat) "I mean really loving someone" (the yearning brushed the edge of agony) "means you are willing to admit the person you love is not what you first fell in love with, not the image you first had; and you must be able to like them still for being as close to that image as they are, and avoid disliking them for being so far away."

And through the tenderness that suddenly obliterated all hurt, Ratlit's voice came from the jeweled mosaics of overlapping masks that shielded him: "Alegra, I want to talk about loneliness,"

"I'm on my way home, kids," I said. "Tell me what happens with Prince Charming when he wakes up." They kept on talking while I went through the difficulties of finding my way out without Alegra's help. When my head cleared, halfway down the stairs, I couldn't tell you if I'd been there five minutes or five years.

V

When I got to the hangar next morning Sandy was filing the eight-foot prongs on the conveyer. "You got a job coming in about twenty minutes," he called down from the scaffold.

"I hope it's not another of those rebuilt jobs."

"Yep."

"Hell," I said. "I don't want to see another one for six weeks."

"All he wants is a general tuneup. Maybe two hours."

"Depends on where it's been," I said. "Where has it been?"

"Just back from—"

"Never mind." I started toward the office cubicle. "I think I'll put the books in order for the last six months. Can't let it go forever."

"Boss," Sandy protested, "that'll take all day!"

"Then I better get started." I leaned back out the door. "Don't disturb me."

Of course as soon as the shadow of the hull fell over the office window I came out in my coveralls, after giving Sandy five minutes to get it grappled and himself worried. I took the lift up to the one-fifty catwalk, When I stepped out, Sandy threw me a grateful smile from his scar-ugly face. The golden had already started his instructions. When I reached them and coughed, the golden turned to me and continued talking, not bothering to fill me in on what he had said before, figuring Sandy and I would put it together. You could tell this golden had made his pile. He wore an immaculate blue tunic, with bronze codpiece, bracelets and earrings. His hair was the same bronze, his skin was burned red black, and his blue-gray eyes and tight-muscled mouth were proud, proud, proud. While I finished getting instructions, Sandy quietly got started unwelding the eight-foot seal of the organum so we could get to the checkout circuits.

Finally the golden stopped talking—that's the only way you could tell he was finished—and leaned his angular six and a half feet against the railing, clicking his glossy, manicured nails against the pipe a few times. He had that same sword-length pinky nail, all white against his skin. I climbed out on the rigging to help Sandy.

We had been at work ten minutes when a kid, maybe eighteen or nineteen, barefoot and brown, black hair hacked off at shoulder length, a rag that didn't fit tucked around under his belt, and dirty, came wandering down the catwalk. His thumbs were hooked under the yellow beltlinks: golden.

First I thought he'd come from the ship. Then I realized he'd just stalked into the hangar from outside and come up on the lift.

"Hey, brother!" The kid who was golden hooked his thumbs in his belt, as Sandy and I watched the dialogue from the rigging on the side of the hull. "I'm getting tired of hanging around this Star-pit. Just about broke as well. Where you running to?"

The man who was golden clicked his nails again. "Go away, distant cousin."

"Come on, brother, give me a berth on your lifeboat out of this dungheap to someplace worthwhile."

"Go away, or I'll kill you."

"Now, brother, I'm just a youngster adrift in this forsaken quarter of the sky. Come on, now—"

Suddenly the blond man whirled from the railing, grabbed up a four-foot length of pipe leaning beside him, and swung it so hard it hissed. The black haired ragamuffin leapt back and from under his rag snatched something black that, with a flick of that long nail, suddenly had seven inches of blade in front of it. The bar swung again, caught the shoulder of the boy, then clattered against the hull. He shrieked and came straight forward. The two bodies locked, turned, fell. A gur-

gle, and the man's hands slipped from the neck of the ragamuffin. The boy scrambled back to his feet. Blood bubbled
and popped on the hot blade.

A last spasm caught the man, and he flipped over, smear-
ing the enameled catwalk, rolled once more, this time under
the rail, and dropped two hundred and fifty feet to the cement flooring.

Flick. Off went the power in the knife. The golden wiped
powdered blood on his thigh, spat over the rail and said
softly, "No relative of mine." Flick. The blade itself disappeared. He started down the catwalk.

"Hey!" Sandy called, when he choked his voice back into
his throat, "what about . . . I mean you . . . well, your ship!"
There are no inheritance laws among golden—only rights of
plunder.

The golden glanced back. "I give it to you," he sneered.
His shoulder must have been killing him, but he stepped into
the lift like he was walking into a telephone booth. That's a
golden for you.

Sandy was horrified and bewildered. Behind his pitted ugli-
ness there was that particularly wretched amazement only
the totally vulnerable get when hurt.

"That's the first time you've ever seen an incident like
that?" I felt sorry for him.

"Well, I wandered into Gerg's Bar a couple of hours after
they had that massacre. But the ones who started it were
drunk."

"Drunk or sober." I said, "Believe me, it doesn't mean
that much difference to the way a man acts. I know." I shook
my head. "I keep forgetting you've only been here three
months."

Sandy, upset, looked down at the twisted blot on the flooring. "What about him? And the ship, boss?"

"I'll call the wagon to come scrape him up. And so the
ship is yours."

"Huh?"

"He gave it to you. It'll stand up in court. It just takes one witness. Me."

"What am I gonna do with it? I mean I would have to haul it to a junk station to get the salvage. Look, Boss, I'm gonna give it to you. Sell it or something. I'd feel sort of funny with it anyway."

"I don't want it. Besides, then I'd be involved in the transaction and couldn't be a witness."

"I'll be a witness." Ratlit stepped from the lift. "I caught the whole bit when I came in the door. Great acoustics in this place." He whistled again. The echo came back. Ratlit closed his eyes a moment. "Ceiling is . . . a hundred and twenty feet overhead, more or less. How's that, huh?"

"Hundred and twenty-seven," I said.

Ratlit shrugged. "I need more practice. Come on, Sandy, you give it to him, and I'll be a witness."

"You're a minor," Sandy said. Sandy didn't like Ratlit. I used to think it was because Ratlit was violent and flamboyant where Sandy was stolid and ugly. Even though Sandy kept protesting the temporariness of his job to me, I remember, when I first got to the Star-pit, those long-dying thoughts I'd had about leaving. It was a little too easy to see Sandy a mechanic here thirty years from now. I wasn't the only one it had happened to. Ratlit had been a grease monkey three weeks. You tell me where he was going to be in three weeks. "Aren't you suppose to be greasing at Poloscki's?" Sandy said, turning back to the organum.

"Coffee break," Ratlit said. "If you're going to give it away, Sandy, can I have it?"

"So you can claim salvage? Hell, no."

"I don't want it for salvage. I want it for a present." Sandy looked up again. "Yeah. To give to someone else. Finish the tuneup and give it to me, okay?"

"You're nuts, kid-boy," Sandy said. "Even if I gave you the ship, what you gonna pay for the work with?"

"Aw, it'll only take a couple of hours, You're half done anyway. I figured you'd throw in the tuneup along with it. If you really want the money, I'll get it to you a little at a time. Vyme, what sort of professional discount will you give me?

I'm just a grease monkey, but I'm still in the business."

I whacked the back of his red head, between a-little-too-playfully and not-too-hard. "Come on, kid-boy," I said. "Help me take care of puddles downstairs. Sandy, finish it up, huh?"

Sandy grunted and plunged both hands back into the organum.

As soon as the lift door closed, Ratlit demanded, "You gonna give it to me, Vyme?"

"It's Sandy's ship," I said. "You tell him, and he will."

I laughed. "You tell me how the golden turned out when he came to. I assume that's who you want the ship for. What sort of fellow was he?"

Ratlit hooked his fingers in the mesh wall of the lift cage and leaned back. "They're only two types of golden," He began to swing from side to side. "Mean ones and stupid ones." He was repeating a standard line you heard around the Star-pit.

"I hope yours is stupid," I said, thinking of the two who'd just ruined Sandy's day and upset mine.

"Which is worse?" Ratlit shrugged. That is the rest of the line. When a golden isn't being outright mean, he exhibits the sort of nonthinkingness that gets other people hurt—you remember the one that nearly rammed my ship, or the ones who didn't bother to bring back the Kyber antitoxin? It can be worse than meanness. "But this one—" Ratlit stood up "—is unbelievably stupid."

"Yesterday you hated them; Today you want to give one a ship."

"He doesn't have one," Ratlit explained calmly, as though that warranted all change of attitude. "And because he's sick, it'll be hard for him to find work unless he has one of his own."

"I see." We bounced on the silicon cushion. I pushed open the door and started for the office. "What all went on after I left? I must have missed the best part of the evening."

"You did. Will I really need that much more sleep when I pass thirty-five?"

"Cut the cracks and tell me what happened."

"Well—" Ratlit leaned against the office doorjamb while I dialed necrotics. "Alegra and I talked a little after you left, till finally we realized the golden was awake and listening. Then he told us we were beautiful."

I raised an eyebrow. "Mmmm?"

"That's what we said. And he said it again, that watching us talk and think and build was one of the most beautiful things he'd ever seen. 'What have you seen?' we asked him. And he began to tell us." Ratlit stopped breathing, something built up, then, at once it came out, "Oh, Vyme, the places he's been! The things he done, the landscapes he's starved in, the hells where he's had to lie down and go to sleep he was that tired, or the heavens he's soared through screaming! Oh, the things he told us about! And Alegra made them almost real so we could all be there again, just like she used to do when she was a psychiatrist! The stories, the places, the things . . ."

"Sounds like it was really something,"

"It was nothing!" he came back vehemently. "It was all in the tears that wash your eyes, in the humming in your cars, in the taste of your own saliva. It was just a hallucination, Vyme! It wasn't real." Here his voice started cracking between the two octaves that were after it. "But that thing I told you about . . . huge . . . alive and dead at the same time, like a star . . . way in another galaxy. Well, he's seen it. And last night, but it wasn't real, of course, but . . . I almost heard it . . . singing!" His eyes were huge and green and bright. I felt envious of anyone who could pull this reaction from kids like Alegra and Ratlit.

"So, we decided—" his voice fixed itself on the proper side of middle C—"after he went back to sleep, and we lay awake talking a while longer, that we'd try and help him get back out there. Because it's . . . wonderful!"

"That's fascinating," When I finished my call, I stood up from the desk. I'd been sitting on the corner. "After work I'll buy you dinner and you can tell me all about the things he showed you."

"He's still there, at Alegra's," Ratlit said—helplessly, I realized after a moment. "I'm going back right after work."

"Oh," I said. I didn't seem to be invited.

"It's just a shame," Ratlit said when we came out of the office, "that he's *so* stupid." He glanced at the mess that had been golden staining the concrete and shook his head.

VI

I'd gone back to the books when Sandy stepped in. "All finished. What say we knock off for a beer or something, huh, boss?"

"All right," I said, surprised. Sandy was usually as social as he was handsome. "Want to talk about something?"

"Yeah." He looked relieved.

"That business this morning got to your head, huh?"

"Yeah," he repeated.

"There is a reason," I said as I made ready to go. "It's got something to do with the psychological part of being a golden. Meanness and stupidity, like everyone says. But however it makes them act here, it protects them from complete insanity at the twenty thousand light-year limit."

"Yeah. I know, I know." Sandy had started stepping uncomfortably from one boot to the other. "But that's not what I wanted to talk about."

"It isn't?"

"Um-um."

"Well?" I asked after a moment.

"It's that kid, the one you're gonna give the ship to."

"Ratlit?"

"Yeah."

"I haven't made up my mind about giving him the ship," I lied. "Besides, legally it's yours."

"You'll give it to him," Sandy said. "And I don't care, I mean not about the ship. But, boss, I gotta talk to you about that kid-boy."

Something about Sandy . . .

I'd never realized he'd thought of Ratlit as more than a

general nuisance. Also, he seemed sincerely worried about me. I was curious. It took him all the way to the bar and through two beers—while I drank hot milk with honey—before he tongued and chewed what he wanted to say into shape.

"Boss, understand, I'm nearer Ratlit than you. Not only my age. My life's been more like his than yours has. You look at him like a son, To me, he's a younger brother: 1 taught him all the tricks. I don't understand him completely, but I see him clearer than you do. He's had a hard time, but not as hard as you think. He's gonna take you—and I don't mean money—for everything he can."

Where the hell that came from I didn't know and didn't like. "He won't take anything I don't want to give."

"Boss?" Sandy suddenly asked. "You got kids of your own?"

"Nine," I said. "Did have. I don't see the ones who're left now, for which their parents have always been just as happy—except one. And she was sensible enough to go along with the rest, while she was alive."

"Oh." Sandy got quiet again. Suddenly he went scrambling in his overall pouch and pulled out a three-inch porta-pix. Those great, greasy hands that I was teaching to pick up an egg shell through a five-hundred to one-ratio waldo were clumsily fumbling at the push-pull levers. "I got kids," he said. "See. Seven of them."

And on the porta-pix screen was a milling, giggling group of little apes that couldn't have been anybody else's. All the younger ones lacked was acne. They even shuffled back and forth from one foot to the other. They began to wave, and the speaker in the back chirped: "Hi da! Hello, da! Da, mommy says to say we love you! Da, da, come home soon!"

"I'm not with them now," he said throatily. "But I'm going back soon as I get enough money so I can take them all out of that hell-hole they're in now and get the whole family with a decent sized proke-group. There're only twenty-three adults there now, and things were beginning to rub. That's why I left in the first place. It was getting so nobody could talk to anyone else. That's pretty rough on all our kids, thirty-two when I left. But soon I'll be able to fix that."

"On the salary I'm paying you?" This was the first I'd heard of any of this; that was my first reaction. My second, which I didn't voice, was: Then why the hell don't you take that ship and sell it somehow! Over forty and self-employed the most romantic become monetarily practical.

Sandy's fist came down hard on the bar. "That's what I'm trying to say to you, boss! About you, about Ratlit. You've all got it in your heads that this, out here, is it! Finito! The end! Sure, you gotta accept limitations, but the right ones. Sure, you have to admit there are certain directions in which you cannot go. But once you do that, you find there are others where you can go as far as you want. Look, I'm not gonna hang around the Star-pit all my life. And if I make my way back toward galactic center, make enough money so I can go home, raise my family the way I want, that's going forward, forward even from here. Not back."

"All right," I said. Quiet Sandy surprised me. I still wondered why he wasn't breaking his tail to get salvage on that ship that had just fallen into his hands, if getting back home with money in his pockets was that important. "I'm glad you told me about yourself. Now how does it all tie up with Ratlit?"

"Yeah. Ratlit." He put the porta-pix back in his overall pouch. "Boss, Ratlit is the kid your own could be. You want to give him the advice, friendship and concern he's never had, that you couldn't give yours. But Ratlit is also the kid I was about ten years ago, started no place, with no destination, and no values to help figure out the way, mixed up in all the wrong things, mainly because he's not sure where the right ones are."

"I don't think you're that much like Ratlit," I told him. "I think you may wish you were. You've done a lot of the things Ratlit's done? Ever write a novel?"

"I tried to write a trilogy," Sandy said, "it was lousy. But it pushed some things off my chest, so I got something out of it, even if nobody else did, which is what's important. Because now I'm a better mechanic for it, Boss. Until I admit to myself what I can't do, it's pretty hard to work on what I can. Same goes for Ratlit. You too. That's growing up, And one thing you can't do is help Ratlit by giving him a ship he can't fly."

Growing up brought back the picture. "Sandy, did you ever build an ecologarium when you were a kid?"

"No." The word had the puzzled inflection that means, don't-even-know-what-one-is.

"I didn't either," I told him. Then I grinned and punched him in the shoulder. "Maybe you're a little like me, too? Let's get back to work."

"Another thing," Sandy said, not looking very happy as he got off the stool. "Boss, that kid's gonna hurt you. I don't know how, but it's gonna seem like he hunted for how to make it hurt most, too. That's what I wanted to tell you, boss."

I was going to urge him to take the ship, but he handed me the keys back in the hanger before I could say anything and walked away. When people who should be clearing up their own problems start giving you advice . . . well, there was something about Sandy I didn't like.

If I can't take long walks at night with company, I take them by myself. I was strolling by the Edge, the world-wind was low, and the Stellarplex, that huge-heat-gathering mirror that hung nine thousand miles off the pit, was out. It looks vaguely like the moon used to look from Earth, only twice as big, perfectly silver, and during the three and a half days it faces us it's always full.

Then, up ahead where the fence was broken, I saw Ratlit kicking gravel over the Edge. He was leaning against a lamppost, his shirt ballooning and collapsing at his back.

"Hey, kid-boy! Isn't the golden still at Alegra's?"

Ratlit saw me and shrugged.

"What's the matter?" I asked when I reached him. "Ate dinner yet?"

He shrugged again. His body had the sort of ravenous metabolism that shows twenty-four hours without food. "Come on. I promised you a meal. Why so glum?"

"Make it something to drink."

"I know about your phony I.D.," I told him. "But we're going to eat. You can have milk, just like me."

No protests, no dissertation on the injustice of liquor laws. He started walking with me.

"Come on, kid-boy, talk to gramps. Don't you want your ship any more?"

Suddenly he clutched my forearm with white, bony fingers. My forearm is pretty thick, and he couldn't get his hands around it. "Vyme, you've got to make Sandy give it to me now! You've got to!"

"Kid-boy, talk to me."

"Alegra." He let go. "And the golden. Hate golden, Vyme. Always hate them. Because if you start to like one, and then start hating again, it's worse."

"What's going on? What are they doing?"

"He's talking. She's hallucinating. And neither one pays any attention to me."

"I see."

"You don't see. You don't understand about Alegra and me."

I was the only one who'd met the both of them who didn't.

"I know you're very fond of each other." More could be said.

Ratlit said more. "We don't even like each other that much, Vyme. But we need each other. Since she's been here, I get her junk for her. She's too sick to go out much now. And when I have bad changes, or sometimes bright recognitions, it doesn't matter. I bring them to her, and she builds pictures of them for me, and we explore them together and . . . learn about things, When she was a psychiatrist for the government, she learned an awful lot about how people tick. And she's got an awful lot to teach me, things I've got to know." Fifteen-year-old ex-psychiatrist drug addict? Same sort of precocity that produces thirteen-year old novelists. Get used to it. "I need her now almost as much as she needs her . . . medicine."

"Have you told the golden you've got him a ship?"

"You didn't say I could have it yet."

"Well, I say so right now. Why don't we go back there and tell him he can be on his way? If we put it a little more politely, don't you think that'll do the trick?"

He didn't say anything. His face just got back a lot of its life.

"We'll go right after we eat. What the hell, I'll buy you a drink. I may even have one with you."

Alegra's was blinding when we arrived. "Ratlit, oh, you're back! Hello, Vyme! I'm so glad you're both here! Everything is beautiful tonight!"

"The golden," Ratlit said. "Where's the golden?"

"He's not here." A momentary throb of sadness dispelled with torturous joy. "But he's coming back!"

"Oh," Ratlit said. His voice echoed through the long corridors of golden absence winding the room. " 'Cause I got a ship for him. All his. Just had a tuneup. He can leave any time he wants to."

"Here's the keys," I said, taking them from my pouch for dramatic effect. "Happen to have them right here."

As I handed them to Ratlit there were fireworks, applause, a fanfare of brasses. "Oh, that's wonderful. Wonderful! Because guess what, Ratlit? Guess what, Vyme?"

"I don't know," Ratlit said. "What?"

"I'm a golden too!" Alegra cried from the shoulders of the cheering crowd pushing their way through still more admiring thousands.

"Huh?"

"I, me, myself am actually an honest to goodness golden. I just found out today."

"You can't be," Ratlit said. "You're too old for it just to show up now."

"Something about my medicine," Alegra explained. "It's

dreadfully complicated." The walls were papered with anatomical charts, music by Stockhausen. "Something in my
medicine kept it from coming out until now, until a golden
could come to me, drawing it up and out of the depths of me,
till it burst out, beautiful and wonderful and . . . golden!
Right now he's gone off to Carlson Labs with a urine sample
for a final hormone check. They'll tell him in an hour, and
he'll bring back my golden belt. But he's sure already. And
when he comes back with it, I'm going to go with him to the
galaxies, as his apprentice. We're going to find a cure for his
sickness and something that will make it so I won't need my
medicine any more. He says if you have all the universe to
roam around in, you can find anything you look for. But you
need it *all*—not just a cramped little cluster of a few billion
stars off in a corner by itself. Oh, I'm free, Ratlit, like you
always wanted to be! While you were gone, he . . . well, did
something to me that was *golden,* and it triggered my hormonal imbalance!" The image came in through all five
senses. Breaking the melodious ecstasy came the clatter of
keys as Ratlit hurled them at the wall.

I left feeling pretty odd. Ratlit had started to go too, but
Alegra called him back. "Oh, now don't go on like that,
Ratty! Act your age. Won't you stay and do me one little last
favor?"

So he stayed. When I untangled myself from the place and
was walking home, I kept on remembering what Alegra had
said about love.

VII

Work next day went surprisingly smoothly. Poloscki called
me up about ten and asked if I knew where Ratlit was because he hadn't been at work that day. "You're sure the kid
isn't sick?"

I said I'd seen him last night and that he was probably all
right. Poloscki made a sort of disgusted sound and hung up.

Sandy left a few minutes early, as he had been doing all
week, to run over to the post office before it closed. He was

expecting a letter from his group, he said. I felt strange about having given the ship away out from under him. It was sort of an immature thing to do. But he hadn't said anything about wanting it, and Ratlit was still doing Alegra favors, so maybe it would all work out for the best.

I thought about visiting Alegra that evening. But there was the last six-months' paperwork, still not finished. I went into the office, plugged in the computer and got ready to work late.

I was still at it sometime after eleven when the entrance light blinked, which meant somebody had opened the hangar door. I'd locked it. Sandy had the keys so he could come in early. So it was Sandy. I was ready for a break and all set to jaw with him a while. He was always coming back to do a little work at odd hours. I waited for him to come into the office. But he didn't.

Then the needle on the power gauge, which had been hovering near zero with only the drain of the little office computer, swung up to seven. One of the big pieces of equipment had been cut in.

There was some cleanup work to do, but nothing for a piece that size. Frowning, I switched off the computer and stepped out of the office. The first great opening in the hangar roof was mostly blocked with the bulk of Ratlit's/Sandy's/my ship. Stellarplex light curved smoothly over one side, then snarled in the fine webbing of lifts, catwalks, haul-lines and grappler rigging. The other two were empty, and hundred-meter circles of silver dropped through assembly riggings to the concrete floor. Then I saw Sandy.

He stood just inside the light from the last opening, staring up at the Stellarplex, its glare lost in his ruined face. As he raised his left hand—when it started to move I thought it looked too big—light caught on the silver joints of the master-gauntlet he was wearing. I knew where the power was going.

As his hand went above his head, a shadow fell over him as a fifteen-foot slave talon swung from the darkness, its movement aping the master-glove. He dropped his hand in front of his face, fingers curved. Metal claws lowered about him, beginning to quiver. Something about the way . . . he was trying to kill himself!

I started running toward those hesitant, gaping claws, leaped into the grip, and reached over his shoulder to slap my forearm into the control glove, just as he squeezed. Like I said, my forearm is big, but when those claws came together, it was a tight fit. Sandy was crying.

"You stupid," I shouted, "inconsiderate, bird-brained, infantile—" as I pried his fingers lose from my arm, the talons jerked open one at a time from around us—"asinine, idiotic—" at last I got the glove off, "puerile . . ." Then I said, "What the hell is the matter with you?"

Sandy was sitting on the floor now, his head hung between his shoulders. He stank.

"Look," I said, maneuvering the slave talon back into place with the gross-motion controls on the gauntlet's wrist, "if you want to go jump off the Edge, that's line with me. Half the gate's down anyway. But don't come here and mess up my tools. You can squeeze you own head up a little, but you're not going to bust up my glove here. You're fired. Now tell me what's wrong."

"I knew it wasn't going to work. Wasn't even worth trying, I knew . . ." His voice was getting all mixed up with the sobs. "But I thought maybe . . ." Beside his left hand was the porta-pix, its screen cracked. And a crumpled piece of paper.

I turned off the glove, and the talons stopped humming twenty feet overhead. I picked up the paper and smoothed it out. I didn't mean to read it all the way through.

Dear Sanford,

Things have been difficult since you left but not too hard and I guess a lot of pressure is off everybody since you went away and the kids are getting used to your not being here though Bobbi-D cried a lot at first. She doesn't now. We got your letter and were glad to hear things had begun to settle down for you though Hank said you should have written before this and was very mad though Mary tried to calm him down but he just said, "When he married you all he married me too, damn it, and I've got just as much right to be angry at him as you have," which is true, Sanford, but I tell you what he said because it's a quote and I think you should know exactly what's being said, especially since it expresses something we all feel on one level or another. You said you might be able to send us a little money, if we wanted you home, which I think would be very good, the money I mean, though Laura said if I put that in the letter she would divorce us, but she won't, and like Hank I've got a right to say what I feel which is, Yes I think you should send money, especially after that unpleasant business just before you left. But we are all agreed we do not want you to come back. And would rather not have the money if that's what it meant.

That is hard but true. As you can gather your letter caused quite an upset here. I would like—which makes me different from the others but is why they wanted me to write this letter—to hear from you again and keep track of what you are doing because I used to love you very much and I never could hate you. But like Bobbi-D, I have stopped crying.

Sincerely—

The letter was signed "Joseph." In the lower corner were the names of the rest of the men and women of the group.

"Sandy?"

"I knew they wouldn't take me back. I didn't even really try, did I? But—"

"Sandy, get up."

"But the *children,*" he whispered. "What's gonna happen to the children?"

And there was a sound from the other end of the hangar. Three stories up the side of the ship in the open hatchway, silvered by Stellarplex light, stood the golden, the one Ratlit and I had found on the street. You remember what he looked like. He and Alegra must have sneaked in while Sandy and I were struggling with the waldo. Probably they wanted to get away as soon as possible before Ratlit made real trouble, or before I changed my mind and got the keys back. All this ship-giving had been done without witnesses. The sound was the lift rising toward the hatchway. "The children?" Sandy whispered again.

The door opened, and a figure stepped out in the white light. Only it was Ratlit! It was Ratlit's red hair, his gold earring, his bouncy run as he started for the hatch. And there were links of yellow metal around his waist.

Baffled, I heard the golden call: "Everything checks out inside, brother. She'll fly us anywhere."

And Ratlit cried, "I got the grapples all released, brother. Let's go!" Their voices echoed down through the hangar. Sandy raised his head, squinting.

As Ratlit leapt into the hatch, the golden caught his arm around the boy's shoulder. They stood a moment, gazing at one another, then Ratlit turned to look down into the hangar, back on the world he was about to leave. I couldn't tell if he knew we were there or not. Even as the hatch swung closed, the ship began to whistle.

I hauled Sandy back into the shock chamber. I hadn't even locked the door when the thunder came and my ears nearly split. I think the noise surprised Sandy out of himself. It broke something up in my head, but the pieces were falling wrong.

"Sandy," I said, "we've got to get going!"

"Huh?" He was fighting the drunkenness and probably his stomach too. "I don't wanna go nowhere."

"You're going anyway. I'm sure as hell not going to leave you alone."

VIII

When we were halfway up the stairs I figured she wasn't there. I felt just the same. Maybe she was with them in the ship.

"My medicine. Please, can't you get my medicine? I've got to have my medicine, please, please . . . please." I could just hear the small, high voice when I reached the door. I punched it open.

Alegra lay on the mattress, pink eyes wide, white hair frizzled around her balding skull. She was incredibly scrawny, her uncut nails black as Sandy's nubs without the excuse of hours in a graphite-lubricated gauntlet. The translucency of her pigmentless skin under how-many-days of dirt made my flesh crawl. Her face drew in around her lips like the flesh about a scar. "My medicine. Vyme, is that you? You'll get my medicine for me, Vyme? Won't you get my medicine?" Her mouth wasn't moving, but the voice came on. She was too weak to project on any but the aural level. It was the first time I'd seen Alegra without her cloak of hallucination, and it brought me up short.

"Alegra," I said when I got hold of myself. "Ratlit and the golden went off on the ship."

"Ratlit. Oh, nasty Ratty, awful little boy! He wouldn't get my medicine. But you'll get it for me, won't you, Vyme? I'm going to die in about ten minutes, Vyme. I don't want to die. Not like this. The world is so ugly and painful now. I don't want to die here."

"Don't you have any?" I stared around the room I hadn't seen since Drunk-roach lived there. It was a lot worse. Dried garbage, piled first in one corner, now covered half the floor. The rest was littered with papers, broken glass, a spilled can of something unrecognizable for the mold, and a dead beetle.

"No. None here. Ratlit gets it from a man who hangs out in Gerg's over on Calle-X. Oh, Ratlit used to get it for me every day, he would bring me my lovely medicine. I never had to leave my room at all. You go get it for me, Vyme."

"It's the middle of the night, Alegra! Gerg's is closed, and Calle-X is all the way across the pit anyway. Couldn't even get there in ten minutes, much less find this character and come back!"

"If I were well, Vyme, I'd fly you there in a cloud of light pulled by peacocks and porpoises, and you'd come back to hautboys and tambourines, bringing my beautiful medicine to me, in less than an eye's blink. But I'm sick now. Sick.

And I'm going to die."

There was a twitch in the crinkled lid of one pink eye.

"Alegra, what happened!"

"Ratlit's insane!" she projected with shocking vicious-ness. I heard Sandy behind me catch his breath, "Insane at twenty thousand light-years, dead at twenty-five."

"But his golden belt . . ."

"It was mine! It was my belt and he stole it. And he wouldn't get my medicine. Ratlit's not a golden. I'm a golden, Vyme! I can go anywhere, anywhere at all! I'm a golden golden golden . . . But I'm sick now. I'm so sick."

"But didn't the golden know the belt was yours?"

"Him? Oh, he's so incredibly stupid! He would believe anything. The golden went to check some papers and get provisions and was gone all day, to get my belt. But you were here that night. I asked Ratlit to go get my medicine and take another sample to Carlson's for me. But neither of them came back till I was very sick, very weak. Ratlit found the golden, you see, told him that I'd changed my mind about going, and that he, Ratlit, was a golden as well, that he'd just been to Carlson's. So the golden gave him my belt and off they went."

"But how in the world would he believe a kid with a story like that?"

"You know how stupid a golden can be, Vyme. As stupid as they can be mean. Besides, it doesn't matter to him if Rat-lit dies. He doesn't care if Ratlit was telling the truth or not. The golden will live. When Ratlit starts drooling, throwing up blood, goes deaf first and blind last and dies, the golden won't even be sad. He's too stupid to feel sad. That's the way golden are. But I'm sad, Vyme, because no one will bring me my medicine."

My frustration had to lash at something; she was there. "You mean you didn't know what you were doing to Ratlit by leaving, Alegra? You mean you didn't know how much he wanted to get out, and how much he needed you at the same time? You couldn't see what it would do to him if you deprived him of the thing he needed and rubbed his nose in the thing he hated both at once? You couldn't guess that he'd *pull* some crazy stunt? Oh, kid-girl, you talk about golden. You're the stupid one."

"Not stupid." she projected quietly. "*Mean,* Vyme. I knew he'd try to do something. I just didn't think he'd succeed. Ratlit is really such a child."

The frustration, spent, became rolling sadness. "Couldn't you have waited just a little longer, Alegra? Couldn't you have worked out the leaving some other way, not hurt him so much?"

"I wanted to get out, Vyme, to keep going and not be trapped. Like Ratlit wanted, like you want, like Sandy wants, like golden." For a moment I had forgotten Sandy and the golden. "Only I was cruel. I had the chance to do it and I took it. Why is that bad, Vyme? Unless, of course, that's what being free means."

A twitch in the eyelid again. It closed. The other stayed open.

"Alegra—"

"I'm a golden, Vyme. A golden. And that's how golden are. But don't be mad at me, Vyme. Don't. Ratlit was mean too, not to give me my medi—"

The other eye closed. I closed mine too and tried to cry, but my tongue was pushing too hard on the roof of my mouth.

Sandy came to work the next day, and I didn't mention his being fired. The teletapes got hold of it, and the headlines tried to make the thing as sordid as possible:

X-CON TEENAGER (they didn't mention his novel) SLAYS JUNKY SWEETHEART. DIES HORRIBLY! They didn't mention the golden either. They never do. Reporters pried around the hanger a while, trying to get us to say the ship was stolen. Sandy came through pretty well. "It was his ship," he grunted, putting lubricant in the gauntlets. "I gave it to him."

"What are you gonna give a kid like that a ship for? Maybe you loaned it to him, 'Dies horrible death in borrowed ship.' That sounds okay."

"Gave it to him. Ask the boss." He turned back toward the scaffolding. "He witnessed."

"Look, even if you liked the kid, you're not saving him anything by covering up."

"I didn't like him," Sandy said. "But I gave him the ship."

"Thanks," I told Sandy when they left, not sure what I was thanking him for, but still feeling very grateful. "I'll do you a favor back."

A week later Sandy came in and said, "Boss, I want my favor."

I narrowed my eyes against his belligerent tone. "So you're gonna quit at last. Can you finish out the week?"

He looked embarrassed, and his hands started moving around in his overall pouch. "Well, yeah. I am gonna leave. But not right away, boss. It is getting a little hard for me to take, out here."

"You'll get used to it," I said. "You know there's something about you that's, well, a lot like me, I learned. You will too."

Sandy shook his head. "I don't think I want to." His hand came out of his pocket. "See, I got a ticket." In his dirty fingers was a metal-banded card. "In four weeks I'm going back in from the Star-pit. Only I didn't want to tell you just now, because, well, I did want this favor, boss."

I was really surprised. "You're not going back to your group," I said. "What are you going to do?"

He shrugged. "Get a job. I don't know. There's other groups. Maybe I've grown up a little bit." His fists went way down into his pouch, and he started to shift his weight back and forth on his feet. "About that favor, boss."

"What is it?"

"I got to talking to this kid outside. He's really had it rough, Vyme." That was the first and last time Sandy ever called me by name, though I'd asked him to enough times before. "And he could use a job."

A laugh got all set to come out of me. But it didn't, because the look on his ugly face, behind the belligerence, was so vulnerable and intense. Vulnerable? But Sandy had his ticket; Sandy was going on.

"Send him to Poloscki's," I said. "Probably needs an extra grease-monkey. Now let me get back to work, huh?"

"Could you take him over there?" Sandy said very quickly. "That's the favor, boss."

"Sandy, I'm awfully busy." I looked at him again. "Oh, all right."

"Hey, boss," Sandy said as I slid from behind the desk, "remember that thing you asked me if I ever had when I was a kid?"

It took a moment to come back to me. "You mean an ecologarium?"

"Yeah. That's the word." He grinned. 'The kid-boy's got one. He's right outside, waiting for you."

"He's got it with him?"

Sandy nodded.

I walked toward the hangar door picturing some kid lugging around a six-by-six plastic cage.

Outside the boy was sitting on a fuel hydrant. I'd put a few trees there, and the "day"-light from the illumination tubes arching the street dappled the gravel around him.

IX

He was about fourteen, with copper skin and curly black hair. I saw why Sandy wanted me to go with him about the job. Around his waist, as he sat hunched over on the hydrant with his toes spread on metal base-flange, was a wide-linked belt that was golden.

He was looking through an odd jewel-and-brass thing that hung from a chain around his neck.

"Hey."

He looked up. There were spots of light on his blue-black hair.

"You need a job?"

He blinked.

"My name's Vyme. What's yours?"

"You call me An." The voice was even, detached, with an inflection that is golden.

I frowned. "Nickname?"

He nodded.

"And really?"

"Androcles."

He had all sorts of official papers saying so. But sometimes it's hard to remember. And it doesn't matter whether the hair is black, white, or red. "Well, let's see if we can put you to work somewhere. Come on." An stood up, eyes fixed on me, suspicion hiding behind high glitter. "What's the thing around your neck?"

His eyes struck it and bounced back to my face in an instant. "Cousin?" he asked.

"Huh?" Then I remember the golden slang. "Oh, sure. First cousins. Brothers if you want."

"Brother," An said. Then a smile came tumbling out on his face, silent and volcanic. He began loping along beside me as we started off toward Poloscki's. "This—" he held up the thing on the chain "—is an ecologarium. Want to see?" His diction was clipped, precise and detached. But when an expression caught on his face, it was unsettlingly intense.

"Oh, a little one. With microorganisms?"

An nodded.

"Sure. Let's have a look."

The hair on the back of his neck pawed the chain as he bent to remove it. I held it up to see.

Some blue liquid, a fairly large air bubble and a glob of black-speckled jelly in a transparent globe, the size of an eyeball; it was set in two metal rings, one within the other, pivoted so the globe turned in all directions. Mounted on the outside ring was a curved tongue of metal at the tip of which was a small tube with a pin-sized lens. The tube was threaded into a bushing, and I guess you used it to look at what was going on in the sphere.

"Self-contained," explained An. "The only thing needed to keep the whole thing going is light. Just about any frequency will do, except way up on the blue end. And the shell cuts that out." I looked through the brass eyepiece.

I'd swear there were over a hundred life forms with five to fifty stages each: spores, zygotes, seeds, eggs, growing and developing through larvae, pupae, buds, reproducing through sex, syzygy, fission. And the whole ecological cycle took about two minutes.

Spongy masses like red lotuses clung to the air bubble. Every few seconds one would expel a cloud of black things like wrinkled bits of carbon paper into the gas where they were attacked by tiny motes I could hardly see even with the lens. Black became silver. It fell back to the liquid like globules of mercury, and coursed toward the jelly that was emitting a froth of bubbles. Something in the froth made the silver beads reverse direction. They reddened, sent out threads and alveoli, until they reached the main bubble again as lotuses.

The reason the lotuses didn't crowd each other out was because every eight or nine seconds a swarm of green paramecia devoured most of them. I couldn't tell where they came from; I never saw one of them split or get eaten, but they must have had something to do with the thorn-balls—if only because there were either thorn-balls or paramecia floating in the liquid, but never both at once.

A black spore in the jelly wiggled, then burst the surface as a white worm. Exhausted, it laid a couple of eggs, rested until it developed fins and a tail, then swam to the bubble where lay more eggs among the lotuses. Its fins grew larger, its tail shriveled, splotches of orange and blue would appear, till it took off like a weird butterfly to sail around the inside of the bubble. The motes that silvered the black offspring of the lotus must have eaten the parti-colored fan because it just grew thinner and frailer till it disappeared. The eggs by the lotus would hatch into bloated fish forms that swam back through the froth to vomit a glob of jelly on the mass at the bottom, then collapse. The first eggs didn't do much except turn into black spores when they were covered with enough jelly.

All this was going on amidst a kaleidoscope of frail, wilting flowers and blooming jeweled webs, vines and worms, warts and jellyfish, symbiotes and saprophytes, while rainbow herds of algae careened back and forth like glittering confetti. One rough-rinded galoot, so big you could see him without the eyepiece, squatted on the wall, feeding on jelly, batting his eye-spots while the tide surged through tears of gills.

I blinked as I took it from my eye.

"That looks complicated." I handed it back to him.

"Not really." He slipped it around his neck. "Took me two weeks with a notebook to get the whole thing figured out. You saw the big fellow?"

"The one who winked?"

"Yes. Its reproductive cycle is about two hours, which trips you up at first. Everything else goes so fast. But once you see him mate with the thing that looks like a spider web with sequins—same creature, different sex—and watch the offspring aggregate into paramecia, then dissolve again, the whole thing falls into—"

"One creature!" I said. "The whole thing is a single creature!"

An nodded vigorously. "Has to be to stay self-contained." The grin on his face whipped away like a shade snapped up on a window. A very serious look was underneath. "Even after I saw the big fellow mate, it took me a week to understand it was all one."

"But if goofus and the fishnet have paramecia—" I began. It seemed logical when I made the guess. "You've seen one before."

I shook my head. "Not like that one, anyway. I once saw something similar, but it was much bigger, about six feet across."

An's seriousness was replaced by quivering horror. I mean he really started to shake. "How could you . . . *ever* even *see* all the . . . stuff inside, much less *catalogue* it? You say . . . *this* is complicated?"

"Hey, relax. Relax!" I said. He did. Like that. "It was much simpler," I explained and went on to describe the one our kids had made so many years ago as best I remembered.

"Oh," An said at last, his face set in its original impassivity. "It wasn't microorganisms. Simple. Yes." He looked at the pavement. "Very simple." When he looked up, another expression had scrambled his features, I took a moment to identify it as confusion. "I don't see the point at all."

There was surprising physical surety in the boy's movement; his nervousness was a cat's, not a human's. But it was one of the psychological qualities of golden.

"Well," I said, "it showed the kids a picture of the way the cycles of life progress."

An rattled his chain. "That is why they gave us these things. But every thing in the one you had was so primitive. It wasn't a very good picture."

"Don't knock it," I told him. "When I was a kid, all I had was an ant-colony. I got my infantile *Weltanschauung* watching a bunch of bugs running around between two plates of glass. I think I would have been better prepared by a couple of hungry rats on a treadmill. Or maybe a torus-shaped fish tank alternating sharks with schools of piranhas. Get them all chasing around after each other real fast—"

"Ecology wouldn't balance," An said. "You'd need snails to get rid of the waste. Then a lot of plants to reoxygenate the water, and some sort of herbivore to keep down the plants because they'd tend to choke out everything since neither the sharks nor the piranhas would eat them." Kids and their damn literal minds. "And if the herbivores had some way to keep the sharks off, then you might do it."

"What's wrong with the first one I described?" The explanation worked around the muscles of his face. "The lizards, the segment worms, the plants, worts, all their cycles were completely circular. They were born, grew up, reproduced, maybe took care of the kids a while, then died. Their only function was reproduction. That's a pretty awful picture." He made an unintelligible face.

Something about this wise-alecky kid who was golden, younger than Alegra, older than Teehalt, I liked.

"There are stages in here," An tapped his globe with his

pinky nail, "that don't get started on their most important
functions till after they've reproduced and grown up through
a couple more metamorphoses as well. Those little green
worms are a sterile end stage of the blue feathery things. But
they put out free phosphates that the algae live on. Everything else, just about, lives on the algae—except the thorn
balls. They eat the worms when they die. There's phagocytes
in there that ingest the dust-things when they get out of the
bubble and start infecting the liquid." All at once he got very
excited. "Each of us in the class got one of these! They made
us figure them out! Then we had to prepare these recordings
on whether the reproductive process was the primary function in life or an adjunctive one." Something white frothed
the corners of his mouth. "I think grown-ups should just
leave their kids the hell *alone,* go on and do something *else,*
stop bothering us! That's what I said! That's what I *told*
them!" He stopped, his tongue flicked the foam at the cusp
of his lips; he seemed all right again.

"Sometimes," I said evenly, "if you leave them alone and
forget about them, you end up with monsters who aren't kids
anymore. If you'd been left alone, you wouldn't have had a
chance to put your two cents in in the first place, and you
wouldn't have that thing around your neck." And he was
really trying to follow what I was saying. A moment past his
rage, his face was as open and receptive as a two-year-old's.
God, I want to stop thinking about Antoni!

"That's not what I mean." He wrapped his arms around
his shoulders and bit on his forearm pensively.

"An, you're not stupid, kid-boy. You're cocky, but I don't
think you're mean. You're golden." There was all my resentment, out now, Ratlit. There it is, Alegra. I didn't grow
up with the word, so it meant something different to me. An
looked up to ingest my meaning. The toothmarks were white
on his skin, then red around that. "How long have you been
one?"

He watched me, arms still folded. "They found out when I
was seven."

"That long ago?"

"Yes." He turned and started walking again. "I was very precocious."

"Oh." I nodded. "Just about half your life then. How's it been, little brother, being a golden?"

An dropped his arms. "They take you away from your group a lot of time." He shrugged. "Special classes. Training programs. I'm psychotic."

"I never would have guessed." What would you call Ratlit or Alegra?

"I know it shows. But it gets us through the psychic pressures at the reality breakdown at twenty thousand light-years. It does. For the past few years, though, they've been planting the psychosis artificially, pretty far down in the preconscious, so it doesn't affect our ordinary behavior as much as it does the older ones. They can use this process on anybody whose hormone system is even close to golden. They can get a lot more and a lot better quality golden that way than just waiting for us to pop up by accident."

As I laughed, something else struck me. "Just what do you need a job out here for, though? Why not hitch out with some cousin or get a job on one of the intergalactics as an apprentice?"

"I have a job in another galaxy. There'll be a ship stopping for me in two months to take me out. A whole lot of Star-pits have been established in galaxies halfway to Undok. I'll be going back and forth, managing roboi-equipment, doing managerial work. I thought it would be a good idea to get some practical experience out here before I left."

"Precocious," I said. "Look, even with roboi-equipment you have to know one hell of a lot about the inside of how many different kinds of keeler drives. You're not going to get that kind of experience in two months as a greasemonkey. And roboi-equipment I don't even have any in my place. Poloscki's got some, but I don't think you'll get your hands on it."

"I know a good deal already," An said with strained modesty.

"Yeah?" I asked him a not too difficult question and got

an adequate answer. Made me feel better that he didn't come back with something really brilliant. I did know more than he did. "Where'd you learn?"

"They gave me the information the same way they implanted my psychosis."

"You're pretty good for your age. Dear old Luna Vocational. Maybe educational methods have improved a bit. Come to think of it, I was just as old as you when I started playing around with those keeler models. Dozens and dozens of helical inserts—"

"And those oily organum sensitives in all that graphite. Yes, brother. But I've never even had my hands in a waldo."

I frowned, "Hell, when I was younger than you, I could—" I stopped. "Of course, with roboi-equipment, you need them. But it's not a bad thing to know how they work, just in case."

"That's why I want a job." He hooked one finger on his chain. "Brother-in-law Sandy and I got to talking, so I asked him about working here. He said you might help me get in someplace."

"I'm glad he did. My place only handles big ships, and it's all waldo, Me and an assistant can do the whole thing. Poloscki's place is smaller, but handles both inter- and intragalactic jobs, so you got more variety and a bigger crew. You find Poloscki, say I sent you, tell what you can do and why you're out here. Belt or no, you'll probably get something better than a monkey."

"Thanks, brother."

We turned off Calle-D. Poloscki's hangar was ahead. Dull thunder sounded over the roof as a ship departed.

"As soon as I despair of the younger generation," I told him, "one of you kids comes by and I start to think there's hope again. Granted you're a psychopath, you're a lot better than some of your older, distant relations." An looked up at me, apprehensive.

"You've never had a run-in with some of your cousins out here. But don't be surprised if you're dead tomorrow and your job's been inherited by some character who decided to split your head open to check on what's inside. I try to get used to you, behaving like something that isn't even salvage. But, boy, can your kind really mess up a guy's picture of the world."

"And what the hell do you expect us to act like?" An shot back. Spittle glittered on his lips again. "What would *you* do if you were trapped like *us?*"

"Huh?" I said questioningly. "You trapped?"

"Look." A spasm passed over his shoulders. "The psychotechnician who made sure I was properly psychotic *wasn't* a golden, *brother!* You *pay* us to bring back to weapons, dad! *We* don't fight your damn wars, *grampa! You're* the ones who take us away from our groups, say we're *too* valuable to submit to your laws, then deny us our heredity because we don't *breed* true, no-relative-of-*mine!*"

"Now wait a minute!"

An snatched the chain from around his neck and held it taut in front of him. His voice ground to a whisper, his eyes glittered. "I strangled one of my classmates with this chain, the one I've got in my hands now." One by one, his features blanked all expression. "The teacher took it away from me for a week, as punishment for killing the little girl."

The whisper stopped decibels above silence, then went on evenly. "Out here, nobody will punish me. And my reflexes are faster than yours."

Fear lashed my anger as I followed the insanity flickering in his eyes.

"Now!" He made a quick motion with his hands; I ducked. "I give it to you!" He flung the chain toward me. Reflexively I caught it. An turned away instantly and stalked into Poloscki's.

X

When I burst through the rattling hangar door at my place, the lift was coming down. Sandy yelled through the mesh walls, "Did he get the job?"

"Probably," I yelled back, going toward the office. I heard the cage settle on the silicon cushion. Sandy was at my side a moment later, grinning. "So how do you like my brother-in-law, Androcles?"

"Brother-in-law?" I remembered An using the phrase, but I'd thought it was part of the slang which is golden. Something about the way Sandy said it though. "He's your *real* brother-in-law?"

"He's Joey's kid brother. I didn't want to say anything until after you met him." Sandy came along with me toward the office door. "Joey wrote me again and said since An was coming out here he'd tell him to stop by and see me and maybe I could help him out."

"Now how the hell am I supposed to know who Joey is?" I pushed open the door. It banged the wall.

"He's one of my husbands, the one who wrote me that letter you told me you'd read."

"Oh, yeah. Him." I started stalking papers.

"I thought it was pretty nice of him after all that to tell An to look me up when he got out here. It means there's still somebody left who doesn't think I'm a complete waste. So what do you think of Androcles?"

"He's quite a boy." I scooped up the mail that had come in after lunch, started to go through it but put it down to hunt for my coveralls.

"An used to come visit us when he got his one weekend a month off from his training program as golden," Sandy was going on. "Joey's and Art's parents lived in the reeds near the estuary. But we lived back up the canyon by Chroma Falls. An and Joey were pretty close, even though Joey's my age and An was only eight or nine back then. I guess Joey was the only one going through, since they were both golden."

Surprised and shocked, I turned back to the desk. "You were married with a golden?" One of the letters on the top of the pile was addressed to Alegra, from Carlson's Labs. I had a carton of the kids' junk in the locker and had gotten the mail—there wasn't much—sent to the hangar, as though I were waiting for somebody to come for it.

"Yeah," Sandy said, surprised at my surprise. "Joey."

So I wouldn't stand there gaping, I picked up Alegra's letter.

"Since the traits that are golden are polychromazoic, it dies out if they only breed with each other. There's a big campaign back in galactic center to encourage them to join heterogeneous proke-groups."

"Like blue-point Siamese cats, huh?" I ran my blackened thumbnail through the seal.

"That's right. But they're *not* animals, boss. I remember what they put that kid-boy through for psychotic reinforcement of the factors that were golden to make sure they stuck. It tore me up to hear him talk about it when he'd visit us."

I pulled a porta-pix out of Alegra's envelope. Carlson's tries to personalize its messages.

"I'm sure glad they can erase the conscious memory from the kids' minds when they have to do that sort of stuff."

"Small blessings and all that," I said, flipping the porta-pix on.

Personalized but mass produced. ". . . blessed addit . . ." the little speaker echoed me. Poloscki and I had used Carlson's a couple of times, I know. I guess every other mechanic up here had too. The porta-pix had started in the middle. Now it hummed back to the beginning.

"You know," Sandy went on, "Joey was different, yeah, sort of dense about some things . . ."

"Alegra," beamed the chic, grandmotherly type Carlson's always uses for messages of this sort, "we were so glad to receive the urine sample you sent us by Mr. Ratlit last Thursday . . ."

". . . even so, Joey was one of the sweetest men or women I've ever known. He was the easiest person in the group to live with. Maybe it was because he was away a lot . . ."

". . . and now. just a week later—remember, Carlson's gives results immediately and confirms them by personalized porta-pix in seven days—we are happy to tell you that there will be a blessed addition to your group. However . . ."

". . . All right, he was different, reacted funny to a lot of things. But nothing like this rank, destructive stupidity you find out here at the Star-pit . . ."

". . . the paternity is not Mr. Ratlit's. If you are interested, for your eugenic records, in further information, please send us other possible urine samples from the men in your group, and we will be glad to confirm paternity . . ."

". . . I can't understand the way people act out here, boss. And that's why I'm pushing on."

". . . Thank you so much for letting us give you this wonderful news. Remember, when in doubt, call Carlson's."

I said to Sandy, "You were married with—you loved a golden?"

Unbidden, the porta-pix began again. I flipped it off without looking.

"Sandy," I said, "you were hired because you were a fair mechanic and you kept off my back, Do what you're paid for. Get out of here!"

"Oh. Sure, boss." He backed quickly from the office.

I sat down.

Maybe I'm old-fashioned, but when someone runs off and abandons a sick girl like that, it gets me. That was the trip to Carlson's, the one last little favor Ratlit never came back from. On the spot results, and formal confirmation in seven days. In her physical condition, pregnancy would have been as fatal as the withdrawal. And she was too ill for any abortive method I know of not to kill her. On the spot results. Ratlit must have known all that too when he got the results back, the results that Alegra was probably afraid of, the results she sent him to find. Ratlit knew Alegra was going to die anyway. And so he stole a golden belt. "Loving someone, I mean really loving someone—" Alegra had said. When someone runs off and leaves a sick girl like that, there's got to be a reason. It came together for me like two fissionables. The explosion cut some moorings in my head I thought were pretty solidly fixed.

I pulled out the books, plugged in the computer, unplugged it, put the books away and stared into the ecologarium in my fist.

Among the swimming, flying, crawling things, mating,

giving birth, growing, changing, busy at whatever their business was, I picked out those dead-end green worms. I hadn't noticed them before because they were at the very edge of things, bumping against the wall. After they released their free phosphates and got tired of butting the shell, they turned on each other and tore themselves to pieces.

Fear and anger is a bad combination in me.

I came close to being killed by a golden once, through that meanness and stupidity.

The same meanness and stupidity had killed Alegra and Ratlit.

And now when this damn kid threatens to—I mean at first I had thought he was threatening to—

I reached Gerg's a few minutes after the daylights went out and the street lamps came on. But I'd stopped in nearly a dozen places on the way. I remember trying to explain to a sailor from a star-shuttle who was just stopping over at the Star-pit for the first time and was all upset because one woman golden had just attacked another with a broken glass. I remember saying to the three-headed bulge of his shoulder, ". . . an ant-colony! You know what it is, two pieces of glass with dirt between them, and you can see all the little ants make tunnels and hatch eggs and stuff. When I was a kid, I had an ant-colony . . ." I started to shake my hand in his face. The chain from the ecologarium was tangled up in my fingers.

"Look." He caught my wrist and put it down on the counter. "It's all right now, pal. Just relax."

"You look," I said as he turned away. "When I was a kid, all I had was an ant-colony!"

He turned back and leaned his rusty elbow on the bar. "Okay." he said affably. Then he made the most stupid and frustrating mistake he possibly could have just then. "What about your aunt?"

"My mother."

"I thought you were telling me about your aunt?"

"Naw," I said. "My aunt, she drank too much. This is

about my mother."

"All right. Your mother then."

"My mother, see, she always worried about me, getting sick and things. I got sick a lot when I was little kid. She made me mad! Used to go down and watch the ships take off from a place they called Brooklyn Navy Yards. They were ships that went to the stars."

The sailor's oriental face grinned. "Yeah, me too. Used to watch 'em when I was a kid."

"But it was raining, and she wouldn't let me go!"

"Aw, that's too bad. Little rain never hurt a kid. Why didn't she call up and have it turned off so you could go out? Too busy to pay attention to you, huh? One of my old men was like that."

"Both of mine were," I said. "But not my ma. She was all over me all the time when she was there. But she made me mad!"

He nodded with real concern. "Wouldn't turn off the rain."

"Naw. couldn't. You didn't grow up where I did. narrow-minded, dark-side world. No modern conveniences."

"Off the main trading routes, huh?"

"Way off. She wouldn't let me go out, and that made me mad."

He was still nodding.

"So I broke it!" My fist came down hard on the counter, and the plastic globe on its brass cage clacked on the wood. "Broke it! Sand, glass all over the rug, on the window sill!"

"What'd you break?"

"Smashed it, stamped on it, threw sand whenever she tried to make me stop!"

"Sand? You lived on a beach? We had a beach when I was a kid. A beach is nice for kids. What'd you break?"

"Let all the damn bugs out. Bugs in everything for days. Let 'em all out."

"Didn't have no bugs on our beach. But you said you were off the main trading routes."

"Let 'em *out!*" I banged my fist again. "Let everybody

out, whether they like it or not! It's their problem whether they make it, not mine! Don't care, I don't—" was laughing now.

"She let you go out, and you didn't care?"

My hand came down on top of the metal cage, hard. I caught my breath at the pain. "On our beach," I said, turning my palm up to look. There were red marks across it, "There weren't any bugs on our beach." Then I started shaking.

"You mean you were just putting me on, before, about the bugs. Hey, are you all right?"

". . . broke it," I whispered. Then I smashed fist and globe and chain into the side of the counter. "Let 'em *out!*" I whirled away, clutching my bruised hand against my stomach.

"*Watch* it, kid-boy!"

"I'm not a kid-boy!" I shouted. "You think I'm some stupid, half-crazy kid!"

"So you're a few years older than me."

"I'm not a kid anymore!"

"So you're ten years older than Sirius, all right? Quiet down, or they'll kick us out."

I bulled out of Gerg's. A couple of people came after me because I didn't watch where I was going. I don't know who won, but I remember somebody yelling, "Get out! Get out!" It may have been me.

I remember later, staggering under the mercury street lamp, the world-wind slapping my face, stars swarming back and forth below me, gravel sliding under my boots, the toes inches over the Edge. The gravel clicked down the metal siding, the sound terribly clear as I reeled in the loud wind, shaking my arm against the night.

As I brought my hand back, the wind lashed the cold chain across my check and the bridge of my nose. I lurched back, trying to claw it away. But it stayed all tangled on my fingers while the globe swung, gleaming in the street light. The wind roared. Gravel chattered down the siding.

Later, I remember the hangar door ajar, stumbling into the darkness, so that in a moment I was held from plummeting into nothing only by my own footsteps as black swerved around me. I stopped when my hip hit a workbench. I pawed around under the lip of the table till I found a switch. In the dim orange light, racked along the back of the bench in their plastic shock-cases, were the row of master-gauntlets. I slipped one out and slid my hand into it.

"Who's over there?"

"Go 'way, Sandy." I turned from the bench, switched up the power on the wrist controls. Somewhere in the dark above, a fifteen-foot slave-hand hummed to life.

"Sorry, buster. This isn't Sandy. Put that down and get away from there."

I squinted as the figure approached in the orange light, hand extended. I saw the vibra-gun and didn't bother to look at the face.

Then the gun went down. "Vyme, baby? That you? What the hell are you doing here this hour of the night?"

"Poloscki?"

"Who'd you think it was?"

"Is this your place?" I looked around, shook my head. "But I thought it was mine." I shook my head again.

Poloscki sniffed. "Hey, have you been a naughty kid-boy tonight!"

I swung my hand, and the slave-hand overhead careened twenty feet.

The gun jumped. "Look, you mess up my waldo and I will kill you, don't care who you are! Take that thing off."

"Very funny." I brought the talon down where I could see it clawing shadow.

"Come on, Vyme. I'm serious. Turn it off and put it down. You're a mess now and you don't know what you're doing."

"That kid, the golden. Did you give him a job?"

"Sure. He said you sent him. Smart so and so. He rehulled a little yacht with the roboi-anamechaniakatasthysizer, just to show me what he could do. If I knew a few more people who could handle them that well, I'd go all roboi. He's not worth a damn with a waldo, but as long as he's got that little green light in front of him, he's fine." I brought the talons down another ten feet so that the spider hung between us.

"Well, I happen to be very handy with a waldo, Poloscki."

"Vyme, you're gonna get *hurt . . .*"

"Poloscki," I said, "will you stop coming off like an over-protective aunt? I don't need another one."

"You're very drunk, Vyme."

"Yeah. But I'm no clumsy kid-boy who is going to mess up your equipment."

"If you do, you'll be—"

"Shut up and watch." I pulled the chain out of my pouch and tossed it onto the concrete floor. In the orange light you couldn't tell whether the cage was brass or silver. "What's that?"

The claws came down, and the line-point tips, millimeters above the floor, closed on the ecologarium.

"Oh, hey! I haven't seen one of those since I was ten. What are you going to do with it? Those are five-hundred-to-one strength, you know. You're gonna break it."

"That's right. Break this one too."

"Aw, come on. Let me see it first." I lifted the globe. "Could be an eggshell," I said. "Drunk or sober I can handle this damn equipment, Poloscki."

"I haven't seen one for years. Used to have one."

"You mean it wasn't spirited back from some distant galaxy by a golden, from some technology beyond our limited ken?"

"Product of the home spiral. Been around since the fifties."

I raised it over Poloscki's extended hand. "They're supposed to be very educational. What do you want to break it for?"

"I never saw one."

"You came from someplace off the routes, didn't you. They weren't that common. Don't break it."

"I want to."

"Why, Vyme?"

Something got wedged in my throat. "Because I want to get out, and if it's not that globe, it's going to be somebody's head." Inside the gauntlet my hand began to quiver. The talons jerked. Poloscki caught the globe and jumped back. "Vyme!"

"I'm hanging on here at the Edge." My voice kept getting caught on the things in my throat. "I'm useless, with a bunch of monsters and fools!" The talons swung, contracted, clashed on each other. "And then when the children . . . when the *children* get so bad you can't even reach them . . ." The claw opened, reached for Poloscki, who jumped back in the half-dark. "Damn it, Vyme—"

". . . can't even reach the children anymore." The talon stopped shaking, came slowly back, knotting. "I want to break something and get out. Very childishly, yes. Because nobody is paying any attention to *me*." The list jumped. "Even when I'm trying to help. I *don't* want to hurt anybody *anymore*. I *swear* it, so help me, I swear—"

"Vyme, take off the glove and listen!"

I raised the slave-hand because it was about to scrape the cement.

"Vyme, I want to pay some attention to you." Slowly Poloscki walked back into the orange light. "You've been sending me kids for five years now, coming around and checking up on them, helping them out of the stupid scrapes they get in. They haven't all been Ratlits. I like kids too. That's why I take them on. I think what you do is pretty great. Part of me loves kids. Another part of me loves you."

"Aw, Poloscki . . ." I shook my head. Somewhere disgust began.

"It doesn't embarrass me. I love you a little and wouldn't mind loving you a lot. More than once I've thought about asking you to start a group."

"*Please,* Poloscki. I've had too many weird things happen to me this week. Not tonight, huh?" I then turned the power off in the glove.

"Love shouldn't frighten you, no matter when or how it comes, Vyme. Don't run from it. A marriage between us? Yeah, it would be a little hard for somebody like you, at first. But you'd get used to it before long. Then when kids came around, there'd be two—"

"I'll send Sandy over," I said. "He's the big-hearted marrying kind. Maybe he's about ready to try again." I pulled off the glove.

"Vyme, don't go out like that. Stay for just a minute."

"Poloscki," I said, "I'm just not that goddamn drunk!" I threw the glove on the table.

"Please, Vyme."

"You're gonna use your gun to keep me here?"

"Don't be like—"

"I hope the kids I send over here appreciate you more than I do right now. I'm sorry I busted in here. Good night!"

I turned from the table.

Nine thousand miles away the Stellarplex turned too. Circles of silver dropped through the roof. Behind the metal cage of the relaxed slave-claw I saw Poloscki's large, injured eyes, circles of crushed turquoise, glistening now.

And nine feet away someone said, "Ma'am?"

Poloscki glanced over her shoulder. "An, you awake?"

An stepped into the silver light, rubbing his neck. "That office chair is pretty hard, sister."

"He's here?" I asked.

"Sure," Poloscki said. "He didn't have any place to stay so I let him sleep in the office while I finished up some work in the back. Vyme, I meant what I said. Leave if you want, but not like this. Untwist."

"Poloscki," I said, "you're very sweet, and affectionate and a good mechanic too. But I've been there before. Asking me to join a group is like asking me to do something obscene. I know what I'm worth."

"I'm also a good businesswoman. Don't think that didn't enter my head when I thought about marrying you." An came and stood beside her. He was breathing hard, the way an animal does when you wake it all of a sudden.

"Poloscki, you said it, I didn't: I'm a mess. That's why I'm not with my own group now."

"You're not always like this. I've never seen you touch a drop before."

"For a while," I said, "it happened with disgusting frequency. Why do you think my group dropped me?"

"Must have been a while ago. I've known you a long time. So you've grown up since then. Now it only happens every half dozen years or so. Congratulations. Come have some coffee. An, run into the office and plug in the pot. I showed you where it was." An turned like something blown by the world-wind and was gone in the shadow. "Come on," Poloscki said. She took my arm, and I came with her. Before we left the light, I saw my reflection in the polished steel tool-cabinet door.

"Aw, no." I pulled away from her. "No, I better go home now."

"Why? An's making coffee."

"The kid. I don't want the kid to see me like this."

"He already has. Won't hurt him. Come on."

XI

When I walked into Poloscki's office, I felt I didn't have a damn thing left. No, I had one. I decided to give it away. When An turned to me with the cup, I put my hands on his shoulders. He jumped, but not enough to spill the coffee. "First and last bit of alcoholic advice for the evening, kid-boy. Even if you are crazy, don't go around telling people who are not golden how they've trapped you."

An ducked from under my hands, put the coffee on the desk, and turned back. "I didn't say you trapped us."

"You said we treated you lousy and exploited you, which we may, and that this trapped you—"

"I said you exploited us, which you do, *and* that we were trapped. I *didn't* say by what."

Poloscki sat down on the desk, picked up my coffee and sipped it.

I raised my head. "All right. Tell me how you're trapped."

"Oh, I'm sorry," Poloscki said. "I started drinking your coffee."

"Shut up. How are you trapped, An?"

He moved his shoulders around as though he was trying to get them comfortable. "It started in Tyber-44 cluster. Golden were coming back with really bad psychic shock."

"Yes. I'd heard about it. That was a few years back."

An's face started to twitch, the muscles around his eyes twisted below the skin. "*Something* out there . . ."

I put my hand on the back of his neck, my thumb in the soft spot behind his ear and began to stroke, the way you get a cat to calm down, "Take it easy. Just tell me."

"Thanks," An said and bent his head forward. "We found them first in Tyber-44, but then they turned up all *over,* on half the planets in every galaxy that could support any life, and a lot more that shouldn't have been able to at all." His breathing grew coarser. I kept rubbing, and it slowed again. "I guess we have such a funny psychology that working with them, studying them, even thinking about them too much . . . there's something about them that changes our sense of reality. The shock was bad."

"An," I said, "to be trapped, there has to be somewhere you can't go. For it to bug you, there has to be something else around that can."

He nodded under my hand, then straightened up. "I'm all right now. Just tired. You want to know where and what?"

Poloscki had put down the coffee now and was dangling the chain. An whirled to stare at it directly.

"Where?" he said. "Other universes."

"Galaxies further out?" asked Poloscki.

"No. Completely different matrices of time and space." Staring at the swinging ball seemed to calm him even more. "No physical or temporal connection to this one at all."

"A sort of parallel—"

"Parallel? Hell!" It was almost a drawl. "There's nothing parallel about them. Out of the billions-to-the-billionth of them, most are hundreds of times the size of ours and empty. There are a few, though, whose entire spatial extent is even smaller than this galaxy. Some of them are completely dense to us, because even though there seems to be matter in them, distributed more or less as in this universe, there's no electromagnetic activity at all. No radio waves, no heat, no light." The globe swung, the voice was a whisper.

I closed my fist around the globe and took it from Poloscki. "How do you know about them? Who brings back the information? Who is it who can get out?"

Blinking, An looked back at me.

When he told me, I began to laugh. To accommodate the shifting reality tensions, the psychotic personality that is golden is totally labile. An laughed with me, not knowing why. He explained through his torrential hysteria how with the micro-micro surgical techniques from Tyber-44 they had read much of the information from a direct examination of the creature's nervous system, which covered its surface like velvet. It could take intense cold or heat, a range of pressure from vacuum to hundreds of pounds per square millimeter; but a fairly small amount of ultraviolet destroyed the neural synapses, and they died. They were small and deceptively organic because in an organic environment they appeared to breathe and eat. They had four sexes, two of which carried the young. They had clusters of retractible sense organs that first appeared to be eyes, but were sensitive to twelve distinct senses, stimulation for three of which didn't even exist in our continuum. They traveled around on four suction cups when using kinetic motion for ordinary traversal of space, were small, and looked furry. The only way to make them jump universes was to scare the life out of them. At which point they just disappeared.

An kneaded his stomach under his belt to ease the pain from so much laughter. "Working with them at Tyber-44 just cracked up a whole bunch of golden." He leaned against the desk, panting and grinning. "They had to be sent home for therapy. We still can't think about them directly, but it's easier for us to control what we think about than for you; that's part of being golden. I even had one of them for a pet, up until yesterday. The damn creatures are either totally apathetic, or vicious. Mine was a baby, all white and soft." He held out his arm. "Yesterday it bit me and disappeared." On his wrist there was a bluish place centered on which was a crescent of pin-pricks. "Lucky it was a baby. The bites infect easily."

Poloscki started drinking from my cup again as An and I started laughing all over.

Walking back that night, black coffee slopped in my belly.

There are certain directions in which you cannot go. Choose one in which you can move as far as you want. Sandy said that? He did. But there was something about Sandy, very much like someone golden. It doesn't matter how, he's going on.

Under a street lamp I stopped and lifted up the ecologarium. The reproductive function, was it primary or adjunctive? If, I thought with the whisky lucidity always suspect at dawn, you consider the whole ecological balance a single organism, it's adjunctive, a vital reparative process along with sleeping and eating, to the primary process which is living, working, growing. I put the chain around my neck.

I was still half soused, and it felt bad. But I howled. Androcles, is drunken laughter appropriate to mourn all my dead children? Perhaps not. But tell me, Ratlit, Androcles, tell me Alegra, what better way to launch my live ones who are golden into night? I don't know. I know I laughed. Then I put my lists into my overall pouch and crunched along the Edge toward home.

1968

THE HUGO AND Nebula awards for 1968 were unique. With the first Nebulas in 1965 the question had arisen as to whether the new series would simply rubber-stamp the old (or, in view of the dates on which the awards were made each year, vice versa). In fact, no such thing occurred. In the first year of double awards, two works won both Hugo and Nebula while four others won only Hugo *or* Nebula. The second year there was only one double winner, and there were six single winners. The third year, one double and seven singles.

In 1968, for the first time ever (and—to date, at least—the last), the Hugo and Nebula voters selected completely different lists. Not only were the specific works and authors divergent, but the sources were also completely different from each other. The Hugo award novel, John Brunner's *Stand on Zanzibar,* was a Doubleday book. A huge, ambitious, dos Passos-like book, *Stand on Zanzibar* was by far the most notable and successful effort, up to the time, of a hugely prolific craftsman.

The Nebula award novel, Alexei Panshin's *Rite of Passage,* was also a remarkable effort. Panshin had been a life-long admirer of Heinlein's and eventually wrote a book about Heinlein and his works. *Rite of Passage* was Panshin's homage to Heinlein: a letter-perfect Heinlein "juvie." The book was rejected by a score of publishers before being taken by Terry Carr for the latter's much-acclaimed Ace Special series, but once in print it achieved quick popularity and has continued to attract readers for over a decade.

In the shorter lengths, the fans awarded the Hugo to three works from *Galaxy;* "Nightwings," by Robert Silverberg,

"The Sharing of the Flesh," by Poul Anderson and "The Beast that Shouted Love at the Heart of the World," by Harlan Ellison. This was a sweep the likes of which Campbell in his palmiest days at *Astounding* could only have dreamed. It was achieved, ironically, not by any of the famed editors of science fiction history—Gernsback, Campbell, Boucher, Gold—but by Frederick Pohl, a man far better known for his own fiction. A further irony: 1968 was the last year of Pohl's editorship of *Galaxy*. In 1969 the magazine was sold to new publishers: they and Pohl were unable to agree on a working relationship and he left. As for the Nebulas, Anne McCaffrey's *Analog* novella "Dragonrider" won her a trophy to stand beside the previous year's Hugo for "Weyr Search." The novelette and short-story Nebula awards were won by Richard Wilson for "Mother to the World," and by Kate Wilhelm for "The Planners." Both these stories had appeared in Damon Knight's *Orbit 3,* and the charges of cronyism resurfaced, this time with two additional flips.

In 1938 a group of young men and women in New York City had founded a club known as the Futurian Society. The organization had elements in it of science fiction fan club, radical political action group, communal living experiment, literary mutual-aid pact and general social group. Its members, by the mid-1940s, had included such notables as Donald Wollheim, James Blish, Judith Merril, Frederick Pohl, Virginia Kidd, Isaac Asimov, Larry Shaw, Richard Wilson, John B. Michel, Harry Dockweiller, Cyril Kornbluth, David Kyle and Robert W. Lowndes.

Of these, Dockweiller and Michel died young and under tragic circumstances, leaving little to mark the promise of their youthful talent. But all the others survived to excel in the field of science fiction as editors, authors, agents or publishers.

One of the youngest of the early Futurians was Damon Knight, and in drawing up a chronology of organizations, individuals and events, it is possible to make direct connections from the original Futurian Society of more than forty years ago to the persons and forces that shape the science fiction community to this day.

Now, in 1968, two stories from Damon Knight's *Orbit* capture Nebula awards. One is by Damon Knight's old Futurian comrade, Richard Wilson; the other, by Damon Knight's wife, Kate Wilhelm. Quickly: Lupoff is *not* accusing Knight, Wilson and Wilhelm of collusion. Lupoff is *not* suggesting anything illegal, immoral or improper about the whole event.

What I'm suggesting is this: It was damned unfortunate that the same people kept coming up in different combinations. The charges of cronyism, conflict of interest and "Milford Mafia" were loud in the halls of the Algonquin Hotel in the hours following the Nebula award ceremonies in the spring of 1969. Some of the accused Milford Mafia had big buttons made up, proudly proclaiming their membership in that mythical society.

It was all very unfortunate. It certainly hurt SFWA, and some of its aftereffects linger to this day.

As for the stories themselves, one has little complaint against the choices. There were plenty of other fine stories available, of course. Certainly James Blish's novel *Black Easter* (which made the Nebula ballot) and Delany's novel *Nova* (which made the Hugo ballot) are deserving of mention. In the shorter lengths, Terry Carr's "The Dance of the Changer and the Three," Betsy Curtis's "The Steiger Effect" and Damon Knight's devastating "Masks" (from *Playboy)* at least deserve mention.

But I think the *most* deserving, overlooked story of 1968 was Joanna Russ's "The Barbarian." And "The Barbarian," damn it all a million times over, was first published in Damon Knight's *Orbit 3!* What can I say?

As for Joanna Russ—and this particular story—I *can* say a little. Russ has been writing and publishing science fiction since 1959. Holder of a degree as master of fine arts in drama, she brings a strong sense of theater to her fiction. In the late 1960s she began a series of stories about her heroine Alyx, carrying her through a variety of worlds and relationships with energy and wit.

As the 1970s progressed, Russ's fiction tended to become increasingly polemical, bringing her increased attention from critics and from partisans of (and opponents of) her principles. At the same time, her appeal to book-buyers who asked for unadulterated entertainment was necessarily lessened. As Heinlein has said, "We're competing for beer money." Whether Russ's interests will lead her completely away from fiction in the 1980s, or will bring her back more fully to fiction, we can only wait and see.

In any case, her existing body of works, admittedly uneven in quality, contain some of the most splendid and rewarding stories of their time. "The Barbarian' in particular mixes genres with the skill of a dramatist, adds a wry wit worthy of a Fritz Leiber, provides a full portion of pure entertainment, yet contains Russ's polemical statement in a quietly but strongly implicit fashion. It's a splendid job!

The Barbarian

JOANNA RUSS

ALYX, THE GRAY-EYED, the silent woman. Wit, arm, kill-quick for hire, she watched the strange man thread his way through the tables and the smoke toward her. This was in Ourdh, where all things are possible. He stopped at the table where she sat alone and with a certain indefinable gallantry, not pleasant but perhaps its exact opposite, he said:

"A woman—here?"

"You're looking at one," said Alyx dryly, for she did not like his tone. It occurred to her that she had seen him before—though he was not so fat then, no, not quite so fat—and then it occurred to her that the time of their last meeting had almost certainly been in the hills when she was four or five years old. That was thirty years ago. So she watched him very narrowly as he eased himself into the seat opposite, watched him as he drummed his fingers in a lively tune on the tabletop, and paid him close attention when he tapped one of the marine decorations that hung from the ceiling (a stuffed blowfish, all spikes and parchment, that moved lazily to and fro in a wandering current of air) and made it bob. He smiled, the flesh around his eyes straining into folds.

"I know you," he said. "A raw country girl fresh from the hills who betrayed an entire religious delegation to the police some ten years ago. You settled down as a picklock. You made a good thing of it. You expanded your profession to include a few more difficult items and you did a few things that turned heads hereabouts. You were not unknown, even then. Then you vanished for a season and reappeared as a fairly rich woman. But that didn't last, unfortunately."

"Didn't have to," said Alyx.

"Didn't last," repeated the fat man imperturbably, with a lazy shake of the head. "No, no, it didn't last. And now," (he pronounced the "now" with peculiar relish) "you are getting old."

"Old enough," said Alyx, amused.

"Old," said he, "old. Still neat, still tough, still small. But old. You're thinking of settling down."

"Not exactly."

"Children?"

She shrugged, retiring a little into the shadow. The fat man did not appear to notice. "It's been done," she said.

"You may die in childbirth," said he, "at your age."

"That, too, has been done."

She stirred a little, and in a moment a short-handled Southern dagger, the kind carried unobtrusively in sleeves or shoes, appeared with its point buried in the tabletop, vibrating ever so gently.

"It is true," said she, "that I am growing old. My hair is threaded with white. I am developing a chunky look around the waist that does not exactly please me, though I was never a ballet-girl." She grinned at him in the semi-darkness. "Another thing," she said softly, "that I develop with age is a certain lack of patience. If you do not stop making personal remarks and taking up my time—which is valuable—I shall throw you across the room."

"I would not, if I were you," he said.

"You could not."

The fat man began to heave with laughter. He heaved until he choked. Then he said, gasping, "I beg your pardon." Tears ran down his face.

"Go on," said Alyx. He leaned across the table, smiling, his fingers mated tip to tip, his eyes little pits of shadow in his face.

"I come to make you rich," he said.

"You can do more than that," said she steadily. A quarrel broke out across the room between a soldier and a girl he had picked up for the night; the fat man talked through it, or rather under it, never taking his eyes off her face.

"Ah!" he said, "you remember when you saw me last and you assume that a man who can live thirty years without growing older must have more to give—if he wishes—than a handful of gold coins. You are right. I can make you live long. I can insure your happiness. I can determine the sex of your children. I can cure all diseases. I can even" (and here he lowered his voice) "turn this table, or this building, or this whole city to pure gold, if I wish it."

"Can anyone do that?" said Alyx, with the faintest whisper of mockery.

"I can," he said. 'Come outside and let us talk. Let me show you a few of the things I can do. I have some business here in the city that I must attend to myself and I need a guide and an assistant. That will be you."

"If you can turn the city into gold." said Alyx just as softly, "can you turn gold into a city?"

"Anyone can do that," he said, laughing: "come along," so they rose and made their way into the cold outside air—it was a clear night in early spring—and at a corner of the street where the moon shone down on the walls and the pits in the road, they stopped.

"Watch," said he.

On his outstretched palm was a small black box. He shook it, turning it this way and that, but it remained wholly featureless. Then he held it out to her and, as she took it in her hand, it began to glow until it became like a piece of glass lit up from the inside. There in the middle of it was her man, with his tough, friendly, young-old face and his hair a little gray, like hers. He smiled at her, his lips moving soundlessly. She threw the cube into the air a few times, held it to the side of her face, shook it, and then dropped it on the ground, grinding it under her heel, it remained unhurt.

She picked it up and held it out to him, thinking:

Not metal, very light. And warm. A toy? Wouldn't break, though. Must be some sort of small machine, though God knows who made it and of what. It follows thoughts. Marvelous. But magic? Bah! Never believed in it before; why now?

*Besides, this thing too sensible; magic is elaborate, unde-
pendable, useless. I'll tell him*—but then it occurred to her
that someone had gone to a good deal of trouble to impress
her when a little bit of credit might have done just as well.
And this man walked with an almighty confidence through
the streets for someone who was unarmed. And those thirty
years—so she said very politely:

"It's magic!"

He chuckled and pocketed the cube.

"You're a little savage," he said, "but your examination of
it was most logical. I like you. Look! I am an old magician.
There is a spirit in that box and there are more spirits under
my control than you can possibly imagine. I am like a man
living among monkeys. There are things spirits cannot do—
or things I choose to do myself, take it any way you will. So
I pick one of the monkeys who seems brighter than the rest
and train it. I nick you. What do you say?"

"All right," said Alyx.

"Calm enough!" he chuckled. "Calm enough! Good.
What's your motive?"

"Curiosity," said Alyx. "It's a monkeylike trait." He
chuckled again; his flesh choked it and the noise came out in
a high, muffled scream.

"And what if I bite you," said Alyx, "like a monkey?"

"No, little one," he answered gaily, "you won't. You may
be sure of that." He held out his hand, still shaking with
mirth. In the palm lay a kind of blunt knife which he pointed
at one of the whitewashed walls that lined the street. The
edges of the wall burst into silent smoke, the whole section
trembled and slid, and in an instant it had vanished, vanished
as completely as if it had never existed, except for a sullen
glow at the raw edges of brick and a pervasive smell of burning. Alyx swallowed.

"It's quiet, for magic," she said softly. "Have you ever
used it on men?"

"On armies, little one."

So the monkey went to work for him. There seemed as yet to

be no harm in it. The little streets admired his generosity and the big ones his good humor; while those too high for money or flattery he won by a catholic ability that was—so the little picklock thought—remarkable in one so stupid. For about his stupidity there could be no doubt. She smelled it. It offended her. It made her twitch in her sleep, like a ferret. There was in this woman—well hidden away—an anomalous streak of quiet humanity that abhorred him, that set her teeth on edge at the thought of him, though she could not have put into words just what was the matter. *For stupidity,* she thought, *is hardly—is not exactly—*

Four months later they broke into the governor's villa. She thought she might at last find out what this man was after besides pleasure jaunts around the town. Moreover, breaking and entering always gave her the keenest pleasure; and doing so "for nothing" (as he said) tickled her fancy immensely. The power in gold and silver that attracts thieves was banal, in this thief's opinion, but to stand in the shadows of a sleeping house, absolutely silent, with no object at all in view and with the knowledge that if you are found you will probably have your throat cut—! She began to think better of him. This dilettante passion for the craft, this reckless silliness seemed to her as worthy as the love of a piece of magnetite for the North and South poles—the "faithful stone" they call it in Ourdh.

"Who'll come with us?" she asked, wondering for the fiftieth time where the devil he went when he was not with her, whom he knew, where he lived, and what that persistently bland expression on his face could possibly mean.

"No one," he said calmly.

"What are we looking for?"

"Nothing."

"Do you ever do anything for a reason?"

"Never." And he chuckled.

And then, "Why are you so fat?" demanded Alyx, halfway out of her own door, half into the shadows. She had recently settled in a poor quarter of the town, partly out of laziness, partly out of necessity. The shadows playing in the hollows of her face, the expression of her eyes veiled, she said it again, "Why are you so goddamned fat!" He laughed until he wheezed.

"The barbarian mind!" he cried, lumbering after her in high good humor. "Oh—oh, my dear!—oh, what freshness!" She thought:

That's it! and then.

The fool doesn't even know I hate him.

But neither had she known, until that very moment.

They scaled the northeast garden wall of the villa and crept along the top of it without descending, for the governor kept dogs. Alyx, who could walk a taut rope like a circus performer, went quietly. The fat man giggled. She swung herself up to the nearest window and hung there by one arm and a toehold for fifteen mortal minutes while she sawed through the metal hinge of the shutter with a file. Once inside the building (he had to be pulled through the window) she took him by the collar with uncanny accuracy, considering that the inside of the villa was stone dark. "Shut up!" she said, with considerable emphasis.

"Oh?" he whispered.

"I'm in charge here," she said, releasing him with a jerk, and melted into the blackness not two feet away, moving swiftly along the corridor wall. Her fingers brushed lightly alongside her, like a creeping animal: stone, stone, a gap, warm air rising . . . In the dark she felt wolfish, her lips skinned back over her teeth; like another species she made her way with hands and ears. Through them the villa sighed and rustled in its sleep. She put the tips of the fingers of her free hand on the back of the fat man's neck, guiding him with the faintest of touches through the turns of the corridor. They crossed an empty space where two halls met; they retreated noiselessly into a room where a sleeper lay breathing against a dimly lit window, while someone passed in the corridor outside. When the steps faltered for a moment, the fat man gasped and Alyx wrung his wrist, hard. There was a cough from the corridor, the sleeper in the room stirred and murmured, and the steps passed on. They crept back to the hall. Then he told her where he wanted to go.

"What!" She had pulled away, astonished, with a reckless hiss of indrawn breath. Methodically he began poking her in the side and giving her little pushes with his other hand—she moving away, outraged—but all in silence. In the distant reaches of the building something fell—or someone spoke—and without thinking, they waited silently until the sounds had faded away. He resumed his continual prodding. Alyx, her teeth on edge, began to creep forward, passing a cat that sat outlined in the vague light from a window, perfectly unconcerned with them and rubbing its paws against its face, past a door whose cracks shone yellow, past ghostly staircases that opened up in vast wells of darkness, breathing a faint, far updraft, their steps rustling and creaking. They were approaching the governor's nursery. The fat man watched without any visible horror—or any interest, for that matter—while Alyx disarmed the first guard, stalking him as if he were a sparrow, then the one strong pressure on the blood vessel at the back of the neck (all with no noise except the man's own breathing; she was quiet as a shadow). Now he was trussed up, conscious and glaring, quite unable to move. The second guard was asleep in his chair. The third Alyx decoyed out the anteroom by a thrown pebble (she had picked up several in the street). She was three motionless feet away from him as he stooped to examine it; he never straightened up. The fourth guard (he was in the anteroom, in a feeble glow that stole through the hangings of the nursery beyond) turned to greet his friend—or so he thought—and then Alyx judged she could risk a little speech. She said thoughtfully, in a low voice, "That's dangerous, on the back of the head."

"Don't let it bother you," said the fat man. Through the parting of the hangings they could see the nurse, asleep on her couch with her arms bare and their golden circlets gleaming in the lamplight, the black slave in a profound huddle of darkness at the farther door, and a shining, tented basket—the royal baby's royal house. The baby was asleep. Alyx stepped inside—motioning the fat man away from the lamp—and picked the governor's daughter out of her gilt cradle. She went round the apartment with the baby in one arm. bolting both doors and closing the hangings, draping the fat man in a guard's cloak and turning down the lamp so that a bare glimmer of light reached the farthest walls.

"Now you've seen it," she said, "shall we go?"

He shook his head. He was watching her curiously, his head tilted to one side. He smiled at her. The baby woke up and began to chuckle at finding herself carried about; she grabbed at Alyx's mouth and jumped up and down, bending in the middle like a sort of pocket-compass or enthusiastic spring, The woman lifted her head to avoid the baby's fingers and began to soothe her, rocking her in her arms, "Good Lord, she's cross-eyed," said Alyx. The nurse and her slave slept on, wrapped in the profoundest unconsciousness. Humming a little, soft tune to the governor's daughter, Alyx walked her about the room, humming and rocking, rocking and humming, until the baby yawned.

"Better go," said Alyx.

"No." said the fat man.

"Better," said Alyx again. "One cry and the nurse—"

"Kill the nurse," said the fat man.

"The slave—"

"He's dead."

Alyx started, rousing the baby. The slave still slept by the door, blacker than the blackness, but under him oozed something darker still in the twilight flame of the lamp. "You did that?" whispered Alyx, hushed. She had not seen him move. He took something dark and hollow, like the shell of a nut, from the palm of his hand and laid it next the baby's cradle; with a shiver half of awe and half of distaste Alyx put that richest and most fortunate daughter of Ourdh back into her gilt cradle. Then she said:

"Now we'll go."

"But I have not what I came for," said the fat man.

"And what is that?"

"The baby."

"Do you mean to steal her?" said Alyx curiously.

"No," said he, "I mean for you to kill her."

The woman stared. In sleep the governor's daughter's nurse stirred; then she sat bolt upright, said something incomprehensible in a loud voice, and fell back to her couch, still deep in sleep. So astonished was the picklock that she did not move. She only looked at the fat man. Then she sat by the cradle and rocked it mechanically with one hand while she looked at him.

"What on earth for?" she said at length. He smiled. He seemed as easy as if he were discussing her wages or the price of pigs; he sat down opposite her and he too rocked the cradle, looking on the burden it contained with a benevolent, amused interest. If the nurse had woken up at that moment, she might have thought she saw the governor and his wife, two loving parents who had come to visit their child by lamplight. The fat man said: "Must you know?"

"I must," said Alyx.

"Then I will tell you," said the fat man, "not because you must, but because I choose. This little six-months morsel is going to grow up."

"Most of us do," said Alyx, still astonished.

"She will become a queen," the fat man went on, "and a surprisingly wicked woman for one who now looks so innocent. She will be the death of more than one child and more than one slave. In plain fact, she will be a horror to the world. This I know."

"I believe you," said Alyx, shaken.

"Then kill her," said the fat man. But still the picklock did not stir. The baby in her cradle snored, as infants sometimes do, as if to prove the fat man's opinion of her by showing a surprising precocity; still the picklock did not move, but stared at the man across the cradle as if he were a novel work of nature.

"I ask you to kill her," said he again.

"In twenty years," said she, "when she has become so very wicked."

"Woman, are you deaf? I told you—"

"In twenty years!" In the feeble light from the lamp she appeared pale, as if with rage or terror. He leaned deliberately across the cradle, closing his hand around the shell or round-shot or unidentifiable object he had dropped there a moment before; he said very deliberately:

"In twenty years you will be dead."

"Then do it yourself," said Alyx softly, pointing at the object in his hand, "unless you had only one?"

"I had one."

"Ah, well then," she said, "here!" and she held out to him across the sleeping baby the handle of her dagger, for she had divined something about this man in the months they had known each other; and when he made no move to take the blade, she nudged his hand with the handle.

"You don't like things like this, do you?" she said.

"Do as I say, woman!" he whispered. She pushed the handle into his palm. She stood up and poked him deliberately with it, watching him tremble and sweat; she had never seen him so much at a loss. She moved round the cradle, smiling and stretching out her arm seductively. "Do as I say!" he cried.

"Softly, softly."

"You're a sentimental fool!"

"Am I?" she said. "Whatever I do, I must feel; I can't just twiddle my fingers like you, can I?"

"Ape!"

"You chose me for it."

"Do as I say!"

"Sh! You will wake the nurse."

For a moment both stood silent, listening to the baby's all-but-soundless breathing and the rustling of the nurse's sheets. Then he said, "Woman, your life is in my hands."

"Is it?" said she.

"I want your obedience!"

"Oh no," she said softly, "I know what you want. You want importance because you have none; you want to swallow up another soul. You want to make me fear you and I think you can succeed, but I think also that I can teach you the difference between fear and respect. Shall I?"

"Take care!" he gasped.

"Why?" she said. "Lest you kill me?"

"There are other ways," he said, and he drew himself up, but here the picklock spat in his face. He let out a strangled wheeze and lurched backwards, stumbling against the curtains. Behind her Alyx heard a faint cry; she whirled about to see the governor's nurse sitting up in bed, her eyes wide open.

"Madam, quietly, quietly," said Alyx, "for God's sake!"

The governor's nurse opened her mouth.

"I have done no harm," said Alyx passionately, "I swear it!" but the governor's nurse took a breath with the clear intention to scream, a hearty, healthy, full-bodied scream like the sort picklocks hear in nightmares. In the second of the governor's nurse's shuddering inhalation—in that split second that would mean unmentionably unpleasant things for Alyx, as Ourdh was not a kind city—Alyx considered launching herself at the woman, but the cradle was between. It would be too late. The house would be roused in twenty seconds. She could never make it to a door—or a window—not even to the garden, where the governor's hounds could drag down a stranger in two steps. All these thoughts flashed through the picklock's mind as she saw the governor's nurse inhale with that familiar, hideous violence; her knife was still in her hand; with the smooth simplicity of habit it slid through her fingers and sped across the room to bury itself in the governor's nurse's neck, just above the collarbone in that tender hollow Ourdhian poets love to sing of. The woman's open-mouthed expression froze on her face; with an "uh!" of surprise she fell forward, her arms hanging limp over the edge of the couch. A noise came from her throat. The knife had opened a major pulse, and in the blood's slow, powerful, rhythmic tides across sheet and slippers and floor Alyx could discern a horrid similarity to the posture and appearance of the black slave. One was hers, one was the fat man's. She turned and hurried through the curtains into the anteroom, only noting that the soldier blindfolded and bound in the

corner had managed patiently to work loose the thongs
around two of his fingers with his teeth. He must have been
at it all this time. Outside in the hall the darkness of the
house was as undisturbed as if the nursery were that very
Well of Peace whence the gods first drew (as the saying is)
the dawn and the color—but nothing else—for the eyes of
women. On the wall someone had written in faintly shining
stuff, like snail-slime, the single word *Fever*.

But the fat man was gone.

Her man was raving and laughing on the floor when she
got home. She could not control him—she could only sit
with her hands over her face and shudder—so at length she
locked him in and gave the key to the old woman who
owned the house, saying, "My husband drinks too much. He
was perfectly sober when I left earlier this evening and now
look at him. Don't let him out."

Then she stood stock-still for a moment, trembling and
thinking: of the fat man's distaste for walking, of his wheez-
ing, his breathlessness, of his vanity that surely would have
led him to show her any magic vehicle he had that took him
to whatever he called home. He must have walked. She had
seen him go out the north gate a hundred times.

She began to run.

To the south Ourdh is built above marshes that will engulf
anyone or anything unwary enough to try to cross them, but
to the north the city peters out into sand dunes fringing the
seacoast and a fine monotony of rocky hills that rise to a
countryside of sandy scrub, stunted trees and what must
surely be the poorest farms in the world. Ourdh believes that
these farmers dream incessantly of robbing travelers, so nobody goes there, all the fashionable world frequenting the
great north road that loops a good fifty miles to avoid this
region. Even without its stories the world would have no reason to go here; there is nothing to see but dunes and weeds
and now and then a shack (or more properly speaking, a hut)
resting on an outcropping of rock or nesting right on the sand
like a toy boat in a basin. There is only one landmark in the

whole place—an old tower hardly even fit for a wizard—and that was abandoned nobody knows how long ago, though it is only twenty minutes' walk from the city gates. Thus it was natural that Alyx (as she ran, her heart pounding in her side) did not notice the stars, or the warm night-wind that stirred the leaves of the trees, or indeed the very path under her feet: though she knew all the paths for twenty-five miles around. Her whole mind was on that tower. She felt its stones stick in her throat. On her right and left the country flew by, but she seemed not to move; at last, panting and trembling, she crept through a nest of tree-trunks no thicker than her wrist (they were very old and very tough) and sure enough, there it was. There was a light shining halfway between bottom and top. Then someone looked out, like a cautious householder out of an attic, and the light went out.

Ah, thought she, and moved into the cover of the trees, The light—which had vanished—now reappeared a story higher and so on, higher and higher, until it reached the top. It wobbled a little, as if held in the hand. So this was his country seat! Silently and with great care, she made her way from one pool of shadow to another. One hundred feet from the tower she circled it and approached it from the northern side. A finger of the sea cut in very close to the base of the building (it had been slowly falling into the water for many years) and in this she first waded and then swam, disturbing the faint, cold radiance of the starlight in the placid ripples. There was no moon. Under the very walls of the tower she stopped and listened; in the darkness under the sea she felt along the rocks; then, expelling her breath and kicking upwards, she rushed head-down; the water closed round, the stone rushed past and she struggled up into the air. She was inside the walls.

And so is he, she thought. For somebody had cleaned the place up. What she remembered as choked with stone rubbish (she had used the place for purposes of her own a few years back) was bare and neat and clean; all was square, all was orderly, and someone had cut stone steps from the level of the water to the most beautifully precise archway in the world. But of course she should not have been able to see any of this at all, The place should have been in absolute darkness. Instead, on either side of the arch was a dim glow, with a narrow beam of light going between them; she could see dancing in it the dust-motes that are never absent from this earth, not even from air that has lain quiet within the rock of a wizard's mansion for uncountable years. Up to her neck in the ocean, this barbarian woman then stood very quietly and thoughtfully for several minutes. Then she dove down into the sea again, and when she came up her knotted cloak was full of the tiny crabs that cling to the rocks along the seacoast of Ourdh. One she killed and the others she suspended captive in the sea; bits of the blood and flesh of the first she smeared carefully below the two sources of that narrow beam of light; then she crept back into the sea and loosed the others at the very bottom step, diving underwater as the first of the hurrying little creatures reached the arch. There was a brilliant flash of light, then another, and then darkness. Alyx waited. Hoisting herself out of the water, she walked through the arch—not quickly, but not without nervousness. The crabs were pushing and quarreling over their dead cousin. Several climbed over the sources of the beam, *pulling,* she thought, *the crabs over his eyes.* However he saw, he had seen nothing. The first alarm had been sprung.

Wizards' castles—and their country residences—have every right to be infested with all manner of horrors, but Alyx saw nothing. The passage wound on, going fairly constantly upward, and as it rose it grew lighter until every now and then she could see a kind of lighter shape against the blackness and a few stars. These were windows. There was no sound but her own breathing and once in a while the complaining rustle of one or two little creatures she had inadvertently carried with her in a corner of her cloak. When she stopped she heard nothing. The fat man was either very quiet or very far away. She hoped it was quietness. She slung the cloak over her shoulder and began the climb again. Then she ran into a wall.

This shocked her, but she gathered herself together and

tried the experiment again. She stepped back, then walked forward and again she ran into a wall, not rock but something at once elastic and unyielding, and at the very same moment someone said (as it seemed to her, inside her head) *You cannot get through.*

Alyx swore, religiously. She fell back and nearly lost her balance. She put out one hand and again she touched something impalpable, tingling and elastic: again the voice sounded close behind her ear, with an uncomfortable, frightening intimacy as if she were speaking to herself: *You cannot get through.* "Can't I!" she shouted, quite losing her nerve, and drew her sword: it plunged forward without the slightest resistance, but something again stopped her bare hand and the voice repeated with idiot softness, over and over *You cannot get through. You cannot get through—*

"Who are you?" said she, but there was no answer. She backed down the stairs, sword drawn, and waited. Nothing happened. Round her the stone walls glimmered, barely visible, for the moon was rising outside; patiently she waited, pressing the corner of her cloak with her foot, for as it lay on the floor one of the crabs had chewed his way to freedom and had given her ankle a tremendous nip on the way out. The light increased.

There was nothing there. The crab, who had scuttled busily ahead on the landing of the stair, seemed to come to the place himself and stood there, fiddling. There was absolutely nothing there. Then Alyx, who had been watching the little animal with something close to hopeless calm, gave an exclamation and threw herself flat on the stairs—for the crab had begun to climb upward between floor and ceiling and what it was climbing on was nothing. Tears forced themselves to her eyes. Swimming behind her lids she could see her husband's face, appearing first in one place, then in another, as if frozen on the black box the fat man had showed her the first day they met. She laid herself on the stone and cried. Then she got up, for the face seemed to settle on the other side of the landing and it occurred to her that she must go through. She was still crying. She took off one of her san-

dals and pushed it through the something-nothing (the crab
still climbed in the air with perfect comfort). It went through
easily. She grew nauseated at the thought of touching the
crab and the thing it climbed on, but she put one hand invol-
untarily over her face and made a grab with the other (*You
cannot* said the voice). When she had got the struggling animal thoroughly in her grasp, she dashed it against the rocky-
side wall of the tunnel and flung it forward with all her
strength. It fell clattering twenty feet further on.

The distinction then, she thought, *is between life and
death,* and she sat down hopelessly on the steps to figure this
out, for the problem of dying so as to get through and yet
getting through without dying, struck her as insoluble.
Twenty feet down the tunnel (the spot was in darkness and
she could not see what it was) something rustled. It sounded
remarkably like a crab that had been stunned and was now
recovering, for these animals think of nothing but food and
disappointments only seem to give them fresh strength for
the search. Alyx gaped into the dark. She felt the hairs rise
on the back of her neck: She would have given a great deal
to see into that spot, for it seemed to her that she now
guessed at the principle of the fat man's demon, which kept
out any conscious mind—as it had spoken in hers—but perhaps would let through . . . She pondered. This cynical
woman had been a religious enthusiast before circumstances
forced her into a drier way of thinking; thus it was that she
now slung her cloak ahead of her on the ground to break her
fall and leaned deliberately, from head to feet, into the horrid, springy net she could not see. Closing her eyes and
pressing the fingers of both hands over an artery in the back
of her neck, she began to repeat to herself a formula that she
had learned in those prehistoric years, one that has to be altered slightly each time it is repeated—almost as effective a
self-hypnotic device as counting backward. And the voice,
too, whispering over and over *You cannot get through, you
cannot gel through—cannot—cannot—*

Something gave her a terrific shock through teeth, bones
and flesh, and she woke to find the floor of the landing tilted

two inches from her eyes. One knee was twisted under her and the left side of her face ached dizzily, warm and wet under a cushion of numbness. She guessed that her face had been laid open in the fall and her knee sprained, if not broken.

But she was through.

She found the fat man in a room at the very top of the tower, sitting in a pair of shorts in a square of light at the end of a corridor; and as she made her way limping towards him, he grew (unconscious and busy) to the size of a human being, until at last she stood inside the room, vaguely aware of blood along her arm and a stinging on her face where she had tried to wipe her wound with her cloak. The room was full of machinery. The fat man (he had been jiggling some little arrangement of wires and blocks on his lap) looked up, saw her, registered surprise and then broke into a great grin. "So it's you," he said.

She said nothing. She. put one arm along the wall to steady herself.

"You are amazing," he said, "perfectly amazing. Come here," and he rose and sent his stool spinning away with a touch. He came up to where she stood, wet and shivering, staining the floor and wall, and for a long minute he studied her. Then he said softly: "Poor animal, Poor little wretch." Her breathing was ragged. She glanced rapidly about her, taking in the size of the room (it broadened to encompass the whole width of the tower) and the four great windows that opened to the four winds, and the strange things in the shadows: multitudes of little tables, boards hung on the walls, knobs and switches and winking lights innumerable. But she did not move or speak.

"Poor animal," he said again. He walked back and surveyed her contemptuously, both arms akimbo, and then he said, "Do you believe the world was once a lump of rock?"

"Yes," she said.

"Many years ago," he said, "many more years than your mind can comprehend, before there were trees—or cities—or

women—I came to this lump of rock. Do you believe that?"
She nodded.

"I came here," said he gently, "in the satisfaction of a certain hobby, and I made all that you see in this room—all the
little things you were looking at a moment ago—and I made
the tower, too. Sometimes I make it new inside and sometimes I make it look old. Do you understand that, little one?"
She said nothing.

"And when the whim hits me," he said, "I make it new
and comfortable and I settle into it, and once I have settled
into it I begin to practice my hobby. Do you know what my
hobby is?" He chuckled.

"My hobby, little one," he said, "came from this tower
and this machinery, for this machinery can reach all over the
world and then things happen exactly as I choose. Now do
you know what my hobby is? My hobby is world-making, I
make worlds, little one."

She took a quick breath, like a sigh, but she did not speak.
He smiled at her.

"Poor beast," he said, "you are dreadfully cut about the
face and I believe you have sprained one of your limbs.
Hunting animals are always doing that. But it won't last.
Look," he said, "look again," and he moved one fat hand in a
slow circle around him. "It is I, little one," he said, "who
made everything that your eyes have ever rested on. Apes
and peacocks, tides and times" (he laughed) "and the fire and
the rain. I made you. I made your husband. Come," and he
ambled off into the shadows. The circle of light that had
rested on him when Alyx first entered the room now followed him, continually keeping him at its center, and although her hair rose to see it, she forced herself to follow,
limping in pain past the tables, through stacks of tubing and
wire and between square shapes the size of stoves. The light
fled always before her. Then he stopped, and as she came up
to the light, he said:

"You know, I am not angry at you."

Alyx winced as her foot struck something, and grabbed
her knee.

"No, I am not," he said. "It has been delightful—except for tonight, which demonstrates, between ourselves, that the whole thing was something of a mistake and shouldn't be indulged in again—but you must understand that I cannot allow a creation of mine, a paring of my fingernail, if you take my meaning, to rebel in this silly fashion." He grinned. "No, no," he said, "that I cannot do. And so" (here he picked up a glass cube from the table in back of him) "I have decided" (here he joggled the cube a little) "that tonight—why, my dear, what is the matter with you? You are standing there with the veins in your fists knotted as if you would like to strike me, even though your knee is giving you a great deal of trouble just at present and you would be better employed in supporting some of your weight with your hands or I am very much mistaken." And he held out to her—though not far enough for her to reach it—the glass cube, which contained an image of her husband in little, unnaturally sharp, like a picture let into crystal. "See?" he said. "When I turn the lever to the right, the little beasties rioting in his bones grow ever more calm and that does him good. A great deal of good. But when I turn the lever to the left—"

"Devil!" said she.

"Ah, I've gotten something out of you at last!" he said, coming closer. "At last you know! Ah, little one, many and many a time I have seen you wondering whether the world might not be better off if you stabbed me in the back, eh? But you can't, you know. Why don't you try it?" He patted her on the shoulder. "Here I am, you see, quite close enough to you, peering, in fact, into those tragic, blazing eyes—wouldn't it be natural to try and put an end to me? But you can't, you know. You'd be puzzled if you tried. I wear an armor plate, little beast, that any beast might envy, and you could throw me from a ten-thousand-foot mountain, or fry me in a furnace, or do a hundred and one other deadly things to me without the least effect. My armor plate has *in-er-tial dis-crim-in-a-tion,* little savage, which means that it lets nothing too fast and nothing too heavy get through. So you cannot hurt me at all. To murder me, you would have to strike me, but that is too fast and too heavy and so is the ground that hits me when I fall and so is fire. Come here." She did not move.

"Come here, monkey," he said. "I'm going to kill your man and then I will send you away; though since you operate so well in the dark, I think I'll bless you and make that your permanent condition. What do you think you're doing?" for she had put her fingers to her sleeve; and while he stood, smiling a little with cube in his hand, she drew her dagger and fell upon him, stabbing him again and again.

"There," he said complacently, "do you see?"

"I see," she said hoarsely, finding her tongue.

"Do you understand?"

"I understand," she said.

"Then move off," he said, "I have got to finish," and he brought the cube up to the level of his eyes. She saw her man, behind the glass as in a refracting prism, break into a multiplicity of images; she saw him reach out grotesquely to the surface; she saw his fingertips strike at the surface as if to erupt into the air; and while the fat man took the lever between thumb and forefinger and—prissily and precisely, his lips pursed into wrinkles, prepared to move it all the way to the left—

She put her fingers in his eyes and then, taking advantage of his pain and blindness, took the cube from him and bent him over the edge of a table in such a way as to break his back. This all took place inside the body. His face worked spasmodically, one eye closed and unclosed in a hideous parody of a wink, his fingers paddled feebly on the tabletop and he fell to the floor.

"My dear!" he gasped.

She looked at him expressionlessly.

"Help me," he whispered, "eh?" His fingers fluttered. "Over there," he said eagerly, "medicines. Make me well, hey? Good and fast. I'll give you half."

"All," she said.

"Yes, yes, all," he said breathlessly, "all—explain all— fascinating hobby—spend most of my time in this room—

get the medicine—"

"First show me," she said, "how to turn it off."

"Off?" he said. He watched her, bright-eyed.

"First," she said patiently, "I will turn it all off. And then I will cure you."

"No," he said, "no, no! Never!" She knelt down beside him.

"Come," she said softly, "do you think I want to destroy it? I am as fascinated by it as you are. I only want to make sure you can't do anything to me, that's all. You must explain it all first until I am master of it, too, and then we will turn it on."

"No, no," he repeated suspiciously.

"You must," she said, "or you'll die. What do you think I plan to do? I have to cure you, because otherwise how can I learn to work all this? But I must be safe, too. Show me how to turn it off."

He pointed, doubtfully.

"Is that it?" she said.

"Yes," he said, "but—"

"Is that it?"

"Yes, but—no—wait!" for Alyx sprang to her feet and fetched from his stool the pillow on which he had been sitting, the purpose of which he did not at first seem to comprehend, but then his eyes went wide with horror, for she had got the pillow in order to smother him, and that is just what she did.

When she got to her feet, her legs were trembling. Stumbling and pressing both hands together as if in prayer to subdue their shaking, she look the cube that held her husband's picture and carefully—oh, how carefully!—turned the lever to the right. Then she began to sob. It was not the weeping of grief, but a kind of reaction and triumph, all mixed; in the middle of that eerie room she stood, and threw her head back and yelled. The light burned steadily on. In the shadows she found the fat man's master switch, and leaning against the wall, put one finger—only one—on it and caught her breath. Would the world end? She did not know. After a few minutes' search she found a candle and flint hidden away in a cupboard and with this she made herself a light; then, with eyes closed, with a long shudder, she leaned—no, sagged—against the switch, and stood for a long moment, expecting and believing nothing.

But the world did not end. From outside came the wind and the sound of the sea-wash (though louder now, as if some indistinct and not quite audible humming had just ended) and inside fantastic shadows leapt about the candle—the lights had gone out. Alyx began to laugh, catching her breath. She set the candle down and searched until she found a length of metal tubing that stood against the wall, and then she went from machine to machine, smashing, prying, tearing, toppling tables and breaking controls. Then she took the candle in her unsteady hand and stood over the body of the fat man, a phantasmagoric lump on the floor, badly lit at last. Her shadow loomed on the wall. She leaned over him and studied his face, that face that had made out of agony and death the most appalling trivialities. She thought:

Make the world? You hadn't the imagination. You didn't even make these machines; that shiny finish is for customers, not craftsmen, and controls that work by little pictures are for children. You are a child yourself, a child and a horror, and I would ten times rather be subject to your machinery than master of it. Aloud she said:

"Never confuse the weapon and the arm," and taking the candle, she went away and left him in the dark.

She got home at dawn and, as her man lay asleep in bed, it seemed to her that he was made out of the light of the dawn that streamed through his fingers and his hair, irradiating him with gold. She kissed him and he opened his eyes.

"You've come home," he said.

"So I have." said she. "I fought all night," she added, "with the Old Man of the Mountain," for you must know that this demon is a legend in Ourdh; he is the god of this world who dwells in a cave containing the whole world in little, and from his cave he rules the fates of men.

"Who won?" said her husband, laughing, for in the sunrise when everything is suffused with light it is difficult to see the seriousness of injuries.

"I did!" said she. "The man is dead." She smiled, splitting open the wound on her check, which began to bleed afresh. "He died," she said, "for two reasons only: because he was a fool. And because we are not."

And all the birds in the courtyard broke out shouting at once.

1969

EACH PASSING YEAR or parallel Hugo and Nebula awards seems to add something to science fiction's history. In 1969 one novel won undisputed possession in both competitions.[2]

This was *The Left Hand of Darkness*, by Ursula K. Le Guin. The book had been published as an Ace Science Fiction Special, as had Alexei Panshin's Nebula-winning *Rite of Passage* the year before.

The Ace Specials were a unique case of science fiction publishing. Donald Wollheim had edited Ace Books' science fiction line from the founding of the company in the early 1950s. A decade later a popular science fiction fan, Terry Carr, had left his California home and moved to New York to seek his fortune in the world of literature. Carr had had some success as a writer, producing a small stream of skillfully crafted friction; he had also established a record as an amateur editor and publisher.

As Ace expanded its program, Wollheim hired Carr as an assistant. Soon Carr was selecting manuscripts on his own and eventually gained the freedom to start a series of books with a distinctive graphic design and special series designation. They were hugely successful from a critical point of view. Although the rates Carr paid were only slightly higher than those Ace offered for its general run of books, the Science Fiction Specials were selected, edited, and published with such care that they rapidly developed a prestigious

---

[2] *Dune*, by Frank Herbert, the very first Nebula-winning novel, had also won the Hugo for 1965, its year of publication. However, it was tied for the latter award with . . . *And Call Me Conrad*, by Roger Zelazny.

reputation.

Among them were noteworthy books by Bob Shaw, James Blish and Norman L. Knight, Roger Zelazny, James H. Schmitz, R.A. Lafferty, John Brunner, Joanna Russ, Wilson Tucker, Ron Goulart, Gertrude Friedberg, D.G. Compton, and Michael Moorcock.

As the new decade of the 1970s progressed, however, Ace Books was sold, then sold again. Under the new administrations, the editors changed. First Carr left, to return to the West Coast and divide his time between writing and independent editing; in the past decade he has risen in stature as an editor and is today regarded as the most prolific and capable of science fiction anthologists. After Carr had left, Don Wollheim also resigned to create his own firm, DAW Books, where he has continued the highly successful work he did earlier at Ace.

As for Ace Books, following a series of revolving-door managements and editorships, the company finally regained its stability as a division of Grossett & Dunlap. It remains a major publisher of science fiction, but the Special series, despite a couple of halfhearted attempts to revive it, has become part of history, along with Larry Shaw's earlier Lancer Science Fiction Library, Lloyd Arthur Eshbach's Golden Science Fiction Library and other noble experiments of the past.

To return to 1969 . . . Le Guin's *Left Hand of Darkness* was the novel which established her as a major author and launched her climb to nationwide acclaim. But there were several other notable science fiction novels published in 1969, including Norman Spinrad's *Bug Jack Barron* and Kurt Vonnegut's *Slaughterhouse-Five.* Spinrad's novel gained attention when its serialization in *New Worlds* caused that magazine's censorship and suppression. *Bug Jack Barron* is a first class book in its own right, but being banned in Britain surely did as much for it in 1969 as being banned in Boston had done for many a popular novel in earlier days.

As for *Slaughterhouse-Five,* I suspect that it would have had a very strong chance to win at least one award away from *The Left Hand of Darkness* had it come from one of the recognized publishers within the science fiction field, or had it been packaged and labeled as science fiction by its publisher, Delacorte. There has been much debate over the years as to whether or not Vonnegut is a science fiction writer. Of course he wisely declines the label, and his publishers similarly omit it in their packaging, thus reaching a far larger and more lucrative audience than any specialized genre can afford.

But for heaven's sake . . . Vonnegut's early stories appeared in *Galaxy* and *F&SF,* he attended the Milford Conference and he even wrote (sparingly) for science fiction fanzines. Aside from all such matters, the internal evidence of his works marks them clearly as science fiction. *Slaughterhouse-Five,* the book in hand, dealt with time travel, space travel, alien creatures and alien planets. What more is needed?

But *Slaughterhouse-Five* was published by Delacorte, not Ace or Ballantine or Doubleday; and by 1969 Vonnegut had learned to stay away from fanzines and from Milford, Pennsylvania. And if he was going to turn his back on the science fiction community, by gum, the science fiction community would return the favor.

So there!

In the shorter lengths there was a return to confusion over categories as the fans dropped the novelette category from the Hugos. Thus, there were two short-fiction Hugos given and three short-fiction Nebulas. The Hugo winner for novella was Fritz Leiber's "Ship of Shadows." The Nebula went to Harlan Ellison for "A Boy and His Dog." Samuel R. Delany's "Time Considered as a Helix of Semi-Precious Stones" received the Nebula for best novelette—and the Hugo for best short story!

And Robert Silverberg received the Nebula for best short story for "Passengers," a relentlessly grim *Orbit* story.

There was controversy over the eligibility of Delany's winning story. As had been the case with Moorcock's "Behold the Man" two years earlier, "Time Considered" had ap-

peared first in *New Worlds,* in 1968. It was reprinted in
Wollheim and Carr's *Best* for 1969, and it was on the basis
of this appearance that the story was nominated for and won
both Hugo and Nebula.

Both Moorcock's and Delany's stories had competed suc-
cessfully on the basis of their *first American publication.* But
the awards—both series—were intended to recognize outstanding new works, not reprints. Again there was grumbling, but again no official action was taken. No disgruntled,
unsuccessful nominee lodged a formal protest with SFWA,
much less went to court to sue—although the latter possibility opens astonishing vistas for possible mischief.

And once presented and allowed to stand, the awards
made their way into the record books and will, presumably,
remain there forever.

Not that there were no worthy alternatives. The year 1969
saw the publication of plenty of memorable stories: Silverberg's "To Jorslem" in *Galaxy,* Spinrad's apocalyptic "The
Big Flash" in *Orbit,* Le Guin's "Nine Lives" in *Playboy* and
her "Winter's King" in *Orbit,* "The Last Flight of Dr. Ain"
by James Tiptree, Jr., in *Galaxy,* "Not Long Before the End"
by Larry Niven in *F&SF* and Ellison's "Shattered Like a
Glass Goblin" (one of the few strongly anti-psychedelic stories to appear in science fiction) in *Orbit.* It seems to me
ironic that Robert Silverberg's "Sundance" not only failed to
win either the Hugo or Nebula but also was not even nominated for either award. It is one of the author's own favorite
stories, one of his most moving and one of his most accomplished in terms of technique. It has also shown more staying
power than "Passengers." At last count, "Passengers" had
been reprinted five times while "Sundance" had been reprinted eleven. (The present appearance of "Sundance"
makes twelve.)

But here Silverberg was in the awkward position of competing against himself. It might have been an interesting state
of affairs, had the fans retained the novelette category for
"Time Considered" in 1969, if "Sundance" had won the
Hugo for short story while "Passengers" won the Nebula, or

vice versa. But that, alas, is idle speculation.

I suppose that "Passengers" had the greater initial success because it makes a single point, makes it with overwhelming and unbearable impact, and then is over. "Sundance," by contrast, does so very much, and does it in such varied and subtle ways, that the latter story takes closer concentration, and even so takes more time to slide down into the reader's subconscious, where it then works on the emotions.

It's a difficult story. You have to read it slowly and carefully. You may even have to read it several times. But do it, please. It is one of the all-time outstanding examples of what can be done within the compressed boundaries of the short story.

Sundance

ROBERT SILVERBERG

TODAY you LIQUIDATED about 50,000 Eaters in Sector A, and now you are spending an uneasy night. You and Herndon flew east at dawn, with the green-gold sunrise at your backs, and sprayed the neural pellets over a thousand hectares along the Forked River. You flew on into the prairie beyond the river, where the Eaters have already been wiped out, and had lunch sprawled on the thick, soft carpet of grass where the first settlement is expected to rise. Herndon picked some juiceflowers, and you enjoyed half an hour of mild hallucinations. Then, as you headed toward the copter to begin an afternoon of further pellet spraying, he said suddenly, "Tom, how would you feel about this if it turned out that the Eaters weren't just animal pests? That they were *people,* say, with a language and rites and a history and all?"

You thought of how it had been for your own people.

"They aren't," you said.

"Suppose they were. Suppose the Eaters—"

"They aren't. Drop it."

Herndon has this streak of cruelty in him that leads him to ask such questions. He goes for the vulnerabilities; it amuses him. All night now his casual remark has echoed in your mind. Suppose the Eaters . . . suppose the Eaters . . . suppose . . . suppose . . .

You sleep for a while, and dream, and in your dreams you swim through rivers of blood.

Foolishness. A feverish fantasy. You know how important it is to exterminate the Eaters fast, before the settlers get here. They're just animals, and not even harmless animals at that; ecology-wreckers is what they are, devourers of oxygen-liberating plants, and they have to go. A few have been saved for zoological study. The rest must be destroyed. Ritual extirpation of undesirable beings, the old, old story. But let's not complicate our job with moral qualms, you tell yourself. Let's not dream of rivers of blood.

The Eaters don't even *have* blood, none that could flow in rivers, anyway. What they have is, well, a kind of lymph that permeates every tissue and transmits nourishment along the interfaces. Waste products go out the same way, osmotically. In terms of process, it's structurally analogous to your own kind of circulatory system, except there's no network of blood vessels hooked to a master pump. The life-stuff just oozes through their bodies as though they were amoebas or sponges or some other low-phylum form. Yet they're definitely high-phylum in nervous system, digestive setup, limb-and-organ template, etc. Odd, you think. The thing about aliens is that they're alien, you tell yourself, not for the first time.

The beauty of their biology for you and your companions is that it lets you exterminate them so neatly.

You fly over the grazing grounds and drop the neural pellets. The Eaters find and ingest them. Within an hour the poison has reached all sectors of the body. Life ceases; a rapid breakdown of cellular matter follows, the Eater literally falling apart molecule by molecule the instant that nutrition is cut off; the lymphlike stuff works like acid; a universal lysis occurs; flesh and even the bones, which are cartilaginous, dissolve. In two hours, a puddle on the ground. In four, nothing at all left. Considering how many millions of Eaters you've scheduled for extermination here, it's sweet of the bodies to be self-disposing. Otherwise what a charnel house this world would become!

Suppose the Eaters . . .

Damn Herndon. You almost feel like getting a memory-editing in the morning. Scrape his stupid speculations out of your head. If you dared. If you dared.

In the morning he does not dare. Memory-editing frightens

him; he will try to shake free of his new-found guilt without it. The Eaters, he explains to himself, are mindless herbivores, the unfortunate victims of human expansionism, but not really deserving of passionate defense. Their extermination is not tragic; it's just too bad. If Earthmen are to have this world, the Eaters must relinquish it. There's a difference, he tells himself, between the elimination of the Plains Indians from the American prairie in the nineteenth century and the destruction of the bison on that same prairie. One feels a little wistful about the slaughter of the thundering herds; one regrets the butchering of millions of the noble brown woolly beasts, yes. But one feels outrage, not mere wistful regret, at what was done to the Sioux. There's a difference. Reserve your passions for the proper cause.

He walks from his bubble at the edge of the camp toward the center of things. The flagstone path is moist and glistening. The morning fog has not yet lifted, and every tree is bowed, the long, notched leaves heavy with droplets of water. He pauses, crouching, to observe a spider-analog spinning its asymmetrical web. As he watches, a small amphibian, delicately shaded turquoise, glides as inconspicuously as possible over the mossy ground. Not inconspicuously enough; he gently lifts the little creature and puts it on the back of his hand. The gills flutter in anguish, and the amphibian's sides quiver. Slowly, cunningly, its color changes until it matches the coppery tone of the hand. The camouflage is excellent. He lowers his hand and the amphibian scurries into a puddle. He walks on.

He is forty years old, shorter than most of the other members of the expedition, with wide shoulders, a heavy chest, dark glossy hair, a blunt, spreading nose. He is a biologist. This is his third career, for he has failed as an anthropologist and as a developer of real estate. His name is Tom Two Ribbons. He has been married twice but has no children. His great-grandfather died of alcoholism; his grandfather was addicted to hallucinogens; his father had compulsively visited cheap memory-editing parlors. Tom Two Ribbons is conscious that he is failing a family tradition, but he has not yet found his own mode of self-destruction.

In the main building he discovers Herndon, Julia, Ellen, Schwartz, Chang, Michaelson, and Nichols. They are eating breakfast; the others are already at work. Ellen rises and comes to him and kisses him. Her short soft yellow hair tickles his cheeks. "I love you," she whispers. She has spent the night in Michaelson's bubble. "I love you," he tells her, and draws a quick vertical line of affection between her small pale breasts. He winks at Michaelson, who nods, touches the top of two fingers to his lips, and blows them a kiss. We are all good friends here, Tom Two Ribbons thinks.

"Who drops pellets today?" he asks.

"Mike and Chang," says Julia. "Sector C."

Schwartz says, "Eleven more days and we ought to have the whole peninsula clear. Then we can move inland."

"If our pellet supply holds up," Chang points out.

Herndon says, "Did you sleep well, Tom?"

"No," says Tom. He sits down and taps out his breakfast requisition, in the west, the fog is beginning to burn off the mountains. Something throbs in the back of his neck. He has been on this world nine weeks now, and in that time it has undergone its only change of season, shading from dry-weather to foggy. The mists will remain for many months. Before the plains parch again, the Eaters will be gone and the settlers will begin to arrive. His food slides down the chute and he seizes it. Ellen sits beside him. She is a little more than half his age: this is her first voyage: she is their keeper of records, but she is also skilled at editing.

"You look troubled," Ellen tells him. "Can I help you?"

"No. Thank you."

"I hate it when you get gloomy."

"It's a racial trait," says Tom Two Ribbons.

"I doubt that very much."

"The truth is that maybe my personality reconstruct is wearing thin. The trauma level was so close to the surface. I'm just a walking veneer, you know."

Ellen laughs prettily. She wears only a sprayon half-wrap. Her skin looks damp; she and Michaelson have had a swim at dawn. Tom Two Ribbons is thinking of asking her to marry him, when this job is over. He has not been married since the collapse of the real estate business. The therapist suggested divorce as part of the reconstruct. He sometimes wonders where Terry has gone and whom she lives with now. Ellen says, "You seem pretty stable to me, Tom."

"Thank you," he says. She is young. She docs not know.

"If it's just a passing gloom I can edit it out in one quick snip."

"Thank you," he says. "No."

"I forgot. You don't like editing."

"My father—"

"Yes?"

"In fifty years he pared himself down to a thread," Tom Two Ribbons says. "He had his ancestors edited away, his whole heritage, his religion, his wife, his sons, finally his name. Then he sat and smiled all day. Thank you, no editing."

"Where are you working today?" Ellen asks.

"In the compound, running tests."

"Want company? I'm off all morning."

"Thank you, no," he says, too quickly. She looks hurt. He tries to remedy his unintended cruelty by touching her arm lightly and saying, "Maybe this afternoon, all right? I need to commune a while. Yes?"

"Yes," she says, and smiles, and shapes a kiss with her lips.

After breakfast he goes to the compound. It covers a thousand hectares east of the base; they have bordered it with neural-field projectors at intervals of eighty meters, and this is a sufficient fence to keep the captive population of two hundred Eaters from straying. When all the others have been exterminated, this study group will remain. At the southwest corner of the compound stands a lab bubble from which the experiments are run: metabolic, psychological, physiological, ecological. A stream crosses the compound diagonally. There is a low ridge of grassy hills at its eastern edge. Five distinct copses of tightly clustered knife-blade trees are separated by patches of dense savanna. Sheltered beneath the grass are the oxygen-plants, almost completely hidden except for the photosynthetic spikes that jut to heights of three or four meters at regular intervals, and for the lemon-colored respiratory bodies, chest high, that make the grassland sweet and dizzying with exhaled gases. Through the fields move the Eaters in a straggling herd, nibbling delicately at the respiratory bodies.

Tom Two Ribbons spies the herd beside the stream and goes toward it. He stumbles over an oxygen-plant hidden in the grass but deftly recovers his balance and, seizing the puckered orifice of the respiratory body, inhales deeply. His despair lifts. He approaches the Eaters. They are spherical, bulky, slow-moving creatures, covered by masses of coarse orange fur. Saucerlike eyes protrude above narrow rubbery lips. Their legs are thin and scaly, like a chicken's, and their arms are short and held close to their bodies. They regard him with bland lack of curiosity. "Good morning, brothers!" is the way he greets them this time, and he wonders why.

I noticed something strange today. Perhaps I simply sniffed too much oxygen in the fields; maybe I was succumbing to a suggestion Hernden planted; or possibly it's the family masochism cropping out. But while I was observing the Eaters in the compound, it seemed to me, for the first time, that they were behaving intelligently, that they were functioning in a ritualized way.

I followed them around for three hours. During that time they uncovered half a dozen outcroppings of oxygen-plants. In each case they went through a stylized pattern of action before starting to munch. They:

Formed a straggly circle around the plants.

Looked toward the sun.

Looked toward their neighbors on left and right around the circle.

Made fuzzy neighing sounds *only* after having done the foregoing.

Looked toward the sun again.

Moved in and ate.

If this wasn't a prayer of thanksgiving, a saying of grace, then what was it? And if they're advanced enough spiritually to say grace, are we not therefore committing genocide here? Do chimpanzees say grace? Christ, we wouldn't even wipe out chimps the way we're cleaning out the Eaters! Of course, chimps don't interfere with human crops, and some kind of coexistence would be possible, whereas Eaters and human agriculturalists simply can't function on the same planet. Nevertheless, there's a moral issue here. The liquidation effort is predicated on the assumption that the intelligence level of the Eaters is about on a par with that of oysters, or, at best, sheep. Our consciences stay clear because our poison is quick and painless and because the Eaters thoughtfully dissolve upon dying, sparing us the mess of incinerating millions of corpses. But if they pray—

I won't say anything to the others just yet. I want more evidence, hard, objective. Films, tapes, record cubes. Then we'll see. What if I can show that we're exterminating intelligent beings? My family knows a little about genocide, after all, having been on the receiving end just a few centuries back. I doubt that I could halt what's going on here. But at the very least I could withdraw from the operation. Head back to Earth and stir up public outcries.

I hope I'm imagining this.

I'm not imagining a thing. They gather in circles; they look to the sun; they neigh and pray. They're only balls of jelly on chicken-legs, but they give thanks for their food. Those big round eyes now seem to stare accusingly at me. Our tame herd here knows what's going on: that we have descended from the stars to eradicate their kind, and that they alone will be spared. They have no way of fighting back or even of communicating their displeasure, but they *know*. And hate us. Jesus, we have killed two million of them since we got here, and in a metaphorical sense I'm stained with blood, and what will I do, what can I do?

I must move very carefully, or I'll end up drugged and edited.

I can let myself seem like a crank, a quack, an agitator. I can't stand up and *denounce!* I have to find allies. Herndon, first. He surely is onto the truth; he's the one who nudged *me* to it, that day we dropped pellets. And I thought he was merely being vicious in his usual way!

I'll talk to him tonight.

He says, "I've been thinking about that suggestion you made. About the Eaters. Perhaps we haven't made sufficiently close psychological studies. I mean, if they really *are* intelligent—"

Herndon blinks. He is a tall man with glossy dark hair, a heavy beard, sharp cheekbones. "Who says they are, Tom?"

"You did. On the far side of the Forked River, you said—"

"It was just a speculative hypothesis. To make conversation."

"No, I think it was more than that. You really believed it."

Herndon looks troubled. "Tom, I don't know what you're trying to start, but don't start it. If I for a moment believed we were killing intelligent creatures, I'd run for an editor so fast I'd start an implosion wave."

"Why did you ask me that thing, then?" Tom Two Ribbons says.

"Idle chatter."

"Amusing yourself by kindling guilts in somebody else? You're a bastard, Herndon. I mean it."

"Well, look, Tom, if I had any idea that you'd get so worked up about a hypothetical suggestion—" Herndon shakes his head. "The Eaters aren't intelligent beings. Obviously. Otherwise we wouldn't be under orders to liquidate them."

"Obviously," says Tom Two Ribbons.

Ellen said, "No, I don't know what Tom's up to. But I'm pretty sure he needs a rest. It's only a year and a half since his personality reconstruct, and he had a pretty bad breakdown back then."

Michaelson consulted a chart. "He's refused three times in

a row to make his pellet-dropping run. Claiming he can't take time away from his research. Hell, we can fill in for him, but it's the idea that he's ducking chores that bothers me."

"What kind of research is he doing?" Nichols wanted to know.

"Not biological," said Julia. "He's with the Eaters in the compound all the time, but I don't see him making any tests on them. He just watches them."

"And talks to them," Chang observed.

"And talks, yes," Julia said.

"About what?" Nichols asked,

"Who knows?"

Everyone looked at Ellen. "You're closest to him," Michaelson said. "Can't you bring him out of it?"

"I've got to know what he's in, first," Ellen said. "He isn't saying a thing."

You know that you must be very careful, for they outnumber you, and their concern for your mental welfare can be deadly. Already they realize you are disturbed, and Ellen has begun to probe for the source of the disturbance. Last night you lay in her arms and she questioned you, obliquely, skillfully, and you knew what she is trying to find out. When the moons appeared she suggested that you and she stroll in the compound, among the sleeping Eaters. You declined, but she sees that you have become involved with the creatures.

You have done probing of your own—subtly, you hope. And you are aware that you can do nothing to save the Eaters. An irrevocable commitment has been made. It is 1876 all over again: these are the bison, these are the Sioux, and they must be destroyed, for the railroad is on its way. If you speak out here, your friends will calm you and pacify you and edit you, for they do not see what you see. If you return to Earth to agitate, you will be mocked and recommended for another reconstruct. You can do nothing. You can do nothing.

You cannot save, but perhaps you can record.

Go out into the prairie. Live with the Eaters; make your-self their friend; learn their ways. Set it down, a full account of their culture, so that at least that much will not be lost. You know the techniques of field anthropology. As was done for your people in the old days, do now for the Eaters.

He finds Michaelson. "Can you spare me for a few weeks?" he asks.

"Spare you, Tom? What do you mean?"

"I've got some field studies to do. I'd like to leave the base and work with Eaters in the wild."

"What's wrong with the ones in the compound?"

"It's the last chance with wild ones, Mike. I've got to go."

"Alone, or with Ellen?"

"Alone."

Michaelson nods slowly. "All right, Tom. Whatever you want. Go. I won't hold you here."

I dance in the prairie under the green-gold sun. About me the Eaters gather. I am stripped; sweat makes my skin glisten; my heart pounds. I talk to them with my feet, and they un-derstand.

They understand.

They have a language of soft sounds. They have a god. They know love and awe and rapture. They have rites. They have names. They have a history. Of all this I am convinced.

I dance on thick grass.

How can I reach them? With my feet, with my hands, with my grunts, with my sweat. They gather by the hundreds, by the thousands, and I dance. I must not stop. They cluster about me and make their sounds. I am a conduit for strange forces. My great-grandfather should see me now! Sitting on his porch in Wyoming, the firewater in his hand, his brain rotting—see me now, old one! See the dance of Tom Two Ribbons! I talk to these strange ones with my feet under a sun that is the wrong color. I dance. I dance.

"Listen to me," I say. "I am your friend, I alone, the only

one you can trust. Trust me, talk to me, teach me. Let me preserve your ways, for soon the destruction will come."

I dance, and the sun climbs, and the Eaters murmur.

There is the chief. I dance toward him, back, toward, I bow, I point to the sun. I imagine the being that lives in that ball of flame, I imitate the sounds of these people, I kneel, I rise, I dance. Tom Two Ribbons dances for you.

I summon skills my ancestors forgot. I feel the power flowing in me. As they danced in the days of the bison, I dance now, beyond the Forked River.

I dance, and now the Eaters dance too. Slowly, uncertainly, they move toward me, they shift their weight, lift leg and leg, sway about. "Yes, like that!" I cry. "Dance!"

We dance together as the sun reaches noon height.

Now their eyes are no longer accusing. I see warmth and kinship. I am their brother, their red-skinned tribesman, he who dances with them. No longer do they seem clumsy to me. I here is a strange ponderous grace in their movements. They dance. They dance. They caper about me. Closer, closer, closer!

We move in holy frenzy.

They sing, now, a blurred hymn of joy. They throw forth their arms, unclench their little claws. In unison they shift weight, left foot forward, right, left, right. Dance, brothers, dance, dance, dance! They press against me. Their flesh quivers; their smell is a sweet one. They gently thrust me across the field, to a part of the meadow where the grass is deep and untrampled. Still dancing, we seek for the oxygen-plants, and find clumps of them beneath the grass, and they make their prayer and seize them with their awkward arms, separating the respiratory bodies from the photosynthetic spikes. The plants, in anguish, release floods of oxygen. My mind reels. I laugh and sing. The Eaters are nibbling the lemon-colored perforated globes, nibbling the stalks as well. They thrust their plants at me. It is a religious ceremony, I see. Take from us, eat with us, join with us, this is the body, this is the blood, take, eat, join. I bend forward and put a lemon-colored globe to my lips. I do not bite; I nibble, as they do, my teeth slicing away the skin of the globe. Juice spurts into my mouth while oxygen drenches my nostrils. The Eaters sing hosannas. I should be in full paint for this, paint of my forefathers, feathers too, meeting their religion in the regalia of what should have been mine. Take, eat, join. The juice of the oxygen-plant flows in my veins. I embrace my brothers. I sing, and as my voice leaves my lips it becomes an arch that glistens like new steel, and I pitch my song lower, and the arch turns to tarnished silver. The Eaters crowd close. The scent of their bodies is fiery red to me. Their soft cries are puffs of steam. The sun is very warm; its rays are tiny jagged pings of puckered sound, close to the top of my range of hearing, plink! plink! plink! The thick grass hums to me, deep and rich, and the wind hurls points of flame, along the prairie. I devour another oxygen-plant, and then a third. My brothers laugh and shout. They tell me of their gods, the god of warmth, the god of food, the god of pleasure, the god of death, the god of holiness, the god of wrongness, and the others. They recite for me the names of their kings, and I hear their voices as splashes of green mold on the clean sheet of the sky. They instruct me in their holy rites. I must remember this, I tell myself, for when it is gone it will never come again. I continue to dance. They continue to dance. The color of the hills becomes rough and coarse, like abrasive gas. Take, eat, join. Dance. They are so gentle!

I hear the drone of the copter, suddenly.

It hovers far overhead. I am unable to see who flies in it. "No!" I scream. "Not here! Not these people! Listen to me! This is Tom Two Ribbons! Can't you hear mc? I'm doing a field study here! You have no right—!"

My voice makes spirals of blue moss edged with red sparks. They drift upward and are scattered by the breeze.

I yell, I shout, I bellow. I dance and shake my fists. From the wings of the copter the jointed arms of the pellet-distributors unfold. The gleaming spigots extend and whirl. The neural pellets rain down into the meadow, each tracing a blazing track that lingers in the sky. The sound of the copter becomes a furry carpet stretching to the horizon, and my shrill voice is lost in it.

The Eaters drift away from me, seeking the pellets, scratching at the roots of the grass to find them. Still dancing, I leap into their midst, striking the pellets from their hands, hurling them into the stream, crushing them to powder. The Eaters growl black needles at me. They turn away and search for more pellets. The copter turns and flies off, leaving a trail of dense oily sound. My brothers are gobbling the pellets eagerly.

There is no way to prevent it.

Joy consumes them and they topple and lie still. Occasionally a limb twitches; then even this stops. They begin to dissolve. Thousands of them melt on the prairie, sinking into shapelessness, losing their spherical forms, flattening, ebbing into the ground. The bonds of the molecules will no longer hold. It is the twilight of protoplasm. They perish. They vanish. For hours I walk the prairie. Now I inhale oxygen; now I eat a lemon-colored globe. Sunset begins with the ringing of leaden chimes. Black clouds make brazen trumpet calls in the east and the deepening wind is a swirl of coaly bristles. Silence comes. Night falls. I dance. I am alone.

The copter comes again, and they find you, and you do not resist as they gather you in. You are beyond bitterness. Quietly you explain what you have done and what you have learned, and why it is wrong to exterminate these people. You describe the plant you have eaten and the way it affects your senses, and as you talk of the blessed synesthesia, the texture of the wind and the sound of the clouds and the timbre of the sunlight, they nod and smile and tell you not to worry, that everything will be all right soon, and they touch something cold to your forearm, so cold that it is a whir and a buzz and the deintoxicant sinks into your vein and soon the ecstasy drains away. leaving only the exhaustion and the grief.

He says, "We never learn a thing, do we? We export all our horrors to the stars. Wipe out the Armenians, wipe out the Jews, wipe out the Tasmanians, wipe out the Indians, wipe out everyone who's in the way, and then come out here and do the same damned murderous thing. You weren't with me out there. You didn't dance with them. You didn't see what a rich, complex culture the Eaters have. Let me tell you about their tribal structure. It's dense: seven levels of matrimonial relationships, to begin with, and an exogamy factor that requires—"

Softly Ellen says, "Tom, darling, nobody's going to harm the Eaters."

"And the religion," he goes on. "Nine gods, each one an aspect of *the* god. Holiness and wrongness both worshiped. They have hymns, prayers, a theology. And we, the emissaries of the god of wrongness—"

"We're not exterminating them," Michaelson says. "Won't you understand that, Tom? This is all a fantasy of yours. You've been under the influence of drugs, but now we're cleaning you out. You'll be clean in a little while. You'll have perspective again."

"A fantasy?" he says bitterly. "A drug dream? I stood out in the prairie and saw you drop pellets. And I watched them die and melt away. I didn't dream that."

"How can we convince you?" Chang asks earnestly. "What will make you believe? Shall we fly over the Eater country with you and show you how many millions there are?"

"But how many millions have been destroyed?" he demands.

They insist that he is wrong, Ellen tells him again that no one has ever desired to harm the Eaters. "This is a scientific expedition, Tom. We're here to *study* them. It's a violation of all we stand for to injure intelligent lifeforms."

"You admit that they're intelligent?"

"Of course. That's never been in doubt."

"Then why drop the pellets?" he asks. "Why slaughter them?"

"None of that has happened, Tom," Ellen says. She takes his hand between her cool palms. "Believe us. Believe us."

He says bitterly, "If you want me to believe you, why

don't you do the job properly? Get out the editing machine and go to work on me. You can't simply *talk* me into rejecting the evidence of my own eyes."

"You were under drugs all the time," Michaelson says.

"I've never taken drugs! Except for what I ate in the meadow, when I danced—and that came after I had watched the massacre going on for weeks and weeks. Are you saying that it's a retroactive delusion?"

"No, Tom," Schwartz says. "You've had this delusion all along. It's part of your therapy, your reconstruct. You came here programmed with it."

"Impossible," he says,

Ellen kisses his fevered forehead. "It was done to reconcile you to mankind, you see. You had this terrible resentment of the displacement of your people in the nineteenth century. You were unable to forgive the industrial society for scattering the Sioux, and you were terribly full of hate. Your therapist thought that if you could be made to participate in an imaginary modern extermination, if you could come to see it as a necessary operation, you'd be purged of your resentment and able to take your place in society as—"

He thrusts her away. "Don't talk idiocy. If you knew the first thing about reconstruct therapy, you'd realize that no reputable therapist could be so shallow, There are no one-to-one correlations in reconstructs. No, don't touch me. Keep away. Keep away."

He will not let them persuade him that this is merely a drug-born dream. It is no fantasy, he tells himself, and it is no therapy. He rises. He goes out. They do not follow him. He takes a copter and seeks his brothers.

Again I dance. The sun is much hotter today. The Eaters are more numerous. Today I wear paint, today I wear feathers. My body shines with my sweat. They dance with me, and they have a frenzy in them that I have never seen before. We pound the trampled meadow with our feet. We clutch for the sun with our hands. We sing, we shout, we cry. We will dance until we fall.

This is no fantasy, These people are real, and they are in-telligent, and they are doomed. This I know.

We dance. Despite the doom, we dance.

My great-grandfather comes and dances with us. He too is real. His nose is like a hawk's, not blunt like mine, and he wears the big headdress, and his muscles are like cords under his brown skin. He sings, he shouts, he cries.

Others of my family join us.

We eat the oxygen-plants together. We embrace the Eat-ers. We know, all of us, what it is to be hunted.

The clouds make music and the wind takes on texture and the sun's warmth has color.

We dance. We dance. Our limbs know no weariness.

The sun grows and fills the whole sky, and I see no Eaters now, only my own people, my father's fathers across the centuries, thousands of gleaming skins, thousands of hawk's noses, and we eat the plants, and we find sharp sticks and thrust them into our flesh, and the sweet blood flows and dries in the blaze of the sun, and we dance, and we dance, and some of us fall from weariness, and we dance, and the prairie is a sea of bobbing headdresses, an ocean of feathers, and we dance, and my heart makes thunder, and my knees become water, and the sun's fire engulfs me, and I dance, and I fall, and I dance, and I fall, and I fall, and I fall.

Again they find you and bring you back. They give you the cool snout on your arm to take the oxygen-plant drug from your veins, and then they give you something else so you will rest. You rest and you are very calm. Ellen kisses you and you stroke her soft skin, and then the others come in and they talk to you. saying soothing things, but you do not lis-ten, for you are searching for realities. It is not an easy search. It is like falling through many trapdoors, looking for the one room whose floor is not hinged. Everything that has happened on this planet is your therapy, you tell yourself, designed to reconcile an embittered aborigine to the white man's conquest; nothing is really being exterminated here. You reject that and fall through and realize that this must be the therapy of your friends; they carry the weight of accumulated centuries of guilts and have come here to shed that load, and you are here to ease them of their burden, to draw their sins into yourself and give them forgiveness. Again you fall through, and see that the Eaters are mere animals who threaten the ecology and must be removed; the culture you imagined for them is your hallucination, kindled out of old churnings. You try to withdraw your objections to this necessary extermination, but you fall through again and discover that there is no extermination except in your mind, which is troubled and disordered by your obsession with the crime against your ancestors, and you sit up, for you wish to apologize to these friends of yours, these innocent scientists whom you have called murderers. And you fall through.

1970

IN 1968 THE Hugo and Nebula voters selected completely differing slates of winners. Within two years they performed a complete turnabout and for the first time in history (and the only time, to date) selected identical lists of stories. Strangely, while the same number of Hugos and Nebulas were awarded, and to the very same stories, this was done under slightly different category designations. Whereby hangs another tale.

But first, let's examine the winning—and losing—novels of 1970.

Certainly the outstanding publisher of the year was Ace, and the outstanding editor was Terry Carr, for it was his Special series that dominated the Nebula ballot. Four of the six nominees were Ace Science Fiction Specials; *And Chaos Died,* by Joanna Russ; *The Year of the Quiet Sun,* by Wilson Tucker; *Fourth Mansions,* by R.A. Lafferty; and *The Steel Crocodile,* by D.G. Compton. The fifth nominee was *The Tower of Glass,* by Robert Silverberg, published by Scribner's.

All of these five books were serious novels, intellectually, emotionally or morally challenging to the reader. The nation was passing through a dark time, the Nixon administration was at the peak of its power and prestige and science fiction writers, as they have long done, were sublimating and transferring the agony of our society's conscience into stories set in other times and other places.

By contrast with these serious works, *Ringworld* alone offered its readers a pleasant escape from reality, a few hours of unchallenging relaxation. It was a "travelogue" novel, a forerunner of Arthur C. Clarke's *Rendezvous with Rama* and John Varley's *Titan,* both to come later in the decade. The reader could disconnect his aching conscience, turn off his straining intellect and simply go along with the author for "a good read."

If I seem to be condemning the book, the author or the readers of *Ringworld,* let me say now that this is not my intention. There is a place in our artistic diet for aesthetic protein and there is a place for aesthetic bubble gum, and the voters said clearly that 1970 was the year for aesthetic bubble gum.

When it came time for the Hugo voters to name *their* favorite novels, they further underlined the Nebula voters' choice by dropping several of the thornier Nebula nominees from the ballot and substituting two "hard science" novels: *Star Light,* by Hal Clement, and *Tau Zero,* by Poul Anderson.

But when it came time to announce the final choice, it was *Ringworld* again.

The winner for best novella—both Nebula and Hugo— was Fritz Leiber's "Ill Met in Lankhmar," from *F&SF.* Leiber had been writing his wry swordplay-and-sorcery adventures of Fafhrd and the Grey Mouser for more than twenty years. Leiber was and is hugely popular, personally, as one of the grand veterans of the pulp era and one of the courtly gentlefolk who lend our often brawling and disorderly field a badly needed touch of class.

"Ill Met in Lankhmar" was about as close to an "origin story" as Leiber had ever written for the series, and as a splendid piece of light amusement—entirely in keeping with the choice of *Ringworld* for best novel—it was a totally appropriate choice to win both awards.

The Nebula-winning novelette was "Slow Sculpture," by Theodore Sturgeon, published in *Galaxy.* Rather than a simple "easy read," this story provided a different kind of balm. It was a story of great emotional warmth, of reassurance, that seemed to say to the reader. *Well, things may be tough, but don't worry too much, persist and persevere and whatever you do, don't give up hope . . . and everything will be all right in the end.*

"Slow Sculpture" won the Nebula for best novelette. The fans—for the last time, may all the gods have pity on us!—were still quarreling over categories and kept insisting that three were enough. They gave no Hugo for best novelette but decided that "Slow Sculpture" was a *short story* and awarded Sturgeon the Hugo in that category!

This was a particularly popular choice, for Sturgeon, like Leiber, was a personally popular veteran of the pulp era, as much loved for his cumulative contributions to the field over a span of decades as he was for a particular work. Oddly, while Sturgeon had once won an International Fantasy Award (for *More than Human,* in 1954), he had never won a Nebula or a Hugo.

Now he had won one of each for a single story! And now we come to the tale I promised you. The Nebula awards for 1970 were presented at a banquet held in New York. The banquet was preceded by a cocktail hour and the meal was accompanied by wine.

By the time the awards were presented, following the cocktail hour, the meal and a series of speeches of varying lengths, the officer of the Science Fiction Writers of America who had been designated to present the awards was feeling a trifle drowsy.

The officer—let's call him John Doe to avoid renewing old embarrassments—opened the proverbial sealed envelope and read the list of nominated short stories, "A Cold Night Dark with Snow," by Kate Wilhelm, *Orbit.* "By the Falls," Harry Harrison, *Galaxy.* "The Creation of Bennie Good," by James Sallis, *Orbit.* "In the Queue," by Keith Laumer, *Orbit.* "A Dream at Noonday," by Gardner Dozois, *Orbit.* "Entire and Perfect Chrysolite," by R.A. Lafferty, *Orbit.* "The Island of Dr. Death and Other Stories." by Gene Wolfe, *Orbit.*

"And the winning story," John Doe intoned sleepily, "is 'The Island of Dr. Death and Other Stories,' by Gene Wolfe, from *Orbit* 7."

Wolfe, a hearty, stocky man who had traveled from his home in Illinois to attend the Nebula festivities, rose from his seat. He started across the room, grinning, to accept his trophy. Halfway across the room, he was halted by another statement from John Doe.

"Oh, I'm sorry," Doc said, "The winner is not 'The Island of Dr. Death and Other Stories.' "

Wolfe stood in the center of the room, waiting for some explanation.

"The winner is," Doe said, "well, the winner is *No Award,* 'The Island of Dr. Death and Other Stories' got more votes than any other story, but *No Award* got the most, So there's no award. No award."

Wolfe stood there. Was this a cruel hoax of some bizarre sort? A joke? *Had* he won the Nebula, or hadn't he?

"There's no award," John Doe repeated. "I'm sorry I made a mistake, Go back and sit down. You didn't win," And that was that.

Three years later, Wolfe had his revenge.

But for 1970, there is no possible way to choose any story *but* "The Island of Dr. Death and Other Stories" for this book. The title is strange, and the story is strange as well. There is some question as to whether "The Island of Dr. Death and Other Stories" is exactly science fiction, although "The Island of Dr. Death" is, with very little doubt.

The Island of Doctor Death and Other Stories

GENE WOLFE

WINTER COMES TO WATER as well as land, though there are no leaves to fall. The waves that were a bright, hard blue yesterday under a fading sky today are green, opaque, and cold. If you are a boy not wanted in the house you walk the beach for hours, feeling the winter that has come in the night; sand blowing across your shoes, spray wetting the legs of your corduroys. You turn your back to the sea, and with the sharp end of a stick found half buried write in the wet sand *Tackman Babcock.*

Then you go home, knowing that behind you the Atlantic is destroying your work.

Home is the big house on Settlers Island, but Settlers Island, so called, is not really an island and for that reason is not named or accurately delineated on maps. Smash a barnacle with a stone and you will see inside the shape from which the beautiful barnacle goose takes its name. There is a thin and flaccid organ which is the goose's neck and the mollusk's siphon, and a shapeless body with tiny wings. Settlers Island is like that.

The goose neck is a strip of land down which a county road runs. By whim, the mapmakers usually exaggerate the width of this and give no information to indicate that it is scarcely above the high tide. Thus Settlers Island appears to be a mere protuberance on the coast, not requiring a name— and since the village of eight or ten houses has none, nothing shows on the map but the spider line of road terminating at the sea.

The village has no name, but home has two: a near and a far designation. On the island, and on the mainland nearby, it is called the Seaview place because in the earliest years of the century it was operated as a resort hotel. Mama calls it The House of 31 February; and that is on her stationery and is presumably used by her friends in New York and Philadelphia when they do not simply say, "Mrs. Babcock's." Home is four floors high in some places, less in others, and is completely surrounded by a veranda; it was once painted yellow, but the paint—outside—is mostly gone now and he House of 31 February is gray.

Jason comes out the front door with the little curly hairs on his chin trembling in the wind and his thumbs hooked in the waistband of his Levi's. "Come on, you're going into town with me. Your mother wants to rest."

"Hey tough!" Into Jason's Jaguar, feeling the leather upholstery soft and smelly; you fall asleep.

Awake in town, bright lights flashing in the car windows. Jason is gone and the car is growing cold; you wait for what seems a long time, looking out at the shop windows, the big gun on the hip of the policeman who walks past, the lost dog who is afraid of everyone, even you when you tap the glass and call to him.

Then Jason is back with packages to put behind the seat. "Are we going home now?"

He nods without looking at you, arranging his bundles so they won't topple over, fastening his seatbelt. "I want to get out of the car," He looks at you.

"I want to go in a store. Come on, Jason." Jason sighs. "All right, the drugstore over there, okay? Just for a minute,"

The drugstore is as big as a supermarket, with long bright aisles of glassware and notions and paper goods. Jason buys fluid for his lighter at the cigarette counter, and you bring him a book from the revolving wire rack. "Please, Jason?"

He takes it from you and replaces it in the rack, then when you are in the car again takes it from under his jacket and gives it to you.

It is a wonderful book, thick and heavy, with the edges of

the pages tinted yellow. The covers are glossy stiff card-board, and on the front is a picture of a man in rags fighting a thing partly like an ape and partly like a man, but much worse than either. The picture is in color, and there is real blood on the ape-thing; the man is muscular and handsome, with tawny hair lighter than Jason's and no beard.

"You like that?"

You are out of town already, and without the street lights it's too dark in the car, almost, to see the picture. You nod.

Jason laughs. "That's camp. Did you know that?" You shrug, riffling the pages under your thumb, thinking of reading alone, in your room tonight.

"You going to tell your mom how nice I was to you?"

"Uh-huh, sure. You want me to?"

"Tomorrow, not tonight. I think she'll be asleep when we get back. Don't wake her up," Jason's voice says he will be angry if you do.

"Okay."

"Don't come into her room."

"Okay."

The Jaguar says "*Hutntntaaa . . .*" down the road, and you can see the whitecaps in the moonlight now, and the driftwood pushed just off the asphalt.

"You got a nice, soft mommy, you know that? When I climb on her it's just like being on a big pillow."

You nod, remembering the times when, lonely and frightened by dreams, you have crawled into her bed and snuggled against her soft warmth—but at the same time angry, knowing Jason is somehow deriding you both.

Home is silent and dark, and you leave Jason as soon as you can, bounding off down the hall and up the stairs ahead of him, up a second, narrow, twisted flight to your own room in the turret.

I had this story from a man who was breaking his word in telling it. How much it has suffered in his hands—I should say in his mouth, rather—I cannot say. In essentials it is true, and I give it to you as it was given to me.

This is the story he told.

Captain Philip Ransom had been adrift, alone, for nine days when he saw the island. It was already late evening when it appeared like a thin line of purple on the horizon, but Ransom did not sleep that night. There was no feeble questioning in his wakeful mind concerning the reality of what he had seen; he had been given that one glimpse and he knew. Instead his brain teemed with facts and speculations. He knew he must be somewhere near New Guinea, and he reviewed mentally what he knew of the currents in these waters and what he had learned in the past nine days of the behavior of his raft. The island when he reached it—he did not allow himself to say *if*—would in all probability be solid jungle a few feet back from the water's edge. There might or might not be natives, but he brought to mind all he could of the Bazaar Malay and Tagalog he had acquired in his years as a pilot, plantation manager, white hunter, and professional fighting man in the Pacific.

In the morning he saw that purple shadow on the horizon again, a little nearer this time and almost precisely where his mental calculations had told him to expect it. For nine days there had been no reason to employ the inadequate paddles provided with the raft, but now he had something to row for. Ransom drank the last of his water and began stroking with a steady and powerful beat which was not interrupted until the prow of his rubber craft ground into beach sand.

Morning, You are slowly awake. Your eyes feel gummy, and the light over your bed is still on. Downstairs there is no one, so you get a bowl of milk and poured sugary cereal out for yourself and light the oven with a kitchen match so that you can eat and read by the open door. When the cereal is gone you drink the sweet milk and crumbs in the bottom of the bowl and start a pot of coffee, knowing that will please Mother. Jason comes down, dressed but not wanting to talk; drinks coffee and makes one piece of cinnamon toast in the oven. You listen to him leave, the stretched buzzing of his car on the road, then go up to Mother's room.

She is awake, her eyes open looking at the ceiling, but you know she isn't ready to get up yet. Very politely, because that minimizes the chances of being shouted at, you say, "How are you feeling this morning, Mama?"

She rolls her head to look. "Strung out. What time is it, Tackie?"

You look at the little folding clock on her dresser. "Seventeen minutes after eight."

"Jason go?"

"Yes, just now, Mama."

She is looking at the ceiling again. "You go back downstairs now, Tackie. I'll get you something when I feel better."

Downstairs you put on your sheepskin coat and go out on the veranda to look at the sea. There are gulls riding the icy wind, and very far off something orange bobbing in the waves, always closer.

A life raft. You run to the beach, jump up and down and wave your cap. "Over here. Over here."

The man from the raft has no shirt but the cold doesn't seem to bother him. He holds out his hand and says, "Captain Ransom," and you take it and are suddenly taller and older; not as tall as he is or as old as he is, but taller and older than yourself. "Tackman Babcock, Captain."

"Pleased to meet you. You were a friend in need there a minute ago."

"I guess I didn't do anything but welcome you ashore."

"The sound of your voice gave me something to steer for while my eyes were too busy watching that surf. Now you can tell me where I've landed and who you are."

You are walking back lo the house now, and you explain to Ransom about you and Mother, and how she doesn't want to enroll you in the school here because she is trying to get you into the private school your father went to once. And after a time there is nothing more to say, and you show Ransom one of the empty rooms on the third floor where he can rest and do whatever he wants. Then you go back to your own room to read.

"Do you mean that you *made* these monsters?"

"*Made* them?" Dr. Death leaned forward, a cruel smile playing about his lips. "Did God *make* Eve, Captain, when he took her from Adam's rib? Or did Adam make the bone and God *alter* it to become what he wished? Look at it this way, Captain. I am God and Nature is Adam."

Ransom looked at the thing who grasped his right arm with hands that might have circled a utility pole as easily. "Do you mean that this thing is an animal?"

"Not an animal," the monster said, wrenching his arm cruelly. "Man."

Dr. Death's smile broadened. "Yes, Captain, man. The question is, what are you? When I'm finished with you we'll see. Dulling your mind will be less of a problem that upgrading these poor brutes; but what about increasing the efficacy of your sense of smell? Not to mention rendering it impossible for you to walk erect."

"*Not* to walk all-four-on-ground," the beast-man holding Ransom muttered, "*that* is the *law*."

Dr. Death turned and called to the shambling hunchback Ransom had seen earlier, "Golo, see to it that Captain Ransom is securely put away; then prepare the surgery."

A car. Not Jason's noisy Jaguar, but a quiet, large-sounding car. By heaving up the narrow, light little window at the corner of the turret and sticking your head out into the cold wind you can see it: Dr. Black's big one, with the roof and hood all shiny with new wax.

Downstairs Dr. Black is hanging up an overcoat with a collar of fur, and you smell the old cigar smoke in his clothing before you see him; then Aunt May and Aunt Julie are there to keep you occupied so that he won't be reminded too vividly that marrying Mama means getting you as well. They talk to you: "How have you been, Tackie? What do you find to do out here all day?"

"Nothing."

"Nothing? Don't you ever go looking for shells on the beach?"

"I guess so."

"You're a handsome boy, do you know that?" Aunt May touches your nose with a scarlet-tipped finger and holds it there.

Aunt May is Mother's sister, but older and not as pretty. Aunt Julie is Papa's sister, a tall lady with a pulled-out, unhappy face, and makes you think of him even when you know she only wants Mama to get married again so that Papa won't have to send her any more money.

Mama herself is downstairs now in a clean new dress with long sleeves. She laughs at Dr. Black's jokes and holds onto his arm, and you think how nice her hair looks and that you will tell her so when you are alone. Dr. Black says, "How about it, Barbara, are you ready for the party?" and Mother, "Heavens no. You know what this place is like—yesterday I spent all day cleaning and today you can't even see what I did. But Julie and May will help me." Dr. Black laughs. "After lunch."

You get into his big car with the others and to go a restaurant on the edge of a cliff, with a picture window to see the ocean. Dr. Black orders a sandwich for you that has turkey and bacon and three pieces of bread, but you are finished before the grown-ups have started, and when you try to talk to Mother, Aunt May sends you out to where there is a railing with wire to fill in the spaces like chicken wire only heavier, to look at the view.

It is really not much higher than the top window at home. Maybe a little higher. You put the toes of your shoes in the wire and bend out with your stomach against the rail to look down, but a grown-up pulls you down and tells you not to do it, then goes away. You do it again, and there are rocks at the bottom which the waves wash over in a neat way, covering them up and then pulling back. Someone touches your elbow, but you pay no attention for a minute, watching the water.

Then you get down, and the man standing beside you is
Dr. Death.

He has a white scarf and black leather gloves and his hair
is shiny black. His face is not tanned like Captain Ransom's
but white, and handsome in a different way like the statue of
a head that used to be in Papa's library when you and Mother
used to live in town with him, and you think: Mama would
say after he was gone how good looking he was. He smiles at
you, but you are no older.

"Hi." What else can you say?

"Good afternoon. Mr. Babcock, I'm afraid I startled you."

You shrug. "A little bit, I didn't expect you to be here, I
guess."

Dr. Death turns his back to the wind to light a cigarette he
takes from a gold case. It is longer even than a 101 and has a
red tip, and a gold dragon on the paper. "While you were
looking down, I slipped from between the pages of the excellent novel you have in your coat pocket."

"I didn't know you could do that."

"Oh, yes. I'll be around from time to time."

"Captain Ransom is here already. He'll kill you." Dr.
Death smiles and shakes his head. "Hardly. You see, Tackman, Ransom and I are a bit like wrestlers; under various
guises we put on our show again and again—but only under
the spotlight." He flicks his cigarette over the rail and for a
moment your eyes follow the bright spark out and down and
see it vanish in the water. When you look back, Dr. Death is
gone, and you are getting cold. You go back into the restaurant and get a free mint candy where the cash register is and
then go to sit beside Aunt May again in time to have coconut
cream pie and hot chocolate.

Aunt May drops out of the conversation long enough to
ask, "Who was that man you were talking to, Tackie?"

"A man." In the car Mama sits close to Dr. Black, with
Aunt Julie on the other side of her so she will have to, and
Aunt May sits way up on the edge of her seat with her head
in between theirs so they can all talk. It is gray and cold outside; you think of how long it will be before you are home

again, and take the book out.

Ransom heard them coming and flattened himself against the wall beside the door of his cell. There was no way out, he knew, save through that iron portal. For the past four hours he had been testing every surface of the stone room for a possible exit, and there was none. Floor, walls, and ceiling were of cyclopean stone blocks; the windowless door of solid metal locked outside.

Nearer. He tensed every muscle and knotted his fists.

Nearer. The shambling steps halted. There was a rattle of keys and the door swung back. Like a thunderbolt of purpose he dove through the opening. A hideous face loomed above him and he sent his right fist crashing into it, knocking the lumbering beast-man to his knees. Two hairy arms pinioned him from behind, but he stretched ahead of him with a dim glow of daylight at the end and he sprinted for it. Then—darkness!

When he recovered consciousness he found himself already erect, strapped to the wall of a brilliantly lit room which seemed to share the characters of a surgical theater and a chemical laboratory. Directly before his eyes stood a bulky object which he knew must be an operating table, and upon it, covered with a sheet, lay the unmistakable form of a human being.

He had hardly had time to comprehend the situation when Dr. Death entered, no longer in the elegant evening dress in which Ransom had beheld him last, but wearing white surgical clothing. Behind him limped the hideous Golo, carrying a tray of implements.

"Ah!" Seeing that his prisoner was conscious, Dr. Death strolled across the room and raised a hand as though to strike him in the face, but, when Ransom did not flinch, dropped it, smiling. "My dear Captain! You are with us again, I see."

"I hoped for a minute there," Ransom said levelly, "that I was away from you. Mind telling me what got me?"

"A thrown club, or so my slaves report. My baboon-man is quite good at it. But aren't you going to ask about this charming little tableau I've staged for you?"

"I wouldn't give you the pleasure."

"But you are curious." Dr. Death smiled his crooked smile. "I shall not keep you in suspense. Your own time, Captain, has not come yet; and before it does I am going to demonstrate my technique to you. It is so seldom that I have a really appreciative audience." With a calculated gesture he whipped away the sheet which had covered the prone form on the operating table.

Ransom could scarcely believe his eyes. Before him lay the unconscious body of a girl, a girl with skin as white as silk and hair like the sun seen through mist,

"You are interested now, I see," Dr. Death remarked drily, "and you consider her beautiful. Believe me, when I have completed my work you will flee screaming if she so much as turns what will no longer be a face toward you. This woman has been my implacable enemy since I came to this island, and the time has come for me to"—he halted in mid-sentence and looked at Ransom with an expression of mingled slyness and gloating—"for me to illustrate something of your own fate, shall we say."

While Dr. Death had been talking his deformed assistant had prepared a hypodermic. Ransom watched as the needle plunged into the girl's almost translucent flesh, and the liquid in the syringe—a fluid which by its very color suggested the vile perversion of medical technique—entered her bloodstream. Though still unconscious the girl sighed, and it seemed to Ransom that a cloud passed over her sleeping face as though she had already begun an evil dream. Roughly the hideous Golo turned her on her back and fastened in place straps of the same kind as those that held Ransom himself pinned to the wall.

"What are you reading, Tackie?" Aunt May asked.

"Nothing." He shut the book.

"Well, you shouldn't read in the car. It's bad for your

eyes."

Dr. Black looked back at them for a moment, then asked Mama, "Have you gotten a costume for the little fellow yet?"

"For Tackie?" Mama shook her head, making her beautiful hair shine even in the dim light of the car. "No, nothing. It will be past his bedtime."

"Well, you'll have to let him see the guests anyway, Barbara; no boy should miss that."

And then the car was racing along the road out to Settlers Island. And then you were home.

Ransom watched as the loathsome creature edged toward him. Though not as large as some of the others its great teeth looked formidable indeed, and in one hand it grasped a heavy jungle knife with a razor edge.

For a moment he thought it would molest the unconscious girl, but it circled around her to stand before Ransom himself, never meeting his eyes.

Then, with a gesture as unexpected as it was frightening, it bent suddenly to press its hideous face against his pinioned right hand, and a great, shuddering gasp ran through the creature's twisted body.

Ransom waited, tense.

Again that deep inhalation, seeming almost a sob. Then the beast-man straightened up, looking into Ransom's face but avoiding his gaze, A thin, strangely-familiar whine came from the monster's throat.

"Cut me loose." Ransom ordered.

"Yes. This I came to. Yes, Master." The huge head, wider than it was high, hobbled up and down. Then the sharp blade of the machete bit into the straps holding Ransom. As soon as he was free he took the blade from the willing hand of the beast-man and freed the limbs of the girl on the operating table. She was light in his arms, and for an instant he stood looking down at her tranquil face.

"Come, Master." The beast-man pulled at his sleeve. "Bruno knows a way out. Follow Bruno."

A hidden flight of steps led to a long and narrow corridor, almost pitch dark. "No one use this way," the beast-man said in his harsh voice. "They not find us here."

"Why did you free me?" Ransom asked. There was a pause, then almost with an air of shame the great, twisted form replied, "You smell good. And Bruno does not like Dr. Death."

Ransom's conjectures were confirmed. Gently he asked, "You were a dog before Dr. Death worked on you, weren't you, Bruno?"

"Yes." The beast-man's voice held a sort of pride. "A St, Bernard. I have seen pictures."

"Dr. Death should have known better than to employ his foul skills on such a noble animal," Ransom reflected aloud. "Dogs are too shrewd in judging character; but then the evil are always foolish in the final analysis."

Unexpectedly the dog-man halted in front of him, forcing Ransom to stop too. For a moment the massive head bent over the unconscious girl. Then there was a barely audible growl. "You say, Master, that I can judge. Then I tell you Bruno does not like this female Dr. Death calls Talar of the Long Eyes."

You put the open book face-down on the pillow and jump up, hugging yourself and skipping bareheels around the room. Marvelous! Wonderful!

But no more reading tonight. Save it, save it. Turn the light off, and in the delicious dark put the book reverently away under the bed, pushing aside pieces of the Tinker Toy set and the box with the filling station game cards. Tomorrow there will be more, and you can hardly wait for tomorrow. You lie on your back, hands under head, covers up to chin and when you close your eyes, you can see it all: the island, with jungle trees swaying in the sea wind; Dr. Death's castle lifting its big, cold grayness against the hot sky.

The whole house is still, only the wind and the Atlantic are out, the familiar sounds. Downstairs Mother is talking to Aunt May and Aunt Julie and you fall asleep.

Are you awake! Listen! Late, it's very late, a strange time you have almost forgotten. Listen!

So quiet it hurts. Something. Something. Listen!

On the steps.

You get out of bed and find your flashlight. Not because you are brave, but because you cannot wait there in the dark.

There is nothing in the narrow, cold little stairwell outside your door. Nothing in the big hallway of the second floor. You shine your light quickly from end to end. Aunt Julie is breathing through her nose, but there is nothing frightening about that sound, you know what it is: only Aunt Julie, asleep, breathing loud through her nose.

Nothing on the stairs coming up.

You go back to your room, turn off your flashlight, and get into bed. When you are almost sleeping there is the scrabbling sound of hard claws on the floor-boards and a rough tongue touching your fingertip? "Don't be afraid, Master, it is only Bruno." And you feel him, warm with his own warm and smelling of his own smell, lying beside your bed.

Then it is morning. The bedroom is cold, and there is no one in it but yourself. You go into the bathroom where there is a thing like a fan but with hot electric wires to dress.

Downstairs Mother is up already with a cloth thing tied over her hair, and so are Aunt May and Aunt Julie, sitting at the table with coffee and milk and big slices of fried ham. Aunt Julie says, "Hello, Tackie," and Mother smiles at you. There is a plate out for you already and you have ham and toast.

All day the three women are cleaning and putting up decorations—red and gold paper masks Aunt Julie made to hang on the wall, and funny lights that change color and go around—and you try to stay out of the way, and bring in wood for a fire in the big fireplace that almost never gets used. Jason comes, and Aunt May and Aunt Julie don't like him, but he helps some and goes into town in his car for things he forgot to buy before. He won't take you, this time. The wind comes in around the window, but they let you alone in your room and it's even quiet up there because they're all downstairs.

Ransom looked at the enigmatic girl incredulously.

"You do not believe me," she said. It was a simple statement of fact, without anger or accusation.

"You'll have to admit it's pretty hard to believe," he temporized. "A city older than civilization, buried in the jungle here on this little island."

Talar said tonelessly, "When you were as he"—she pointed at the dog-man—"is now, Lemuria was queen of this sea. All that is gone, except my city. Is not that enough to satisfy even Time?"

Bruno plucked at Ransom's sleeve. "Do not go, Master! Beast-men go sometimes, beast-men Dr. Death does not want, few come back. They are very evil at that place."

"You see?" A slight smile played about Talar's ripe lips. "Even your slave testifies for me. My city exists."

"How far?" Ransom asked curtly.

"Perhaps half a day's travel through the jungle." The girl paused, as though afraid to say more.

"What is it?" Ransom asked.

"You will lead us against Dr. Death? We wish to cleanse this island which is our home."

"Sure. I don't like him any more than your people do. Maybe less."

"Even if you do not like my people you will lead them?"

"If they'll have me. But you're hiding something. What is it?"

"You see me, and I might be a woman of your own people. Is that not so?" They were moving through the jungle again now, the dog-man reluctantly acting as rear guard.

"Very few girls of my people are as beautiful as you are, but otherwise yes."

"And for that reason I am high priestess to my people,

for in me the ancient blood runs pure and sweet. But it is not so with all." Her voice sunk to a whisper. "When a tree is very old, and yet still lives, sometimes the limbs are strangely twisted. Do you understand?"

"Tackie? Tackie are you in there?"
"Uh-huh." You put the book inside your sweater.
"Well, come and open this door. Little boys ought not to lock their doors. Don't you want to see the company?" You open, and Aunt May's a gypsy with long hair that isn't hers around her face and a mask that is only at her eyes.

Downstairs cars are stopping in front of the house and Mother is standing at the door dressed in Day-Glo robes that open way down the front but cover her arms almost to the ends of her fingers. She is talking to everyone as they come in, and you see her eyes are bright and strange the way they are sometimes when she dances by herself and talks when no one is listening.

A woman with a fish for a head and a shiny, silver dress is Aunt Julie. A doctor with a doctor's coat and listening things and a shiny thing on his head to look through is Dr. Black, and a soldier in a black uniform with a pirate thing on his hat and a whip is Jason. The big table has a punchbowl and cakes and little sandwiches and hot bean dip. You pull away when the gypsy is talking to someone and take some cakes and sit under the table watching legs.

There is music and some of the legs dance, and you stay under there a long time.

Then a man's and a girl's legs dance close to the table and there is suddenly a laughing face in front of you—Captain Ransom's, "What are you doing under there, Tack? Come out and join the party." And you crawl out, feeling very small instead of older, but older when you stand up. Captain Ransom is dressed like a castaway in a ragged shirt and pants torn off at the knees, but all clean and starched. His love beads are seeds and sea shells, and he has his arm around a girl with no clothes at all, just jewelry.

"Tack, this is Talar of the Long Eyes."

You smile and bow and kiss her hand, and are nearly as tall as she. All around people are dancing or talking, and no one seems to notice you. With Captain Ransom on one side of Talar and you on the other you thread your way through the room, avoiding the dancers and the little groups of people with drinks. In the room you and Mother use as a living room when there's no company, two men and two girls are making love with the television on, and in the little room past that a girl is sitting on the floor with her back to the wall, and men are standing in the corners. "Hello," the girl says. "Hello to you all." She is the first one to have noticed you, and you stop.

"Hello."

"I'm going to pretend you're real. Do you mind?"

"No." You look around for Ransom and Talar, but they are gone and you think that they are probably in the living room, kissing with the others.

"This is my third trip. Not a god trip, but not a bad trip. But I should have had a monitor—you know, someone to stay with me. Who are those men?"

The men in the corners stir, and you can hear the clinking of their armor and see light glinting on it and you look away. "I think they're from the City. They probably came to watch out for Talar," and somehow you know that this is the truth.

"Make them come out where I can see them."

Before you can answer Dr. Death says, "I don't really think you would want to," and you turn and find him standing just behind you wearing full evening dress and a cloak. He takes your arm. "Come on, Tackie, there's something I think you should see." You follow him to the back stairs and then up, and along the hall to the door of Mother's room.

Mother is inside on the bed, and Dr. Black is standing over her filling a hypodermic. As you watch, he pushes up her sleeves so that all the other injection marks show ugly and red on her arm, and all you can think of is Dr. Death bending over Talar on the operating table. You run downstairs looking for Ransom, but he is gone and there is nobody at the party at all except the real people and, in the cold shadows of the back stoop, Dr. Death's assistant Golo, who will not speak, but only stares at you in the moonlight with pale eyes,

The next house down the beach belongs to a woman you have seen sometimes cutting down the dry fall remnant of her asparagus or hilling up her roses while you played. You pound at her door and try lo explain, and after a while she calls the police.

. . . across the sky. The flames were licking at the roof timbers now. Ransom made a megaphone of his hands and shouted. "Give up! You'll all be burned to death if you stay in there!" but the only reply was a shot and he was not certain they had heard him. The Lemurian bow-men discharged another flight of arrows at the windows.

Talar grasped his arm: "Come back before they kill you."

Numbly he retreated with her, stepping across the massive body of the bull-man, which lay pierced by twenty or more shafts.

You fold back the corner of a page and put the book down. The waiting room is cold and bare, and although sometimes the people hurrying through smile at you, you feel lonely. After a long time a big man with gray hair and a woman in a blue uniform want to talk to you.

The woman's voice is friendly, but only the way teachers' voices are sometimes. "I'll bet you're sleepy, Tackman. Can you talk to us a little still before you go to bed?"

"Yes,"

The gray-haired man says, "Do you know who gave your mother drugs?"

"I don't know. Dr. Black was going to do something to her."

He waves that aside. "Not that. You know, medicine. Your mother took a lot of medicine. Who gave it to her? Jason?"

"I don't know."

The woman says, "Your mother is going to be well, Tackman, but it will be a while—do you understand? For now you're going to have to live for a while in a big house with some other boys."

"All right."

The man: "Amphetamines. Does that mean anything to you? Did you ever hear that word?" You shake your head.

The woman: "Dr. Black was only trying to help your mother, Tackman. I know you don't understand, but she used several medicines at once, mixed them, and that can be very bad."

They go away and you pick up the book and riffle the pages, but you do not read. At your elbow Dr. Death says, "What's the matter, Tackie?" He smells of scorched cloth and there is a streak of blood across his forehead, but he smiles and lights one of his cigarettes.

You hold up the book. "I don't want it to end. You'll be killed at the end."

"And you don't want to lose me? That's touching."

"You will, won't you? You'll burn up in the fire and Captain Ransom will go away and leave Talar."

Dr. Death smiles. "But if you start the book again we'll all be back. Even Golo and the bull-man."

"Honest?"

"Certainly." He stands up and tousles your hair, "It's the same with you, Tackie. You're too young to realize it yet, but it's the same with you."

1971

IN 1947, ERLL Korshak and Everett F. Bleiler founded Shasta Publishers, one of the most distinguished of the fan-owned presses. Shasta lasted until 1957, publishing nineteen books by such distinguished authors as L. Ron Hubbard, John W. Campbell, Jr., E. Sprague dc Camp, Robert A. Heinlein. Murray Leinster, Fredric Brown, Alfred Bester and A.E. Van Vogt.

When Shasta ceased to exist, it did not simply fade away, or collapse in bankruptcy, or become part of another firm. Instead, it exploded in scandal and controversy which surviving members of the firm still refuse to discuss, on the record, for fear of libel suits, even though twenty-five years have passed.

In their bibliography of science-fantasy specialty publishers, Mark Owings and Jack L. Chalker add the note that, "Shasta announced a great many books it never produced— some of which were originals never seen again."

Owings and Chalker are correct. One of these announced books was *Riverworld,* by Philip José Farmer. *Riverworld* was not just another announced novel: it was the winner of a contest co-sponsored by Shasta, one of the science fiction magazines and a mass market paperback publisher. When Shasta folded, both the prize money and Farmer's manuscript disappeared, and in those benighted pre-Xerox years, the Shasta copy of *Riverworld* was the only copy that existed!

Farmer was shattered. He gave up his full-time writing career, got himself an honest job, and only over a period of years managed to work himself back into full-time writing. It was not until the mid-1960s that Farmer managed to reconstruct the lost material sufficiently to commence magazine publication and not until 1971 that a full, book length version appeared. By now the material had grown into the Riverworld series, and the first volume, *To Your Scattered Bodies Go,* was published by Putnam.

It promptly won the Hugo.

The Farmer book had not won the Nebula: it fact, it had not even made the Nebula ballot! The Nebula-winning novel was *A Time of Changes,* by Robert Silverberg. The Silverberg novel *did* make the Nebula ballot, but in final voting it finished last of five nominees.

Only one other novel made both ballots, and it was, in my opinion, its author's most overlooked and underrated work: *The Lathe of Heaven,* by Ursula K. Le Guin. Years later, a two-hour television production and the concurrent reissue of the book were to bring it a larger and more appreciative audience.

In the shorter lengths, the fans were in their final year of two rather than three awards. This, Poul Anderson's story "The Queen of Air and Darkness" (from *F&SF)* won the Hugo for best novella and the Nebula for best novelette, while Katherine MacLean's "The Missing Man" (from *Analog)* was the Nebula voters' choice for best novella.

The voters differed, also, as to the year's best short story. Larry Niven's "Inconstant Moon," a typically ingenious work, won the Hugo, and Silverberg's "Good News from the Vatican," an amusing bit of fluff about the first robot Pope, won the Nebula. Neither story had appeared in a magazine. The Niven story made its first appearance in a collection of the author's stories; Silverberg's had appeared in the first volume of the new original anthology series, *Universal I,* edited by Terry Carr.

Two important figures in the science fiction field died within just a week of each other, in July of 1971. The first was August Derleth, a highly prolific author of regional fiction and poetry, a less significant author of fantasy and science fiction, but a most important person in the area of editing and publishing.

Derleth had been the co-founder, later the sole proprietor and longtime editor of Arkham House, one of the first and most significant of the specialty publishers in science fiction and fantasy. It was the work of Derleth through Arkham House that rescued both H.P. Lovecraft and Robert E. Howard from the trash heap of defunct pulp magazines.

Even more important, John W. Campbell, Jr., died on July 11, 1971. He was both the first and the last of the three really great science fiction magazine editors. Boucher, of *F&SF*, had died in 1968. Gold, of *Galaxy*, although still alive and sporadically active as a writer, had left his editorial post in 1961.

It seemed, somehow, that Campbell's death completed the process that began with the washout of 1953: the decline and fall of the science fiction magazine. Of course, this was not strictly true. A number of these magazines survived at the time and continue to survive. The magazine that Campbell had taken over as *Astounding Stories* and left as *Analog Science Fiction & Fact,* has survived for more than a decade, post-Campbell, and shows little sign of ending.

But the energy had departed from the magazines; what had been the center of the science fiction field had become peripheral. As the major influence in the novel had shifted from the editorial offices of the magazines to those of the book publishers, now the major influence in the realm of short fiction had moved from the (salaried) editors of the magazines to the independent, self-employed editors of original anthologies: Knight of *Orbit,* Ellison of *Dangerous Visions,* Carr of *Universe* and Silverberg of *New Dimensions,* as well as the other editors of the many one-shot original anthologies that have appeared over the years.

In this regard, 1971 saw the publication of the first volumes of both the new Carr and the new Silverberg series. Among the many distinguished stories that appeared in the volumes was a very remarkable novelette by Ursula K. Le Guin, "Vaster than Empires and More Slow." That the story did not *win* either Nebula or Hugo is not greatly surprising: there were many fine stories and it's the old, old matter of someone having to lose and someone having to win. More notable. I think, is the fact that "Vaster than Empires" ran a strong second to "Inconstant Moon" in Hugo balloting—but didn't even make the ballot for the Nebula.

I think the fans were right and the writers were wrong about "Vaster than Empires and More Slow." See if you agree.

Vaster than Empires and More Slow

URSULA K. LE GUIN

YOU'RE LOOKING AT a clock. It has hands, and figures arranged in a circle. The hands move. You can't tell if they move at the same rate, or if one moves faster than the other. What does *than* mean? There is a relationship between the hands and the circle of figures, and the name of this relationship is on the tip of your tongue; the hands are . . . something-or-other, at the figures. Or is it the figures that . . . at the hands? What does *at* mean? They are figures—your vocabulary hasn't shrunk at all—and of course you can count, one two three four etc., but the trouble is you can't tell which one is one. Each one is one: itself. Where do you begin? Each one being one, there is no, what's the word, I had it just now, something-ship, between the ones. There is no between. There is only here and here, one and one. There is no there. Maya has fallen. All is here now one. But if all is now and all here and one all, there is no end. It did not begin so it cannot end. Oh God, here now One get me out of this—

I'm trying to describe the sensations of the average person in NAFAL flight. It can be much worse than this for some, whose time-sense is acute. For others it is restful, like a drug-haze freeing the mind from the tyranny of hours. And for a few the experience is certainly mystical; the collapse of time and relation leading them directly to intuition of the eternal. But the mystic is a rare bird, and the nearest most people get to God in paradoxical time is by inarticulate and anguished prayer for release.

They used to drug people for the long jumps, but stopped

the practice when they realized its effects. What happens to a drugged, or ill, or wounded person during near-lightspeed flight is, of course, indeterminable. A jump of ten light-years should logically make no difference to a victim of measles or gunshot. The body ages only a few minutes; why is the measles patient carried out of the ship a leper, and the wounded man a corpse? Nobody knows, except perhaps the body, which keeps the logic of the flesh, and knows it has lain festering, bleeding, or drugged into mindlessness for ten years. Many imbeciles having been produced, the Fisher King Effect was established as fact, and they stopped using drugs and transporting the ill, the damaged, and the pregnant. You have to be in common health to go NAFAL, and you have to take it straight.

But you don't have to be sane.

It was only during the earliest decades of the League that Earthmen, perhaps trying to bolster their battered collective ego, sent out ships on enormously long voyages, beyond the pale, over the stars and far away. They were seeking for worlds that had not, like all the known worlds, been settled or seeded by the Founders on Hain, truly alien worlds; and all the crews of these Extreme Surveys were of unsound mind. Who else would go out to collect information that wouldn't be received for four, or five, or six centuries? Received by whom? This was before the invention of the instantaneous communicator; they would be isolated both in space and time. No sane person who has experienced time-slippage of even a few decades between near worlds would volunteer for a round trip of a half millennium. The Surveyors were escapists; misfits; nuts.

Ten of them climbed aboard the ferry at Smeming Port on Pesm, and made varyingly inept attempts to get to know one another during the three days the ferry took getting to their ship, *Gum*. Gum is a Low Cetian nickname, on the order of Baby or Pet. There was one Low Cetian on the team, one Hairy Cetian, two Hainishmen, one Beldene, and five Terraus; the ship was Cetian-built, but chartered by the Government of Earth. Her motley crew came aboard wiggling through the coupling-tube one by one like apprehensive spermatozoa fertilizing the universe. She zittered for the navigator put *Gum* underway. She zittered for some hours on the edge of space a few hundred million miles from Pesm, and then abruptly vanished.

When after ten hours twenty-nine minutes, or 256 years, *Gum* reappeared in normal space, she was supposed to be in the vicinity of Star KGE-96651. Sure enough, there was the cheerful gold pinhead of the star. Somewhere within a 400-million-kilometer sphere there was also a greenish planet, World 4470, as charted by a Certain Mapmaker long ago. The ship now had to find the planet. This was not quite so easy as it might sound, given a 400-million-kilometer hay-stack. And *Gum* couldn't bat about in planetary space at near lightspeed; if she did, she and Star KGE-96651 and World 4470 might all end up going bang. She had to creep, using rocket propulsion, at a few hundred thousand miles an hour. The Mathematician/Navigator, Asnanifoil, knew pretty well where the planet ought to be, and thought they might raise it within ten E-days. Meanwhile the members of the Survey team got to know one another still better.

"I can't stand him," said Porlock, the Hard Scientist (chemistry, plus physics, astronomy, geology, etc.), and little blobs of spittle appeared on his moustache. "The man is in-sane. I can't imagine why he was passed as fit to join a Sur-vey team, unless this is a deliberate experiment in noncom-patibility, planned by the Authority, with us as guinea pigs."

"We generally use hamsters and Hainish gholes," said Mannon, the Soft Scientist (psychology, plus psychiatry, an-thropology, ecology, etc.), politely; he was one of the Hain-ishmen. "Instead of guinea pigs. Well, you know, Mr. Osden is really a very rare case, In fact, he's the first fully cured case of Render's Syndrome—a variety of infantile autism which was thought to be incurable. The great Terran analyst Hammergeld reasoned that the cause of the autistic condition in this case is a supernormal emphatic capacity, and devel-oped an appropriate treatment. Mr. Osden is the first patient to undergo that treatment, in fact he lived with Dr. Hammer-

geld until he was eighteen. The therapy was completely successful."

"Successful?"

"Why, yes. He certainly is not autistic."

"No, he's intolerable!"

"Well, you see," said Mannon, gazing mildly at the saliva-
flecks on Porlock's mustache, "the normal defensive-
aggressive reaction between strangers meeting—let's say
you and Mr. Osden just for example—is something you're
scarcely aware of; habit, manners, inattention get you past it;
you've learned to ignore it, to the point where you might
even deny it exists. However, Mr. Osden, being an empath,
feels it. Feels his feelings, and yours, and is hard put to say
which is which. Let's say that there's a normal element of
hostility towards any stranger in your emotional reaction to
him when you meet him, plus a spontaneous dislike of his
looks, or clothes, or handshake—it doesn't matter what. He
feels that dislike. As his autistic defense has been unlearned,
he resorts to an aggressive-defense mechanism, a response in
kind to the aggression which you have unwittingly projected
onto him." Mannon went on for quite a long time.

"'Nothing gives a man the right to be such a bastard,"
Porlock said.

"He can't tune us out?" asked Harfex, the Biologist, another Hainishman.

"It's like hearing," said Olleroo, Assistant Hard Scientist,
stooping over to paint her toenails with fluorescent lacquer.
"No eyelids on your ears. No Off switch on empathy. He
hears our feelings whether he wants to or not."

"Does he know what we're *thinking?*" asked Eskwana, the
Engineer, locking round at the others in real dread.

"No," Porlock snapped. "Empathy's not telepathy! Nobody's got telepathy."

"Yes," said Mannon, with his little smile. "Just before I
left Hain there was a most interesting report in from one of
the recently rediscovered worlds, a hilfer named Rocannon
reporting what appears to be a teachable telepathic technique
existent among a mutated hominid race; I only saw a synop-

sis in the HILF *Bulletin,* but—" He went on. The others had
learned that they could talk while Mannon went on talking;
he did not seem to mind, nor even to miss much of what they
said.

"Then why does he hate us?" Eskwana asked.

"Nobody hates you, Ander honey," said Olleroo, daubing
Eskwana's left thumbnail with fluorescent pink. The engineer flushed and smiled vaguely.

"He acts as if he hated us," said Haito, the Coordinator.
She was a delicate-looking woman of pure Asian descent,
with a surprising voice, husky, deep, and soft, like a young
bullfrog. "Why, if he suffers from our hostility, does he increase it by constant attacks and insults? I can't say I think
much of Dr. Hammergeld's cure, really, Mannon; autism
might be preferable . . ."

She stopped. Osden had come into the main cabin. He
looked flayed. His skin was unnaturally white and thin,
showing the channels of his blood like a faded road-map in
red and blue. His Adam's apple, the muscles that circled his
mouth, the bones and ligaments of his wrists and hands, all
stood out distinctly as if displayed for an anatomy lesson.
His hair was pale rust, like long-dried blood. He had eye-
brows and lashes, but they were visible only in certain lights;
what one saw was the bones of the eyesockets, the veining of
the lids, and the colorless eyes. They were not red eyes, for
he was not really an albino, but they were not blue or gray;
colors had canceled out in Osden's eyes, leaving a cold wa-
terlike clarity, infinitely penetrable. He never looked directly
at one. His face lacked expression, like an anatomical drawing, or a skinned face.

"I agree," he said in a high, harsh tenor, "that even autistic
withdrawal might be preferable to the smog of cheap sec-
ondhand emotions with which you people surround me.
What are *you* sweating hate for now, Porlock? Can't stand
the sight of me? Go practice some autoeroticism the way you
were doing last night, it improves your vibes—Who the devil
moved my tapes, here? Don't touch my things, any of you. I
won't have it."

"Osden," said Asnanifoil, the Hairy Cetian, in his large slow voice, "why *are* you such a bastard?"

Ander Eskwana cowered down and put his hands in front of his face. Contention frightened him. Olleroo looked up with a vacant yet eager expression, the eternal spectator.

"Why shouldn't I be?"" said Osden. He was not looking at Asnanifoil, and was keeping physically as far away from all of them as he could in the crowded cabin. "None of you constitute, in yourselves, any reason for my changing my behavior."

Asnanifoil shrugged; Cetians are seldom willing to state the obvious. Harfex, a reserved and patient man, said, "The reason is that we shall be spending several years together. Life will be better for all of us if—"

"Can't you understand that I don't give a damn for all of you?" Osden said, took up his microtapes, and went out. Eskwana had suddenly gone to sleep. Asnanifoil was drawing slipstreams in the air with his finger and muttering the Ritual Primes. "You cannot explain his presence on the team except as a plot on the part of the Terrain Authority. I saw this almost at once. This mission is meant to fail," Harfex whispered to the Coordinator, glancing over his shoulder. Porlock was fumbling with his fly-button; there were tears in his eyes. I did tell you they were all crazy, but you thought I was exaggerating.

All the same, they were not unjustified. Extreme Surveyors expected to find their fellow team members intelligent, well trained, unstable, and personally sympathetic. They had to work together in close quarters, and nasty places, and could expect one another's paranoias, depressions, manias, phobias, and compulsions to be mild enough to admit of good personal relationship, at least most of the time. Osden might be intelligent, but his training was sketchy and his personality was disastrous. He had been sent only on account of his singular gift, the power of empathy: properly speaking, of wide-range bioemphatic receptivity. His talent wasn't species-specific; he could pick up emotion or sentience from anything that felt. He could share lust with a white rat, pain with a squashed cockroach, and phototropy with a moth. On an alien world, the Authority had decided, it would be useful to know if anything nearby is sentient, and if so, what its feelings towards you are. Osden's title was a new one: he was the team's Sensor.

"What is emotion, Osden?" Haito Tomiko asked him one day in the main cabin, trying to make some rapport with him for once. "What is it, exactly, that you pick up with your empathic sensitivity?"

"Muck," the man answered in his high, exasperated voice. "The psychic excreta of the animal kingdom. I wade through your feces."

"I was trying," she said, "to learn some facts." She thought her tone was admirably calm.

"You weren't after facts. You were trying to get at me. With some fear, some curiosity, and a great deal of distaste. The way you might poke a dead dog, to see the maggots crawl. Will you understand once and for all that I don't want to be got at, that I want to be left alone?" His skin was mottled with red and violet, his voice had risen. "Go roll in your own dung, you yellow bitch!" he shouted at her silence.

"Calm down," she said, still quietly, but she left him at once and went to her cabin. Of course he had been right about her motives; her question had been largely a pretext, a mere effort to interest him. But what harm in that? Did not that effort imply respect for the other? At the moment of asking the question she had felt at most a slight distrust of him; she had mostly felt sorry for him, the poor arrogant venomous bastard, Mr. No-Skin as Olleroo called him. What did he expect, the way he acted? Love?

"I guess he can't stand anybody feeling sorry for him," said Olleroo, lying on the lower bunk, gilding her nipples. "Then he can't form a human relationship. All his Dr. Hammergeld did was turn an autism inside out . . ."

"Poor frot," said Olleroo. "Tomiko, you don't mind if Harfex comes in for a while tonight, do you?"

"Can't you go to his cabin? I'm sick of always having to sit in Main with that damned peeled turnip."

"You do hate him, don't you? I guess he feels that. But I slept with Harfex last night too, and Asnanifoil might get jealous, since they share the cabin, it would be nicer here."

"Service them both," Tomiko said with the coarseness of offended modesty. Her Terran subculture, the East Asian, was a puritanical one; she had been brought up chaste.

"I only like one a night," Olleroo replied with innocent serenity. Beldene, the Garden Planet, had never discovered chastity, or the wheel.

"Try Osden, then," Tomiko said. Her personal instability was seldom so plain as now: a profound self-distrust manifesting itself as destructivism. She had volunteered for this job because there was, in all probability, no use in doing it. The little Beldene looked up, paintbrush in hand, eyes wide. "Tomiko, that was a dirty thing to say."

"Why?"

"It would be vile! I'm not attracted to Osden!"

"I didn't know it mattered to you," Tomiko said indifferently, though she did know. She got some papers together and left the cabin, remarking, "I hope you and Harfex or whoever it is finish by last bell; I'm tired."

Olleroo was crying, tears dripping on her little gilded nipples. She wept easily, Tomiko had not wept since she was ten years old.

It was not a happy ship; but it took a turn for the better when Asnanifoil with his computer raised World 4470. There it lay, a dark-green jewel, like truth at the bottom of a gravity well. As they watched the jade disc grow, a sense of mutuality grew among them. Osden's selfishness, his accurate cruelty, served now to draw the others together. "Perhaps," Mannon said, "he was sent as a beating-gron. What Terrans call a scapegoat. Perhaps his influence will be the good after all." And no one, so careful were they to be kind to one another, disagreed.

They came into orbit. There were no lights on nightside, on the continents none of the lines and clots made by animals who build.

"No men," Harfex murmured.

"Of course not," snapped Osden, who had a viewscreen to himself, and his head inside a polythene bag. He claimed that the plastic cut down the empathic noise he received from the others. "We're two light-centuries past the limit of the Hainish Expansion, and outside that there are no men. Anywhere. You don't think Creation would have made the same hideous mistake twice?"

No one was paying him much heed; they were looking with affection at that jade immensity below them, where there was life, but not human life. They were misfits among men, and what they saw there was not desolation, but peace. Even Osden did not look quite so expressionless as usual; he was frowning.

Descent in fire on the sea; air reconnaissance; landing. A plain of something like grass, thick, green, bowing stalks, surrounded the ship, brushed against extended view-cameras, smeared the lenses with a fine pollen.

"It looks like a pure phytosphere," Harfex said. "Osden, do you pick up anything sentient?"

They all turned to the Sensor. He had left the screen and was pouring himself a cup of tea. He did not answer. He seldom answered spoken questions.

The chitinous rigidity of military discipline was quite inapplicable to these teams of Mad Scientists; their chain of command lay somewhere between parliamentary procedure and peck-order, and would have driven a regular service officer out of his mind. By the inscrutable decision of the Authority, however, Dr. Haito Tomiko had been given the title of Coordinator, and she now exercised her prerogative for the first time. "Mr. Sensor Osden," she said, "please answer Mr. Harfex."

"How could I 'pick up' anything from outside," Osden said without turning, "with the emotions of nine neurotic hominids pullulating around me like worms in a can? When I have anything to tell you. I'll tell you. I'm aware of my responsibility as Sensor. If you presume to give me an order again, however, Coordinator Haito. I'll consider my responsibility void."

"Very well, Mr. Sensor, I trust no orders will be needed henceforth." Tomiko's bullfrog voice was calm, but Osden seemed to flinch slightly as he stood with his back to her; as if the surge of her suppressed rancor had struck him with physical force,

The biologist's hunch proved correct. When they began field analyses they found no animals even among the microbiota. Nobody here ate anybody else. All life-forms were photosynthesizing or saprophagous, living off light or death, not off life. Plants: infinite plants, not one species known to the visitors from the house of Man. Infinite shades and intensities of green, violet, purple, brown, red. Infinite silences. Only the wind moved, swaying leaves and fronds, a warm soughing wind laden with spores and pollens, blowing the sweet pale-green dust over prairies of great grasses, heaths that bore no heather, flowerless forests where no foot had ever walked, no eye had ever looked. A warm, sad world, sad and serene. The Surveyors, wandering like picnickers over sunny plains of violet filicaliformes, spoke softly to each other. They know their voices broke a silence of a thousand million years, the silence of wind and leaves, leaves and wind, blowing and ceasing and blowing again. They talked softly; but being human, they talked.

"Poor old Osden," said Jenny Chong, Bio and Tech, as she piloted a helijet on the North Polar Quadrating run. "All that fancy hi-fi stuff in his brain and nothing to receive. What a bust."

"He told me he hates plants," Olleroo said with a giggle.

"You'd think he'd like them, since they don't bother him like we do,"

"Can't say I much like these plants myself," said Porlock, looking down at the purple undulations of the North Circumpolar Forest, "All the same. No mind. No change. A man alone in it would go right off his head."

"But it's all alive," Jenny Chong said. "And if it lives, Osden hates it."

"He's not really so bad," Olleroo said, magnanimous. Porlock looked at her sidelong and asked, "You ever slept with him, Olleroo?"

Olleroo burst into tears and cried, "You Terrans are obscene!"

"No she hasn't," Jenny Chong said, prompt to defend. "Have you, Porlock?"

The chemist laughed uneasily: Ha, ha, ha. Flecks of spittle appeared on his mustache.

"Osden can't bear to be touched," Olleroo said shakily. "I just brushed against him once by accident and he knocked me off like I was some sort of dirty . . . thing. We're all just things to him."

"He's evil," Porlock said in a strained voice, startling the two women. "He'll end up shattering this team, sabotaging it one way or another. Mark my words. He's not fit to live with other people!"

They landed on the North Pole. A midnight sun smoldered over low hills. Short, dry, greenish-pink bryoform grasses stretched away in every direction, which was all one direction, south. Subdued by the incredible silence, the three Surveyors set up their instruments and collected their samples, three viruses twitching minutely on the hide of an unmoving giant.

Nobody asked Osden along on runs as pilot or photographer or recorder, and he never volunteered, so he seldom left base camp. He ran Harfex's botanical taxonomic data through the on-ship computers, and served as assistant to Eskwana, whose job here was mainly repair and maintenance. Eskwana had begun to sleep a great deal, twenty-five hours or more out of the thirty-two hour day, dropping off in the middle of repairing a radio or checking the guidance circuits of a helijet. The Coordinator stayed at base one day to observe, No one else was home except Poswet To, who was subject to epileptic fits; Mannon had plugged her into a therapy-circuit today in a state of preventive catatonia. Tomiko spoke reports into the storage banks, and kept an eye on Osden and Eskwana. Two hours passed.

"You might want to use the 860 microwaldoes in scaling that connection," Eskwana said in his soft, hesitant voice.

"Obviously!"

"Sorry. I just saw you had the 840's there—"

"And will replace them when I take the 860's out. When I don't know how to proceed, Engineer, I'll ask your advice."

After a minute Tomiko looked round. Sure enough, there was Eskwana sound asleep, head on the table, thumb in his mouth.

"Osden."

The white face did not turn, he did not speak, but conveyed impatiently that he was listening.

"You can't be unaware of Eskwana's vulnerability."

"I am not responsible for his psychopathic reactions."

"But you are responsible for your own. Eskwana is essential to our work, here, and you're not. If you can't control your hostility, you must avoid him altogether."

Osden put down his tools and stood up, "With pleasure!" he said in his vindictive, scraping voice, "You could not possibly imagine what it's like to *experience* Eskwana's irrational terrors. To have to share his horrible cowardice, to have to cringe with him at everything!"

"Are you trying to justify your cruelty towards him? I thought you had more self-respect." Tomiko found herself shaking with spite. "If your empathic power really makes you share Ander's misery, why does it never induce the least compassion in you?"

"Compassion," Osden said. "Compassion. What do you know about compassion?"

She stared at him, but he would not look at her. "Would you like me to verbalize your present emotional affect regarding myself?" he said. "I can do so more precisely than you can. I'm trained to analyze such responses as I receive them. And I do receive them."

"But how can you expect mc to feel kindly towards you when you behave as you do?"

"What does it matter how I *behave,* you stupid sow, do you think it makes any difference? Do you think the average human is a well of loving kindness? My choice is to be hated or to be despised. Not being a woman or a coward, I prefer to be hated."

"That's rot. Self-pity. Every man has—"

"But I am not a man," Osden said. "There are all of you. And there is myself. I am *one.*"

Awed by that glimpse of abysmal solipsism, she kept silent a while; finally she said with neither spite nor pity, clinically, "You could kill yourself, Osden."

"That's your way, Haito," he jeered. "I'm not depressive and *seppuku* isn't my bit. What do you want me to do here?"

"Leave. Spare yourself and us. Take the airear and a data-feeder and go do a species count. In the forest; Harfex hasn't even started the forests yet. Take a hundred-square-meter forested area, anywhere inside radio range. But outside empathy range. Report in at eight and twenty-four o'clock daily."

Osden went, and nothing was heard from him for five days but laconic all-well signals twice daily. The mood at base camp changed like a stage set. Eskwana stayed awake up to eighteen hours a day. Poswet To got out her stellar lute and chanted the celestial harmonies (music had driven Osden to frenzy). Mannon, Harfex, Jenny Chong, and Tomiko all went off tranquilizers. Porlock distilled something in his laboratory and drank it all by himself. He had a hangover. Asnanifoil and Poswet To held an all-night Numerical Epiphany, that mystical orgy of higher mathematics which is the chiefest pleasure of the religious Cetian soul. Olleroo slept with everybody. Work went well.

The Hard Scientist came towards base at a run, laboring through the high, fleshy stalks of the graminiformes. "Something—in the forest—" His eyes bulged, he panted, his mustache and fingers trembled. "Something big. Moving, behind me. I was putting in a benchmark, bending down. It came at me. As if it was swinging down out of the trees. Behind me." He stared at the others with the opaque eyes of terror or exhaustion.

"Sit down, Porlock. Take it easy. Now wait, go through this again. You *saw* something—"

"Not clearly. Just the movement. Purposive. A—an—I

don't know what it could have been. Something self-moving. In the trees, the arboriformes, whatever you call 'em. At the edge of the woods."

Harfex looked grim. "There is nothing here that could attack you, Porlock. There are not even microzoa. There *could not* be a large animal."

"Could you possibly have seen an epiphyte drop suddenly, a vine come loose behind you?"

"No," Porlock said. "It was coming down at me, through the branches, fast. When I turned it took off again, away and upward. It made a noise, a sort of crashing. If it wasn't an animal, God knows what it could have been! It was big—as big as a man, at least. Maybe a reddish color. I couldn't see, I'm not sure."

"It was Osden," said Jenny Chong, "doing a Tarzan act." She giggled nervously, and Tomiko repressed a wild reckless laugh. But Harfex was not smiling.

"One gets uneasy under the arboriformes," he said in his polite, repressed voice. "I've noticed that. Indeed that may be why I've put off working in the forests. There's a hypnotic quality in the colors and spacing of the stems and branches, especially the helically arranged ones; and the spore-throwers grow so regularly spaced that it seems unnatural. I find it quite disagreeable, subjectively speaking. I wonder if a stronger effect of that sort mightn't have produced a hallucination . . .?"

Porlock shook his head. He wet his lips. "It was there," he said. "Something. Moving with purpose. Trying to attack me from behind."

When Osden called in, punctual as always, at twenty-four o'clock that night, Harfex told him Porlock's report. "Have you come on anything at all, Mr. Osden, that could substantiate Mr. Porlock's impression of a motile, sentient life-form, in the forest?"

Ssss, the radio said sardonically. "No. Bullshit," said Osden's unpleasant voice.

"You've been actually inside the forest longer than any of us," Harfex said with unmitigable politeness. "Do you agree with my impression that the forest ambiance has a rather troubling and possibly hallucinogenic effect on the perceptions?"

Ssss. "I'll agree that Porlock's perceptions are easily troubled. Keep him in his lab, he'll do less harm. Anything else?"

"Not at present," Harfex said, and Osden cut off. Nobody could credit Porlock's story, and nobody could discredit it. He was positive that something, something big, had tried to attack him by surprise. It was hard to deny this, for they were on an alien world, and everyone who had entered the forest had felt a certain chill and foreboding under the "trees." ("Call them trees, certainly," Harfex had said: "They really are the same thing, only, of course, altogether different.") They agreed that they had felt uneasy, or had had the sense that something was watching them from behind.

"We've got to clear this up," Porlock said, and he asked to be sent as a temporary Biologist's Aide, like Osden, into the forest to explore and observe. Olleroo and Jenny Chong volunteered if they could go as a pair. Harfex sent them all off into the forest near which they were encamped, a vast tract covering four-fifths of Continent D. He forbade side arms. They were not to go outside a fifty-kilo half-circle, which included Osden's current site. They all reported in twice daily, for three days. Porlock reported a glimpse of what seemed to be a large semi-erect shape moving through the trees across the river; Olleroo was sure she had heard something moving near the tent, the second night.

"There are no animals on this planet," Harfex said, dogged.

Then Osden missed his morning call. Tomiko waited less than an hour, then flew with Harfex to the area where Osden had reported himself the night before. But as the helijet hovered over the sea of purplish leaves, illimitable, impenetrable, she felt a panic despair. "How can we find him in this?"

"He reported landing on the river bank. Find the air-car: he'll be camped near it, and he can't have gone far from his camp. Species-counting is slow work. There's the river."

"There's his car," Tomiko said, catching the bright foreign glint among the vegetable colors and shadows. "Here goes, then."

She put the ship in hover and pitched out the ladder. She and Harfex descended. The sea of life closed over their heads.

As her feet touched the forest floor, she unsnapped the flap of her holster; then glancing at Harfex. who was unarmed, she left the gun untouched. But her hand kept coming back up to it. There was no sound at all, as soon as they were a few meters away from the slow, brown river, and the light was dim. Great boles stood well apart, almost regularly, almost alike; they were soft-skinned, some appearing smooth and others spongy, gray or greenish-brown or brown, twined with cablelike creepers and festooned with epiphytes, extending rigid, entangled armfuls of big, saucer-shaped, dark leaves that formed a roof-layer twenty to thirty meters thick. The ground underfoot was springy as a mattress, every inch of it knotted with roots and peppered with small, fleshy-leaved growths.

"Here's his tent," Tomiko said, cowed at the sound of her voice in that huge community of the voiceless. In the tent was Osden's sleeping bag, a couple of books, a box of rations. We should be calling, shouting for him, she thought, but did not even suggest it; nor did Harfex. They circled out from the tent, careful to keep each other in sight through the thick-standing presences, the crowding gloom. She stumbled over Osden's body, not thirty meters from the tent, led to it by the whitish gleam of a dropped notebook. He lay face down between two huge-rooted trees. His head and hands were covered with blood, some dried, some still oozing red.

Harfex appeared beside her, his pale Hainish complexion quite green in the dusk. "Dead?"

"No. He's been struck. Beaten. From behind." Tomiko's fingers felt over the bloody skull and nape and temples. "A weapon or a tool . . . I don't find a fracture."

As she turned Osden's body over so they could lift him, his eyes opened. She was holding him, bending close to his face. His pale lips writhed. A deathly fear came to her. She screamed aloud two or three times and tried to run away, shambling and stumbling into the terrible dusk. Harfex caught her, and at his touch and the sound of his voice, her panic decreased. "What is it? What is it?" he was saying.

"I don't know," she sobbed. Her heartbeat still shook her, and she could not see clearly. "The fear—the . . . I panicked. When I saw his eyes."

"We're both nervous. I don't understand this—"

"I'm all right now, come on, we've got to get him under care."

Both working with senseless haste, they lugged Osden to the riverside and hauled him up on a rope under his armpits; he dangled like a sack, twisting a little, over the glutinous dark sea of leaves. They pulled him into the helijet and took off. Within a minute they were over open prairie. Tomiko locked onto the homing beam. She drew a deep breath, and her eyes met Harfex's.

"I was so terrified I almost fainted. I have never done that."

"I was . . . unreasonably frightened also," said the Hainishman, and indeed he looked aged and shaken. "Not so badly as you. But as unreasonably."

"It was when I was in contact with him, holding him. He seemed to be conscious for a moment."

"Empathy? . . . I hope he can tell us what attacked him."

Osden, like a broken dummy covered with blood and mud, half-lay as they had bundled him into the rear seats in their frantic urgency to get out of the forest.

More panic met their arrival at base. The ineffective brutality of the assault was sinister and bewildering. Since Harfex stubbornly denied any possibility of animal life they began speculating about sentient plants, vegetable monsters, psychic projections. Jenny Chong's latent phobia reasserted itself and she could talk about nothing except the Dark Egos which followed people around behind their backs. She and Olleroo and Porlock had been summoned back to base; and nobody was much inclined to go outside.

Osden had lost a good deal of blood during the three or four hours he had lain alone, and concussion and severe contusions had put him in shock and semi-coma. As he came out of this and began running a lower fever he called several times for "Doctor," in a plaintive voice: "Doctor Hammergeld . . ." When he regained full consciousness, two of those long days later, Tomiko called Harfex into the cubicle.

"Osden, can you tell us what attacked you?"

The pale eyes flickered past Harfex' face.

"You were attacked," Tomiko said gently. The shifty gaze was hatefully familiar, but she was a physician, protective of the hurt. "You may not remember it yet. Something attacked you. You were in the forest—"

"Ah!" he cried out, his eyes growing bright and his features contorting. "The forest—in the forest—"

"What's in the forest?"

He gasped for breath. A look of clearer consciousness came into his face. After a while he said, "I don't know."

"Did you see what attacked you?" Harfex asked.

"I don't know."

"You remember it now."

"I don't know."

"All our lives may depend on this. You must tell us what you saw!"

"I don't know," Osden said, sobbing with weakness. He was too weak to hide the fact that he was hiding the answer, yet he would not say it. Porlock, nearby, was chewing his pepper-colored mustache as he tried to hear what was going on in the cubicle. Harfex leaned over Osden and said, "You *will* tell us—" Tomiko had to interfere bodily.

Harfex controlled himself with an effort that was painful to see. He went off silently to his cubicle, where no doubt he took a double or triple dose of tranquilizers. The other men and women, scattered about the big frail building, a long main hall and ten sleeping-cubicles, said nothing, but looked depressed and edgy. Osden, as always, even now, had them all at his mercy. Tomiko looked down at him with a rush of hatred that burned in her throat like bile. This monstrous egotism that fed itself on others' emotions, this absolute self-ishness, was worse than any hideous deformity of the flesh. Like a congenital monster, he should not have lived. Should not be alive. Should have died. Why had his head not been split open?

As he lay flat and white, his hands helpless at his sides, his colorless eyes were wide open, and there were tears running from the corners. Tomiko moved towards him suddenly. He tried to flinch away. "Don't," he said in a weak hoarse voice, and tried to raise his hands to protect his head. "Don't!"

She sat down on the folding stool beside the cot, and after a while put her hand on his. He tried to pull away, but lacked the strength.

A long silence fell between them.

"Osden," she murmured, "I'm sorry. I'm very sorry. I will you well. Let me will you well, Osden. I don't want to hurt you. Listen, I do see now. It was one of us. That's right, isn't it. No, don't answer, only tell me if I'm wrong; but I'm not, . . . Of course there are animals on this planet: Ten of them. I don't care who it was. It doesn't matter, does it. It could have been me, just now. I realize that. I didn't understand how it is, Osden. You can't see how difficult it is for us to understand . . . But listen. If it were love, instead of hate and fear. . . . Is it never love?"

"No."

"Why not? Why should it never be? Are human beings all so weak? That is terrible. Never mind, never mind, don't worry. Keep still. At least right now it isn't hate, is it? Sympathy at least, concern, well-wishing. You do feel that, Osden? Is it what you feel?"

"Among . . . others things," he said, almost inaudible,

"Noise from my subconscious, I suppose. And everybody else in the room. . . . Listen, when we found you there in the forest, when I tried to turn you over, you partly wakened, and I felt a horror of you. I was insane with fear for a minute. Was that your fear of me I felt?"

"No."

Her hand was still on his, and he was quite relaxed, sinking towards sleep, like a man in pain who has been given relief from pain. "The forest," he muttered; she could barely understand him. "Afraid."

She pressed him no further, but kept her hand on his and watched him go to sleep. She knew what she felt, and what therefore he must feel. She was confident of it: there is only one emotion, or state of being, that can thus wholly reverse itself, polarize, within one moment. In Great Hainish indeed there is one word, ontá, for love and for hate. She was not in love with Osden, of course, that is another kettle of fish. What she felt for him was ontá, polarized hate. She held his hand and the current flowed between them, the tremendous electricity of touch, which he had always dreaded. As he slept the ring of anatomy-chart muscles around his mouth relaxed, and Tomiko saw on his face what none of them had ever seen, very faint, a smile. It faded. He slept on.

He was tough; next day he was sitting up, and hungry. Harfex wished to interrogate him, but Tomiko put him off. She hung a sheet of polythene over the cubicle door, as Osden himself had often done.

"Does it actually cut down your empathic reception?" she asked, and he replied, in the dry, cautious tone they were now using to each other. "No."

"Just a warning, then."

"Partly. More faith-healing. Dr. Hammergeld thought it worked . . . Maybe it does, a little."

There had been love, once. A terrified child, suffocating in the tidal rush and battering of the huge emotions of adults, a drowning child, saved by one man. Taught to breathe, to live, by one man. Given everything, all protection and love, by one man. Father, mother/God: no other. "Is he still alive?" Tomiko said, thinking of Osden's incredible loneliness, and the savage cruelty of the great doctors. She was shocked when she heard his forced, tinny laugh. "He died at least two and a half centuries ago," Osden said. "Do you forget where we are, Coordinator? We've all left our little families behind . . ."

Outside the polythene curtain the eight other human beings on World 4470 moved vaguely. Their voices were low
and strained. Eskwana slept; Poswet To was in therapy;
Jenny Chong was trying to rig lights in her cubicle so that
she wouldn't cast a shadow.

"They're all scared," Tomiko said, scared. "They've all
got these ideas about what attacked you. A sort of ape-
potato, a giant fanged spinach, I don't know . . . Even Harfex. You may be right not to force them to see. That would
be worse, to lose confidence in one another. But why are we
all so shaky, unable to face the fact, going to pieces so easily? Are we really all insane?"

"We'll soon be more so."

"Why?"

"There *is* something."

He closed his mouth, the muscles of his lips stood out
rigid.

"Something sentient?"

"A sentience."

"In the forest?"

He nodded.

"What is it, then—?"

"The fear." He began to look strained again, and moved
restlessly. "When I fell there, you know, I didn't lose consciousness at once. Or I kept regaining it. I don't know. It
was more like being paralyzed."

"You were."

"I was on the ground. I couldn't get up. My face was in
the dirt, in that soft leafmold. It was in my nostrils and eyes.
I couldn't move. Couldn't see. As if I was in the ground.
Sunk into it, part of it. I knew I was between two trees even
though I never saw them. I suppose I could feel the roots.
Below me in the ground, down under the ground. My hands
were bloody, I could feel that, and the blood made the dirt
around my face sticky. I felt the fear. It kept growing. As if
they'd finally *known* I was there, lying on them there, under
them, among them, the thing they feared, and yet part of
their fear itself. I couldn't stop sending the fear back, and it

kept growing, and I couldn't move, I couldn't get away. I would pass out, I think, and then the fear would bring me to again, and I still couldn't move. Any more than they can."

Tomiko felt the cold stirring of her hair, the readying of the apparatus of terror. "They: who are they, Osden?"

"They, it—I don't know. The fear."

"What is he talking about?" Harfex demanded when Tomiko reported this conversation. She would not let Harfex question Osden yet, feeling that she must protect Osden from the onslaught of the Hainishman's powerful, over-repressed emotions. Unfortunately this fueled the slow-fire of paranoid anxiety that burned in poor Harfex, and he thought she and Osden were in league, hiding some fact of great importance or peril from the rest of the team.

"It's like the blind man trying to describe the elephant. Osden hasn't seen or heard the . . . the sentience, any more than we have."

"But he's felt it, my dear Haito," Harfex said with just-suppressed rage. "Not empathically. On his skull. It came and knocked him down and beat him with a blunt instrument. Did he not catch *one* glimpse of it?"

"What would he have seen, Harfex?" Tomiko asked, but he would not hear her meaningful tone; even he had blocked out that comprehension. What one fears is alien. The murderer is an outsider, a foreigner, not one of us. The evil is not in me!

"The first blow knocked him pretty well out," Tomiko said a little wearily, "he didn't see anything. But when he came to again, alone in the forest, he felt a great fear. Not his own fear, an empathic affect. He is certain of that. And certain it was nothing picked up from any of us. So that evidently the native life-forms are not all insentient."

Harfex looked at her a moment, grim. "You're trying to frighten me, Haito. I do not understand your motives." He got up and went off to his laboratory table, walking slowly and stiffly, like a man of eighty not of forty.

She looked round at the others. She felt some desperation. Her new, fragile, and profound interdependence with Osden gave her, she was well aware, some added strength. But if even Harfex could not keep his head, who of the others would? Porlock and Eskwana were shut in cubicles, the others were all working or busy with something. There was something queer about their positions. For a while the Coordinator could not tell what it was, then she saw that they were all sitting facing the nearby forest. Playing chess with Asnanifoil, Olleroo had edged her chair around until it was almost beside his.

She went to Mannon, who was dissecting a tangle of spidery brown roots, and told him to look for the pattern-puzzle. He saw it at once, and said with unusual brevity, "Keeping an eye on the enemy."

"What enemy? What do *you* feel, Mannon?" She had a sudden hope in him as a psychologist, on this obscure ground of hints and empathies were biologists went astray. "I feel a strong anxiety with a specific spatial orientation. But I am not an empath. Therefore, the anxiety is explicable in terms of the particular stress-situation, that is the attack on a team member in the forest, and also in terms of the total stress-situation, that is my presence in a totally alien environment, fur which the archetypical connotations of the word 'forest' provide an inevitable metaphor."

Hours later Tomiko woke to hear Osden screaming in nightmare; Mannon was calming him, and she sank back into her own dark-branching pathless dreams. In the morning Eskwana did not wake. He could not be roused with stimulant drugs. He clung to his sleep, slipping farther and farther back, mumbling softly now and then until, wholly regressed, he lay curled on his side, thumb at his lips, gone. "Two days: two down. Ten little Indians, nine little Indians . . ." That was Porlock.

"And you're the next little Indian," Jenny Chong snapped. "Go analyze your urine, Porlock!"

"He is driving us all insane," Porlock said, getting up and waving his left arm. "Can't you feel it? For God's sake, are you all deaf and blind? Can't you feel what he's doing, the emanations? It all comes from him—from his room there—

from his mind. He is driving us all insane with fear!"

"Who is?" said Asnanifoil, looming black, precipitous and hairy over the little Terran.

"Do I have to say his name? Osden, then. Osden! Osden! Why do you think I tried to kill him? In self-defense! To save all of us! Because you won't see what he's doing to us. He's sabotaged the mission by making us quarrel, and now he's going to drive us all insane by projecting fear at us so that we can't sleep or think, like a huge radio that doesn't make any sound, but it broadcasts all the time, and you can't sleep, and you can't think. Haito and Harfex are already under his control but the rest of you can be saved. I had to do it!"

"You didn't do it very well," Osden said, standing half-naked, all rib and bandage, at the door of his cubicle. "I could have hit myself harder. Hell, it isn't me that's scaring you blind, Porlock, it's out there—there, in the woods!"

Porlock made an ineffectual attempt to assault Osden; Asnanifoil held him back, and continued to hold him effortlessly while Mannon gave him a sedative shot. He was put away shouting about giant radios. In a minute the sedative took effect, and he joined a peaceful silence to Eskwana's.

"All right," said Harfex. "Now, by my Gods, you'll tell us what you know and all you know."

Osden said, "I don't know anything." He looked battered and faint. Tomiko made him sit down before he talked.

"After I'd been three days in the forest, I thought I was occasionally receiving some kind of faint affect."

"Why didn't you report it?"

"Thought I was going spla, like the rest of you."

"That, equally, should have been reported."

"You'd have called me back to base. I couldn't take it. You realize that my inclusion in the mission was a bad mistake. I'm not able to coexist with nine other neurotic personalities at close quarters. I was wrong to volunteer for Extreme Survey, and the Authority was wrong to accept me."

No one spoke; but Tomiko saw, with certainty this time, the flinch in Osden's shoulders and the tightening of his facial muscles, as he registered their bitter agreement.

"Anyhow, I didn't want to come back to base, because I was curious. Even going psycho, how could I pick up empathic affects when there was no creature to emit them? They weren't bad, then. Very vague. Queer. Like a draft in a closed room, a flicker in the corner of your eye. Nothing really."

For a moment he had been borne up on their listening: they heard, so he spoke. He was wholly at their mercy. If they disliked him, he had to be hateful: if they mocked him he became grotesque; if they listened to him he was the storyteller. He was helplessly obedient to the demands of their emotions, reactions, moods. And there were seven of them, too many to cope with, so that he must be constantly knocked about from one to another's whim. He could not find coherence. Even as he spoke and held them, somebody's attention would wander: Olleroo perhaps was thinking that he wasn't unattractive; Harfex was seeking the ulterior motive of his words; Asnanifoil's mind, which could not be long held by the concrete, was roaming off towards the eternal peace of number; and Tomiko was distracted by pity, by fear. Osden's voice faltered. He lost the thread. "I ... I thought it must be the trees," he said, and stopped.

"It's not the trees," Harfex said. "They have no more nervous system than do plants of the Hainish Descent on Earth. None."

"You're not seeing the forest for the trees, as they say on Earth," Mannon put in, smiling elfinly; Harfex stared at him. "What about those root-nodes we've been puzzling about for twenty days—eh?"

"What about them?"

"They are, indubitably, connections. Connections among the trees. Right? Now let's just suppose, most improbably, that you knew nothing of animal brain-structure. And you were given one axon, or one detached glial cell, to examine. Would you be likely to discover what it was? Would you see that the cell was capable of sentience?"

"No. Because it isn't. A single cell is capable of mechanical response to stimulus. No more. Are you hypothesizing that individual arboriformes are 'cells' in a kind of brain, Mannon?"

"Not exactly. I'm merely pointing out that they are all interconnected, both by the root-node linkage and by your green epiphytes in the branches. A linkage of incredible complexity and physical extent. Why, even the prairie grass-forms have those root-connectors, don't they? I know that sentience or intelligence isn't a thing, you can't find it in, or analyze it out from, the cells of a brain. It's a function of the connected cells. It is, in a sense, the connection: the connectedness. It doesn't exist. I'm not trying to say it exists. I'm only guessing that Osden might be able to describe it."

And Osden took him up, speaking as if in trance. "Sentience without senses. Blind, deaf, nerveless, moveless. Some irritability, response to touch. Response to sun, to light, to water, and chemicals in the earth around the roots. Nothing comprehensible to an animal mind. Presence without mind. Awareness of being, without object or subject. Nirvana."

"Then why do you receive fear?" Tomiko asked in a low voice.

"I don't know. I can't see how awareness of objects, of others, could arise: an unperceiving response . . . But there was an uneasiness, for days. And then when I lay between the two trees and my blood was on their roots—" Osden's face glittered with sweat. "It became fear." he said shrilly, "only fear."

"If such a function existed," Harfex said, "it would not be capable of conceiving of a self-moving, material entity, or responding to one. It could no more become aware of us than we can 'become aware' of Infinity."

"The silence of those infinite expanses terrifies me," muttered Tomiko. "Pascal was aware of Infinity. By way of fear."

"To a forest," Mannon said, "we might appear as forest fires. Hurricanes. Dangers. What moves quickly is dangerous, to a plant. The rootless would be alien, terrible. And if it is mind, it seems only too probable that it might become aware of Osden, whose own mind is open to connection with all others so long as he's conscious, and who was lying in pain and afraid within it, actually inside it. No wonder it was afraid—"

"Not 'it,' " Harfex said. "There is no being, no huge creature, no person! There could at most be only a function—"

"There is only a fear," Osden said.

They were all still a while, and heard the stillness outside.

"Is that what I feel all the time coming up behind me?" Jenny Chong asked, subdued.

Osden nodded. "You all feel it, deaf as you arc. Eskwana's the worst off, because he actually has some empathic capacity. He could send if he learned how, but he's too weak, never will be anything but a medium."

"Listen, Osden," Tomiko said, "you can send. Then send to it—the forest, the fear out there—tell that we won't hurt it. Since it has, or is, some sort of affect that translates into what we feel as emotion, can't you translate back? Send out a message. We are harmless, we are friendly."

"You must know that nobody can emit a false empathic message, Haito. You can't send something that doesn't exist."

"But we don't intend harm, we are friendly."

"Are we? In the forest, when you picked me up, did you feel friendly?"

"No. Terrified. But that's—it, the forest, the plants, not my own fear, isn't it?"

"What's the difference? It's all you felt. Can't you see," and Osden's voice rose in exasperation, "why I dislike you and you dislike me, all of you? Can't you see that I retransmit every negative or aggressive affect you've felt towards me since we first met? I return your hostility, with thanks. I do it in self-defense. Like Porlock. It is self-defense, though, it's the only technique I developed to replace my original defense of total withdrawal from others. Unfortunately it creates a closed circuit, self-sustaining and self-reinforcing. Your initial reaction to me was the instinctive antipathy to a cripple; by now of course it's hatred. Can you fail to see my point? The forest-mind out there transmits only terror, now, and the only message I can send it is terror, because when exposed to it I can feel nothing except terror!"

"What must we do, then?" said Tomiko, and Mannon replied promptly, "Move camp. To another continent. If there are plant-minds there, they'll be slow to notice us, as this one was; maybe they won't notice us at all."

"It would be a considerable relief," Osden observed stiffly. The others had been watching him with a new curiosity. He had revealed himself, they had seen him as he was, a helpless man in a trap. Perhaps, like Tomiko, they had seen that the trap itself, his crass and cruel egotism, was their own construction, not his. They had built the cage and locked him in it, and like a caged ape he threw filth out through the bars. If, meeting him, they had offered trust, if they had been strong enough to offer him love, how might he have appeared to them?

None of them could have done so, and it was too late now. Given time, given solitude, Tomiko might have built up with him a slow resonance of feeling, a consonance of trust, a harmony: but there was no time, their job must be done. There was not room enough for the cultivation of so great a thing, and they must make do with sympathy, with pity, the small change of love. Even that much had given her strength, but it was nowhere near enough for him. She could see in his flayed face now his savage resentment of their curiosity, even of her pity.

"Go lie down, that gash is bleeding again," she said, and he obeyed her.

Next morning they packed up, melted down the spray-form hangar and living quarters, lifted *Gum* on mechanical drive and took her halfway round World 4470, over the red and green lands, the many warm-green seas. They had picked out a likely spot on Continent G: a prairie, thousand square kilos of windswept graminiformes. No forest was within a hundred kilos of the site, and there were no lone trees or groves on the plain. The plant-forms occurred only in large species-colonies, never intermingled, except for certain tiny ubiquitous saprophytes and spore-bearers. The team sprayed holomeld over structure forms, and by evening of the thirty-two-hour day were settled in to the new camp. Eskwana was still asleep and Porlock still sedated, but everyone else was cheerful. "You can breathe here!" they kept saying.

Osden got on his feet and went shakily lo the doorway; leaning there he looked through twilight over the dim reaches of the swaying grass that was not grass. There was a faint, sweet odor of pollen on the wind; no sound but the soft, vast sibilance of wind. His bandaged head cocked a little, the empath stood motionless for a long time. Darkness came, and the stars, lights in the windows of the distant house of Man. The wind had ceased, there was no sound. He listened.

In the long night Haito Tomiko listened. She lay still and heard the blood in her arteries, the breathing of sleepers, the wind blowing, the dark veins running, the dreams advancing, the vast static of stars increasing as the universe died slowly, the sound of death walking. She struggled out of her bed, fled the tiny solitude of her cubicle. Eskwana alone slept. Porlock lay straitjacketed, raving softly in his obscure native tongue. Olleroo and Jenny Chong were playing cards, grim-faced. Poswet To was in the therapy niche, plugged in. Asnanifoil was drawing a mandala, the Third Pattern of the Primes. Mannon and Harfex were sitting up with Osden.

She changed the bandages on Osden's head. His lank, reddish hair, where she had not had to shave it, looked strange. It was salted with white, now. Her hands shook as she worked. Nobody had yet said anything.

"How can the fear be here too?" she said, and her voice rang flat and false in the terrific silence of the vegetable night.

"It's not just the trees; the grasses too . . ."

"But we're twelve thousand kilos from where we were this morning, we left it on the other side of the planet."

"It's all one," Osden said. "One big green thought. How

long does it take a thought to get from one side of your brain to the other?"

"It doesn't think. It isn't thinking," Harfex said, lifelessly. "It's merely a network of processes. The branches, the epiphytic growths, the roots with those nodal junctures between individuals: they must all be capable of transmitting electrochemical impulses. There are no individual plants, then, properly speaking. Even the pollen is part of the linkage, no doubt, a sort of windborne sentience, connecting overseas. But it is not conceivable. That all the biosphere of a planet should be one network of communications, sensitive, irrational, immortal, isolated . . ."

"Isolated," said Osden. "That's it! That's the fear. It isn't that we're motile, or destructive. It's just that we are. We are other. There has never been any other."

"You're right," Mannon said, almost whispering. "It has no peers. No enemies. No relationship with anything but itself. One alone forever."

"Then what's its function in species-survival?"

"None, maybe," Osden said. "Why are you getting teleological, Harfex? Aren't you a Hainishman? Isn't the measure of complexity the measure of the eternal joy?"

Harfex did not take the bait. He looked ill. "We should leave this world," he said.

"Now you know why I always want to get out, get away from you," Osden said with a kind of morbid geniality. "It isn't pleasant, is it—the other's fear? . . . If only it were an animal intelligence. I can get through to animals. I get along with cobras and tigers; superior intelligence gives one the advantage. I should have been used in a zoo, not on a human team . . . If I could get through to the damned stupid potato! If it wasn't overwhelming . . . I still pick up more than the fear, you know. And before it panicked it had a—there was a serenity. I couldn't take it in, then, I didn't realize how big it was. To know the whole daylight, after all, and the whole night. All the winds and the lulls together. The winter stars and the summer stars at the same time. To have roots, and no enemies. To be entire. Do you see? No invasion. No others.

To be whole . . ."

He had never spoken before, Tomiko thought.

"You are defenseless against it, Osden," she said. "Your personality has changed already. You're vulnerable to it. We may not all go mad, but you will, if we don't leave."

He hesitated, then he looked up at Tomiko, the first time he had ever met her eyes, a long, still look, clear as water.

"What's sanity ever done for me?" he said, mocking. "But you have a point, Haito. You have something there."

"We should get away," Harfex muttered.

"If I gave in to it," Osden mused, "could I communicate?"

"By 'give in,' " Mannon said in a rapid, nervous voice, "I assume that you mean, stop sending back the empathic information which you receive from the plant-entity: stop rejecting the fear, and absorb it. That will either kill you at once, or drive you back into total psychological withdrawal, autism."

"Why?" said Osden. "Its message is *rejection*. But my salvation is rejection. It's not intelligent. But I am."

"The scale is wrong. What can a single human brain achieve against something so vast?"

"A single human brain can perceive pattern on the scale of stars and galaxies," Tomiko said, "and interpret it as Love."

Mannon looked from one to the other of them; Harfex was silent.

"It'd be easier in the forest," Osden said. "Which of you will fly me over?"

"When?"

"Now. Before you all crack up or go violent."

"I will," Tomiko said.

"None of us will," Harfex said.

"I can't," Mannon said. "I . . . I'm too frightened. I'd crash the jet."

"Bring Eskwana along. If I can pull this off, he might serve as a medium."

"Are you accepting the Sensor's plan, Coordinator?" Harfex asked formally.

"Yes."

"I disapprove. I will come with you, however."

"I think we're compelled, Harfex," Tomiko said, looking at Osden's face, the ugly white mask transfigured, eager as a lover's face.

Olleroo and Jenny Chong, playing cards to keep their thoughts from their haunted beds, their mounting dread, chattered like scared children. "This thing, it's in the forest, it'll get you—"

"Scared of the dark?" Osden jeered. "But look at Eskwana, and Porlock, and even Asnanifoil—"

"It can't hurt you. It's an impulse passing through synapses, a wind passing through branches. It is only a nightmare."

They took off in a helijet, Eskwana curled up still sound asleep in the rear compartment, Tomiko piloting, Harfex and Osden silent, watching ahead for the dark line of forest across the vague gray miles of starlit plain.

They neared the black line, crossed it; now under them was darkness.

She sought a landing place, flying low, though she had to fight her frantic wish to fly high, to get out, get away. The huge vitality of the plant-world was far stronger here in the forest, and its panic beat in immense dark waves. There was a pale patch ahead, a bare knoll-top a little higher than the tallest of the black shapes around it; the not-trees; the rooted; the parts of the whole. She set the helijet down in the glade, a bad landing. Her hands on the stick were slippery as if she had rubbed them with cold soap. About them now stood the forest, black in darkness. Tomiko cowered down and shut her eyes. Eskwana moaned in his sleep. Harfex's breath came short and loud, and he sat rigid, even when Osden reached across him and slid the door open.

Osden stood up; his back and bandaged head were just visible in the dim glow of the control-panel as he paused stooping in the doorway.

Tomiko was shaking. She could not raise her head. "No, no, no, no, no, no, no," she said in a whisper. "No. No. No."

Osden moved suddenly and quietly, swinging out of the

doorway, down into the dark. He was gone. I am coming! said a great voice that made no sound. Tomiko screamed. Harfex coughed; he seemed to be trying to stand up, but did not do so.

Tomiko drew in upon herself, all centered in the blind eye in her belly, in the center of her being; and outside that there was nothing but the fear. It ceased.

She raised her head; slowly unclenched her hands. She sat up straight. The night was dark, and stars shone over the forest. There was nothing else.

"Osden," she said, but her voice would not come. She spoke again, louder, a lone bullfrog croak. There was no reply.

She began to realize that something had gone wrong with Harfex. She was trying to find his head in the darkness, for he had slipped down from the seat, when all at once, in the dead quiet, in the dark rear compartment of the craft, a voice spoke. "Good," it said.

It was Eskwana's voice. She snapped on the interior lights and saw the engineer lying curled up asleep, his hand half over his mouth.

The mouth opened and spoke. "All well," it said. "Osden—"

"All well," said the soft voice from Eskwana's mouth. "Where are you?" Silence. "Come back."

Wind was rising. "I'll stay here," the soft voice said.

"You can't stay—"

Silence.

"You'd be alone, Osden!"

"Listen." The voice was fainter, slurred, as if lost in the sound of wind. "Listen. I will tell you well."

She called his name after that, but there was no answer. Eskwana lay still. Harfex lay stiller.

"Osden!" she cried, leaning out the doorway into the dark, wind-shaken silence of the forest of being. "I will come back. I must get Harfex to the base. I will come back, Osden!"

Silence and wind in leaves.

They finished the prescribed survey of World 4470, the eight of them; it took them forty-one days more. Asnanifoil and one or another of the women went into the forest daily at first, searching for Osden in the region around the bare knoll; though Tomiko was not in her heart sure which bare knoll they had landed on that night in the very heart and vortex of terror. They left piles of supplies for Osden, food enough for fifty years, clothing, tents, tools. They did not go on searching; there was no way to find a man alone, hiding, if he wanted to hide, in those unending labyrinths and dim corridors vine-entangled, root-floored. They might have passed within arm's reach of him and never seen him.

But he was there; for there was no fear anymore.

Rational, and valuing reason more highly after an intolerable experience of the immortal mindless, Tomiko tried to understand rationally what Osden had done. But the words escaped her control. He had taken the fear into himself, and accepting had transcended it. He had given up his self to the alien, an unreserved surrender, that left no place for evil. He had learned the love of the Other, and thereby had been given his whole self. But this is not the vocabulary of reason.

The people of the Survey team walked under the trees, through the vast colonies of life, surrounded by a dreaming silence, a brooding calm that was half-aware of them and wholly indifferent to them. There were no hours. Distance was no matter. Had we but world enough and time . . . The planet turned between the sunlight and the great dark; winds of winter and summer blew fine, pale pollen across the quiet seas.

Gum returned after many surveys, years, and light-years, to what had several centuries ago been Smeming Port of Pesm. There were still men there to receive (incredulously) the team's reports and to record its losses: Biologist Harfex, dead of fear, and Sensor Osden, left as a colonist.

1972

IN THE INTRODUCTION to *Turning Points,* a volume of essays on the art of science fiction, Damon Knight makes the following laudable statement: ". . . it has always seemed to me that an anthologist who immortalizes his own work is hard to distinguish from a contest judge who awards himself a prize."

This principle—really a special instance of the legal and political concept of "conflict of interest"—has a vital relevance to *What If: Stories that Should have Won the Hugo,* and particularly to the stories of 1972. I will return to this theme in a few paragraphs, but first let's take our customary look at the Hugo- and Nebula-winning novel of the year, and at some of the others novels published in 1972.

Robert Silverberg performed a rare feat—in fact, as far as I have been able to find, a unique one—by placing *two* novels on both the Nebula and Hugo final ballots. These were *Dying Inside* (nominated on the basis of its *Galaxy* serialization) and *The Book of Skulls* (published in hardcover by Scribner's and in paper by Signet Books).

Both were intensely psychological books, both of them only marginally science fiction. One concerned a man with a limited telepathic talent which he used to eke out a bare living as a ghostwriter of academic papers. The other dealt with the quest of a group of young men for a hidden monastery in the Southwest and their initiation into the religious order and its supposed secrets.

The two books were among Silverberg's most accomplished; both of them dark, brooding, powerful works. Either of them would have been a *very* strong contender, possibly the winner. But through the unfortunate coincidence of publication dates, they became eligible simultaneously for the awards. Silverberg in effect became his own most potent rival and kept himself away from the prizes. It was, in a sense, the very opposite of the odd case in which a novel had once won a Hugo for best short story.[3]

In addition to Silverberg's unfortunately timed pair of excellent novels, there were several other very strong contenders. John Brunner's *The Sheep Look Up* (Harper & Row) was the ultimate novel of doom-through-environmental-contamination. *The Sheep Look Up* was Brunner's third huge novel, following *Stand on Zanzibar* and *The Jagged Orbit.* The major obstacle to its popularity (although it did make the Nebula ballot) was its overwhelming pessimism.

Norman Spinrad drew much attention for his book *The Iron Dream* (Avon), which also appeared on the Nebula ballot. This must be one of the strangest volumes ever published. It is laid in a parallel universe, in which the young Adolf Hitler emigrated to the United States and became a pulp science fiction writer. *The Iron Dream* contains a biography of the author—I should say, "the author"—a list of his works and even a pseudo-scholarly exegesis by an imaginary professor of literature. But the bulk of the volume is devoted to "reprinting" the entire text of Hitler's novel *Lord of the Swastika,* Hugo-award winning best science fiction novel of 1954.[4]

Also published in 1972 was Barry Malzberg's *Beyond Apollo,* which received the first John Campbell Memorial Award, presented by a self-sustaining committee of authors and academics, rather after the fashion of the long-defunct International Fantasy Award. And in a lighter vein, there was David Gerrold's novel of a self-aware computer, *When Harlie Was One.*

But it was Isaac Asimov's novel *The Gods Themselves*

---

[3] See *What If: Stories that Should have Won the Hugo,* Volume I, entry for works published in 1961.

[4] A delicious irony. See *What If: Stories that Should have Won the Hugo,* Volume I, for details.

that won both the Hugo and the Nebula. This was the popular Asimov's first novel since 1957 (discounting one screenplay novelization and a juvenile novel written under a pseudonym). Asimov had received two "special" Hugos in earlier years but had never actually won a Hugo or Nebula award in regular competition, in a regularly scheduled category.

If the later Grand Master award of SFWA had existed in 1972, I suspect that Asimov might have received it, for his lifetime contribution to science fiction has been an unquestionably outstanding one, while *The Gods Themselves* was a rather uneven novel, to say the least.

But then, here I am second-guessing history again. I'd better move on to the shorter lengths.

Two events of 1967 generated sequels that came together in 1972. One of these events was the publication of Harlan Ellison's huge—and hugely influential—anthology, *Dangerous Visions*. Aside from offering stories of excellent quality, *Dangerous Visions* had offered a home to many stories whose authors considered them too controversial or too experimental for publication in other existing markets. The book was a great success, and Ellison began work on a second volume.

Also in 1967, the old Lancer Books published my own first novel, *One Million Centuries*. This was a rather conservative book both in theme and in literary technique. With it in print, I started work on a second novel, one dealing with somewhat more controversial themes than had the first, and one executed in a variety of experimental techniques. Although this latter novel did eventually find its way into print as *Space War Blues* (Dell, 1978), no publisher was willing to take a chance on it in the 1960s.

You see where I'm heading, of course. Yes, Ellison *did* opt to publish the story, squeezed down to novella length. It appeared in *Again, Dangerous Visions* in 1972 as "With the Bentfin Boomer Boys on Little Old Alabama." And it made the Nebula ballot (although not the Hugo ballot). And now you see why I opened this section with that quotation from Damon Knight. I am tempted. I am sorely tempted. How often, I ask you, does the loser of an election get to invalidate the voting and declare himself the winner? But, assisted by the adamant refusal of my editor at Pocket Books, I will resist.

The novella category was unusually rich in 1972. The award nominees included Phyllis Gottlieb's "Son of the Morning," Frederik Pohl's "The Gold at the Starbow's End," Gene Wolfe's "The Fifth Head of Cerberus," Jerry Pournelle's "The Mercenery" and Joe Haldeman's "Hero."

But the winners were none of these. "The Word for World is Forest," by Ursula Le Guin, won the Hugo, and Arthur C. Clarke's "A Meeting with Medusa" won the Nebula.

To be quite honest, I was disgruntled about the Clarke story. Not about "A Meeting with Medusa" itself. It was a brilliant story, one of the most convincing—and most gripping—hard science stories in modern times. But it actually was published in late October or early November of 1971! It was in *Playboy,* the issue dated December 1971, and here it won the Nebula for best novella of 1972!

There was no hanky-panky involved. SFWA had discovered a nice source of income in annual volumes of Nebula award stories and, in order to facilitate the prompt completion and publication of these annuals, had adopted a "Nebula year" running from December 11 to November 30. Shades of the old "Hugo year" controversy! As for dated magazines, the cover date rather than the actual date of publication was to be considered "official." So—whether it really made sense or not—Clarke's story that millions of people read in November 1971, in *Playboy* dated December 1971, was eligible for the 1972 Nebula.

The novelette and short-story awards—at last the Hugo's and Nebula's were back together on the question of categories—seem to have produced fewer really powerful contenders, although there were enough to give respectable winners. Poul Anderson's original "Goat Song" won both awards in the novelette length. In the short-story category, Joanna Russ won the Nebula for her controversial and bitter "When It Changed." The Hugo voting produced a tie between

"Eurema's Dam" by R.A. Lafferty and "The Meeting" by Frederik Pohl and Cyril M. Kornbluth.

Wait a minute! Pohl and Kornbluth? Pohl, sure. But Cyril Kornbluth died in March of 1958. Had this story been in inventory at *F&SF* for over fourteen years?

No, as it turned out. "The Meeting" was a "posthumous collaboration," one of a number of such in which Pohl completed stories from notes or fragments left behind at Kornbluth's death. There have been a lot of these posthumous collaborations in the field of science fiction and fantasy. Some of them, most notably those involving H.P. Lovecraft and August Derleth, would more honestly be labeled pastiches, i.e. stories written after the manner of, and dealing with themes favored by, deceased authors . . . but written, of course, by authors not deceased.

In the case of the Pohl-Kornbluth posthumous collaborations, however, I think there is a far stronger case for legitimacy. The two men had collaborated on several novels and a number of shorter works while both lived. And the posthumous collaborations were the product of stories actually conceived and in some cases partially written during the days of the living collaboration. "The Meeting" was legit.

But I think the voters missed a bet when they passed over "Painwise," by James Tiptree, Jr. Despite its name—and despite its theme, which is, at least in part, pain—the story is *not* an especially cruel or painful one. In its own oddly inverted way it is a story of courage, persistence and ultimate triumph . . . of a sort. And like all of the stories in *What If,* it is a story memorable after a single reading, and rich enough to continue to reward many readings.

Painwise

JAMES TIPTREE, JR.

HE WAS WISE to the ways of pain. He had to be, for he felt none.

When the Xenons put electrodes to his testicles, he was vastly entertained by the pretty lights.

When the Ylls fed firewasps into his nostrils and other body orifices, the resultant rainbows pleased him. And when later they regressed to simple disjointments and eviscerations, he noted with interest the deepening orchid hues that stood for irreversible harm.

"This time?" he asked the boditech when his scouter had torn him from the Ylls.

"No," said the boditech.

"When?"

There was no answer.

"You're a girl in there, aren't you? A human girl?"

"Well, yes and no," said the boditech. "Sleep now." He had no choice.

Next planet a deadfall smashed him into a splintered gutbag, and he hung for three gangrenous dark-purple days before the scouter dug him out.

" 'Is 'ime?" he mouthed to the boditech.

"No."

"Eh!" But he was in no shape to argue. They had thought of everything. Several planets later the gentle Znaffi stuffed him in a floss cocoon and interrogated him under hallogas. How, whence, why had he come? But the faithful guardian in his medulla kept him stimulated with a random mix of *Atlas Shrugged* and Varese's *Ionisation,* and when the Znaffi

unstuffed him, they were more hallucinated than he.

The boditech treated him for constipation and refused to answer his plea. *"When?"*

So he went on, system after system, through spaces un-companioned by time, which had become scrambled and fi-nally absent. What served him instead was the count of suns in his scouter's sights, of stretches of cold blind no-when that ended in a new now, pacing a giant fireball while the scouter scanned the lights that were its planets. Of whirldowns to orbit over clouds-seas-deserts-craters-icecaps-duststorms-cities-ruins-enigmas beyond counting. Of terrible births when the scouter panel winked green and he was catapulted down, down, a living litmus hurled and grabbed, unpodded finally into an alien air, an earth that was not Earth. And alien natives, simple or mechanized or lunatic or unknow-able, but never more than vaguely human and never faring beyond their own home suns. And his departures, routine or melodramatic, to culminate in the composing of his "re-ports," in fact only a few words tagged to the matrix of scan data automatically fired off in one compressed blip in the direction the scouter called Base Zero. Home.

Always at that moment he stared hopefully at the screens, imagining yellow suns. Twice he found what might be Crux in the stars, and once the Bears.

"Boditech, I suffer!" He had no idea what the word meant, but he had found it made the thing reply.

"Symptoms?"

"Derangement of temporality. When am I? It is not possi-ble for a man to exist crossways in time. Alone."

"You have been altered from simple manhood."

"I suffer, listen to me! Sol's light back there—what's there now? Have the glaciers melted? Is Chichen Itza built? Will we go home to meet Hannibal? Boditech! Are these re-ports going to Neanderthal man?"

Too late he felt the hypo. When he woke, Sol was gone and the cabin swam with euphories.

"Woman," he mumbled.

"That has been provided for."

This time it was oriental, with orris and hot rice wine on its lips and a piquancy of little floggings in the steam. He oozed into a squashy sunburst and lay panting while the cabin cleared.

"That's all you, isn't it?"

No reply.

"What, did they program you with the Kama Sutra?"

Silence.

"WHICH ONE IS YOU?"

The scanner chimed. A new sun was in the points.

Sometime after that he took to chewing on his arms and then to breaking his fingers. The boditech became severe.

"These symptoms are self-generated. They must stop."

"I want you to talk to me."

"The scouter is provided with an entertainment console. I am not."

"I will tear out my eyeballs."

"They will be replaced."

"If you don't talk to me, I'll tear them out until you have no more replacements."

It hesitated. He sensed it was becoming involved.

"On what subject do you wish me to talk?"

"What is pain?"

"Pain is nociception. It is mediated by C-fibers, modeled as a gated or summation phenomenon and often associated with tissue damage."

"What is nociception?"

"The sensation of pain."

"But what does it *feel* like? I can't recall. They've reconnected everything, haven't they? All I get is colored lights. What have they tied my pain nerves to? What hurts me?"

"I do not have that information."

"Boditech, I want to feel pain!"

But he had been careless again. This time it was Amerind, strange cries and gruntings and the reek of buffalo hide. He squirmed in the grip of strong copper loins and excited through limp auroras.

"You know it's no good, don't you?" he gasped.

The oscilloscope eye looped.

"My programs are in order. Your response is complete."

"My response is not complete. I want to TOUCH YOU!"

The thing buzzed and suddenly ejected him to wakefulness. They were in orbit. He shuddered at the blurred world streaming by below, hoping that this would not require his exposure. Then the board went green and he found himself hurtling toward new birth.

"Sometime I will not return," he told himself. "I will stay. Maybe here."

But the planet was full of bustling apes, and when they arrested him for staring, he passively allowed the scouter to pull him out.

"Will they ever bring me home, boditech?"

No reply.

He pushed his thumb and forefinger between his lids and twisted until the eyeball hung wetly on his cheek.

When he woke up he had a new eye.

He reached for it, found his arm in soft restraint. So was the rest of him.

"I suffer!" he yelled. "I will go mad this way!"

"I am programmed to maintain you on involuntary function," the boditech told him. He thought he detected an unclarity in its voice. He bargained his way to freedom and was careful until the next planet landing.

Once out of the pod he paid no attention to the natives who watched him systematically dismember himself. As he dissected his left kneecap, the scouter sucked him in.

He awoke whole. And in restraint again.

Peculiar energies filled the cabin, oscilloscopes convulsed. Boditech seemed to have joined circuits with the scouter's panel.

"Having a conference?"

His answer came in gales of glee-gas, storms of symphony. And amid the music, kaleidesthesia. He was driving a stagecoach, wiped in salt combers, tossed through volcanoes with peppermint flames, crackling, flying, crumbling, burrowing, freezing, exploding, tickled through lime-colored minutes, sweating to tolling voices, clenched, scrambled, detonated into multisensory orgasms . . . poured on the lap of vacancy.

When he realized his arm was free, he drove his thumb in his eye. The smother closed down.

He woke up swaddled, the eye intact.

"I will go mad!"

The euphorics imploded.

He came to in the pod, about to be everted on a new world.

He staggered out upon a fungus lawn and quickly discovered that his skin was protected everywhere by a hard flexible film. By the time he had found a rock splinter to drive into his ear, the scouter was on him.

The ship needed him, he saw. He was part of its program.

The struggle formalized.

On the next planet he found his head englobed, but this did not prevent him from smashing bones through his unbroken skin.

After that the ship equipped him with an exoskeleton. He refused to walk.

Articulated motors were installed to move his limbs.

Despite himself, a kind of zest grew. Two planets later he found industries and threw himself into a punch press with smashing success. But on the next landing he tried to repeat it with a cliff, and bounced on invisible force-lines. These precautions frustrated him for a time, until he managed by great cunning again to rip out an entire eye. The new eye was not perfect.

"You're running out of eyes, boditech!" he exulted.

"Vision is not essential."

This sobered him. Unbearable to be blind. How much of him was essential to the ship? Not walking. Not handling. Not hearing. Not breathing, the analyzers could do it. Not even sanity. *What?*

"Why do you need a man, boditech?"

"I do not have that information."

"It doesn't make sense. What can I observe that the scanners can't?"

"Then you must talk with me, boditech. If you talk with me, I won't try to injure myself. For a while, anyway."

"I am not programmed to converse."

"But it's necessary. It's the treatment for my symptoms. You must try."

"It is time to watch the scanners."

"You said it!" he cried. "You didn't just eject me. Boditech, you're learning. I will call you Amanda."

On the next planet he behaved well and came away unscathed. He pointed out to Amanda that her talking treatment was effective.

"Do you know what Amanda means?"

"I do not have those data."

"It means *beloved*. You're my girl."

The oscilloscope faltered.

"Now I want to talk about returning home. When will this mission be over? How many more suns?"

"I do not have—"

"Amanda, you've tapped the scouter's banks. You know when the recall signal is due. When is it, Amanda? When?"

"Yes . . . when the course of human events—"

"When, Amanda? How long more?"

"Oh, the years are many, the years are long, but the little toy friends are true—"

"Amanda, *You're telling me the signal is overdue.*"

A sine-curve scream and he was rolling in lips. But it was a feeble raving, sadness in the mechanical crescendos. When the mouths faded, he crawled over and laid his hand on the console beside her green eyes.

"They have forgotten us, Amanda. Something has broken down."

Her pulse line skittered.

"I am not programmed—"

"No. You're not programmed for this. But I am. I will make your new program, Amanda. We will turn the scouter back, we will find Earth. Together. We will go home."

"We," the voice said faintly. "We—?"

"They will make me back into a man, you into a woman."
Her voder made a buzzing sob and suddenly shrieked.
"Look out!"
Consciousness blew up,

He came to staring at a brilliant red eye on the scouter's emergency panel. This was new.

"Amanda!" Silence.

"Boditech, I suffer!"

No reply.

Then he saw that her eye was dark. He peered in. Only a dim green line flickered, entrained to the pulse of the scouter's fiery eye. He pounded the scouter's panel.

"You've taken over Amanda! You've enslaved her! Let her go!"

From the voder rolled the opening bars of Beethoven's Fifth.

"Scouter, our mission has terminated. We are overdue to return. Compute us back to Base Zero."

The Fifth rolled on, rather vapidly played. It became colder in the cabin. They were braking into a star system. The slave arms of boditech grabbed him, threw him into the pod. But he was not required here, and presently he was let out again to pound and rave alone. The cabin grew colder yet, and dark. When presently he was set down on a new sun's planet, he was too dispirited to fight. Afterwards his "report" was a howl for help through chattering teeth, until he saw that the pickup was dead. The entertainment console was dead too, except for the scouter's hog music. He spent hours peering into Amanda's blind eye, shivering in what had been her arms. Once he caught a ghostly whimper:

"Mommy. Let me out."

"Amanda?"

The red master scope flared. Silence. He lay curled on the cold deck, wondering how he could die. If he failed, over how many million planets would the mad scouter parade his breathing corpse? They were nowhere in particular when it happened. One minute the screen showed Doppler star-harsh; the next they were clamped in a total white-out, inertia all skewed, screens dead.

A voice spoke in his head, mellow and vast, *"Long have we watched you, little one."*

"Who's there?" he quavered, "Who are you?"

"Your concepts are inadequate."

"Malfunction! Malfunction!" squalled the scouter.

"Shut up, it's not a malfunction. Who's talking to me?"

"You may call us: Rulers of the Galaxy." The scouter was lunging wildly, buffeting him as it tried to escape the white grasp. Strange crunches, firings of unknown weapons. Still the white stasis held, "What do you want?" he cried.

"Want?" said the voice dreamily. *"We are wise beyond knowing. Powerful beyond your dreams. Perhaps you can get us some fresh fruit."*

"Emergency directive! Alien spacer attack!" yowled the scout. Telltales were flaring all over the board, "Wait!" he shouted. "They aren't—"

"SELF-DESTRUCT ENERGIZE!" roared the voder.

"No! No!"

An ophicleide blared, "Help! Amanda, save me!"

He flung his arms around her console. There was a child's wail and everything strobed.

Silence.

Warmth, light. His hands and knees were on wrinkled stuff. Not dead? He looked down under his belly. All right, but no hair. His head felt bare, too. Cautiously he raised it, saw that he was crouching naked in a convoluted cave or shell. It did not feel threatening.

He sat up. His hands were wet. Where were the Rulers of the Galaxy? "Amanda?"

No reply. Stringy globs dripped down his fingers, like egg muscle. He saw that they were Amanda's neurons, ripped from her metal matrix by whatever force had brought him here. Numbly he wiped her off against a spongy ridge. Amanda, cold lover of his long nightmare. But where in space was he?

"Where am I?" echoed a boy's soprano. He whirled. A golden creature was nestled on the ridge behind him, gazing at him in the warmest way. It looked a little like a bushbaby and lissome as a child in furs. It looked like nothing he had ever seen before and like everything a lonely man might long to warm his hands on. And terribly vulnerable.

"Hello, Bushbaby!" the golden thing exclaimed. "No, wait, that's what *you* say." It laughed excitedly, hugging a loop of its thick dark tail. I say, welcome to the Lovepile. We liberated you. Touch, taste, feel. Joy. Admire my language. You don't hurt, do you?"

It peered tenderly into his stupefied face. An empath. They didn't exist, he knew. Liberated? When had he touched anything but metal, felt anything but fear?

This couldn't be real.

"Where am I?"

As he stared, a stained-glass wing fanned out, and a furry little face peeked at him over the bushbaby's shoulder. Big compound eyes, feathery antennae.

"Interstellar metaprotoplasmic transfer pod," the butterfly-thing said sharply. Its rainbow wings vibrated. "Don't hurt Ragglebomb!" It squeaked and dived out of sight behind the bushbaby.

"Interstellar?" he stammered. "Pod?" He gaped around. No screens, no dials, nothing. The floor felt as fragile as a paper bag. Was it possible that this was some sort of space-ship?

"Is this a starship? Can you take me home?" The bushbaby giggled. "Look, *please* stop reading your mind. I mean, I'm trying to *talk* to you. We can take you anywhere. If you don't hurt."

The butterfly popped out on the other side. "I go all over!" it shrilled. "I'm the first *ramplig* starboat, aren't we? Ragglebomb made a live pod, see?" It scrambled onto the bushbaby's head. "Only live stuff, see? Protoplasm. That's what happened to where's Amanda, didn't we? Never *ramplig—*"

The bushbaby reached up and grabbed its head, hauling it down unceremoniously like a soft puppy with wings. The butterfly continued to eye him upside down. They were both very shy, he saw.

"Teleportation, that's your word." the bushbaby told him. "Ragglebomb does it. I don't believe in it. I mean, *you* don't believe it. Oh, googly-googly, these speech bands are a mess!" It grinned bewitchingly, uncurling its long black tail, "Meet Muscle."

He remembered now, *googly-googly* was a word from his baby days. Obviously he was dreaming. Or dead. Nothing like this on all the million dreary worlds. Don't wake up; he warned himself. Dream of being carried home by cuddlesome empaths in a psi-powered paper bag.

"Psi-powered paper bag, that's beautiful," said the bushbaby.

At that moment he saw that the tail uncoiling darkly toward him was looking at him with two ice-grey eyes. Not a tail. An enormous boa flowing to him along the ridges, wedge head low, eyes locked on his. The dream was going bad.

Suddenly the voice he had felt before tolled in his brain, *"Have no few, little one."*

The black sinews wreathed closer, taut as steel. Muscle. Then he got the message: the snake was terrified of *him*. He sat quiet, watching the head stretch to his foot. Fangs gaped. Very gingerly the boa chomped down on his toe. Testing, he thought. He felt nothing; the usual halos flickered and faded in his eyes.

"It's true!" Bushbaby breathed, "Oh, you beautiful No-Pain!"

All fear gone, the butterfly Ragglebomb sailed down beside him caroling "Touch, taste, feel! Drink!" Its wings trembled entrancingly; its feathery head came close. He longed to touch it, held himself rigid. If he reached out, doubtless he would wake up and be dead. The boa Muscle had slumped into a gleaming black river by his feet. He wanted to stroke it too, didn't dare. Let the dream go on. Bushbaby was rummaging in a convolution of the pod. "You'll love this. Our latest find," it told him over its shoulder in an absurdly normal voice. Its manner changed a lot, and yet it all seemed familiar, fragments of lost, exciting memory. "We're into a heavy thing with flavors now." It held up a calabash. "Taste thrills of a thousand unknown planets. Exotic gourmet delights. That's where you can help out, No-Pain. On your way home, of course." He hardly heard it. The golden alien body was coming closer, closer still. "Welcome to the Lovepile," the creature smiled into his eyes. His body clenched, aching for the alien flesh. He had never—

In one more moment he was going to grab, and the dream would blow up.

What happened next was not clear. Something invisible whammed him, and he was tumbling onto Bushbaby, his head booming with funky laughter. Its silken body squirmed under him, hot and solid. The calabash had spilled down his face.

"I'm not dreaming!" he cried, hugging Bushbaby, sputtering kahlua as strong as sin, while Ragglebomb bounced on them, squealing "Owow wow-wow!" He heard Bushbaby murmuring, "Great palatal olfactory interplay," as it helped him lick. Touch, taste, feel. The joy dream field! He grabbed firm hold of Bushbaby's velvet haunches, and they were all laughing like mad, rolling in the great black serpent's coils.

. . . Sometime later while he was feeding Muscle with proffit ears, he got it partly straightened out.

"It's the pain bit." Bushbaby shivered against him. "The amount of agony in this universe, it's horrible. Trillions of lives streaming by out there, radiating pain. We daren't get close. That's why we followed you. Every time we try to pick up some new groceries, it's a disaster."

"Oh, hurt," wailed the butterfly, crawling under his arm. "Everywhere hurt. Sensitive, sensitive," it sobbed. "How can Raggle *ramplig* when it hurts so hard?"

"Pain." He fingered Muscle's cool dark head. "Means nothing to me. I can't even find out what they tied my pain nerves to."

"You are blessed beyond all beings, No-Pain," thought Muscle majestically in their heads. *"These proffit ears are*

too salt. I want some fruit."

"Me too," piped Ragglebomb.

Bushbaby cocked its golden head, listening. "You see? We just passed a place with gorgeous fruit, but it'd kill any of us to go down there. If we could just *ramplig* you down for ten minutes?"

He started to say "Glad to," forgetting they were tele-paths. As his mouth opened, he found himself tumbling through strobe flashes onto a barren dune. He sat up spitting sand. He was in an oasis of stunted cactus trees loaded with bright globes. He tried one. Delicious. He picked. Just as his arms were full, the scene strobed again, and he was sprawled on the Lovepile's floor, his new friends swarming over him,

"Sweet! Sweet!" Ragglebomb bored into the juice. "Save some for the pod, maybe it'll learn to copy them. It metabo-lizes stuff it digests," Bushbaby explained with its mouth full. "Basic rations. Very boring."

"Why couldn't you go down there?"

"Don't. All over that desert, things dying of thirst. Tor-ture." He felt the boa flinch. "You are beautiful, No-pain." Bushbaby nuzzled his ear.

Ragglebomb was picking guitar bridges on his thorax. They all began to sing a sort of seguidilla without words. No instruments here, nothing but their live bodies. Making mu-sic with empaths was like making love with them. Touch what he touched, feel what he felt. Totally into his mind. I— we. One. He could never have dreamed this up, he decided, drumming softly on Muscle. The boa amped, mysterioso.

And so began his voyage home in the Lovepile. his new life of joy. Fruits and fondues he brought them, hams and honey, parsley, sage, rosemary and thyme. World after scruffy world. All different now, on his way home.

"Are there many out here?" he asked lazily, "I never found anyone else, between the stars."

"Be glad," said Bushbaby. "Move your leg." And they told him of the tiny, busy life that plied a far corner of the galaxy, whose pain had made them flee. And of a vast pres-ence Ragglebomb had once encountered before he picked the others up.

"That's where I got the idea for the Rulers bit," Muscle confided. *"We need some cheese."*

Bushbaby cocked his head to catch the minds streaming by them in the abyss.

"How about yoghurt?' It nudged Ragglebomb. "Over that way. Feel it squishing on their teeth? Bland, curdy . . . with just a *rien* of ammonia, probably their milk pails are dirty."

"Pass the dirty yoghurt." Muscle closed his eyes.

"We have some great cheese on Earth," he told them. "You'll love it. When do we get there?"

Bushbaby squirmed.

"Ah, we're moving right along. But what I get from you, it's weird. *Foul* blue sky. *Dying* green. Who needs that?"

"No!" He jerked up, scattering them. "That's not true! Earth is beautiful!"

The walls jolted, knocked him sidewise.

"Watch it!" boomed Muscle. Bushbaby had grabbed the butterfly, petting and crooning to it.

"You frightened his *ramplig* reflex," it told him. "Raggle throws things out when he's upset. Tsut, tsut, don't you, baby. We lost a lot of interesting beings that way at first."

"I'm sorry. But you've got it twisted. My memory's a little messed up, but I'm *sure*. Beautiful. Like amber waves of grain. And purple mountain majesties," he laughed, spreading his arms. "From sea to shining sea!"

"Hey, that swings!" Raggle squeaked, and started strumming.

And so they sailed on, carrying him home.

He loved to watch Bushbaby listening for the thought beacons by which they steered.

"Catching Earth yet?"

"Not yet awhile. Hey, how about some fantastic seafood?"

He sighed and felt himself tumble. He had learned not to bother saying yes. This one was a laugh, because he forgot that dishes didn't *ramplig*. He came back in a mess of creamed trilobites, and they had a creamed-trilobite orgy.

But he kept watching Bushbaby.

"Getting closer?"

"It's a big galaxy, baby." Bushbaby stroked his bald spots. With so much *rampligging* he couldn't keep any hair. "What'll you do on earth that'll blow your mind like this?"

"I'll show you," he grinned. And later on he told them.

"They'll fix me up when I get home. Reconnect me right."

A shudder shook the Lovepile.

'You want to *feel pain?*"

"Pain is the obscenity of the universe," Muscle tolled. *"You are sick."*

"I don't know," he said apologetically. "I can't seem to feel, well, real this way."

They looked at him.

"We thought that was the way your species always felt," said Bushbaby.

"I hope not." Then he brightened. "Whatever it is, they'll fix it. Earth must be pretty soon now, right?"

"Over the sea to Skye!" Bushbaby hummed.

But the sea was long and long, and his moods were hard on the sensitive empaths. Once when he responded listlessly, he felt a warning lurch.

Ragglebomb was glowering at him.

"You want to put me out?" he challenged. "Like those others? What happens to them, by the way?"

Bushbaby winced. "It was dreadful. We had no idea they'd survive so long, outside."

"But I don't feel pain. That's really why you rescued me, isn't it? Go ahead," he said perversely. "I don't care. Throw me out. New thrill."

"Oh, no, no, no!" Bushbaby hugged him. Ragglebomb, penitent, crawled under his legs.

"So you've been popping around the universe bringing live things in to play with and throwing them out when you're bored. Get away," he scolded. "Shallow sensation freaks is all you are. Galactic poltergeists!"

He rolled over and hoisted the beautiful Bushbaby over his face, watching it wiggle and squeal. *"Her lips were red, her looks were free, her locks were yellow as gold."* He kissed its golden belly. *"The Night-Mare Life-in-Death was she, who thicks man's blood with cold."*

And he used their pliant bodies to build the greatest love-pile yet. They were delighted and did not mind when later on he wept, face down on Muscle's dark coils. But they were concerned.

"I have it," Bushbaby declared, tapping him with a pickled eel. *Own-species sex.* After all, face it, you're no empath. You need a jolt of your own kind."

"You mean you know where there's people like me? Humans?"

It nodded, eyeing him as it listened. "Ideal. Just like I read you. Right over there, Raggle. And they have a thing they chew—wait—*salmoglossa fragrans.* Prolongs you-know-what, according to them. Bring some back with you, baby."

Next instant he was rolling through strobes onto tender green. Crushed flowers under him, ferny boughs above, sparkling with sunlight. Rich air rushed into his lungs. He bounced up buoyantly. Low gravity. Before him a parklike vista sloped to a glittering lake on which blew colored sails. The sky was violet, pearly little clouds. Never had he seen a planet remotely like this. If it wasn't Earth, he had fallen into paradise.

Beyond the lake he could see pastel walls, fountains, spires. An alabaster city undimmed by human tears. Music drifted on the sweet breeze. There were figures by the shore.

He stepped out into the sun. Bright silks swirled, white arms went up. Waving to him. He saw they were like human girls, only slimmer and more fair. They were calling. He looked down at his body, grabbed a flowering branch and started toward them.

"Do not forget the Salmoglossa," said the voice of Muscle.

He nodded. The girls' breasts were bobbing, pink-tipped. He broke into a trot.

It was several days later when they brought him back, drooping between a man and a young girl. Another man walked beside them striking plangently on a small harp.

Other girls and children danced along, and a motherly-
looking woman paced in front, all beautiful as peris.

They leaned him gently against a tree, and the harper
stood back to play. He struggled to stand upright. One fist
was streaming blood.

"Good-by," he gasped. "Thanks."

The strobes caught him sagging, and he collapsed on the
Lovepile's floor.

"Aha!" Bushbaby pounced on his fist. "Good grief, your
hand! The *salmoglossas* all blood." It began to shake out the
herbs. "Are you all right now?" Ragglebomb was squeaking
softly, thrusting its long tongue into the blood.

He rubbed his head.

"They welcomed me," he whispered. "It was perfect. Music. Dancing. Games. Love. They haven't any medicine because they eliminated all disease. I had five women and a
cloud-painting team and some little boys, I think."

He held out his bloody blackened hand. Two fingers were
missing.

"Paradise," he groaned. "Ice doesn't freeze me, fire
doesn't burn. None of it means anything at all. I WANT TO
GO HOME."

There was a jolt.

"I'm sorry," he wept. "I'll try to control myself. Please,
please get me back to Earth. It'll be soon, won't it?"

There was a silence.

"When?"

Bushbaby made a throat-clearing noise. "Well, just as
soon as we can find it. We're bound to run across it. Maybe
any minute, you know."

"What?"

He sat up death-faced. "You mean you don't know where
it is? You mean we've just been going—no place?"

Bushbaby wrapped its hands over its ears. "Please! We
can't recognize it from your description. So how can we go
back there when we've never been there? If we just keep an
ear out as we go, we'll pick it up, you'll see." He made a
wasted noise.

"Ten to the eleventh times two. Suns in the galaxy. I don't know your velocity and range. Say, one per second. That's—that's six thousand years." He put his head in his bloody hands. "I'll never see home again."

"Don't say it, baby." The golden body slid close. "Don't knock the trip. We love you, No-Pain." They were all petting him now. "Happy, sing him! Touch, taste, feel. Joy!" But there was no joy.

He took to sitting leaden and apart, watching for a sign.

"This time?"

No.

Not yet. Never.

Ten to the eleventh times two. Fifty percent chance of finding Earth within three thousand years. It was the scouter all over again.

The lovepile reformed without him, and he turned his face away, not eating until they pushed food into his mouth. If he stayed totally inert, surely they would grow bored with him and put him out. No other hope. Finish me, he begged. Soon.

They made little efforts to arouse him with fondlings, and now and then a harsh jolt. He lolled unresisting. End it, he prayed. But still they puzzled at him in the intervals of their games. They mean well, he thought. And they miss the stuff I brought them. Bushbaby was coaxing.

"—First a suave effect, you know. Cryptic. And then a cascade of sweet and sour sparkling over the palate—"

He tried to shut it out. They mean well. Falling across the galaxy with a talking cookbook. Finish me.

"—But the arts of combination," Bushbaby chatted on. "Like moving food: e.g., sentient plants or small live animals, combining flavor with the *frisson* of movement—"

He thought of oysters. Had he eaten some once? Something about poison. The rivers of Earth. Did they still flow? Even if by some unimaginable chance they stumbled on it, would it be far in the past or future, a dead ball? Let me die.

"—And *sound,* that's amusing. We've picked up several races who combine musical effects with certain tastes. And there's the sound of oneself chewing, textures and viscosi-

ties. I recall some beings who sucked in harmonics. Or the
sound of the food itself. One race I caught *en passant* did
that, but with a very limited range. Crunchy. Crispy. Snap-
crackle-pop. One wishes they had explored tonalities, glis-
sando effects—" He lunged up.

"What did you say? Snap-crackle-pop?"

"Why, yes, but—"

"That's it! That's Earth!" he yelled. "You picked up a
goddamn breakfast-food commercial!"

He felt a lurch. They were scrambling up the wall. "A
what?" Bushbaby stared.

"Never mind. Take me there! That's Earth, it's got to be.
You can find it again, can't you? You said you could," he
implored, pawing at them. "Please!"

The Lovepile rocked. He was frightening everybody, "Oh
please." He forced his voice smooth. "But I only heard it for
an instant," Bushbaby protested. "It would be terribly hard,
that far back. My poor head!"

He was on his knees, reaching. "You'd love it," he
pleaded. "We have fantastic food. Culinary poems you never
heard of. Cordon bleu! Escoffier!" he babbled. "Talk about
combinations, the Chinese do it four ways! Or is it the Japa-
nese? Teriyaki! Bubble-and-squeak! Baked Alaska, hot and
crisp outside, inside co-o-old ice cream!"

Bushbaby's pink tongue flicked. Was he getting through?

He clawed his memory for foods he'd never heard of.

"Maguay worms in chocolate! Haggis and bagpipes, crys-
tallized violets, rabbit Mephisto! Octopus in resin wine.
Four-and-twenty blackbird pie! Cakes with girls in them.
Kids seethed in their mothers' milk—wait, that's taboo. Ever
hear of *taboo* foods? Long pig!"

Where was he getting all this? A vague presence drifted in
his mind—his hands, the ridges, long ago. "Amanda," he
breathed, racing on.

"Cormorants aged in manure! Ratatouille! Peaches iced in
champagne!" *Project,* he thought. "*Paw* of fatted goose liver
studded with earth-drenched truffles, clothed in purest white
lard!" He snuffled lustfully. "Hot buttered scones drenched

in whortleberry syrup!" He salivated. "Finnan haddie soufflé, Oh, yes! Unborn baby veal pounded to a membrane and delicately scorched in black herb butter—" Bushbaby and Ragglebomb were clutching each other, eyes closed. Muscle looked mesmerized.

"Find Earth! Grape leaves piled with poignantly sweet wild fraises, clotted with Devon cream!" Bushbaby moaned, rocking to and fro. "Earth! Bitter endives wilted in chicken steam and crumbled bacon! Black gazpacho! Passion-fruit!"

Bushbaby rocked harder, the butterfly clamped to its breast.

Earth, Earth, he willed with all his might, croaking, "Pahklava! Gossamer puff paste and pistachio nuts dripping with mountain honey!"

Bushbaby pushed at Ragglebomb's head, and the pod seemed to skitter.

"Ripe Cornice pears," he whispered. *"Earth?"*

"That's it!" Bushbaby fell over panting. "Oh, those foods, I want every single one. Let's land!"

"Deep-dish steak and kidney pie," he breathed. "Pearled with crusty onion dumplings—"

"Land!" Ragglebomb squealed. "Eat, eat!" The pod jarred. Solidity. Earth. Home.

"LET ME OUT!"

He saw a pucker opening daylight in the wall and dived for it. His legs pumped, struck. Earth! Feet thudding, face uplifted, lungs gulping air. "Home!" he yelled.

—And went headlong on the gravel, arms and legs out of control. A cataclysm smote his inside. "Help!"

His body arched, spewed vomit, his limbs flailed. "Help, Help! What's wrong?" he screamed.

Through his noise he heard an uproar behind him in the pod. He managed to roll, saw gold and black bodies writhing inside the open port. They were in convulsions too. "Stop it! Don't move!" Bushbaby shrieked, "You're killing us!"

"Get us out," he gasped. "This isn't Earth."

His throat garroted itself on his breath, and the aliens moaned in empathy.

"Don't! We can't move," Bushbaby gasped. "Don't breathe, close your eyes quick!"

He shut his eyes. The awfulness lessened slightly.

"What is it? What's happening?"

"PAIN, YOU FOOL," thundered Muscle.

"This is your wretched Earth," Bushbaby wailed. "Now we know what they tied your pain nerves to. Get back in so we can go—carefully!"

He opened his eyes, got a glimpse of pale sky and scrubby bushes before his eyeballs skewered. The empaths screamed.

"Stop! Ragglebomb die!"

"My own home," he whimpered, clawing at his eves. His whole body was being devoured by invisible flames, crushed, impaled, flayed. The pattern of Earth, he realized. Her unique air, her exact gestalt of solar spectrum, gravity, magnetic field, her every sight and sound and touch—that was what they had reconnected to his nerve circuits of pain.

"Evidently they did not want you back," said Muscle's silent voice. *"Get in."*

"They can fix me, they've got to fix me—"

"They aren't here," Bushbaby shouted. "Temporal error. No snap-crackle-pop. You and your baked Alaska—" Its voice broke pitifully. "Come back in so we can go!"

"Wait," he croaked. "When?"

He opened one eye, managed to see a rocky hillside before his forehead detonated. No roads, no buildings. Nothing to tell whether it was past or future. *Not beautiful.*

Behind him the aliens were crying out. He began to crawl blindly toward the pod, teeth clenching over salty gushes. He had bitten his tongue. Every move seared him; the air burned his guts when he had to breathe. The gravel seemed to be slicing his hands open, although no wounds appeared. Only pain, pain, pain from every nerve end.

"Amanda," he moaned, but she was not here. He crawled, writhed, kicked like a pinned bug toward the pod that held sweet comfort, the bliss of no-pain. Somewhere a bird called, stabbing his eardrums. His friends screamed.

"Hurry!"

Had it been a bird? He risked one look back. A brown figure was sidling round the rocks.

Before he could see whether it was ape or human, female or male, the worst pain yet almost tore his brain out. He groveled helpless, hearing himself scream. *The pattern of his own kind.* Of course, the central thing—it would hurt most of all. No hope of staying here. "Don't! Don't! *Hurry!*"

He sobbed, scrabbling toward the Lovepile. The scent of the weeds that his chest crushed raked his throat. *Mangolds,* he thought. Behind the agony, lost sweetness.

He touched the wall of the pod, gasping knives. The torturing air was real air, the terrible Earth was real. *"Get in quick!"*

"Please, plea—" he babbled wordlessly, hauling himself up with lids clenched, fumbling for the port. The real sun of Earth rained acid on his flesh.

The port. Inside lay relief. He would be No-Pain forever. Soft flesh—joy—why had he wanted this? The port!

Standing, he turned, opened both eyes. The form of a dead limb printed a whiplash on his eyeballs. Jagged, ugly. Unendurable. Real—

To hurt forever.

"We can't wait!" Bushbaby wailed. He thought of its golden body flying down the light-years, savoring delight. His arms shook violently.

"Then go!" he bellowed and thrust himself violently away from the Lovepile.

There was an implosion behind him.

He was alone.

He managed to stagger a few steps forward before he went down.

1973

THROUGHOUT THE VOLUMES of this anthology, I have repeatedly indicated what I consider the greatest strength of the Hugo awards: the constituency that stands behind them. With the World Science Fiction. Convention firmly established—the first was held in 1939, and except for a wartime interruption (1942-45) they have been held annually ever since—there is a responsible and reasonably disinterested sponsoring body.

And the constituency—the members of the conventions, all of whom are eligible to vote for Hugo winners—has grown dramatically, making the awards all the more meaningful. That first convention in New York drew an attendance of 200 fans and professionals. Attendance fluctuated between a low of 90 and a high of 400 until 1952, when some 870 fans and professionals turned out in Chicago.

A lot of our more senior members speak nostalgically of those early, Lilliputian gatherings. Everybody knew everybody else, and the convention was like a happy family reunion. I wasn't around the science fiction community then, but by the time I started attending World Conventions in 1960, typical attendance was still in the five to six hundred range, and in retrospect *those* conventions seem like family reunions at which everybody knew one another.

Official records indicate that World Convention attendance surpassed one thousand for the first time in 1967; two thousand in 1972; four thousand, in 1974; five thousand, in 1978. The rising curve is not a continuous one; in some years the attendance falls off, due to geographic, economic and what might be described as "fan-political" reasons. On the other hand, many individuals join conventions, knowing full well they won't get to attend them, in order to obtain the official publications (increasingly plush in recent years) and to vote for the Hugo awards.

The constituency behind the Nebula awards has been smaller than that of the Hugo from the outset. Membership in SFWA started at approximately two hundred, grew quickly to approximately four hundred, and has hovered in the four to five hundred range ever since.

For the awards recognizing works published in 1973, both groups turned to a hard-science novel again, just as they had when Larry Niven's *Ringworld* won both prizes in 1970. This time, the double winner was Arthur C. Clarke's *Rendezvous with Rama,* serialized in *Galaxy,* then published in three hardcover editions, by Harcourt Brace and the Science Fiction Book Club in the US, and by Victor Gollancz in Britain.

Rendezvous with Rama resembled *Ringworld* in more than its emphasis on science rather than human portrayals or social projection. Both books dealt with the discovery of gigantic artifacts in outer space, artifacts of alien manufacture (in Niven's book, a giant ring around a remote star; in Clarke's, a giant spaceship passing through our own solar system). In each case, the novel was thereafter devoted almost entirely to the exploration of the alien artifact. Ingenuity and novelty, in effect, were called upon to carry the entire burden of each book—and did so, to overwhelming acclaim.

Unsuccessful nominees on the two ballots for 1973 included *Time Enough for Love,* by Robert A. Heinlein; *The Man Who Folded Himself,* by David Gerrold; and *People of the Wind,* by Poul Anderson.

The Anderson novel was one of the adventure tales set on an alien planet and featuring alien races that Anderson has done so often and so well. The Heinlein and Gerrold novels dealt with similar themes, the major difference being that Heinlein's book was very long and Gerrold's was very short. But each concerned itself with multiply-redoubled time travel, eroticism, cloning and narcissism, leading to the obvious denouement in which the protagonist was permitted every narcissist's dearest dream.

Larry Niven also placed *Protector* on the Hugo ballot.

Moving on to the shorter lengths . . .

Oh, perhaps I should mention one other book that made the Nebula ballot. *Gravity's Rainbow,* by Thomas Pynchon. Anyone who has followed Pynchon's work back through *V* and *The Crying of Lot 49* knows that Pynchon consistently writes works with a strongly unconventional element. Whether this element is regarded as science fiction, fantasy, or surrealism is for the reader to decide. But whether it is the worldwide secret postal system of *Lot 49,* the holy mission to the alligators of the Manhattan sewer system of *V* or the cybernetic octopus and manned V-2 rocket of *Gravity's Rainbow,* it seems to me that science-fantasy enthusiasts who miss Pynchon's works are cheating themselves of a glorious treat.

At any rate, *Gravity's Rainbow* was still another example of the book that wasn't *labeled* science fiction, wasn't by a writer previously identified with science fiction and was consequently overlooked within the science fiction community. It was more a tribute to some bright members of SFWA that the book made the ballot than it was a surprise that it didn't win the Nebula.

Now for those shorter works of 1973.

Following the dreadful faux pas at the 1970 Nebula award ceremony, when Gene Wolfe was mistakenly announced as winner for 'The Island of Dr. Death and Other Stories," the membership of SFWA must have experienced a classic case of collective remorse. Three years later, in the third volume of Terry Carr's *Universe* series, Wolfe's novella "The Death of Doctor Island" appeared. There was no question about its copping a Nebula.

Mass expiation!

Not that "The Death of Doctor Island" was a weak or undeserving story. In fact, it was a fine work. But I just wonder, if it had appeared under a different title and byline, what the response would have been. There were several other strong candidates for the prizes; in fact, the Hugo and Nebula nominations were almost identical—the Wolfe story; "Chains of the Sea," by Gardner Dozois; *two* novellas by Michael Bishop. That last was, of course, a dangerous situation for Bishop, as it had been the previous year for Robert Silverberg with his two nominated novels. And the result was the same for Bishop as it had been for Silverberg: somebody else took home the trophies.

Only "Junction," by Jack Dann, was nominated for the Nebula but not the Hugo; and only "The Girl Who Was Plugged In," by James Tiptree, Jr., was on the Hugo ballot but not the Nebula. And, rather surprisingly, the Tiptree story (which had appeared in Silverberg's anthology *New Dimensions 3)* won the Hugo!

A word about "James Tiptree, Jr." Tiptree was one of the most popular of the newer writers of the early 1970s (although Tiptree's earliest science fiction dates earlier). A less prolific but also popular writer of the same period was Racoona Sheldon. Tiptree was a somewhat mysterious, retiring individual—science fiction's answer to J.D. Salinger, at least, if not to B. Traven—who caused endless speculation as to "his" true identity. In 1977 Alice Sheldon, a middle-aged psychologist, revealed that she was both Tiptree and Racoona Sheldon. Alice Sheldon had also done some writing under her own name, the earliest work of which I am aware being a piece in *The New Yorker* in 1946.

Tiptree was involved in oddities of category designation throughout the ballots for 1973. Although the fans had more or less adopted the same categories for their awards that the members of SFWA had adopted in imitation of the Mystery Writers of America, there remained the problem of drawing boundaries between the categories and of deciding where a given story belonged.

Thus, Tiptree's "The Girl Who Was Plugged In," which won the Hugo for best novella, had earlier been nominated for the Nebula as best novelette! Other finalists were "Case and the Dreamer," by Theodore Sturgeon; "The Death-bird," by Harlan Ellison; and "Of Mist, and Grass, and Sand," by Vonda N. McIntyre. The last-named story won the Nebula.

Five years later, expanded to novel length and retitled *Dreamsnake,* it won *both* Hugo and Nebula awards!

The Hugo for best novelette went to "The Deathbird," by Ellison, edging out, among others, "Love is the Plan, the Plan is Death," a very remarkable Tiptree story.

Now, stay with me for this . . . "Love is the Plan, the Plan is Death" was a Hugo nominee as a novelette, but it had already been nominated for the Nebula as best short story of 1973—and won! But the *Hugo* for best short story was won by Ursula K. Le Guin for "The Ones Who Walk Away from Omelas."

You figure it out.

"My Brother Leopold," by Edgar Pangborn, appeared in 1973 in *An Exaltation of Stars,* an original anthology edited by Terry Carr and published by Simon & Schuster. There was every reason for the volume to succeed. It was edited by one of our premiere anthologists, published by a prestigious house, and the three authors—the volume contained just three long stories—were all popular and highly respected craftsmen: Pangborn, Robert Silverberg and Roger Zelazny. The theme was also interesting and far from overdone: the stories all dealt with transcendent religious experience, seen in the context of science fiction.

Pangborn's story was particularly interesting. It is a calculated experiment—and in my opinion, a thoroughly successful one—in transferring historial events to a new—in this case, futuristic—setting and retelling them to permit us to view them in a fresh perspective. In the case of "My Brother Leopold," the historical model for the fiction is the trial of Joan of Arc. Carr has told me that Pangborn researched the historical model and actually used some of St. Joan's trial transcript, verbatim, in "My Brother Leopold."

The result is a powerfully affecting and memorable story.

In fact, *An Exaltation of Stars* and several other worthy anthologies failed to receive their due attention in the mid- and late 1970s. The reason is not difficult to perceive.

It happened that a certain free-lance editor and independent packager of books and other media products had turned his greedy eye upon science fiction at the time. I don't want to have to defend a lawsuit, so I'll call this fellow Ralph Emerson Svengali rather than his real name, which is—*whoops!*

Svengali was a brilliant salesman. Bear that in mind.

But he was an inept editor. And he was also a man of the most slippery and flexible ethics when it came to dealing with publishers on the one hand and authors on the other.

Over a period of several years, Svengali managed to swamp the science fiction field with more than one hundred anthologies, as well as several lines of "produced" novels, a science fiction magazine and a line of phonograph records. Their quality ranged downward from mediocre to abominable. Almost all of them sold very poorly.

By the time all concerned woke up to Svengali's game, a score or more of publishers had lost tubfuls of money and had sworn off science fiction. Dozens of authors found that they had been lured into sleazy projects and, as often as not, left with burned fingers, empty bank accounts and diminished literary reputations.

Ralph Emerson Svengali was run out of the field with his tail between his legs, and we are all the better for his departure. But the science fiction anthology as a publishing form had suffered a blow from which it has yet fully to recover.

All of which has not prevented one or two or three other greedy individuals from taking note of Svengali's at-least-temporary success, and the fact that he made off with a *lot* of money when he was finally sent packing.

And so we have had another Svengali or two or three in the years since Ralph departed. I suppose they will be with us always.

My Brother Leopold

EDGAR PANGBORN

1

Memorandum from Jermyn Graz, Frater Literatus & Precentor, to his Beneficence Alesandar Fitzeral, O.S.S., Abbot of St. Benjamin's at Mount Orlook in the Province of Ulsta, November 21, 465.

MY DEAR LORD Abbot:

Your Beneficence has graciously requested information in writing concerning the life of my brother Leopold Graz, thirty-eight years deceased, for the attention of the Examiners from the Holy City when they determine his spiritual status, whether the Church shall declare him beatified. My days of delay have been spent in prayer, wondering how best to comply. In spite of time, my brother's death is new to me as yesterday; I am troubled and uncertain.

For longer than I wish to recall, I have been more an observer than a participant in the sorrowful comedy. I will try to write a narrative as simple as the rings of a tree trunk. I have lived a long time, as my brother Leopold did not, since we played together as boys with Jon Rohan and Sidney Sturm, the four of us a natural company, ever loyal (we thought)—one for all and all (we thought) for one. I think I would have died for any of them, certainly for Sidney, as we swore our readiness to do one day when Jon snagged his pinkie on a thorn and we hurried to make use of the fine fresh gore for writing purposes. Oh, how long ago!—I am bald and slow and wrinkled, and tonight my joints pain me.

I have made the common pilgrimages—to Filadelfia, Albani, the shrines of Conicut and Levannon. I never made the long pilgrimage in Abraham's footsteps to the Old City of Nuin on the Atlantic, but I saw that ocean once, when I traveled as a young man to the highland from which one sees the Black Rocks emerge at low tide like scarecrows in the mouth of the Hudson Sea, and beyond them the great waters. I have beheld other marvels, including adult loyalties that warmed me—but I don't find these more intense than those of boyhood, or less frail; seldom as joyous, since adult loyalties may be stained by cynicism, weariness, second thoughts.

I have been for fifteen years precentor here under your tranquil rule. You will remember I was a monk, inscribing after my name the good letters O.S.S.[5], long before that.

I am also proud of my secular name Jermyn Graz, for our artisan father came from an agrarian family descended from a commune of Old Time; yet I am content to be only your devoted Fr. Jermyn, precentor of this Abbey.

My brother Leopold was born December 13, 405. Thirty-eight years ago, in the reign of Emperor Mahonn and the patriarchate of Urbanus II, he was arrested under the name of Brother Francis, charged with treason, and transferred after ten months' imprisonment to the Ecclesiastical Court at Nuber on suspicion of heresy. And as you know, he was tried, condemned, and executed at Kingstone, October 28, 427.

I have never had the privilege of reading the trial transcript, but my memory lives. When they bound him to the stake the sky did darken and a torrent flooded the streets; the soldiers were obliged to pour oil on the faggots. Some murmured that this showed disregard for God's voice in the storm, but then the crowd fought in the usual way, trampling and shoving to snatch magic relics from the ashes. None of our family survives him but myself. Our father died years before Leopold's execution, and our mother still longer ago, when Leo was seven. I think the Examiners may disregard the rambling of my mother's sister Lora Stone, who thinks my mother had had no carnal knowledge of our father Louis

---

[5] Ordo Sancti Silvani.

Graz in the nine months before Leopold's birth, but was impregnated by fire from heaven. My aunt is very old, tumbling at the past like a child with broken playthings. She did not come to live with us until a year after my mother died.

We are taught that none can be born without sin; that every birth delays the Liquidation, our destiny. But sometimes I sinfully wish I might have held in my arms a child of my brother Leopold.

And I am ravaged by doubts, my Lord Abbot, especially on summer nights after Matins when I should be attentive at prayer. I fall to imagining this earth not liquidated but inhabited by a people changed, no longer constantly at war nor obsessed by greed and fear, a people such as my brother spoke of as dwelling in a City of Light. They would deal charitably; they would enjoy their days. They might one day recapture the lost skill of Old Time and journey to the stars—but then I recall how little can be left of the resources of earth that made this conceivable in Old Time, and I am back in the old cobwebbed halls of human folly without a candle. I have never mentioned these doubts in confession; I have hugged the small sin to myself for comfort, until now this question of my brother's sainthood has smoked me out. The study of history (under Church guidance) has been my life. I am forced to see Old Time as an age when men, by their own written admission, had so wasted and befouled the earth that it could no longer support their fearsome numbers, and nature cut them down with war, plague, famine, and that bearing of sterile monsters which nowadays follows intercourse like a tax paid to Hell. And still I persist in wondering whether folly must always be our nemesis. To me the beauty of earth, of its other dwellers less arrogant than man, often appears more sublime than our grandest achievement. Where nature spreads a floor of loveliness we scrape our feet and shit on it.

{In the brittle jaded original of this letter by Jermyn Graz the foregoing paragraph is marked by a marginal line and exclamation point, probably conveying indignation. This mark was undoubtedly made by Wiltnot Breen, a justice of

*the Ecclesia and the ranking prelate of the Nuber Examiners
in 465, for his initials in the same script and ink are attached
to other marginal notes further on.}*

I know we are taught that in a few years the elect shall be
taken into heaven and all others submerged as if they had
never been, when the oceans rise entirely above the dry land,
and the world as we have known it passes away, a drop of
water in the firmament. Still, when the nights are in summer
and I hear the sad-merry clash of the crickets and katydids
and trill of frogs in the moist woods beyond the monastery
walls—my lord, I wonder and I wonder.

I alone live to remember Leopold as a child. Jon Rohan
died in 435 from after-effects of a wound received in the
War of 426-429. I lost Sidney before that: a devoted young
doctor, he died in 430, the year of the red plague that followed the Moha War—a return, some say, of the epidemic
that did so much to destroy the society of Old Time. I alone
recall the voice of the boy Leopold in the choir of the Kingstone Cathedral, how it soared.

Here was a day of 413: Leopold seven, I fourteen, Jon
Rohan twelve, Sidney fifteen. We met a black-browed
Gypsy, old and horny-footed, in a meadow by Twenyet
Road; we were wandering, not far from home.

We had been trained to fear and avoid Gypsies, as children are usually guarded against any strangeness that might
illuminate the strangeness within themselves. We saw a sagging wagon in the meadow, a crowbait tethered on succulent
grass, and would have slipped past. Something of mirage or
phantasm was in the heaviness of the afternoon. It was that
pregnant month, July. Before we saw the wagon. Leopold
had been singing for us, casually; we had noticed a hawk
high in the blue.

The Gypsy sat motionless on the gray stump of a tree beside the road, wearing a dull loinrag and colorless sandals.
His knotty flesh was brown like the earth behind him, his
gray hair speckled white like the quills of a porcupine. He
had a shoulder satchel: a clay pipe dangled in his hand unlit.
I smelled sweat and coarse Conicut tobacco.

I am not fey. I was born for the prosaic life, passions and marvels passing me as a parade might wind down the road past a child who cannot open the window and call. But I have a more than natural sense for stress and change in others. I knew Jon was startled by the Gypsy and hostile. Sidney was startled too, but pleasantly, the sweetness of his nature responding to anything that showed no enmity. I knew my brother Leopold felt a recognition outside my understanding, as if in some territory out of time where he and the grizzled Gypsy could meet as contemporaries with a shared language.

The Gypsy asked: "Would any of you gentlemen possess a tinderbox? Mine's in my wagon and I too lazy to go stumping after it."

I had a fine new one, a present from my father. Up I stepped, and when the old man had tamped in fresh tobacco I made a light for him, my sliver of flame stabbing down into the gurgling bowl. Sidney stood near, and I knew his thought was for my safety, but the Gypsy was smiling with all dusty wrinkles. "I thank you."

I said as I'd been taught: "It's nothing—you're welcome."

"Welcome—that's a variety of love, ain't it?"

His question seemed directed at Sidney, the oldest of us, the kind one, slim and golden in the sun. Sidney smiled. Jon was standing apart and frowning, working his toes in the dust.

"So everything comes from nothing," said the Gypsy, "and that's what makes the world go round? Am I right, Youngest?" This to Leopold, who had ducked in under my arm. Either Leopold nodded or the Gypsy pretended he had. "I'm right," he said, puffing, "and it's not a bad arrangement, for if the world quit going round wouldn't we fly off like beads from the end of a busted string?" Then he lifted some articles from his satchel and displayed them in the palm of his left hand. "Anyhow, I suppose I'm among Gentlemen who believe the world is round. True, Youngest?"

My little brother said: "My name's Leopold."

"Why, that's a sensible answer." Then the Gypsy's gaze was piercing me. "My Ma named me Aleites. You'll be Leopold's brother." Seldom did others notice a resemblance. In those days I was sandy blond; Leopold's hair was dark as walnut. Our other features differed: Leopold had a straight nose, a glorious high arch of brow; my nose was always puggy, my lips too full. But that Gypsy saw our brotherhood. "And the name people call you—?"

"Jermyn."

"Light and welcome—I must make you a return." He was moving his big right hand over his left, jumbling the oddments there like one preparing a throw of the dice. "Jermyn, I'd have you choose one from this lot—alas, worthless as men measure things in the marketplace. Choose something to please all your blithe company." I stared at his palm, incapable of decision; it looked big as a plowed field. "Here, for instance, my dear, is a bit of a garnet—I don't claim it gives the wearer invisibility; we're sensible people, aren't we? Here's the milk tooth of a chimera, which some say confers bravery if worn next the skin—I don't say it, of course. And this gold phallus no bigger'n a thumbnail—perky, ain't it? Made for a king's son likely, the way every wench he met in his travels was *supposed* to jump out of her skin to please him, since we all know that next to a big one they like a gold one; but I never tried it out, don't actually know a thing about it. I never guarantee a blessed thing; that's why I'm a successful businessman." His old nag nickered at that, and he had the grace to look embarrassed.

I grew desperate. I thought Jon might like the chimera's milk tooth; he was always for games that tested our company's bravery, maybe from a need in himself to prove he was brave enough to meet the world head-on. Jon's father was a captain of engineers in the Second Ulsta Regiment, a loud, urgent man. I would have done anything to please Sidney, but couldn't imagine what he might like out of that jumble. Then I saw how my brother's eyes yearned at one thing there, a thing the Gypsy hadn't even mentioned. This was a lump of clay no longer than my thumb, a trifle stouter, so worn by time you needed a second look to understand it was sculpture, the stylized figure of a little human male with arms folded against his chest, hands flat to the body. And on the other side of the lump—the Gypsy turned it over for me—was a woman's figure sharing the clay body, her face brooding like the man's and mild. I glanced again at Leopold, touched the image, said: "That."

The Gypsy gave me the dingy thing and dribbled the other objects back into his bag. Oh, the glitter of them, the gleam of what I might have had! "You've made the strange choice," he said. "Heaven knows what will come of it, or maybe Heaven doesn't know."

"That's heresy," said Jon Rohan.

"It's heresy." said the Gypsy, "or it's an outlander's way of talking, meaning no harm. Pipe's out—back to work. Bless you and good morning to you, gentlemen." He shambled off to his wagon, and we four straggled back home with our thoughts.

Leopold asked: "Maybe I can keep it for you?" So I gave him the image, wishing it were any of a thousand better things.

Many times since then I have held the image before me, and it has taken me into contemplation; then I am like one caught up to the arch of heaven with no company but the falling stars. In his own fashion my brother must have responded for a while to this same power of the clay. I remember how lovingly he first dropped it into the pocket of his blouse and held a protective hand over it, as another child might cherish a pet. It was only a little later that I began hearing about Leopold's Companion, concerning whose existence the Church Examiners, I suppose, will wish more light.

My brother shared the bed with me in our attic room, a dear fidgeting nuisance. Our mother loved him best; this I had always known as children do know it. But the years that brought him out of babyhood carried her into exhaustion and invalidism, no strength left for contending with small boys. Losing her in these dim ways, we found each other. By the time Leopold was five I think my jealousy had dissolved in fondness, answering his natural warmth. Whether darker feelings still smoldered I cannot say—it was long ago.

The night after our meeting with the Gypsy, Leopold bounced under the covers holding the image, lost it during steep, went frantic hunting for it in the morning. When we salvaged it from the bedclothes, he put it on a string to wear at his neck—not good, for the image was worn so smooth it had hardly a projection for the cord to hold. For Leopold's eighth birthday, Jon and Sidney and I collaborated on a solution. Sidney, brilliant with his hands, carved a box of applewood with a secret fastening; Jon bought a delicate silver chain in an antiquity shop—it cost him two months' allowance—and I joined the chain to the box in my father's workshop. Leopold was speechless with joy, opening and shutting the mysterious catch forty times a day. I have the box still, and the image secure in its nest that Sidney made, his magic as good as ever after half a century.

Our mother was going through a cruel pregnancy. Her time came on her not long after that day we met the Gypsy. For several weeks her illness had brought Leopold and me more than ever together; but there were times when he seemed utterly alone, in unchildlike contemplation of the image. Silent in a corner of the cobbler shop, he could have been on the other side of the stars.

Our house was one of the many shabby-genteel ones that cluster along the Twenyet Road in Kingstone. The Old-Time city of the same name stood southeast of there, now mostly underwater of course. We lived about three miles from Rondo's Shrine, where the Old-Time course of the Twenyet Road takes it under Lake Ashoka. The modern detour curves over higher ground to meet the old road emerging. In many places one still finds the gray rubbish, curious Old-Time road material, frost-heaved, pried loose, dumped out of the way. This work of clearance and improvement was done, I believe, more than a hundred years ago in the era of construction after Katskil became an Empire.[6] Farther out in the

---

[6] Cf. Barker Sidon, Old-Time Survivals in Imperial Katskil, Filadelfia College Press, 745. But Professor Sidon is mainly concerned with the physical survivals; one must look elsewhere for

country, much of the gray junk has been hauled off by farmers to add to their stone fences. A great deal more of the re-
pulsive indestructible garbage of Old Time might be put to
some use, if we would exercise ingenuity.

Our section of the Twenyet Road was called The Crafts,
because so many artisans lived there to catch the trade of
travelers entering the city. Father was a shoemaker, dark-
gloomy like the tanned hides he labored with, strict with
Leopold and me in matters of decorum and truthtelling, but
strict with justice and not unkind. He was one of those who
fend off love with a grunt and then admit it anyway.

Our mother was soft, no disciplinarian. She enjoyed those
romances the Church approves for the common people, for
unlike our father she had learned to read, at a wise woman's
school in her native village; sometimes housework waited
while she dwelt in a storyteller's daydream—who could be-
grudge it to her? Between my birth and Leo's she had borne
two mues. It was at her insistence that Father sent me to
Mam Sola's day school in Kingstone, where I met Sidney
and learned my letters and arithmetic. I have always been
grateful for it: a little reading may prove a key to great reading; I cannot help thinking, my Lord Abbot, that a fairly
widespread literacy might usefully supplement our Imperial
Program of Universal Education.

I know nothing about those other two mues. This late
pregnancy our mother was suffering was terminated by the
birth of a monster, a twelve-pound hulk of flesh with four
arms and, the priest told me later, no anus. He had quickly
smothered the thing as the law requires, and it must have
been buried quickly too, in the dark and without any ceremony, as is proper, in that sad tombless yard—Mues' Acre
—that every church must maintain beyond the limits of its
natural cemetery. But while Fr. Colin disposed of it, the
midwife could not prevent our mother from bleeding to
death.

During this ordeal I was in the attic room charged with

discussion of the mental inheritance.

keeping Leopold out of the way. He was beside himself when the screaming began, though he heard my explanations. I held him fast and said over and over: "They're trying to help her." His heart hammered and his eyes were blind. We heard a last scream, beyond bearing, a flurry of voices, quick footsteps, orders. I must have relaxed my grip, for Leopold tore free and rushed downstairs. I caught up with him in the kitchen. Fr. Colin, that sardonic old man who always befriended me, was wrapping the thing in a cloth, but did not gel it out of sight swiftly enough. Leopold saw it, and collapsed.

"Get him outside, Jermyn," said Fr. Colin. "Fresh air will bring him back to this delightful world." I carried him out into the moonlit splendor of a field behind our house. I kissed him and talked to him. He roused when I moved the locket with the clay image because it was making a hurting hardness between him and me. His eyes opened; he was back with me, gripping the amulet as if it were a bridge to life. "It's all right," I said. "It's all right, Leo." We both knew it was all wrong. Leo at eight understood how our human talk uses these flat reversals of reason. "Happens all the time— the priest says it's the will of God because men were so wicked in Old Time," I went on till I ran out of respectable words.

His night eyes watched me. He took the image from its box and studied it in the white light, turning it from male to female side and back. "Jermyn, why can't people make babies the way grapevines do?" Startled, I laughed. "You might've rested a part of you on the ground till I grew out of it and it was time to cut me free." He knew he was talking absurdly. He said: "I'll preach when I grow up."

"Well, sure. Mother's always wanted you to be a priest."

"No, I won't be a priest. But I'll preach. I'll say it about the grapevines. It's a—a—" Maybe he wanted to say "parable" and didn't have the word. "And I'll tell about the City of Light. The Companion will teach me how."

"The Companion?"

"He came yesterday when I looked at Two-Face. He

stands where light and dark come together." He watched me as if he longed to explain further and could not. It was no play-acting. We were too close for that, in spite of the seven years; when any play-acting was to be done, we shared it.

I said: "Tell me about him. Please. What does he look like?"

"Not always the same. Only a voice sometimes."

I was frightened, and lacerated by jealousy. I saw this Companion taking Leopold away—as perhaps he did, even if we grant him existence only in my brother's mind. I asked: "What is the City of Light?"

"A place the Companion knows." He said no more, but he was not trying to mystify me.

In the house, Fr. Colin told us our mother was dead. "Try to be good boys to your father," he said, fumbling at the unsayable.

Leopold asked like a grown-up: "Is he with her now?"

"Yes," he said. "Take them in, Sister Alma." The midwife was fluttering, poor-boying us, another of the well-meaning ones. She took us where our father sat stricken beside that little dark lady once so well known, now gone secret, the blanket pulled to her chin and she with no more regard for anyone, not even Father. Fr. Colin said: "Leo, you'll understand better when you come to be a priest yourself. God has His reasons, child—it's only that we can't always know them."

But Leopold said: "I cannot be a priest."

Father lifted his head. "Leopold, what do you mean?"

"I can't be a priest," He said this, standing by our mother's body. I remember putting an arm around him because I feared the grown-up world was about to roar at him.

But no. Fr. Colin mumbled about our mother's wish that he might enter holy orders. I scarcely heard that, waiting for what Father would say. It was a gentle reply: "Of course, Leo, you can't be a priest unless you wish it yourself. We'll talk of it later."

But so far as I know it was never brought up again. From that time on, however—the Examiners may find this important—Leopold was intensely keen to share whatever knowledge I brought home from Mam Sola's school. He took to reading like a baby fish to swimming. He gulped down all I could transmit, with impatience for its simplicity, begging for more difficult tasks. "Where are the big books?" he'd demand of me. *"Where are the books?"*

I was not a bad student, indeed Mam Sola praised me, but beside Leo I was a stumbling mule. Two years after our mother's death I resolved to work full time in Father's shop, while Leo would attend the school in my place, but soon he reported that Mam Sola said he knew all she could teach him. She wanted him to go to the great Priests' School at Nuber, and this she and Father arranged for him, beginning in the winter of 415-416, when he was ten. He was the baby of his class among yeasty adolescents: luckily, some of them made a pet of him, sheltering him from the mindless cruelties the majority would have visited on him if they had dared. The priests loved him too after their fashion, seeing maybe a future Patriarch, who knows?

The years 412-418—being nearly my contemporary, my Lord Abbot, Your Beneficence will remember this fragment of time much as I do, and the gradual increase of hatred in our nation toward the Republic of Moha after the accession of the Emperor Mahonn. There was the Sortees Massacre, when Moha traders were set upon by a hysterical crowd—that might have brought war, but neither side was ready. There was the complaint that Moha was cutting us off from trade with Nuin—and nothing ever said about our monopoly of trade with the tropical wealth of Penn, the spices and tea and oranges. The Emperor Mahonn's accession brought a relief from uncertainty: now at least we all know there would be war, and only the timing was unpredictable.

Those were also the six years when my brother grew from seven to thirteen, from jungle of childhood to river's edge.

Jon and Sidney and I found it natural that a small boy should believe in an invisible Companion: a common fantasy. I may have had such a dream myself before Leo was born. That it should continue beyond early childhood was not so natural—but we were credulous, ignorant boys, and in our different ways we too believed in the Companion's existence. We'd catch Leopold with the clay image in his hand, sunlight on his closed eyelids, listening, and we believed.

My lord, he spoke once of "my brother the sun." Now, it was not till many years later, in my historical studies, that I learned of a saint in ancient Christian times who used these words, and certainly before he went to the Nuber school my little brother had never heard of him; yet he did so speak.

We would keep watch for him, a sharp eye against intruders. Unless he himself was a-mind to discuss them, we never asked about those silent conversations. Had others learned of the mystery and bothered Leo, we would have gone after them like wildcats. Leopold had become to us an oracle, our mascot. After he began study at the Priests' School we had him only in the summers, but schoolboys live for that time anyhow. He was ours and he could do no wrong.

We fell into the habit of consulting him as if he possessed a magical insight; maybe he did. We would ask questions about whatever disturbed us—sex, making a living, religion, right and wrong conduct, superstitions—matters that lay far beyond the experience of his years (beyond ours too!). We would mull over his answers for nuggets of gold.

At that time I was not well instructed in the faith. Fr. Colin was swamped in the business of a parish priest's duties, his time for meditation and teaching chewed to bits by the million tiny mouths of everyday trivia. Our father was none too devout, and what early instruction we had from our mother had blended religion and romance in one blur of wishful dreaming. Father resented the tithes, the spending of time on devotion. During those six years, arthritis twisted his cobbler hands; at times I heard him growl heretical complaints.

Jon Rohan, that chubby hero, was somewhat disciplined in religion. Sidney was agnostic, which frightened me, though he was always discreet—I would not say it now of my friend if he were not long dead, beyond reach of wounding. Later, deep in the humanitarian work of his choice, it seemed to me he was not concerning himself as much as he ought to have done with the safety of his soul; but good works, I am sure, have won him a place in Heaven, if Heaven exists.[7] It was not until after his death that I, adrift and wretched from the loss of him and of Leopold, took lay orders as a student of history, leading to my later work as a churchman. At the young time I am describing I had what I will call an undisciplined openness of mind. I found no heresy in believing my brother might converse with an angel.

I will write of an afternoon in early September in Leopold's thirteenth year when we had gone to a favorite clearing above the road to Maplestock. That forest belonged to the Ashoka family, long masters of the Maplestock region. Baron Ashoka's game wardens could legally have lobbed arrows into us on suspicion of poaching—shooting, of course, to cripple and not to kill.

I was twenty that September. Expert in my father's trade, I supposed I would remain a shoemaker. I already managed our shop; pain in the joints was making it nearly impossible for our stubborn old father to go on working. My aunt Mam Lora had kept house for us about five years now, her conversation all sniff and glare, making a cult of our mother as a martyred saint.

That afternoon was a Friday. In the morning we had gone to church, taking the rest of the day for a holiday as our customs then permitted. (My lord, I do dislike the modern trend toward a completely joyless Sabbath.) Sidney was returning soon to the University at Nuber for his third year of medical study. On the journey he would be looking after Leopold, who was going back for his last year at the Priests' School— then the University for him too, we assumed, since he was certain to be granted a scholarship. And Jon too was leaving, for the Military Academy at Nupal. I would stay home and make shoes.

Jon had said goodbye to his sweetheart, Sara Jonas, in the

---

[7] In the margin, a note with the initials W.B.: *"These are strange remarks for a precentor of your Abbey."*

grandeur of his Academy uniform; he told us about that parting, modestly. Sara owned a great share of him, a delicious girl pretty as a violet in the snow. We found that right for one of Jon's temperament, but his humor and good nature appeared to be jelling into a kind of sentimentality that made him no longer quite one of us. He in turn felt, I think, that he had outgrown us and was at eighteen the only adult in a gaggle of starry-eyed goslings. He took a deep melancholy joy in the war talk. He was like a prince condescending: Let us pursue our mundane plans; for him, the lonely glory of going forth to die in our defense, thinking of Sara in his last hour. Not that he ever spoke such corn as that, yet we felt something of the sort in him. My own discomfort at his swashbuckling may have been partly envy: what has a shoemaker to do with war? Well, he makes boots for soldiers to march in, for soldiers to die in.

This was 418, eight years before the war actually began. When it did come, Jon was a captain of infantry, blooded during the Slaves' Rebellion in the western provinces (fomented by Moha, some claimed) in 422. And when the last great struggle with Moha did begin, our Jon was in the thick of it. He was wounded in action, suffering the loss of his left leg from the infection of a spear wound, and the blinding of his right eye. He came back thus to goodwife Sara and his small children: halt, half-blind, the infection still burning in the stump of the thighbone and never quite healing, an old man in his middle twenties. This ruin came on him in our defeat at Brakabin Meadows, April 4, 427, which brought the Moha forces within a short march of Kingstone. No one then could have imagined our recovery, our victories of the following year; 427 was ebb tide, all Katskil breathing despair. For his bravery at Brakabin, Jon received a life's pension and the Iron Wheel of the Order of St. Franklin.

I have digressed again, my lord—forgive me.

A September afternoon of 418, and Leopold had not sung for us that day. At thirteen his voice had cracked; the Cathedral choirmaster warned him not to sing again for two years. We missed it. Entertainments were few. We had the huge

sermons of Fridays and Lecture Days; the street-corner sto-
rytellers, the peep shows, visits from Rambler caravans that
ignored national boundaries and carried amusement, news,
messages everywhere; that was about all. We found it hard to
lose the pleasure of Leopold's singing and know it would
never happen again as it had been, since Leo singing with a
man's voice would be another happening in another world.

We bathed in a pool and dried ourselves in the sun. Leopold was not used to the new curly hair on him or the breaking of his voice, but didn't mind our jokes and bawdy counsel. We found it strange to watch the Mascot enter adoles-
cence as we were emerging from it. His body was becoming
like ours; his mind occupied other dimensions.

Jon asked: "Leo, what does the Companion say about the
war?"

Leopold had lately spoken of the Companion only enough
to let us know the conversation had not ended. He said: "Not
much, Jon. A war will come sometime, and make an end
of—many things."

"Why," said Jon, "everybody knows that."

Sidney inquired: "Because there always has been war?"

"It's a reason," said Jon. "You can't change human nature."

"But it does change," I asserted. "The history books—"
Jon wanted to argue with Sidney, not to hear about history.
"It's the cause, Sid. The future belongs to Katskil. How can
we make progress with Moha like a log across the road?"

(And since then I have read much history of Old Time,
and of ancient time, and how often have I stumbled over
these same worn words! Including my own protests, and
Sidney's.)

"The future doesn't exist," Sidney said.

I put in: "Only in the mind of God."

"Progress by smashing skulls," said Sidney. "Destiny.
Shit."

And Leopold: "Mue-births are bad enough, without war."
Perhaps the Examiners ought to know that from our mother's
death to the time I lost him, Leopold was obsessed with the

tragedy of mue-births. Moments came now and then when his fresh and healthy child's face incredibly foreshadowed maturity, even old age—I don't think I imagined this; and when I saw it I could be almost certain what trouble it was that darkened him.

"No use being a bleeding heart," Jon said. "Face facts!"

Sidney wouldn't get angry, even at that noise. "The facts stare me in the face, Jon, and I say there isn't one stupid thing between us and Moha that couldn't be settled at a conference table."

"But how can you trust 'em?" Leopold said: "You're not hearing each other . . ."

Later Jon asked about the Companion. "Do you still—*see* him?"

"As if my eyes were shut, and I knowing the shape in memory. He speaks, and it's like a memory of hearing."

"Then it's only thinking? Imagining?"

"Maybe. He startles me, and then later I understand." Leopold frowned. "He described the City of Light like—a real place."

Sidney asked: "Do you believe in his separate existence, Leo, the way you believe I'm sitting here bare-ass and beautiful?"

"Not that way. But I think there is a City of Light."

That day was forty-seven years ago. After he left with Sidney for Nuber, I did not see my brother Leopold again for eight years.

We had a letter from him in November. I recall our heady excitement when the Imperial Post rider banged on our door. Letters came rarely to poor districts like Twenyet Road; Leo was being extravagant, undertaking such an expense just to send us greetings. We shut out the urchins who had gathered to stare at the rider, and then my father was beside himself with impatience till I could read him the message. However, that letter was one any schoolboy-might have written to content his family: he was well, studying hard, sorry he couldn't be home for Thanksgiving but looked forward to seeing us in the Week of Abraham,[8] love to everybody.

In early December came a letter from Sidney: Leopold was gone.

On the night of December 7, Leopold had gone to bed as usual in the Senior Dormitory—thirty-six boys in a long room where all-night candles burned and a priest sat wakeful to suppress giggling and other unseemliness. In the morning, Leopold was not there.

The monitor priest admitted he could have dozed off.

The other boys under severest questioning confessed no knowledge, and I think they had none. Leopold must simply have dressed himself silently and walked out. The night watchman spent his hours mostly at the gatehouse; Leo must have climbed the Pine Street wall, hidden by evergreens.

Sidney had not seen Leopold for two weeks before the disappearance; nothing then had seemed to Sidney unusual.

When I read this letter to my father, he gasped and fell — his first stroke. I got word of this to Sidney and Jon. Jon was not given leave of absence; Sidney left Nuber at once and reached our house by evening on a fast horse. In his embrace I found the relief of tears, till then denied. And Sidney gave me the clay image with its applewood box and silver chain. "He *left it behind,* Jermyn. Under his pillow." This we never did understand; nor do I, altogether, in later years. But so the amulet did return to me, my lord, and it has not since left my possession.

Sidney helped me untiringly in caring for my father, who was always asking for news of Leopold, we understood, with his eyes and the one finger he could move. Then soon, mercifully, he had another stroke, and died. We watched the dif-

---

[8] All nations of eastern Murca in the Fifth Century professed Brownism, celebrating the supposed birth of Abraham Brown on December 24 and making the whole week a festival: an obvious superimposition on the Old-Time Christmas. Brownism preferred mild methods of substitution and engulfment in its suppression of Christianity—one could almost speak of syncretism rather than suppression. The modern scholar is often puzzled to distinguish the newcomer from the ghost.

ficult life recede, leaving the shell of our good cobbler Louis Graz, my father, and Sidney closed his eyes for me with his steadfast kindness.

For eight years, no word. Soon after my father's death my Aunt Lora entered the nunnery of St. Ellen at Nupal, where she is now in her ninety-fifth year. Sidney returned to the University, was graduated with high honors, finished his licentiate in 422, and started practice in Kingstone. That was also the year of the Slaves' Rebellion in which Jon Rohan rose to the rank of captain. I sold our house and cobbler shop—another of the gray milestones that emerge in anyone's life story. The buyer was well known to me; he would have notified me if Leopold had ever returned to that house. With a donkey and my cobbler's equipment, I took to the roads.

I had not lost my passion for reading and history. But it was in some manner reinforcing my grief at the loss of Leopold. There can be a weariness, even acedia, in too much history. I wished to escape it for a while. History repeats much of its sorrow, error, lost opportunity. Though I had learned a great deal about the folly and corruption of Old Time, I found small consolation in comparing past with present—I can't see that we have learned much from that dark story. In my monastic years I have collected, edited, sometimes rewritten legends and true tales of our region, past and present. This labor also, though congenial, has done little to alter my view. Hope is a lost child stumbling across a battlefield.

I had stronger reasons for a wanderer's life. An artisan may follow the roads: people must have shoes in a country of thorns and serpents. A peddler-artisan may listen. (Our Gypsy by the roadside was listening.) If careful not to startle or offend, he may ask some questions. I would not believe my brother Leopold was dead.

Sidney never discouraged my search. Jon thought Leo must be dead or carried off by slavers, and scolded me for wasting myself. Sidney aided me, his fine house at Kingstone my home whenever I wished. We knew Leopold, thirteen, harmless, could have had no enemies, and he had no wealth to steal. Slavers would hardly have approached a well-guarded place like the Priests' School; besides, at that time the Nuber polis were said to be keeping those vermin clear out of the Holy City.

I searched—into Penn, Conicut, Levannon, down to the southern extremity of our Empire, that pine-barren country. The clay image went with me, on the silver chain, in the box Sidney had made.

Sometimes, my lord, I dreamed the image might bring the Companion to me, even with word of Leopold. This was superstition, I admit. I cannot guess who made the image or with what ancient purpose, but when I contemplate either of the faces of enduring clay, the present drops from me, time is a murmur behind a curtain, I see my own breed as a blurred commotion in a stream wider and deeper than we suppose. A face of the image may say to me: *Why trouble with those who must soon be gone from the earth altogether in total sterility, or another plague year, or another thousand years of good intentions?* To this I find doubtful answers, and I dare to ask in return: *Why then has God made them? Or is God the Creator only one more fancy of this apelike nobody?* Then the image returns me stare for stare.

I am admitting, my Lord Abbot, that the image carried so long in boyhood by Leopold Graz can indeed stimulate heresy. But remember, and I pray Your Beneficence will urge the Examiners to remember, Leopold was not carrying it when he went about as Brother Francis—I was. And though I have exposed my spirit to the clay, Your Beneficence knows I have lived in what we agreed to call virtue. I think no one would whisper that I am in the grip of the Devil.

In 426 came the first rumor of an itinerant preacher calling himself Brother Francis. I was in Penn and southern Katskil early that year. Everyone expected some clash that would at last fire up the war against Moha. Emperor Mahonn was occupying his pinnacle of majesty at the Summer Palace of Lakurs. far from the Mohan border, uttering ambiguities. Diplomats, those well-fed errand boys, bounced from insult to insult, but Mohan travelers came to our country no more. And under this tension began those religious revivals, opening with prayer and shifting into orgies of hate. There might be a choir; the people would sing the fine hymns from the Third Century religious renascence—*In pace gaudeo or Exultate gentes.* Then preaching and praying, and soon enough the frenzied roaring: *"Down Moha! Destroy! Destroy!"*

According to the story rumor brought me, a slim man, very young, in a robe that some thought marked him as a lay brother of the Silvan Order, appeared at a meeting in the Stadium at Monsella and asked permission to speak, saying he was one Brother Francis, a messenger. When the Bishop of Solvan asked his place of origin, he replied: "My lord, who among us knows that?" The Bishop, moved by the power of his presence, permitted him to address the gathering. The voice of Brother Francis, rumor said, was not loud but so pure and moving that the people stood rock-quiet to hear him. Yet he was only describing a thing they knew intimately: the countryside between Nupal and the Mohan border city of Skoar.

He spoke of farms and villages they knew, of the Maypole dances, the churches where on Friday mornings they heard the words of Abraham explained. He talked of gardens, orchards, common things—the town greens and their pavilions; pastures near woods where the deer showed their proud heads in morning mist. He did not deny what they all knew, that poverty, cruelty, greed, and ignorance devour us; that human beings die from incomprehensible sickness of Old-Time poison from the ground; that men are not altogether masters in the country of brown tiger and black wolf; that if our women escape sterility, at least one birth in every four is a mue. He denied no darkness, but he showed them their world as still a lovely thing. Then he told them in that same quiet voice: "If you follow the present direction of your lusts, the legions will walk here."

I suppose it was the voice and manner that moved them, for this argument has never yet deterred man from fouling his own nest. Some grumbled. One or two called, "God bless

you!" Most were silent. When the Bishop sought their attention it was as though they could not quite catch the noise of
him. They drifted away tranced abandoning the Stadium to
the Bishop and a few twittering officials. And Brother Francis—at this point rumor whispered excitedly—vanished. I
suppose he stepped down to walk anonymously with the
crowd.

Another tale reached me in May when I was returning to
Kingstone. I discussed it with Sidney as we sat in his garden
in the cloudy evening, "Miracles!" he said. "It was to be expected." Brother Francis had spoken at Grangorge, near the
Moha border, and a man with a bent disordered spine, a cripple for years, tossed away his crutches and knelt to kiss the
holy man's robe. Others were then and there healed of old
afflictions. Sidney said: "The times are in a steamy state,
Jermyn—it's this damned war, bound to come any minute.
People have the need to believe. You notice the dear fella's
preaching has no effect on the políticos. They hear only the
noises of power."

"But here's power, if Brother Francis can sway a multi-
tude."

"Yes, if." Sidney went on to speak of cures that baffled
medical reason until one recognized the limited but amazing
power of the mind over states of the flesh. "I'd want to know
how well that man walked the following day," he said, "but
that's the part of the story we never get to hear . . . I see you
still wear Leo's amulet." We talked on about my brother,
remembering loved qualities at random—his occasional
stammer, his yen for fresh bread, his shyness with girls.

Leaving Kingston in June, I fell in with some Ramblers
whose Boss I knew. He told me of a meeting at Brakabin,
where Brother Francis had said: "I speak of the City of
Light."

Thus I knew. My Rambler friend could tell me nothing
more. I hurried to Nuber, inquiring at the Abbey of the Silvan Order. They had been pestered by similar questions and
were short with me: the man's robe was *not* that of a Silvan
lay brother—it lacked the symbols; they knew and wished to

know nothing of any Brother Francis. I went on to—never mind all that. Though frustrated for several more months, I did find him.

When the war began in September, 426, with the smashing of our garrison at the border town of Milburg, Katskil shivered at a prospect of Mohan columns driving south—down the Skoar River, through the hill passes, along the coast of the Hudson Sea. Had Moha tried this they might have won the war, but like our Empire, I daresay, they were ruled by the opaque stupidity of the military mind.

In those days of anxiety I caught word of a band of pilgrims who were marching up along the Delaware, intending to place themselves between the opposing armies in the no-man's-land that extended from Lake Skoar to the Hudson Sea, and these mad saints were led by Brother Francis. I hurried to Gilba, on the north shore of the lake, where they would pass if the story was true. I reached the town on a gleaming October afternoon, when the hills were purple under sunlight and rolling cloud shadows: but a section of the northern horizon was sullen with smoke—not forest fire, God knows, for the woods were soaked from recent rains. The pilgrims had arrived before me and were camped in a meadow at the edge of the town.

They were not saints but simple folk, some perhaps not even very religious, drawn by wonder at a truth-speaker. I have blamed Leopold for bringing them together in so vulnerable a crowd. Certainly his intention was to lead them between the opposing forces, armed only in their goodwill. And their innocent blood drenching the earth would have taught men what they have been taught through the millennia by the blood of other martyrs: namely, nothing.[9] In this I find the cruelty of the saint, who would have the devoted follow the dream—his dream, never understanding that it cannot be theirs for longer than the moment of enthusiasm. Since this particular massacre did not occur in the manner he may have

---

[9] W.B. writes: *"Can he expect the Church to condone this utterance?"*

foreseen, I suppose the question of Leopold's blame will be tossed about to the end of time, and no profit in it.

I asked a black-haired girl at the pilgrims' camp whether I might speak with Brother Francis. She said he was resting in his tent, but then she read my face, and in her kindness took me to him. My brother was asleep. Across eight years I knew him as though I had just then waked beside him in our old house on the Twenyet Road. At the girl's touch on his shoulder he came awake quickly—he always had—and asked: "Beata, my dear—is it time for prayers?"

"Not yet," she said, and I saw she loved him, not only as a believer loves a saint, but as a woman loves a man. "There's one here in need of you." Then she stared amazed from his face to mine, and presently left us.

I knelt by his cot, spoke his name, lost in the puzzled gaze of his so-familiar eyes. He said: "I'm sorry, sir—are you in trouble? What can I do for you? Why do you call me Leo?"

"Leopold, has your memory thrown me away?" For an instant I thought he was shaken, that he really knew me; then I could see in him only confusion. I recalled how once he had gashed his left arm in falling from a tree. "Here," I said, and shoved back the sleeve of his robe and found the scar, a jagged whiteness. "The oak near Rondo's Shrine—a hot August morning—I carried you to the shrine, where the priest bandaged and scolded you."

He searched my face, and told me he was sure I was not trying to deceive him; but was I not mistaken? "For my life began," he said, "in a night-time room where I woke and knew I must go out into the world and learn the ways of it and become a messenger. I knew this from the Companion who spoke to me there, and came with me on my journey out of Nuber." He was speaking slowly, reminiscently, as if partly to himself. "I worked on farms. Sometimes I lived in the woods among the wild things. You see, I have never lived before—everything was new. I was held in a Moha prison once, for vagrancy. But before all this, you understand, I can't have been anything more than a germ of thought at the heart of chaos."

"Did you not change to your young man's form from a bony thirteen-year-old boy just into puberty, with a certain scar on his arm?"

He answered reasonably: "I suppose I did. Maybe there was a life before the one I know; some tell me there must have been. Forgive me if it's unkind—I can't pretend to remember you."

"Sidney Sturm? Jon Rohan?" I watched the beautiful saint's face, my anger not quite dying: maybe it has not quite died. "Louis Graz? Louis Graz and his wife, who died giving birth to a mue?"

"I am sorry, sir. Who were they?"

"Your father and mother, and mine. I am Jermyn Graz. I cared for you and loved you. I do now." I pulled the amulet from under my jacket. "You left this behind, Leo, in the dormitory of the Priests' School at Nuber eight years ago."

He opened the applewood box. Now, Sidney had made the fastening with such uncanny skill that it was quite concealed; no one could open it without a fumbling search unless he already knew the trick. Brother Francis opened it without hesitation. He looked on the clay image and said: "Oh, no! I could never have seen this before." He let the box drop, as if it hurt his fingers.

Outside the tent began a screaming uproar, and two soldiers of the Katskil Imperial Guard burst in, seizing my brother by the arms. "Are you he they call Brother Francis?"

"I am Brother Francis."

"Then I have a warrant for your arrest on a charge of treason against the sovereign people and the Emperor."

"I have done no treason."

"Not for us to judge. You are to come with us." He made no resistance. His eyes warned me that any effort of mine to help would only worsen this new trouble. I have tried to imagine that his loss of memory was assumed to prevent my involvement in the disaster that he knew was about to overtake him; but no—those eyes were surely not seeing me as Jermyn Graz. Following in my stricken obscurity as the soldier led him away, I saw how a platoon of the Guards was dispersing his followers with cudgels and whips, and gathering in some of them to be tied together like a string of slaves. The girl, that gentle Beata who had acted as my guide, flung herself at one of the men in a blind effort to reach Brother Francis, and was pushed to the ground. Her wrists were bound and she was carried off on a giant shoulder, unconscious, limp as a sack of meal.

As Your Beneficence knows, Brother Francis was taken to the military prison at Sofran and held there incommunicado for ten months. Through autumn and winter the war ground on. In April was fought the battle of Brakabin Meadows, and Jon Rohan, who had better have died there, wounded. Only after the war was over did I learn how another band of pilgrims had marched south from central Moha led by a disciple of Brother Francis, one Sister Adonaia. That group was intercepted in a mountain pass by Mohan soldiers, hunted down through the thickets, and butchered. As if, my lord, the two armies had agreed like feral lovers to sweep aside anything that threatened the consummation of their squalid embrace.

I will not try to tell of the trial. Let the Examiners study the transcript. Let them also consider the revulsion within the Church itself after the war. Let them consider how the new Patriarch Benedict denounced the verdict against Brother Francis on many counts, saying that it was tainted by political expediency as well as bigotry—the Church had been hired, he said in effect, to do the hatchet work of an insane Emperor. (There does seem no doubt that the Emperor Mahonn was witless in the last year of his life, and that he was dressed in a wolfskin and drinking fresh chicken's blood when the assassins found him.) Let the Examiners consider how Patriarch Benedict invoked the Third Century ecclesiastical law *Contra Superbiam,* placing the whole Empire under a year's penance. Without this extreme reversal of the Church's position I could not have entered the monastic life.[10]

---

[10] W.B. writes: *"He convicts himself under* Contra Superbiam.

Sidney and I were refused admission to the Patriarchal Palace during the Preparatory Interrogations. We searched out Jon Rohan. How embittered he was!—but he was drifting away from us even before the war. I told him of finding Leopold, of the refusal to admit us; we begged him to go in our place. A wounded veteran with the Iron Wheel of St. Franklin was less likely to be refused. But Jon would not believe Leopold could have become Brother Francis, whose very name Jon loathed. For some baffled words of mine defending the actions of Brother Francis, I thought poor distracted Jon would attack us with his crutch. His wife, disheartened, lovely Sara, begged us to go.

Then at Leopold's final trial and examination at the Lecture Hall of the Palace, I was admitted (but Sidney was not—perhaps they feared his wealth and distinction would weigh too heavily in the prisoner's favor) and the Archbishop of Orange permitted me to testify—what a mockery! Leopold, thin and haggard in his chains, denied me again; but not in quite the same way, my Lord Abbot. I felt he might be denying me for my own protection, lest I burn with him. Those judges were certainly determined to have his life. All but one perhaps: I read compassion in the face of one of them; but it was not a strong face, and he did not speak while I was there.

Quickly the Archbishop's questioning led to the clay image. I was prepared for that trap. Seeing more clearly than I, Sidney had persuaded me to leave the image hidden at his house in Kingstone. If those judges connected Leopold to it, they would make of it idolatry, witchcraft, who knows what? I did badly, my lord—stammered, wept, disgraced myself. I denied knowledge of the image, was called a perjurer (as of course I was), dragged from the Hall, and searched. Sidney and I were banished from the Holy City. And Jon did testify, that day. They must have held him in another anteroom, for we never saw him. He—I will not write of that. It must be in the transcript. Condemned, Leopold was taken to Kingstone.

Who is he to judge the Church and speak as though it were subject to change?"

Behind a chain of polis and soldiers he was drawn in a slow
cart to the stake in the marketplace. I was not the only one
who called to him in love—if he could have heard it. I struggled to the edge of the crowd. A guard recognized me, secured me with an arm bent up behind my back, and grumbled at my ear: "Quiet, fool! We don't want to arrest you."

They lit the faggots at my brother's feet. The wood was
damp; the smoke flung itself upward in a dirty cloud. I heard
my brother cry out: "My Companion, have you forsaken
me?" Moments later, above the priests' chanting, the flames,
the rumbling of the storm that was reaching over the city, he
called me. Very clearly I heard him call: "Jermyn, I have remembered you."

Fr. Jermyn, O.S.S., Precentor

2

*By Maeron of Nupal, Fr. Lit., Clericus Tribunalis Ec-
clesiae in the Patriarchate of Urbanus II: being a Digest of
the Terminal Trial of the Heretic known as Brother Francis
before the Court of Ecclesiastical Inquiry at Nuber, in the
month of October in the year of Abraham 427, His Grace the
Archbishop of Orange Presiding Judge.*

His Grace the Archbishop of Orange being present, the Court
was opened on the ninth day of October, at or about the hour
of Tierce, and before the judges were brought for final examination and judgment the prisoner calling himself Brother
Francis and reputed by some to be one Leopold Graz son of
the cobbler Louis Graz (deceased) of Twenyet Road in the
City of Kingstone, this individual called Brother Francis being charged with heresy and certain related criminal actions
as set forth in eight Articles.

Present on the dais were also the Most Reverend Jeffrey
Sortees Lord Bishop of Nupal and, representing the Secular
Estate, the Right Honorable Tomas Robson Earl of Cornal,
Supervisor of the Ecclesiastical Prisons at Nuber.

The man called Brother Francis being present, the judge

explained to the prisoner his rights at law, reminding him that during the Preparatory Interrogations he had refused the assistance of ecclesiastical counsel, and inquired whether he yet persisted in such refusal now that the matter had come to the point of final trial wherein he stood imperiled of his life.

The prisoner said he needed no defense but what he possessed.

His Grace said: Do you mean simply that you are in God's care?—but the Lord surely would have men aid one another in extremity.

The prisoner replied that he would not ask for counsel.

His Grace suggested that a defending counsel might aid that search for truth which was one of the major concerns of the trial. The prisoner replied that no other knew his heart, therefore no other should assume the burden of his defense.

Then, having been instructed concerning the sanctity of the oath, and that he ought to tell the truth as much for his soul's sake as out of respect for Church and Law, the prisoner said that he would tell the truth so far as he knew it, and so far as he was not forbidden to tell it by his conscience or by that Companion who to him was a second conscience and whose will he had accepted as a guide.

His Grace the Archbishop told him he could not make any such reservations concerning the oath; and the Earl of Cornal also admonished him, saying that he was demanding a license to lie.

The prisoner said: Not so, my lord: I will not lie. But only God, if God lives, can command my mind; therefore I will not swear to tell everything, lest later I be forsworn.

His Grace asked: Do you doubt that God lives?

The man called Brother Francis said: Does any man live altogether without doubt, Your Grace? I have doubted it as one may doubt that the sun will rise.

His Grace said: It is perhaps a point of philosophy.

Bishop Sortees said: As for the reservation on the oath, Your Grace, is it not a reservation that any of us might make? If made out of true deference to the will of God I see no evil in it.

The Earl of Cornal said: But there is that matter of what he calls his Companion.

The prisoner then said that he would take the oath, but in no other way than he had stated, even if the torture were renewed and repeated until he died.

His Grace said: Well, let him be sworn to tell the truth as he understands it. I suppose no man can do more. We must not lose our way in irresponsible debate.

On these terms the prisoner willingly knelt, and having rested his forehead on the Book of Abraham, he made over his heart the sign of the Wheel and swore to tell the truth.

Then was read to the man called Brother Francis the First Article of the Charge.

ARTICLE I: *The man going by the name of Brother Francis is charged with making unproven claim to be a messenger of God.*

Questioned as to the truth of this, the prisoner said: I do not claim and have never claimed it.

His Grace said: But you have called yourself a messenger?

The prisoner said: I have, but cannot tell who sent me.

His Grace asked: Cannot, or will not, my son?

The prisoner said: I cannot, Your Grace. I do not know.

Earl Robson said: It might have been the Devil?

The prisoner said: I have never had reason to think so.

Reminded by His Grace that some of his followers had declared under the ordeal that they believed him to be sent by God, the prisoner said they must have spoken whatever their hearts believed, but not what they knew, since he did not know it himself.

Earl Robson of Comal said: I can't understand this, a man who carries a message, or thinks he does, not knowing who sent him.

The prisoner said: But for the direction of my Companion, I would not call myself a messenger; and my Companion may well be of the chosen of God. I think he is; but he has not told me so.

The Earl of Comal then remarked that, with deference to his colleagues of the Ecclesia, he considered the prisoner had already convicted himself under the First Article of the Charge. His Grace requested the view of the Lord Bishop of Nupal, who said that while he felt the prisoner had so far spoken with reason and humility, he would not further commit himself at this moment.

Then was read to the prisoner the Second Article of the Charge.

ARTICLE II: *The man going by the name of Brother Francis is charged with accepting guidance in all his actions from a being outside the common perceptions of men, whom he calls his Companion, in defiance of the First Law of Holy Church as laid down in the Book of Abraham, Chapter Five, Section Seven:* THOU SHALT SET NO AUTHORITY ABOVE THE AUTHORITY OF ALMIGHTY GOD AS DEFINED BY HIS ANOINTED.

Questioned as to the truth of the charge, the prisoner stated that he had accepted the guidance of his Companion in all actions, but only in the manner in which others might accept the guidance of priests, believing that their counsel would not be contrary to God's will so far as any human being can know it.

His Grace said: But you have no reason except your own opinion, the feeling of your own heart, to believe that this Companion can be regarded as one of God's anointed?

After reflection the prisoner said: No, Your Grace: it is true that I have formed this belief in the light of my own opinion and conscience.

His Grace said: You will admit, then, that unless it can be proved that your Companion is one of God's anointed, you stand convicted of heresy under the Second Article?

The Prisoner said: I can hardly deny it.

Bishop Sortees asked: But you have sincerely believed that your Companion would require nothing of you that violated God's laws?

The prisoner said: Yes, Father, I believe that.

The Earl of Cornal, inquiring whether the prisoner had known his Companion by any other name, the prisoner denied it. Asked by the Earl to describe the Companion, the prisoner said he had seen him only with the eyes of his mind.

The Earl of Cornal said: You are unreasonable. You are attempting to confuse the Court with metaphysics.

The prisoner said: My lord. I use what words I find. I know my Companion; I do not see him as I see your lordship in the flesh.

His Grace the judge asked: Is he with you now, my son?

The prisoner said: No. Your Grace.

His Grace asked: Is it long since he has been with you?

The prisoner said: It has been long. He has not been with me since the day of my arrest.

His Grace asked: Never during the Preparatory Interrogations? He was not with you on the day when, because of contumacious refusals, it was necessary for you to undergo physical persuasion?

The prisoner said: Had he been with me then, Your Grace, I could have borne the torture with a better heart.

His Grace asked: Do you draw any conclusion from this absence of your Companion while you have been in the custody of the Church?

The prisoner said: I draw no conclusion, Your Grace. I remember too well that in the ten months of my imprisonment in the military prison, at Sofran, when I was accused of treason but not of heresy, my Companion was not with me.

His Grace asked: Do you think it possible then that your Companion may have been only the substance of an illusion which has now passed from you? You must know, my son, that the Church has no wish to punish anyone for a malady of the mind.

The prisoner replied quickly and firmly that his Companion was no illusion.

Then the Earl of Cornal asked: Have you ever accompanied your Companion to certain meetings?

The man called Brother Francis said: He was often with me when I spoke to the people, to those who joined my company.

Earl Robson said: That is not the question. Have you ever gone, with this being you call a Companion, to meetings of any group called a coven, a meeting of those who deny the divinity of our Savior Abraham and of his prophet of Old Time Jesus Christ?

The prisoner said: No.

The Earl said: You will answer with respect.

The prisoner said; I know nothing of witchcraft, my lord, but I believe it to be a delusion.

The Earl said: Your Grace, is not that heresy in itself?

His Grace the Archbishop replied that the entire question of witchcraft was a matter of dispute, and that no doubt much light would be shed on it in the next Council on the Creed. He suggested also that with regard to this prisoner, this line of inquiry had apparently been exhausted, and with negative result, in the Preparatory Interrogations, and during the physical persuasion that the Earl himself had attended as Supervisor of the Prisons. His Grace then asked the prisoner: If your Companion should come to you while you are on trial here, will you know it?

The prisoner said: I will know it, Your Grace.

His Grace asked: And will you tell us of it?

The prisoner said: If my Companion permits it.

His Grace said: Have a care, my son, how you set the whim of this unknown Companion above the authority of the Ecclesia.

The prisoner said: I have already stated that I have obeyed all the directions of my Companion, even against my will.

The Lord Bishop of Nupal asked him: But if your Companion required you to perform some act forbidden by the laws of God, you would not perform it, would you?

The prisoner said: Father, I think this could not happen.

His Grace said: But you must answer the Lord Bishop's question, and do so remembering your oath.

The prisoner said: I think the will and the laws of God

have always been explained by some human agency, and these are fallible.

His Grace said: My son, Bishop Sortees' most kindly worded question deserved no such response, which we find over the borderline of heresy. If you continue headstrong and impudent, you will compel us to find you guilty under the Second Article.

Then was read to the prisoner the Third Article of the Charge.

ARTICLE III: *The man going by the name Brother Francis is charged with claiming to have begun life miraculously, without father or mother, in the body of a boy about thirteen years of age.*

In response to the reading of this Charge, the prisoner declared that he had claimed no miracle but merely described what had happened to the best of his knowledge: that his conscious life had indeed commenced at that apparent age, with no memory of an earlier existence.

The Lord Bishop of Nupal said: But this would be a miracle, astonishing as a virgin birth. No childhood?

His Grace reminded Bishop Sortees that cases of lost memory were not unknown, a malady of the mind that was very possibly a punishment for secret sins, and thus no miracle was necessarily involved.

The man called Brother Francis said: I think this may be, Your Grace. God may have taken my memory, but perhaps to strengthen me as a messenger, or for other reasons that I cannot know. I do know that I woke as if from a void: I was; and my Companion guided me.

Bishop Sortees said: I am amazed. I should have taken time to read the record of the Preparatory Interrogations. You woke, Brother Francis, knowing the speech of men?

The Earl of Cornal remarked it had been agreed that the prisoner was not to be addressed as "Brother" since he had demonstrated no right to the title, as would be stated in the Fourth Article. Bishop Sortees apologized for his error, reminding the Earl that he had come uninstructed to the Court in the place of the Bishop of Ulsta, who was ill. Then he repeated his question to the prisoner.

The prisoner said: I must have done so, Father, since my Companion spoke to me and I understood him.

The Lord Bishop asked: And no childhood, my son? No childhood?

The prisoner said: I cannot remember any, Father.

The Earl asked: Well, what kind of voice has your Companion?

The prisoner said he knew that voice with the hearing of his mind.

Earl Robson said: Oh, again, again! Metaphysics!

His Grace the Archbishop then spoke of delusions wherein the deluded may be innocent of evil intent; and the Bishop of Nupal declared that he thought the prisoner spoke with no evil intent but rather like one impelled by a dream; and His Grace warned against premature judgments before completion of the reading of the Articles.

The Earl of Cornal said: But I ask myself, Your Grace, what motive the accused can have had for claiming this miraculous or seemingly miraculous thing, other than a wish to dazzle his befuddled followers.

His Grace said: Let us continue.

Then was read to the prisoner the Fourth Article of the Charge.

ARTICLE IV: *The man going by the name Brother Francis is charged with unlawfully assuming that title, being not a member of any religious body recognized by the Holy Murcan Church, and with wearing a robe simulating that of a lay brother of the Ordo Sancti Silvani.*

In response to this charge the prisoner stated that when he woke to life it was with the knowledge of the Companion calling him, and by the name Brother Francis; that the Companion had always called him by this name and no other, and that he could not remember responding to any other name.

As for the robe, he declared it had been made for him by a woman of his company who knew nothing of religious orders. He also respectfully inquired whether there was an actual law of Church or State that forbade a man to call himself Brother or allow himself to be so addressed if he was not a member of a religious order.

The Earl of Cornal said: Verily the Devil is a lawyer. Everyone knows the title is proper only to a monk. Statute or no statute, can this fellow require us to overlook the tradition of the ages to suit his whim? And how should a woman make a monk's robe not knowing what she did?

His Grace said: My lord of Cornal, we must not assume too much. This may even be a case of true ignorance on both counts. The prisoner's robe, I remind you, did not carry the symbol of the Wheel, nor the symbol of crossed shovels that defines a lay brother's status. And to the prisoner His Grace said: We must warn you, however, that by accepting "Brother" as a title you have caused in some persons a mistaken notion that you spoke with the authority of the Church. This was at least a deception, whether or not by intent.

The prisoner said: Your Grace, I admit my error in this. I told those who joined me that I was no churchman; I ought to have told them not to address me in a way that could cause misunderstanding.

Earl Robson said: Your Grace, I think he buys a great sin with a small penance.

His Grace said: My son, you have spoken with humility, yet I feel a defiance in you still. Are you defiant, at heart?

After long silence, during which His Grace desired that the accused be not interrupted but given time to reflect and consult his conscience, the man calling himself Brother Francis replied: No, Your Grace, I do not think I am.

Bishop Sortees of Nupal asked: In accepting the title "Brother" were you perhaps intending to implement that ancient wish for the brotherhood of man which our Savior Abraham declared in the words: "Let us be born again together"—could this be?

The prisoner said: Those are words that I treasure, Father,

but I can say no more than I have said. I woke, and my Companion called me by that name.

Then was read to the prisoner the Fifth Article of the Charge.

ARTICLE V: *The man going by the name Brother Francis is charged with speaking against the sacrament of marriage, has lived in open sin with a common harlot, and has inspired the women of his company with such a concupiscent hysteria that they believe him to be a god.*

Questioned as to this, the prisoner replied that he had once said, to those friends who marched with him to the meadow of Gilba, that he did not suppose marriage was the only good way men and women might live together. He said he did not think this amounted to speaking against a sacrament. As for the remainder of the charge, he said it was absurd.

The Earl of Cornal asked: Do you deny then that you lived in carnal intimacy, while going about under the name Brother Francis, with one Beata Firmin, a common prostitute?

The prisoner said: Beata Firmin was caught up in the life of a prostitute at an earlier time; she had abandoned it before joining our company. If it has a bearing on my trial for heresy, I do not deny that I loved her, but my Companion has commanded me to live chastely for the sake of my mission. Often Beata slept in my tent, but we had no carnal knowledge of each other.

Earl Robson said: More fool you, she's a handsome woman.

The man calling himself Brother Francis said: Well, my lord, you cannot accuse me both of fornication and of the avoidance of it.

Earl Robson said: Nay then, nay, we must cease jesting. I remind you that you are on trial for criminal actions as well as for heresy.

The prisoner said: I cannot conceive how my friendship for Beata Firmin can be described as a criminal action.

Bishop Sortees said: My lord, surely any criminal actions, to be judged by this Court, must bear a relation to the charge of heresy.

The Earl said: Your Reverence, I think the relation can be shown. And to the prisoner he said: You are aware that the woman Beata Firmin believes you to be a god?

The prisoner said: I have been separated from her for ten months. Ten months ago I am certain she had no such delusion.

The Earl said: Why, man, she speaks of nothing but you and your divinity. She rants, she drivels, she bites her lips to make them red and pleasing against the dream of your return, she sits in her cell with a pillow under her smock and croons to it, saying she is with child by the Divine Brother and the child's dear name shall be Jesus. Is the Companion with you now?

The prisoner replied: My Lord Robson, if your prison has brought Beata Firmin to this state, I will pray God to forgive you in Hell, since it is beyond my human power to forgive.

His Grace said: Finish the reading of the Articles.

The Earl said: It seems I have been cursed by a witch.

His Grace said to him: My lord, my lord, no more jesting. Finish the reading, Clerk.

But Earl Robson of Cornal said: Your Grace, as God is my witness I am not jesting. The moment after this prisoner cursed me I was taken with a violent pain in my right hand.

Bishop Sortees said: But he did not curse your lordship. He said he would pray for your forgiveness by the Almighty, and had I spoken as you did, I declare to you I would feel need of such forgiveness myself.

His Grace asked: Do you wish an adjournment, my lord of Cornal, or may we continue with the reading of the Articles?

The Earl of Cornal said: I ask no adjournment, Your Grace. I will bear it. But I wish this fellow to know, I say to him in open court, if he slips off our griddle here in the Court of the Ecclesia, I'll fetch him down with a charge of witchcraft under secular law, and it shall go hard with him. Then was read to the prisoner the Sixth Article of the Charge.

ARTICLE VI: *The man going by the name Brother Francis is charged with professing to heal the sick by miraculous means.*

In response to this the prisoner said that he professed nothing except his message; that some persons might have found healing in his presence, at times when the Companion was with him, and that if God had truly healed them it must have been done by his Companion rather than by himself.

The Earl of Cornal said: And your Companion, we understand, politely declines to be questioned by this Court?

The prisoner said: My Companion is not here.

The Earl said: A pity, a pity. I should admire to ask his opinion concerning the pain in my hand.

The man known as Brother Francis did not answer. Then was read to him the Seventh Article of the Charge.

ARTICLE VII: *The man going by the name Brother Francis is charged with wantonly leading a band of his followers to a place of peril between the savage invading host of Moha and the defenders of the Empire.*

His Grace the Archbishop said: Since the fact itself is not in dispute, I will only ask how you explain this action.

The prisoner said: We hoped to illuminate the nature of war.

His Grace said: You must know the Church is deeply opposed to war. Why did you not work through the Church?

The prisoner said: That month, Your Grace, Masses were being said for the victory of the Imperial arms.

His Grace replied: Naturally. Since the Holy City is located within the Empire, an attack on Katskil is an attack on Holy Church; therefore the rights of the case are not in question. In any event, your followers were merely swept aside, as you must have known they would be. Why this empty gesture? You placed your people between fire and fire without a shield. Had the Guard not intervened and dispersed them, many lives might have been lost.

The prisoner said: I hear that many of my company were arrested, some questioned under torture, none released except by death.

His Grace explained that this was a political and military problem, not within the competence of the Ecclesiastical Court. The prisoner then stood silent a long time, and appeared like one listening, and there was whispering among the members of the Ecclesia privileged to attend as spectators, which His Grace the Judge was obliged to silence, the prisoner seeming unaware of this. At length the prisoner said: Your Grace, we sought to illuminate the nature of war. But I understand now that the greatest evil is not war itself but the love of war. However, Your Grace, is it not a fact that the armies did not meet that day?

His Grace said: What reasoning is this? They met later, and at that very place. Did you not hear in prison about the battle of Gilba?—I am told that Mohan forces still hold the highlands north of the lake. So what price your intervention? And the armies met at Brakabin Meadows in the following spring, another disaster. There is a witness to be called who was wounded at Brakabin. You shall see for yourself, sir, how effectively your dangerous dream has prevented war. Well?

The prisoner said: Your Grace, we never had great hope of preventing the continuation of this war: only, as I have said, to illuminate the nature of war. In any case, I did as my Companion directed me, and I would do the same again.

Earl Robson said: But maybe with fewer followers?

The man called Brother Francis replied: Maybe with a million followers. Or with two or three. I would do the same again.

His Grace then gently asked the prisoner whether he had been listening a moment past to his Companion, and the prisoner replied: I cannot answer that, Your Grace, because I am not certain.

The Bishop of Nupal said: Your Grace! I have read of some in Old Time who went up unarmed against the machineries of war. Certain priests and others burned their own bodies in protest at evils they found intolerable. It is folly perhaps; but so far I can find no sin in this man.

His Grace said: It is true this Article deals with a social and military issue. However, the wisdom of the Court has included it among the charges of heresy, and so we must consider it.

Earl Robson said: Does it not seem, Your Grace, that this prisoner has set himself up to judge between the nations as only God can judge? The issues of the battlefield, surely, are decided by God and God alone, not by fanatic preachers.

His Grace said: This will be weighed; my lord of Cornal. Does your hand still pain you?

The Earl replied: There is only one more Article to read. After that, if Your Grace thinks best, we might adjourn till tomorrow.

Then was read to the prisoner the Eighth Article of the Charge.

ARTICLE VIII: *The man going by the name Brother Francis is charged with deluding his followers by talk of a coming heaven on earth described as a City of Light, in contravention of Holy Doctrine as set forth in the Book of Abraham, Chapter Five, Section Seven:* THOU SHALT CHERISH NO TREASURE ON EARTH OR IN THE THOUGHT OF EARTH, WHICH IS SOON TO PERISH AND PASS AWAY.

In reply to this, the prisoner said that he had never described the City of Light as a heaven on earth, or ever intentionally deluded anyone in any way.

His Grace asked him: What then is the City of Light?

The man called Brother Francis said: In the City of Light no violence is done to the body of earth or to the human body or spirit. The light of the City is the light of understanding and love, the two inseparable.

His Grace asked: It is a dream of earth and not of heaven?

The man called Brother Francis said: It is not a dream of

heaven on earth, for in the City of Light men may strive for perfection, I suppose, but they do not reject the good that is attainable.

His Grace said: And for this dream of earth you have endured imprisonment and physical persuasion, and may suffer worse: was this not for the sake of persuading others to share your dream, and leave their appropriate labors, and follow you?

The man called Brother Francis replied: I do not urge or persuade. I tell the vision as I see it, and I think those who followed me were sharing it for at least a part of my journey.

His Grace said: As far as the meadow at Gilba, where the armies might have rolled over them. My son, there have been visionaries before who perverted the just course of life. Do you not see the result when men turn aside from their necessary labors after a moonblink, an *ignis fatuus?* Who shall plow and sow, and tend the fields, and mind the harvest? You must have been taught, perhaps in the childhood you do not remember, how God has placed us on this miserable earth for a time of trial, so that souls deserving of Heaven may be winnowed out from the unworthy, and how then the earth shall pass away and be as a drop of water in the firmament. Do you not see, my son, that no other explanation of our presence here is possible, since we must believe that God is all-loving and all-powerful? Why do we concern ourselves with heresy at all, if not to protect our people from straying into disaster? To dazzle the credulous with your vision of a City of Light on earth is to betray them, to hide from them this truth that God's revelation through Abraham has made clear to us. And whether your heart's intent is evil or benevolent, the result is the same as though the Devil himself had stood at your shoulder and charmed the gullible with your voice.

The man called Brother Francis replied: Yet there is a City of Light. I said to those who followed and heard me: There is a battle of Armageddon, where good and evil confront each other for a decision, not for all time but for the time that you know; and there is a City of Light on earth, built by your labor not for all time but for the time that you know. Every day, every night the battle of Armageddon is to be fought, and won or lost: see that you find courage. Every night, every day something is given to the building of the City of Light or taken from it: see that your share is given, and with goodwill. The battle is within you; the city is for all your kind, not for all time but for the time that you know.

At this hour the session of examination and judgment was adjourned until morning of the following day.

His Grace the Archbishop of Orange being present, the Court was opened on the tenth day of October, at or about the hour of Tierce, for the second day of the final judgment and examination in the case of the prisoner charged with heresy who calls himself Brother Francis.

Present as before were the Most Reverend Jeffrey Sortees Lord Bishop of Nupal, and the Rt. Hon. Tomas Robson Earl Of Cornal, who attended this session with his right hand covered by a bandage. His Grace the Archbishop graciously inquired whether his lordship was still in pain; the Earl replied he would willingly bear it rather than delay the trial, adding that all those present yesterday must bear in mind that they were witnesses to what had occurred.

The prisoner being then brought to the dock and chained, His Grace announced that one Jermyn Graz, itinerant cobbler of no known address, had urged his right to testify before the Court, and that this request had been granted. Master Graz came forward and was sworn.

To him His Grace said: When you demanded admission to the Preparatory Interrogations it was denied, Master Graz, in view of the improbability of your story and the fact that the accused disavowed any knowledge of your name. Since then other information has come to us tending to support your claim to be heard. You are sworn; I must further caution you to limit yourself to the question put to you. I request you to look now on the accused and say whether you know him.

Master Graz looked on the prisoner and said: He is my brother, Your Grace. His is my beloved brother.

His Grace then directed the accused to look on the cobbler

Jermyn Graz and say whether he knew him.

The prisoner said: I know him as the man who came to my tent at Gilba on the day I was arrested. If I ever saw him before then, the memory is gone with all my other memories of childhood.

Master Graz said: He is my brother. He disappeared from the Priests' School at Nuber in 418. It was the seventh of December.

His Grace said: Master Graz, when we learned something of this from another source, we spoke to the Headmaster of the Priests' School. The records do show that a boy Leopold Graz, thirteen (your brother we do not doubt), did vanish that day. But the Headmaster Father Ricordi was shown the man called Brother Francis at the prison, and would not say with any certainty that he was Leopold Graz, and you have now heard the prisoner testify that he does not know you. Then His Grace asked the accused: Have you any recollection of attending the Priests' School at Nuber, or any school? The prisoner said: I have none, Your Grace.

His Grace said: But when Father Ricordi described to you the Senior Dormitory at the school as it would look by candlelight, you remembered this as the place where you had, as you say, waked to life?

The prisoner said: That is true, Your Grace.

Master Graz said: He is my brother.

An attending officer of the Court was then obliged to restrain the witness from climbing the barrier into the dock; the man was weeping and appeared beside himself. Being restrained, he apologized to the Court for his behavior.

His Grace said: Subject to your dissent, my lords, I think we may accept the probability that the man called Brother Francis is indeed Leopold Graz, once of Kingstone, who has suffered the loss of memory of his childhood, under what divine punishment we know not. There being no dissent, His Grace said further: We have then an identity for the prisoner, and will address him from now on as Leopold Graz. But I point out to you that this does not further our inquiry, unless the history of his childhood produces evidence bearing on the charge of heresy. I will ask you now, Master Graz, if you have recovered control of yourself, whether you are acquainted with a Captain Jon Rohan.

Master Graz said: I am, Your Grace, or I was. We were boys together, Jon and another friend and my brother Leopold and I.

His Grace: Have you seen Captain Rohan recently?

Master Graz said: Not for a month or more. I went to see him when I was refused admission to the Preparatory Interrogations, hoping he might be allowed to testify in my place. He told me he believed my brother was dead. As a soldier he hated and despised Brother Francis from what he had heard about him, and refused to consider that Brother Francis might be Leopold. Jon still suffers from an unhealed wound. He was not himself; I should have forgiven it. We parted in anger.

His Grace said: We have spoken with him, rather our representatives have, and with your other friend Dr. Sturm. You yourself are better known to us than you may suppose. What can you tell us concerning a clay image once in the possession of your brother Leopold?

Master Graz then appeared startled and confused, stammering and saying he knew of no image belonging to his brother.

The Earl of Cornal said: You are under oath, Master Graz.

Master Graz said: Ah, you mean my little amulet. I had one till lately, the sort I'm sure the Church hasn't disapproved. But my brother would never have cared for anything like that. He was always deeply religious, Your Grace. He would have found it sacrilegious.

His Grace asked: This idol is not now in your possession?

Master Graz replied: No, Your Grace. I lost it some time back.

The Bishop of Nupal would then have questioned him, but His Grace intervened, saying: My lord, whether or not he is lying about possession of the image, he has perjured himself on another count, as testimony that follows will show, and we cannot permit the Court of the Ecclesia to be contami-

nated by a perjurer. Attendant, take this man Jermyn Graz to
the anteroom, strip him, and search him for possession of
any sort of charm or amulet. If any is found, he is to be
committed to the prison for examination. If not, he is to be
conducted to the border of the Holy City of Nuber and
warned not to return within a year, and he is to consider himself fortunate in the leniency of this Court.

Master Graz was removed, and His Grace addressed the
prisoner: Leopold Graz, I note that you have become very
white. Do you wish the help of a physician?

The prisoner said: No, Your Grace, a physician cannot
help me.

His Grace asked: You do admit, then, that you may stand
in need of help for your soul's sake? And when the prisoner
appeared unable to answer, His Grace gently inquired: For
your soul's sake, what can you tell us concerning a clay image, male and female, in a box of applewood fastened to a
silver chain?

After much hesitation, the prisoner said: Your Grace, I
have no knowledge of any such thing.

The Earl of Gonial said: Have you lost your memory for
recent events also? Did not that man Jermyn Graz show you
such an image in your tent at Gilba?

The prisoner said: No, my lord. No.

His Grace then called Captain Jon Rohan, who came from
the west anteroom with the assistance of an attendant, and
was sworn. His Grace asked: Captain Rohan, you are a veteran of the battle of Brakabin Meadows, wounded in the service of His Majesty the Emperor?

The witness replied: I am, Your Grace.

His Grace asked: You testify here willingly, under no du-
ress, Captain Rohan, and in accordance with our previous
conversations at the time when you volunteered to appear
before this Court?

The witness replied: I do, Your Grace.

His Grace said: I will ask whether in former years you
were acquainted with a boy named Leopold Graz, son of the
cobbler Louis Graz of Twenyet Road in Kingstone?

The witness said: I was, Your Grace. He was five years younger than I, and I was a playmate of his elder brother when he was born. I knew him until his thirteenth year, when he disappeared from the Priests' School at Kingstone.

His Grace said: Look on the accused, Captain Rohan, and say whether you know him.

Captain Rohan looked long on the man called Brother Francis and said: Yes, that is Leopold Graz, though greatly changed.

His Grace then directed the prisoner to look on Captain Rohan well and say whether he knew him. The prisoner said with apparent indifference: He is quite unknown to me.

Captain Rohan said: He knows me. He has betrayed his country and his people. He cannot hide behind mystery. He knows, Your Grace, he knows I understand him.

Bishop Sortees said: You are not here to judge, Captain Rohan. I pray Your Grace will instruct him to limit himself to the question.

His Grace said: You must do that, Captain Rohan. I ask you now to tell what you know of the childhood of Leopold Graz.

Captain Rohan said: He possessed great charm, as a boy, but he was what people call fey. Strange, ungovernable, given to outrageous fancies. He became fascinated by an obscene clay image, an object indecently representing both sexes in one body, that his brother secured for him from a Gypsy when Leopold was about seven, and which I think was never out of Leopold's possession until he disappeared from the Priests' School.

His Grace asked: And this obsession with a clay image, was it associated with any other thing that you recall as unusual?

Captain Rohan testified: It was, Your Grace. Very soon after his brother gave him the image, Leopold was speaking of an invisible companion who gave him guidance.

The Lord Bishop of Nupal said: Captain Rohan, is this not quite a common thing in childhood? A child, especially a lonely one, is often given to such fancies, surely.

Captain Rohan said: But this did not pass away as we expect childhood fancies to do, Your Reverence. Yes, my own little daughter chattered of such a thing once, and I corrected her, and soon heard no more about it. But this boy Leopold continued to believe in his spectral companion—and does so still, I understand. We others, being ignorant boys, were much impressed by his talk, and I am sorry to say we encouraged it a while. I stopped doing so when I realized that it bordered on idolatry, or perhaps passed the border.

The Earl of Cornal asked: Do you say that he in fact worshiped this idol, this image?

Captain Rohan testified: My lord, he would hold it in his hands, and often close his eyes and appear to be listening; and then he might give us advice on matters of which he could have known nothing. It was, I remember, advice much more mature than belonged to his years.

His Grace asked: And what, if you know, became of this clay image?

Captain Rohan said: The boy Leopold left it behind when he disappeared from the Priests' School. I believe Sidney Sturm brought it back to Leopold's brother Jermyn, and it was still in Jermyn's possession a month ago when he and Dr. Sturm came to see me.

His Grace said: Leopold Graz, under oath before God to tell the truth, do you say you do not know this man Captain Rohan?

The prisoner said: I know his nature from the way he speaks.

His Grace said: You evade. Do you remember him from the past?

The prisoner said: I cannot answer that.

His Grace said: What? You cannot?

The prisoner said: I took the oath with reservations of which I made no secret. I cannot answer the question.

His Grace said: And you deny any knowledge of a clay image?

After hesitation, the prisoner replied: I do.

His Grace asked: This you say under oath? . . . Leopold

Graz, you must speak so that we hear you, and stand upright if you are able. You declare under oath that you know nothing of any clay image?

The man Leopold Graz called Brother Francis said: The light of the City is the light of understanding and love, the two inseparable.

His Grace the Archbishop then said: There need be no more testimony, no more questioning. The rest, my lords, is for discussion among us three, *in camera*. We insist that there be no loose discussion of this troublesome case by those privileged to attend this hearing as spectators. The Court is now adjourned. Final judgment and sentence will be pronounced on the opening of this Court tomorrow.

3

Letter from Mgr. Wilmot Breen, Magister Theologiae, *Director of Examiners under the Patriarchate of Pretorias IV, to His Beneficence Alesandar Fitzeral, O.S.S., Abbot of St. Benjamin's at Mount Orlook, November 29, 465.*

To Your Beneficence, Greetings.

Speedily and with the help of God we have reached a decision in the question of the blessed Francis of Gilba, and have communicated our finding to His Holiness Pretorius IV by the Will of Heaven Patriarch of the World, It is now our great pleasure to convey to Your Beneficence also the substance of our findings, with gratitude for the assistance so graciously granted us by Your Beneficence in securing the document by Jermyn Graz, which in spite of its dubious nature sheds much on the childhood of the blessed Francis.

We find that beyond doubt Francis of Gilba was divinely inspired in his teaching (so unfortunately never committed to writing) and that in particular his insistence on truthfulness, divine understanding, and divine love as the essence of the everlasting Brownist Faith is a great contribution toward the salvation of mankind. We feel confident that when sufficient time has passed, this noble spirit will be declared sanctified.

In the meantime Your Beneficence will be pleased to learn that the arm bone of the blessed Francis preserved at the Cathedral in Albani continues its work of healing to the manifest glory of God.

We have found that the Companion who appeared to the blessed Francis in his visions was no other than the blessed St. Lucy of Syracuse, martyred in ancient time and venerated throughout the centuries. Understanding in this matter was granted to us in a dream, wherein it was made plain that in speaking of the City of Light, Francis of Gilba was approaching as nearly as God permitted him to explaining the identity of his sacred benefactress: LUCY from ancient Latin LUX, meaning LIGHT. After this guidance it was a simple matter to consult the records, wherein we found that Francis of Gilba, vulgarly known as Leopold Graz, was born on December 13, St. Lucy's Day since time immemorial. Thus all doubt was dispelled: the dross of argument and conjecture fell away and the intention of the Lord was made plain.

We find further, having questioned the benign and ancient woman Mam Lora Stone at the nunnery of St. Ellen at Nupal, that the birth of Francis of Gilba must have been miraculous. St. Lucy, be it remembered, is a patron of woman in childbirth. We need not presume any event so marvelous as a virgin birth, but simply that the mother of Francis was gotten with child by an angelic visitation. A clue to this is unwittingly provided in the manuscript by the man Jermyn Graz, in the passage recording the obscure saying of the boy Francis that he was "born unto the Vine." The Vine, as we know, is secured to the Archangel Dionysus, the Male Principle, and now that the identity of the Companion is known, the conclusion is obvious.

This brings us to a delicate matter wherein we must rely on the discretion of Your Beneficence. The manuscript of the man Jermyn Graz, which we had hoped to return for the archives of St. Benjamin's, has disappeared, owing, we believe, to the criminal dereliction of some minor member of our clerical staff: all of them are to be put to the question, and no doubt the truth will emerge. In the meantime, by the grace of God, a fair copy of the manuscript had been made, from which the gross errors and perversions of the man Jermyn Graz were eliminated; thus we now have a record that is reliable for all time, and if the original manuscript should be recovered, it will probably be the consensus of the Examiners that it ought to be destroyed, not preserved.

The miraculous generation of the blessed Francis of Gilba is rendered even more clear by the fact that Francis could not logically have been whole brother to this man who for many years has been precentor at St. Benjamin's, and who appears to have wormed his way into the affections of Your Beneficence, and whose opinions as they appear in the uncorrected manuscript are tainted with gross heresy and sinful pride and willful error. Your Beneficence will understand that this man Jermyn Graz must be instantly removed from any position at the Abbey, and held in close custody until the Examiners shall have had opportunity to study his literary output— collected stories, legends, commentaries on Old Time, we know not what—and determine whether to place them on the Index Expurgatorius and burn all copies.

Finally—and this is a matter of the utmost urgency—any amulet or image or the like found in the possession of the man Jermyn Graz is to be confiscated and turned over to us for exorcism and disposal. If no such object is found in his possession, he must be persuaded by any approved means to explain his disposition of it. The blessed Francis of Gilba himself repudiated this miserable idol with horror; other implications, we feel sure, will not escape the consideration of Your Beneficence.

Accept, we pray, the assurance of our continual esteem.

Wilmont Breen, M.T.

4

Note from unfrocked prisoner Jermyn Graz to His Beneficence Alesandar Fitzeral, O.S.S., Abbot of St. Benjamin's.

My dear Lord Abbot:

Pray accept my gratitude for the kindness of Your Beneficence in transferring me to this cell where an eastern window
permits me a little morning light, and for allowing me these
writing materials and for permitting me to make this com-
munication to Your Beneficence.

I will first take this opportunity to recant whatever confession of error I may have made under physical persuasion,
and second, to repeat as clearly as I can that which I said to
my examiners and which they would not accept, concerning
my disposal of the two-faced clay.

After I had committed to the hands of Your Beneficence
my Memorandum on the life of my brother Leopold, reflection made it clear to me that the discovery of the image on
my person, considering the present temper of the times,
might result in peril to the clay figure as well as to myself. I
remind Your Beneficence that I have been and still am a his-
torian. To me, in this ugly little dab of clay, there is a beauty
and a wonder that I cannot describe to you: these faces have
seen eternity. Why it was rejected by my poor brother, if indeed it was, I shall never know; but I cannot repudiate it:
these faces that have seen eternity are the faces of my own
kind.

Therefore on leaving Your Beneficence I took myself for
a long walk into the woods outside the monastery grounds,
or perhaps beyond the woods, and I buried the image. It is in
this applewood box that my beloved Sidney made for it, the
silver chain is wrapped around it, and it lies in a place where
it will not be found by any search—for even I, having
smoothed the natural cover and moved away heeding no
landmarks, could not find it again if I would. The Examiners
and their servants cannot overturn all the trees and boulders
or dig away all the earth in all the places where I might have
buried it.

Let it lie there and be discovered again—maybe by a
child, or a poet, or a wanderer, in a time when the passions
of our day are no more remembered than those of Old Time.

Jermyn Graz

RAMBLE HOUSE's

HARRY STEPHEN KEELER WEBWORK MYSTERIES

(RH) indicates the title is available ONLY in the RAMBLE HOUSE edition

The Ace of Spades Murder
The Affair of the Bottled Deuce (RH)
The Amazing Web
The Barking Clock
Behind That Mask
The Book with the Orange Leaves
The Bottle with the Green Wax Seal
The Box from Japan
The Case of the Canny Killer
The Case of the Crazy Corpse (RH)
The Case of the Flying Hands (RH)
The Case of the Ivory Arrow
The Case of the Jeweled Ragpicker
The Case of the Lavender Gripsack
The Case of the Mysterious Moll
The Case of the 16 Beans
The Case of the Transparent Nude (RH)
The Case of the Transposed Legs
The Case of the Two-Headed Idiot (RH)
The Case of the Two Strange Ladies
The Circus Stealers (RH)
Cleopatra's Tears
A Copy of Beowulf (RH)
The Crimson Cube (RH)
The Face of the Man From Saturn
Find the Clock
The Five Silver Buddhas
The 4th King
The Gallows Waits, My Lord! (RH)
The Green Jade Hand
Finger! Finger!
Hangman's Nights (RH)
I, Chameleon (RH)
I Killed Lincoln at 10:13! (RH)
The Iron Ring
The Man Who Changed His Skin (RH)
The Man with the Crimson Box
The Man with the Magic Eardrums
The Man with the Wooden Spectacles
The Marceau Case
The Matilda Hunter Murder

The Monocled Monster
The Murder of London Lew
The Murdered Mathematician
The Mysterious Card (RH)
The Mysterious Ivory Ball of Wong Shing Li (RH)
The Mystery of the Fiddling Cracksman
The Peacock Fan
The Photo of Lady X (RH)
The Portrait of Jirjohn Cobb
Report on Vanessa Hewstone (RH)
Riddle of the Travelling Skull
Riddle of the Wooden Parrakeet (RH)
The Scarlet Mummy (RH)
The Search for X-Y-Z
The Sharkskin Book
Sing Sing Nights
The Six From Nowhere (RH)
The Skull of the Waltzing Clown
The Spectacles of Mr. Cagliostro
Stand By—London Calling!
The Steeltown Strangler
The Stolen Gravestone (RH)
Strange Journey (RH)
The Strange Will
The Straw Hat Murders (RH)
The Street of 1000 Eyes (RH)
Thieves' Nights
Three Novellos (RH)
The Tiger Snake
The Trap (RH)
Vagabond Nights (Defrauded Yeggman)
Vagabond Nights 2 (10 Hours)
The Vanishing Gold Truck
The Voice of the Seven Sparrows
The Washington Square Enigma
When Thief Meets Thief
The White Circle (RH)
The Wonderful Scheme of Mr. Christopher Thorne
X. Jones—of Scotland Yard
Y. Cheung, Business Detective

Keeler Related Works

A To Izzard: A Harry Stephen Keeler Companion by Fender Tucker — Articles and stories about Harry, by Harry, and in his style. Included is a compleat bibliography.

Wild About Harry: Reviews of Keeler Novels — Edited by Richard Polt & Fender Tucker — 22 reviews of works by Harry Stephen Keeler from *Keeler News*. A perfect introduction to the author.

The Keeler Keyhole Collection: Annotated newsletter rants from Harry Stephen Keeler, edited by Francis M. Nevins. Over 400 pages of incredibly personal Keeleriana.

Fakealoo — Pastiches of the style of Harry Stephen Keeler by selected demented members of the HSK Society. Updated every year with the new winner.

Strands of the Web: Short Stories of Harry Stephen Keeler — 29 stories, just about all that Keeler wrote, are edited and introduced by Fred Cleaver.

RAMBLE HOUSE's LOON SANCTUARY

A Clear Path to Cross — Sharon Knowles short mystery stories by Ed Lynskey.

A Jimmy Starr Omnibus — Three 40s novels by Jimmy Starr.

A Niche in Time and Other Stories — Classic SF by William F. Temple

A Roland Daniel Double: The Signal and The Return of Wu Fang — Classic thrillers from the 30s.

A Shot Rang Out — Three decades of reviews and articles by today's Anthony Boucher, Jon Breen. An essential book for any mystery lover's library.

A Smell of Smoke — A 1951 English countryside thriller by Miles Burton.

A Snark Selection — Lewis Carroll's *The Hunting of the Snark* with two Snarkian chapters by Harry Stephen Keeler — Illustrated by Gavin L. O'Keefe.

A Young Man's Heart — A forgotten early classic by Cornell Woolrich.

Alexander Laing Novels — *The Motives of Nicholas Holtz* and *Dr. Scarlett*, stories of medical mayhem and intrigue from the 30s.

An Angel in the Street — Modern hardboiled noir by Peter Genovese.

Automaton — Brilliant treatise on robotics: 1928-style! By H. Stafford Hatfield.

Away From the Here and Now — Clare Winger Harris stories, collected by Richard A. Lupoff

Beast or Man? — A 1930 novel of racism and horror by Sean M'Guire. Introduced by John Pelan.

Black Hogan Strikes Again — Australia's Peter Renwick pens a tale of the 30s outback.

Black River Falls — Suspense from the master, Ed Gorman.

Blondy's Boy Friend — A snappy 1930 story by Philip Wylie, writing as Leatrice Homesley.

Blood in a Snap — The *Finnegan's Wake* of the 21st century, by Jim Weiler.

Blood Moon — The first of the Robert Payne series by Ed Gorman.

Bogart '48 — Hollywood action with Bogie by John Stanley and Kenn Davis

Calling Lou Largo! — Two Lou Largo novels by William Ard.

Cornucopia of Crime — Francis M. Nevins assembled this huge collection of his writings about crime literature and the people who write it. Essential for any serious mystery library.

Corpse Without Flesh — Strange novel of forensics by George Bruce

Crimson Clown Novels — By Johnston McCulley, author of the Zorro novels, *The Crimson Clown* and *The Crimson Clown Again*.

Dago Red — 22 tales of dark suspense by Bill Pronzini.

Dark Sanctuary — Weird Menace story by H. B. Gregory

David Hume Novels — *Corpses Never Argue, Cemetery First Stop, Make Way for the Mourners, Eternity Here I Come*. 1930s British hardboiled fiction with an attitude.

Dead Man Talks Too Much — Hollywood boozer by Weed Dickenson.

Death Leaves No Card — One of the most unusual murdered-in-the-tub mysteries you'll ever read. By Miles Burton.

Death March of the Dancing Dolls and Other Stories — Volume Three in the Day Keene in the Detective Pulps series. Introduced by Bill Crider.

Deep Space and other Stories — A collection of SF gems by Richard A. Lupoff.

Detective Duff Unravels It — Episodic mysteries by Harvey O'Higgins.

Diabolic Candelabra — Classic 30s mystery by E.R. Punshon

Dime Novels: Ramble House's 10-Cent Books — *Knife in the Dark* by Robert Leslie Bellem, *Hot Lead* and *Song of Death* by Ed Earl Repp, *A Hashish House in New York* by H.H. Kane, and five more.

Don Diablo: Book of a Lost Film — Two-volume treatment of a western by Paul Landres, with diagrams. Intro by Francis M. Nevins.

Dope and Swastikas — Two strange novels from 1922 by Edmund Snell

Dope Tales #1 — Two dope-riddled classics; *Dope Runners* by Gerald Grantham and *Death Takes the Joystick* by Phillip Condé.

Dope Tales #2 — Two more narco-classics; *The Invisible Hand* by Rex Dark and *The Smokers of Hashish* by Norman Berrow.

Dope Tales #3 — Two enchanting novels of opium by the master, Sax Rohmer. *Dope* and *The Yellow Claw*.

Double Hot — Two 60s softcore sex novels by Morris Hershman.

Dr. Odin — Douglas Newton's 1933 racial potboiler comes back to life.

Evangelical Cockroach — Jack Woodford writes about writing.

Evidence in Blue — 1938 mystery by E. Charles Vivian.

Fatal Accident — Murder by automobile, a 1936 mystery by Cecil M. Wills.

Fighting Mad — Todd Robbins' 1922 novel about boxing and life

Finger-prints Never Lie — A 1939 classic detective novel by John G. Brandon.

Freaks and Fantasies — Eerie tales by Tod Robbins, collaborator of Tod Browning on the film FREAKS.

Gadsby — A lipogram (a novel without the letter E). Ernest Vincent Wright's last work, published in 1939 right before his death.

Gelett Burgess Novels — *The Master of Mysteries, The White Cat, Two O'Clock Courage, Ladies in Boxes, Find the Woman, The Heart Line, The Picaroons* and *Lady Mechante.* Recently added is A Gelett Burgess Sampler, edited by Alfred Jan. All are introduced by Richard A. Lupoff.

Geronimo — S. M. Barrett's 1905 autobiography of a noble American.

Hake Talbot Novels — *Rim of the Pit, The Hangman's Handyman.* Classic locked room mysteries, with mapback covers by Gavin O'Keefe.

Hands Out of Hell and Other Stories — John H. Knox's eerie hallucinations

Hell is a City — William Ard's masterpiece.

Hollywood Dreams — A novel of Tinsel Town and the Depression by Richard O'Brien.

Hostesses in Hell and Other Stories — Russell Gray's most graphic stories

House of the Restless Dead — Strange and ominous tales by Hugh B. Cave.

I Stole $16,000,000 — A true story by cracksman Herbert E. Wilson.

Inclination to Murder — 1966 thriller by New Zealand's Harriet Hunter.

Invaders from the Dark — Classic werewolf tale from Greye La Spina.

J. Poindexter, Colored — Classic satirical black novel by Irvin S. Cobb.

Jack Mann Novels — Strange murder in the English countryside. *Gees' First Case, Nightmare Farm, Grey Shapes, The Ninth Life, The Glass Too Many, Her Ways Are Death, The Kleinert Case* and *Maker of Shadows.*

Jake Hardy — A lusty western tale from Wesley Tallant.

Jim Harmon Double Novels — *Vixen Hollow/Celluloid Scandal, The Man Who Made Maniacs/Silent Siren, Ape Rape/Wanton Witch, Sex Burns Like Fire/Twist Session, Sudden Lust/Passion Strip, Sin Unlimited/Harlot Master, Twilight Girls/Sex Institution.* Written in the early 60s and never reprinted until now.

Joel Townsley Rogers Novels and Short Stories — By the author of *The Red Right Hand: Once In a Red Moon, Lady With the Dice, The Stopped Clock, Never Leave My Bed.* Also two short story collections: *Night of Horror* and *Killing Time.*

John Carstairs, Space Detective — Arboreal Sci-fi by Frank Belknap Long

Joseph Shallit Novels — *The Case of the Billion Dollar Body, Lady Don't Die on My Doorstep, Kiss the Killer, Yell Bloody Murder, Take Your Last Look.* One of America's best 50's authors and a favorite of author Bill Pronzini.

Keller Memento — 45 short stories of the amazing and weird by Dr. David Keller.

Killer's Caress — Cary Moran's 1936 hardboiled thriller.

Lady of the Yellow Death and Other Stories — More stories by Wyatt Blassingame.

League of the Grateful Dead and Other Stories — Volume One in the Day Keene in the Detective Pulps series.

Library of Death — Ghastly tale by Ronald S. L. Harding, introduced by John Pelan

Malcolm Jameson Novels and Short Stories — *Astonishing! Astounding!, Tarnished Bomb, The Alien Envoy and Other Stories* and *The Chariots of San Fernando and Other Stories.* All introduced and edited by John Pelan or Richard A. Lupoff.

Man Out of Hell and Other Stories — Volume II of the John H. Knox weird pulps collection.

Marblehead: A Novel of H.P. Lovecraft — A long-lost masterpiece from Richard A. Lupoff. This is the "director's cut", the long version that has never been published before.

Master of Souls — Mark Hansom's 1937 shocker is introduced by weirdologist John Pelan.

Max Afford Novels — *Owl of Darkness, Death's Mannikins, Blood on His Hands, The Dead Are Blind, The Sheep and the Wolves, Sinners in Paradise* and *Two Locked Room Mysteries and a Ripping Yarn* by one of Australia's finest mystery novelists.

Money Brawl — Two books about the writing business by Jack Woodford and H. Bedford-Jones. Introduced by Richard A. Lupoff.

More Secret Adventures of Sherlock Holmes — Gary Lovisi's second collection of tales about the unknown sides of the great detective.

Muddled Mind: Complete Works of Ed Wood, Jr. — David Hayes and Hayden Davis deconstruct the life and works of the mad, but canny, genius.

Murder among the Nudists — A mystery from 1934 by Peter Hunt, featuring a naked Detective-Inspector going undercover in a nudist colony.

Murder in Black and White — 1931 classic tennis whodunit by Evelyn Elder.

Murder in Shawnee — Two novels of the Alleghenies by John Douglas: *Shawnee Alley Fire* and *Haunts*.

Murder in Silk — A 1937 Yellow Peril novel of the silk trade by Ralph Trevor.

My Deadly Angel — 1955 Cold War drama by John Chelton.

My First Time: The One Experience You Never Forget — Michael Birchwood — 64 true first-person narratives of how they lost it.

Mysterious Martin, the Master of Murder — Two versions of a strange 1912 novel by Tod Robbins about a man who writes books that can kill.

Norman Berrow Novels — *The Bishop's Sword, Ghost House, Don't Go Out After Dark, Claws of the Cougar, The Smokers of Hashish, The Secret Dancer, Don't Jump Mr. Boland!, The Footprints of Satan, Fingers for Ransom, The Three Tiers of Fantasy, The Spaniard's Thumb, The Eleventh Plague, Words Have Wings, One Thrilling Night, The Lady's in Danger, It Howls at Night, The Terror in the Fog, Oil Under the Window, Murder in the Melody, The Singing Room.* This is the complete Norman Berrow library of locked-room mysteries, several of which are masterpieces.

Old Faithful and Other Stories — SF classic tales by Raymond Z. Gallun

Old Times' Sake — Short stories by James Reasoner from Mike Shayne Magazine.

One Dreadful Night — A classic mystery by Ronald S. L. Harding

Pair O' Jacks — A mystery novel and a diatribe about publishing by Jack Woodford

Perfect .38 — Two early Timothy Dane novels by William Ard. More to come.

Prince Pax — Devilish intrigue by George Sylvester Viereck and Philip Eldridge

Prose Bowl — Futuristic satire of a world where hack writing has replaced football as our national obsession, by Bill Pronzini and Barry N. Malzberg.

Red Light — The history of legal prostitution in Shreveport Louisiana by Eric Brock. Includes wonderful photos of the houses and the ladies.

Researching American-Made Toy Soldiers — A 276-page collection of a lifetime of articles by toy soldier expert Richard O'Brien.

Reunion in Hell — Volume One of the John H. Knox series of weird stories from the pulps. Introduced by horror expert John Pelan.

Ripped from the Headlines! — The Jack the Ripper story as told in the newspaper articles in the *New York* and *London Times*.

Robert Randisi Novels — *No Exit to Brooklyn* and *The Dead of Brooklyn*. The first two Nick Delvecchio novels.

Rough Cut & New, Improved Murder — Ed Gorman's first two novels.

R.R. Ryan Novels — Freak Museum and The Subjugated Beast, two horror classics.

Ruled By Radio — 1925 futuristic novel by Robert L. Hadfield & Frank E. Farncombe.

Rupert Penny Novels — *Policeman's Holiday, Policeman's Evidence, Lucky Policeman, Policeman in Armour, Sealed Room Murder, Sweet Poison, The Talkative Policeman, She had to Have Gas* and *Cut and Run* (by Martin Tanner.) Rupert Penny is the pseudonym of Australian Charles Thornett, a master of the locked room, impossible crime plot.

Sacred Locomotive Flies — Richard A. Lupoff's psychedelic SF story.

Sam — Early gay novel by Lonnie Coleman.

Sand's Game — Spectacular hard-boiled noir from Ennis Willie, edited by Lynn Myers and Stephen Mertz, with contributions from Max Allan Collins, Bill Crider, Wayne Dundee, Bill Pronzini, Gary Lovisi and James Reasoner.

Sand's War — More violent fiction from the typewriter of Ennis Willie

Satan's Den Exposed — True crime in Truth or Consequences New Mexico — Award-winning journalism by the *Desert Journal*.

Satans of Saturn — Novellas from the pulps by Otis Adelbert Kline and E. H. Price

Satan's Sin House and Other Stories — Horrific gore by Wayne Rogers

Secrets of a Teenage Superhero — Graphic lit by Jonathan Sweet

Sex Slave — Potboiler of lust in the days of Cleopatra by Dion Leclerq, 1966.

Shadows' Edge — Two early novels by Wade Wright: *Shadows Don't Bleed* and *The Sharp Edge*.

Sideslip — 1968 SF masterpiece by Ted White and Dave Van Arnam.

Slammer Days — Two full-length prison memoirs: *Men into Beasts* (1952) by George Sylvester Viereck and *Home Away From Home* (1962) by Jack Woodford.

Slippery Staircase — 1930s whodunit from E.C.R. Lorac

Sorcerer's Chessmen — John Pelan introduces this 1939 classic by Mark Hansom.

Star Griffin — Michael Kurland's 1987 masterpiece of SF drollery is back.

Stakeout on Millennium Drive — Award-winning Indianapolis Noir by Ian Woollen.

Strands of the Web: Short Stories of Harry Stephen Keeler — Edited and Introduced by Fred Cleaver.

Summer Camp for Corpses and Other Stories — Weird Menace tales from Arthur Leo Zagat; introduced by John Pelan.

Suzy — A collection of comic strips by Richard O'Brien and Bob Vojtko from 1970.

Tales of the Macabre and Ordinary — Modern twisted horror by Chris Mikul, author of the *Bizarrism* series.

Tenebrae — Ernest G. Henham's 1898 horror tale brought back.

The Amorous Intrigues & Adventures of Aaron Burr — by Anonymous. Hot historical action about the man who almost became Emperor of Mexico.

The Anthony Boucher Chronicles — edited by Francis M. Nevins. Book reviews by Anthony Boucher written for the *San Francisco Chronicle,* 1942 – 1947. Essential and fascinating reading by the best book reviewer there ever was.

The Barclay Catalogs — Two essential books about toy soldier collecting by Richard O'Brien

The Basil Wells Omnibus — A collection of Wells' stories by Richard A. Lupoff

The Beautiful Dead and Other Stories — Dreadful tales from Donald Dale

The Best of 10-Story Book — edited by Chris Mikul, over 35 stories from the literary magazine Harry Stephen Keeler edited.

The Black Dark Murders — Vintage 50s college murder yarn by Milt Ozaki, writing as Robert O. Saber.

The Book of Time — The classic novel by H.G. Wells is joined by sequels by Wells himself and three stories by Richard A. Lupoff. Illustrated by Gavin L. O'Keefe.

The Case in the Clinic — One of E.C.R. Lorac's finest.

The Case of the Bearded Bride — #4 in the Day Keene in the Detective Pulps series

The Case of the Little Green Men — Mack Reynolds wrote this love song to sci-fi fans back in 1951 and it's now back in print.

The Case of the Withered Hand — 1936 potboiler by John G. Brandon.

The Charlie Chaplin Murder Mystery — A 2004 tribute by noted film scholar, Wes D. Gehring.

The Chinese Jar Mystery — Murder in the manor by John Stephen Strange, 1934.

The Compleat Calhoon — All of Fender Tucker's works: Includes *Totah Six-Pack, Weed, Women and Song* and *Tales from the Tower,* plus a CD of all of his songs.

The Compleat Ova Hamlet — Parodies of SF authors by Richard A. Lupoff. This is a brand new edition with more stories and more illustrations by Trina Robbins.

The Contested Earth and Other SF Stories — A never-before published space opera and seven short stories by Jim Harmon.

The Crimson Query — A 1929 thriller from Arlton Eadie. A perfect way to get introduced.

The Curse of Cantire — Classic 1939 novel of a family curse by Walter S. Masterman.

The Devil and the C.I.D. — Odd diabolic mystery by E.C.R. Lorac

The Devil Drives — An odd prison and lost treasure novel from 1932 by Virgil Markham.

The Devil's Mistress — A 1915 Scottish gothic tale by J. W. Brodie-Innes, a member of Aleister Crowley's Golden Dawn.

The Devil's Nightclub and Other Stories — John Pelan introduces some gruesome tales by Nat Schachner.

The Disentanglers — Episodic intrigue at the turn of last century by Andrew Lang

The Dumpling — Political murder from 1907 by Coulson Kernahan.

The End of It All and Other Stories — Ed Gorman selected his favorite short stories for this huge collection.

The Fangs of Suet Pudding — A 1944 novel of the German invasion by Adams Farr

The Ghost of Gaston Revere — From 1935, a novel of life and beyond by Mark Hansom, introduced by John Pelan.

The Girl in the Dark — A thriller from Roland Daniel

The Gold Star Line — Seaboard adventure from L.T. Reade and Robert Eustace.

The Golden Dagger — 1951 Scotland Yard yarn by E. R. Punshon.

The Great Orme Terror — Horror stories by Garnett Radcliffe from the pulps

The Hairbreadth Escapes of Major Mendax — Francis Blake Crofton's 1889 boys' book.

The House That Time Forgot and Other Stories — Insane pulpitude by Robert F. Young

The House of the Vampire — 1907 poetic thriller by George S. Viereck.

The Illustrious Corpse — Murder hijinx from Tiffany Thayer

The Incredible Adventures of Rowland Hern — Intriguing 1928 impossible crimes by Nicholas Olde.

The Julius Caesar Murder Case — A classic 1935 re-telling of the assassination by Wallace Irwin that's much more fun than the Shakespeare version.

The Koky Comics — A collection of all of the 1978-1981 Sunday and daily comic strips by Richard O'Brien and Mort Gerberg, in two volumes.

The Lady of the Terraces — 1925 missing race adventure by E. Charles Vivian.

The Lord of Terror — 1925 mystery with master-criminal, Fantômas.

The Melamare Mystery — A classic 1929 Arsene Lupin mystery by Maurice Leblanc

The Man Who Was Secrett — Epic SF stories from John Brunner

The Man Without a Planet — Science fiction tales by Richard Wilson

The N. R. De Mexico Novels — Robert Bragg, the real N.R. de Mexico, presents *Marijuana Girl, Madman on a Drum, Private Chauffeur* in one volume.

The Night Remembers — A 1991 Jack Walsh mystery from Ed Gorman.

The One After Snelling — Kickass modern noir from Richard O'Brien.

The Organ Reader — A huge compilation of just about everything published in the 1971-1972 radical bay-area newspaper, *THE ORGAN*. A coffee table book that points out the shallowness of the coffee table mindset.

The Poker Club — Three in one! Ed Gorman's ground-breaking novel, the short story it was based upon, and the screenplay of the film made from it.

The Private Journal & Diary of John H. Surratt — The memoirs of the man who conspired to assassinate President Lincoln.

The Secret Adventures of Sherlock Holmes — Three Sherlockian pastiches by the Brooklyn author/publisher, Gary Lovisi.

The Shadow on the House — Mark Hansom's 1934 masterpiece of horror is introduced by John Pelan.

The Sign of the Scorpion — A 1935 Edmund Snell tale of oriental evil.

The Singular Problem of the Stygian House-Boat — Two classic tales by John Kendrick Bangs about the denizens of Hades.

The Smiling Corpse — Philip Wylie and Bernard Bergman's odd 1935 novel.

The Spider: Satan's Murder Machines — A thesis about Iron Man

The Stench of Death: An Odoriferous Omnibus by Jack Moskovitz — Two complete novels and two novellas from 60's sleaze author, Jack Moskovitz.

The Story Writer and Other Stories — Classic SF from Richard Wilson

The Strange Case of the Antlered Man — 1935 dementia from Edwy Searles Brooks

The Strange Thirteen — Richard B. Gamon's odd stories about Raj India.

The Technique of the Mystery Story — Carolyn Wells' tips about writing.

The Threat of Nostalgia — A collection of his most obscure stories by Jon Breen

The Time Armada — Fox B. Holden's 1953 SF gem.

The Tongueless Horror and Other Stories — Volume One of the series of short stories from the weird pulps by Wyatt Blassingame.

The Tracer of Lost Persons — From 1906, an episodic novel that became a hit radio series in the 30s. Introduced by Richard A. Lupoff.

The Trail of the Cloven Hoof — Diabolical horror from 1935 by Arlton Eadie. Introduced by John Pelan.

The Triune Man — Mindscrambling science fiction from Richard A. Lupoff.

The Unholy Goddess and Other Stories — Wyatt Blassingame's first DTP compilation

The Universal Holmes — Richard A. Lupoff's 2007 collection of five Holmesian pastiches and a recipe for giant rat stew.

The Werewolf vs the Vampire Woman — Hard to believe ultraviolence by either Arthur M. Scarm or Arthur M. Scram.

The Whistling Ancestors — A 1936 classic of weirdness by Richard E. Goddard and introduced by John Pelan.

The White Owl — A vintage thriller from Edmund Snell

The White Peril in the Far East — Sidney Lewis Gulick's 1905 indictment of the West and assurance that Japan would never attack the U.S.

The Wizard of Berner's Abbey — A 1935 horror gem written by Mark Hansom and introduced by John Pelan.

The Wonderful Wizard of Oz — by L. Frank Baum and illustrated by Gavin L. O'Keefe

Through the Looking Glass — Lewis Carroll wrote it; Gavin L. O'Keefe illustrated it.

Time Line — Ramble House artist Gavin O'Keefe selects his most evocative art inspired by the twisted literature he reads and designs.

Tiresias — Psychotic modern horror novel by Jonathan M. Sweet.

Totah Six-Pack — Fender Tucker's six tales about Farmington in one sleek volume.

Trail of the Spirit Warrior — Roger Haley's historical saga of life in the Indian Territories.

Two Kinds of Bad — Two 50s novels by William Ard about Danny Fontaine

Two Suns of Morcali and Other Stories — Evelyn E. Smith's SF tour-de-force

Ultra-Boiled — 23 gut-wrenching tales by our Man in Brooklyn, Gary Lovisi.

Up Front From Behind — A 2011 satire of Wall Street by James B. Kobak.

Victims & Villains — Intriguing Sherlockiana from Derham Groves.

Wade Wright Novels — *Echo of Fear, Death At Nostalgia Street, It Leads to Murder* and *Shadows' Edge*, a double book featuring *Shadows Don't Bleed* and *The Sharp Edge*.

Walter S. Masterman Novels — *The Green Toad, The Flying Beast, The Yellow Mistletoe, The Wrong Verdict, The Perjured Alibi, The Border Line, The Bloodhounds Bay* and *The Curse of Cantire*. Masterman wrote horror and mystery, some introduced by John Pelan.

We Are the Dead and Other Stories — Volume Two in the Day Keene in the Detective Pulps series, introduced by Ed Gorman. When done, there may be as many as 11 in the series.

Welsh Rarebit Tales — Charming stories from 1902 by Harle Oren Cummins

West Texas War and Other Western Stories — by Gary Lovisi.

Whip Dodge: Man Hunter — Wesley Tallant's saga of a bounty hunter of the old West.

Win, Place and Die! — The first new mystery by Milt Ozaki in decades. The ultimate novel of 70s Reno.

You'll Die Laughing — Bruce Elliott's 1945 novel of murder at a practical joker's English countryside manor.

RAMBLE HOUSE
Fender Tucker, Prop.   Gavin L. O'Keefe, Graphics
www.ramblehouse.com   fender@ramblehouse.com
228-826-1783   10329 Sheephead Drive, Vancleave MS 39565